A
Broken
Circle

Jerry Harris

A Broken Circle

* * * * *

Disclaimer

This is a work of fiction, a product of the author's imagination. Any resemblance or similarity to any actual events or persons, living or dead, is purely coincidental.

* * * * *

Cover Photo Courtesy of Shutterstock

Formatting and Cover Design by Debora Lewis arenapublishing.org

ISBN-13: 978-1496193292
ISBN-10: 1496193296

To Audrey, Paige, and Alexis

Contents

CHAPTER ONE
VERA CHANEY
MARCH 18, 2012

Vera enjoyed the early morning. She always liked being out of bed before the first shining light of the new day. Today was Sunday, usually the highlight of her week. But Vera knew there would be no highlights or fond memories emanating from today's events. She sat in her kitchen drinking orange juice and eating a piece of dry wheat toast. She was waiting for Big Roscoe. She had called him last week from the hospital in Yazoo City and told him what she needed. She knew he would be in her driveway in a few minutes and she sat and waited for the sound of his car.

The two children and the babysitter were asleep. She had checked on them already. She knew she would take one last look before she left. A light rain was falling. Just hard enough not to be a drizzle. Steady and insistent, the rain and dark sky kept any thought of light and sun and color away. Vera reached across the table and picked up the reddish brown folder she and Gorman Ballard had prepared for the Memphis detective. She walked into the den and picked up the final draft of the letter she had written her father and put it into a large white envelope she retrieved from her oak desk.

She wrote "FATHER" in plain printed capital letters across the front of the envelope. The word took up much of the space of the envelope's front. But in the right hand corner of the envelope, she wrote "Private" in smaller letters. She did not seal the letter. She would tell the detective not to read it. If she thought of something else to put in the letter during the ride to Memphis, she would not have to tear into the envelope. She had room to write a few more lines on the bottom of the last page. She knew that.

Vera took the letter and put it into the file and secured it with a large rubber band. The kitchen was quiet but she could hear the soft, reassuring drone of the refrigerator. A limb on the cedar tree just outside the picture window was slowly waving. She had hoped for a sunny day. Birds in the trees. A dry yard for the kids to play in. Yellow and white jonquils were in full bloom along both sides of the front fence.

She hoped she would be back from Memphis before dark. She had no idea how long the meeting with the detective would take. Vera had made up her mind that if he acted like she was stupid because she was black and a woman or if she thought he was playing her for a sucker because she was a doctor she was coming back home in a hurry. All she knew was his name was Ethan Cheatham and he was just starting out as a private detective and had a nice office on Front Street. A white boy. Had to be with a name like Ethan.

A few minutes after five thirty, Vera heard tires rumbling through the gravel in her driveway. She walked to the front door and waved at Big Roscoe. She went and checked on her children. Her son, Roscoe, was five years old. He was the main reason she was going to Memphis to hire a detective to find her father. When her husband was alive and living in the house, Roscoe was always laughing and getting into something. Hiding her purse. Pulling his sister's hair. Throwing rocks at the banty rooster. Laughing and running. Falling down. All over the house, the porch, the barn, and the driveway. Trying to keep up with and pass his father.

That was all over now. It ended when her husband, Elton Chaney, and his National Guard Unit got the call up to Iraq. Then seven months later, Elton was dead. Blown up by a roadside bomb. When Vera was told of his death, she waited a few hours on that bright

October day in 2010 before telling Roscoe. She had taken him by the right hand and walked with him into the back yard. They sat under the big pecan tree near the back fence on a wooden bench that Elton kept there for cleaning fish and rabbits and squirrels and dove and quail and the occasional deer.

She expected tears when she told him. He did not cry. Yes, there were a few small tears in the corners of his eyes, but Vera remembered a look of shock and, then, retreat in his eyes. He went into a world she could not find. Try as she could, she never felt like she was really a part of his life after that. He did not misbehave. He just would not come out of his world. She did not know what to do. A psychiatrist in New Orleans had tested him and talked to him for a few hours last month. His advice: Wait. The psychiatrist said he was hiding. Just like you would expect a child to do if he or she were scared of a sound or an animal. The psychiatrist had said he was just breaking it down to her in the simplest terms. He had told her about a trip to Washington when he had happened by the Vietnam Memorial and sat on a bench and watched the men and women come by. Some had cried. Some left a single flower and knelt and prayed. Some stared with rage in their eyes. One man touched a name and wept. One woman touched a name, dropped a single rose, and walked off with a smile on her face and tears on her cheeks.

Vera was tired of waiting. Here it was almost Spring. Time for a young boy to be outside. The farm they lived on was almost fifteen miles from Yazoo City and thirty-five from Jackson. Almost two thousand acres that had been in the Chaney family since before World War One. Trees and hollows and a pond and a barn and rose bushes in the yard. Roscoe had no interest in any of that. He stayed in his room when he was not in kindergarten. He did his chores. Fed the chickens. Brought the eggs in. Went to the mailbox and got the mail. Helped his sister load and unload the dishwasher. Made his own bed. Already knew to fold his clothes and keep his room picked up.

She knew she needed help with the boy. Help no New Orleans psychiatrist could give. Help she was seeking from probably the most unlikely and perhaps dangerous source in the Universe. Her father. She looked in on Roscoe. He was asleep but even in sleep she did not feel he was at rest or at peace. It was like he had finally surrendered to the reality and inevitability of sleep. She pulled his quilt over him and kissed him on the forehead and left his room.

She was going to Ann's room when she heard Big Roscoe's heavy footsteps on the front porch. Roscoe on the porch had been Elton's best friend. He had grown up down the road near the Chaney farm. Elton and Roscoe were born a few months apart in 1978. They had grown up together, stealing watermelons from Robert Ertle's patch, riding horses all over the back roads between Bentonia and Little Yazoo and Anding , playing football at the County High School, chasing girls at the small town dances in the little communities all over Yazoo County and even as far away as Jackson and Canton. Roscoe scuffed around after high school and eventually bought a juke joint at Three Points. Three Points was where the road from Little Yazoo dead-ended with the road from Bentonia to Sartaria. Roscoe ran it clean. Beer and big screen TVs over the bar. Three pool tables. Barbecue on Saturdays. Fried catfish on Fridays. A juke box with no gangsta rap on it. No firearms. No fights. No dope. He said he had tried to keep the knives out of the place as best he could.

Roscoe was not that big. Just a little over six feet. But he was smart and he was quick. He could stand behind his bar and smell out trouble, male or female, before it ever sat down or ordered a beer. The Sheriff's car never stopped unless they wanted some food. Vera had named her son Roscoe. It was not her idea. Elton asked her if she would do it when she was around six months along. She wanted to name the boy, Martin, if in fact; it was a boy, as they had been told. Martin after Dr. King. When he brought it up, Elton was in the den watching the Jets and the Bills one Sunday afternoon. He had muted the sound and thrown his big voice into the kitchen. She went into the den and told him she could not see going through life with two Roscoes. Elton had gotten real serious and his voice had softened as he looked into her eyes and said, "There are three reasons I want to name him Roscoe. Number one, he is my best friend. Number two, I am scared there won't be two Roscoes in your life for a long time. You run a juke joint at Three Points and what you think is your future? Somebody gonna shoot him, knife him, run him over with a truck, hit him over the head with a stick, or throw one of them firebombs in that joint. I want him to sell it but he won't. Plus, he is lending money. Five today. Pay back six on payday. That little nickel-ass business will get you waylaid and dead, too. And last, number three, is I ain't never give him nothing. Cept a quarter or so when we were kids and he wanted a drink. That is my three reasons."

Later that afternoon, he came out on the back porch where she was reading and told her, "just like with Ann. You get the final say so. Whatever you pick will be fine." Then he walked back inside and watched some more football.

Nothing else was said and she made up her mind to call the boy Martin, but when she saw him for the first time, she smiled at Elton in the hospital room and named him Roscoe. But, she told Elton that no one would be allowed to call him Little Roscoe or Junior or anything stupid. They would call Elton's lifelong friend Big Roscoe. And no middle name for their son. She felt like Roscoe was enough name for a person. That and Chaney. That was all.

So while one Roscoe was sleeping and the other Roscoe was on the porch, she went in and checked on Ann, her seven-year-old daughter. She lay peacefully in the bed. Her small face strong and serene. Vera had been told to savor these years. Mother and daughter close. Even best friends at this stage. Wait till she is a teenager and gets on your last nerve. That was the conventional beauty shop wisdom. It might turn out that way but Vera felt that it could be different.

Ann had cried loudly after Vera had told her about her father's death. But by the time of the funeral, she had become watchful of her mother and brother. She and her mother had shared their worries over Roscoe. Roscoe did not seem to be listening anymore when Ann talked to him. Vera had not told Ann why she was going to Memphis. Only that it was business. And that Big Roscoe was driving.

The baby sitter, Carolyn, was fifteen and lived down the road a mile or so from the Anding Bridge. A bridge over railroad tracks. Carolyn was sleeping on a pallet Vera had made up for her. She was being paid eight dollars an hour. Even for the sleeping time. She knew where to find the food for the children and not to answer the door if she did not know who was outside. Vera had called the Sheriff and asked him to send a car by in the afternoon to check on the children.

She locked the front door and turned and looked in the driveway. Roscoe's ride was a black Escalade. It was glistening in the early morning rain. It was barely daylight and there was no sun. The rain refused to stop or slow down. Just that steady, slow, southern rain. Elton had put a security light above the garage door. The yellow light was shining on the Escalade through the silent rain.

Roscoe was wearing a pale blue suit, a faded yellow, button down shirt, no tie, and freshly shined black cowboy boots., He was past thirty but looked younger., His face was round and friendly. He was just past six feet tall and weighed less than two hundred pounds. You knew when you first saw him; he was a man of energy and enterprise. And outside the box. Whatever box you visualized or imagined, Roscoe was outside it., He loved women, but he was respectful. He loaned money out by the day, week or month. Always the same. Twenty percent. One day. One month. One week. He hated dope. What it had done to his friends. What it was doing to Yazoo County. He kept the small time sellers and packagers out of his place. He called his place, Roscoe's. He was past happy. He was content. Except he missed his friend, Elton.

Roscoe was glad he was going to spend his day with Vera. She had always accepted him. Kidded him. Acted outraged at his antics. Nagged him about his personal habits. But there had never been any question about him being a part of her life. Ever since they, she and Elton and Roscoe had come together that hot, August Sunday out on Highway 49 just south of Mile Hill and north of Little Yazoo. It was nine years ago. She was just past twenty-eight and in her last year of Residency at St. Dominic Hospital in Jackson. She was on her way back from Yazoo City. She had filled in at the Emergency room in the local hospital when a friend had wanted to go visit her family in Gulfport for a weekend.

She was headed back to Jackson when the right front tire on her little blue Altima blew out. She had braked and slowed down but the car had still slipped into the shallow ditch that was filled with Kudzu, beer bottles, fast food wrappers, and discarded supermarket flyers. She got flustered and was standing on the side of the road behind her car crying when an old brown Ford 150 passed heading north. It stopped and turned around and came back. It stopped a few yards behind her. Roscoe was driving. He took her keys from her and opened her trunk and soon he had the car jacked up and was changing the tire before Elton even left the truck.

Elton walked up to the back of the Altima and asked Vera, "You a Nurse at the Hospital in Yazoo City? You got Hinds County plates on that car."

Vera told him she was taking an instant dislike to him and no, she was not a nurse. She was a doctor in her last year of residency in General Surgery. Elton walked over to Roscoe and said, "See now your tip for changing that tire is going up. You got you a doctor's car. And you know she is smart. She got a real rim and a real tire for a spare. Get her all the way back to Jackson. A tire she can drive a long way. So you know she is going to give you a nice tip."

Roscoe turned and said, "Well, does this mean you are going to get down in this ditch and help me? I am almost through. "

Elton had said, "No, I am resting for when I have to get under that dinky-ass car and wrap that chain you got in the floor board of your truck around her bumper. Then I got to hitch it to your bumper and last I got to make sure you don't tear up both of these inferior vehicles while you are pulling her out of that ditch. Also, I am studying on how much I am going to charge for towing her out of this ditch."

When the tire was changed and the Altima pulled out of the ditch, Elton asked Roscoe for his notebook. The one he kept the records of all his loans in. It was a small green tablet that Roscoe had no trouble keeping in his back left pants pocket. Elton took the book, wrote some numbers down, added them up, tore the sheet out, handed the notebook back to Roscoe, and handed the single sheet with the figures on it to Vera. He stood behind her as she read the sheet. He explained the total was ninety-four dollars. Sixty-five for pulling her out of the ditch, four for Roscoe changing the tire, fifteen for him tying the chain right, and ten for lost time.

Vera took the sheet of paper and crumpled it and then smoothed it back out and handed it to Roscoe and told him to figure it up. Elton took the paper from Roscoe and told her he would make a swap. She told him he was a fool if he thought a country ass nigger like him could outswap her. He acted like he never heard the insult. He said he would call it even if she would agree to let him buy her dinner one night the next week. She asked him if he had forgotten Roscoe and he told her Roscoe owed him seven dollars from last night and he would handle Roscoe. She wrote phone numbers on the back of the tablet paper that had passed for a bill and then she tore the paper up and stuck the scraps of paper in her purse. She had told him to give her his phone number and she might call, but for him not to place any bets on it. Roscoe told her to take her car into a tire shop soon because her tire was shot and it would never serve as a spare. She thanked Roscoe and he had smiled and told Elton he did not know how four dollars got to be seven in less than twelve hours Elton told him he could not be expected to understand high math when he dropped out of junior college in his freshman year when his only excuse was that football season was over and he was bored.

It was almost two weeks later when she called Elton and agreed to go out with him. When he picked her up that first night, Roscoe was waiting in the black Cadillac. He drove them to an Outback near the Reservoir and went inside and sat at the bar while they ate. Vera slowly gave into Elton's charm. They were married the next June and she moved out to the farm and when she finished her residency, she found an old storefront on Main Street in Yazoo City and opened her office. She was a general practitioner and a general surgeon and an ophthalmologist. Depending on the patient. Her business grew fast.

Her income was nothing compared to what most doctors made. Most of her patients had poor insurance or no insurance. Most were black and poor. Yazoo County only had around thirty thousand people and most of them went to one of the white doctors. But she was happy with her life until Elton died. She saw no reason to leave Yazoo County and move to a big city. She just wanted her son back. To lose her husband was bad enough. To lose them both was incomprehensible.

Roscoe eased the Escalade out of the driveway and down the winding country road until he came to Little Yazoo. Little Yazoo was a one-store town. It had lost its post office back in the eighties. One store. Two gas pumps. Just a few miles North of Bentonia and a few miles south of Yazoo City. The store and the few residences were all nestled close to Highway 49. Highway 49 would carry them all the way to Clarksdale and Gorman Ballard's office.

Once Roscoe was headed north on 49, he leaned back in his seat and said, "Now Doc, don't get the wrong idea. This ain't my permanent ride. I bought it off Jimmy Tyson. Tysons are white trash live down near Satartia. Jimmy is about twenty-five. I had to run him off my parking lot twice. He was trying to sell that crack and some meth. Anyway, Jimmy came to me last week with the title to this Escalade. He is going away next Friday. Going to Federal Court in Jackson and get his time. I checked the title and gave him eight grand cash money for it. It is worth more than that but the tires was shot and it has some miles on it. Just two years old. Anyway, I done put almost two thousand dollars back in it. New tires, an air filter; oil change and tire alignment just got me started. I will sell it fast. Costs too much to maintain. It won't hold up to all these Yazoo County bad roads anyway. It's a city car."

"Roscoe, all we been through. Why won't you call me Vera? You know I do not require friends to call me Doctor. I do not need all of that." Vera said.

"How many doctors you think I know? Why should I lose the only chance I will probably have? You the only black doctor in Yazoo County," Roscoe said.

"But we are friends and we have been through a lot and you have always been there for Elton and then me and Elton and now kids and me." Vera said. Roscoe did not say anything else and they passed through Yazoo City and turned north out of the hills into the gray, rainy Delta. The crops had not been planted yet. The land still lay dormant. A few dead cotton stalks stood in the stark fields. Soon the tractors and the seeds and the fertilizers and the water and the sun would fill the fields with bustling green plants. Soy beans. Some rice. Mostly cotton. But today the only green Vera saw was stately cedars and stunted pines she saw growing close to dark houses.

They passed through Tchula and Greenwood and Glendora and shortly after eight, Roscoe pulled up in front of Gorman Ballard's law office on First Street in Clarksdale. The office was on the south side of First and just east of the Coahoma County Circuit Court Building. Ballard's office was an old two story brick, ante-bellum, in design. An iron fence, with a rusty iron gate, separated the office from the street.

Vera got out of the car and put the file under her arm. She asked Roscoe to come in, but he said, "Last time I went in his office, it cost me seven hundred dollars. I'll wait."

By the time Vera got to the brick front steps, Gorman Ballard was standing in the doorway. He was a small man in his mid-fifties. His hair was still black and he wore bow ties he ordered from New York City when he went to court or had clients come into the office., Today, he was wearing a camel's hair blazer, a blue dress shirt, and blue, neatly pressed, trousers. Gorman looked past Vera and waved for Roscoe to come in.

"He won't come in. He's pouting. Said the last time he was here, it cost him seven hundred dollars."

When Vera was seated comfortably in a leather chair in front of the crackling fireplace, Gorman said, "I will go get him. He can wait out in the lobby unless you want him in here."

"No, but bring him into the lobby, so he can complain to you."

Gorman walked through the rain under a small black umbrella to the driver's side of the Escalade. Roscoe took a long time rolling the window down. "I already see what you after. I get under that umbrella. That is probably a hundred dollars and no telling what you got planned for me inside."

"I got chocolate donuts, cinnamon rolls, and hot coffee and a warm fire. All for free." Gorman said.

"Alright, but I didn't bring no seven hundred dollars with me." Roscoe said.

"Last time you was here, you was driving that old rusted out brown 150 truck. If you had driven up in that ride, I would have charged you three thousand. Minimum," Gorman said.

They both laughed and Roscoe got out of the Escalade and took the umbrella from Gorman and hunched down. They walked into the office and Roscoe sat down in front of the hearth in the lobby and picked up the Sunday Clarion-Ledger. Gorman came back with a silver tray with a small pot of coffee and a plate of pastries. He sat them down on a cherry end table and walked into his office.

"I see you brought the file and you probably wrote that letter and I assume it is in the folder." Gorman said.

"I have looked into the background of Ethan Cheatham and I am satisfied and comfortable with him as our choice. He is short on experience, long on character, and has a sterling family pedigree. I know you are not buying a horse, but trust is important. His father, Ellis Cheatham, is head of the Memphis Police Department's Homicide Division. His mother is divorced from Ellis and has remarried. Her husband is a big planter. In the old style. Owns cotton and soybean farms all up and down the Delta. Ethan went to Millsaps and majored in English. Then he went down to Perdido Key in Florida and had a charter business. His father got shot in the line of duty a few years back and Ethan came back to Memphis. He tried his hand with the Memphis Police Department but quit after fifteen months. I strongly suspect he was put off by the regimentation and the routine."

"He is a drinking buddy of Bill Nolan. One of my college friends from Tallahatchie County. He settled in Memphis and is a good lawyer. Has a partner named Tommy Briggs. Both of them good lawyers. They hit a good settlement a few years ago and moved from some rented space in the One Hundred North Main Building and bought this old house on Front Street near Beale. Good view of the river. It is a two-story building. A lot like mine. Red brick and bad plumbing. They had an extra office and so Ethan set up his private investigative service there after he left the Police Department., He remodeled the second floor and lives there. He is not pretentious. He looks like he ought to be playing guitar for Jimmy Buffet. Talking about Ethan. I think he is around twenty-seven or twenty-eight. Nice looking boy. Around six foot two. Weighs around one eighty-five. Hair is a little long. Black like his daddy's," Gorman said.

"His daddy the one that married the black Sheriff of Shelby County last spring? I saw a picture of them in the Clarion Ledger. They run off and got married in New Orleans and stayed three days and came back and she announced the marriage in a four line press release," Vera said.

"Those are the ones. Her name was Sharon Graham. Now all the signs in the Criminal Justice Center and the jail and the substations all were changed to Sharon Cheatham," Gorman said.

"We get in the car; I am going to tell Roscoe why we are going. I told him where. He has never asked why but you know he wants to know," Vera said.

Vera rode in the front passenger seat and Gorman sat in the back, behind and between Vera and Roscoe. They were just out of Clarksdale when Roscoe said, "Lawyer, what if I made a suggestion. You wouldn't charge me would you? I know them day old donuts and that good coffee is going to cost me. I expect a bill in my mailbox by Tuesday."

"Roscoe, I am always open to suggestions. Something my father taught me. He bought that building I practice out of way back in the forties. Just after the war. He was a lawyer and then a Federal Judge down in New Orleans. So let me hear your suggestion." Gorman said.

"That card you got. The one that says "Gorman Ballard, Attorney at Law" on the front. And in smaller letters gives your address and phone number. Then on the back it says "Delta Lawyer". Well, I took some of those cards back to Yazoo County. You know half of Yazoo County is hills and bottomland and half is pure Delta. Well, I live in the poor half. The hill part. I show these cards to my customers and nothing happens. Most of my customers can't afford the gas money from Yazoo City to Clarksdale and back anyway. But some can. But they ain't coming with that Delta Lawyer on the back of that card. So what I suggest is you put in small letters that you will take a limited number of hill folks, too," Gorman said.

"Well, Roscoe, that is a lot better suggestion than I usually get. Folks that never opened a law book are always telling me how to practice my profession. I will take that under advisement." Gorman said.

"Well, I am thinking about buying a store, a little house, and nine acres on the highway from Yazoo City to Canton. About a mile east of Benton. So I will be needing you later this spring. My goal is to get out of the juke joint business in ten years. There is a lot of money in it. But too much risk and too much stress. We closed this morning around three. I got with my bartender after we closed and we counted the beer so when I get back tonight I can reconcile the cash register. He supposed to keep a record of all the money that comes in the front door and be sure nothing, money or merchandise, goes out the back door," Roscoe said.

"Roscoe, let's be serious for a few minutes," Vera said.

"Sho Doc, no problem."

"You come all this way on short notice on one of your busy days and I appreciate it. I also appreciate the fact that we have come almost two hundred miles and you have not asked why we are coming. I will tell you but it is our business. If I think anybody else in Yazoo County needs to know, I will tell them." Vera said.

"I have a father. I have not seen him in a great many years. He has been out of my life for so long, but now I want to see him. And I do not know where he is. I thought I knew but he has left there and I have no idea where he is. We are going to see a detective in Memphis. I will hire him unless he makes me mad. From what Gorman tells me, he will be fine. Do you know where Front and Beale is?" Vera asked.

"Sure." Roscoe said.

"Well, his office is just north of there, up on the bluff, not too far south of the Confederate Park. South of Union. We will probably be there in an hour and a half or two hours. Maybe less. Do you have your cell? I know you do, but it has not rang since we left." Vera said.

"I turned it off. I will turn it back on. I am walking down to Beale Street and then I will eat a bowl of chili and some tamales at the Beale Street Café. Call me when you are through." Roscoe said.

"So you are not going to question me about what I am doing. Not going to call me foolish. Not tell me in that male condescending way that I am wasting my money." Vera said.

"Naw, none of that. I was just thinking that if this detective can find people's fathers, he can make a lot of money. That is for sure." Roscoe said.

When they left Clarksdale, they turned North on Highway 61 and went past Tunica and the casinos and the State Line and the hard South Memphis streets and finally, just before ten o'clock they were on Front Street in front of a two story brick house that had a second story balcony and a spacious front porch. A wooden sign greeted visitors when they entered the neat green yard in front of the office. The sign was swaying gently in the wind. It said, "Nolan and Briggs, Attorneys at Law". A separate and smaller sign said, "Ethan Cheatham, Private Investigator."

Ethan Cheatham walked out of the office and waited for them at the sidewalk. After Gorman introduced Vera and Roscoe, Cheatham took them into the office. His office was on the left of the lobby. Briggs and Nolan had taken separate offices on the right side of the hallway and behind the lobby. The rain had stopped but the gray clouds kept the sun away. Roscoe asked Cheatham if he was going to give him a tour of his office like Gorman had. Cheatham laughed and said sure. Nolan's office was just past the front lobby and Briggs' was in the rear behind Nolan's. Both were spacious. Nolan's was neat and Briggs' was full of files and opened law books and one chair was filled with trial transcripts. The floors throughout the office were dark oak.

Behind Cheatham's office was a library and behind the library was a kitchen. Roscoe found the bathroom in the kitchen and Vera,

Cheatham, and Gorman went to Cheatham's office. Cheatham had a dark wooden desk in the middle of his office. A smaller, roll top desk was in a corner behind the large desk. Cheatham had comfortable red leather chairs for his clients and other visitors. A large window gave him a view of the Big River and the fields west of the River. Vera was clutching the file in her lap. Gorman waited until Roscoe left before starting the meeting.

"As you know, Dr. Vera Chaney is your prospective client. What she wants is for you to find her father. His name is Robert Lee Whitfield. He is roughly fifty-eight years old. This is an approximation because I could not find a birth certificate for him in Hardaman County, Mississippi, where he says he was born. He has spent the last twenty-seven years in Parchman Prison down near Tutwiler. He was released in January of this year. He was instructed to report to my office when he was released as I had, pro bono, worked to get his clemency papers approved. Through neglect, or whatever, he was released without my knowledge. Dr. Chaney had no reason to know of my efforts to have Robert released. But she called me two weeks ago on Roscoe's recommendation and I thought of you when I heard what she wanted. We have prepared a file for you to read and hopefully, it will give you some leads to assist you in your investigation." Gorman said.

Vera handed the file to Ethan and said, "Last fall, my husband, Elton Chaney was killed in Iraq. By one of those IEDs. He was one of the last to die in that conflict. We have two children. Or perhaps I should say we are the parents of two children. A girl, age seven. Her name is Ann. She is named after her maternal great grandmother. One of her daughters, Louise Stepter, was, or is, my mother. I do not know which is appropriate. She left me with my grandmother, Ann Stepter, when I was an infant. She left before Christmas and said she would be back by the spring. She went to Gary, Indiana or Atlanta, Georgia and we never heard back from her. I have no interest in her status at all."

"My son is five years old. His name is Roscoe. He was named after the Roscoe you just met. He, the older Roscoe, was my husband's best friend. I relented and named my son Roscoe. After Elton was killed, my son has withdrawn into a world I cannot penetrate. My father was a good man who did a bad thing. He committed a crime. He killed a man who had a wife and four children. The jury gave him ninety-nine years and he has done close to thirty of those years. So I may be compounding my problems. Bringing him back to my life. But I will take the chance. If I am making a mistake by bringing him back into my life, I know Big Roscoe and Mr. Ballard will help me."

"I have checked with the Sheriff of Hardaman County and he says Robert is not in the county and has not been there. I have checked with the Highway Patrol and one of the Governor's Special Investigators and we have not found him. No arrest record since his release. No car accident. No clues as of now." Gorman said.

"Well?" Vera asked.

"No promises. I will start on it this afternoon. Read the file and go from there. Dr. Chaney, I would like some contact information from you. And I would like to know if you want me to contact Mr. Ballard or you. Let's set something up so there is as little confusion as possible. You are the client, but you are also a doctor and I hate to be bothering you with trivial details. I do not want to get your hopes up too high nor do I want you to be discouraged. Finding people is an inexact science. He may be in Memphis working for a funeral home or he could be in Canada working on a ranch. Luck plays into this. Luck and patience", Cheatham said.

"A couple of things I have not gotten to yet. There is a letter from me to my father in the file. It is not sealed, but I do not want you to read it. It is very personal and I will be available to answer any questions you have as best I can. I work six hard days. I do scheduled surgery on Tuesdays and Thursdays. I will not be able to return a call on those days until late at night and I may be too tired then. So you will need to be patient with me. And, I want you to find him, deliver the letter, and offer to bring him back to me from wherever he is and then leave the rest to him. I love him despite what he has done. But I will not beg him or anyone else on the face of God's Earth to help me. I just do not want to lose a child of my own. I have lost a couple of patients who were children. That is bad enough, but to lose your own child, gradually, just slipping away right in front of you. I am helpless."

She did not cry. She looked straight ahead into Cheatham's blue eyes. Gorman Ballard got up and walked to the window. "I can see a barge heading down the river. Riding high so I guess it is empty. They usually fill up again before they come back down. How did you get this office? A great view. Hardwood floors, eleven-foot ceilings. This is nice," Gorman said.

"My dad and Bill Nolan and Tommy Lee Briggs have been friends for over thirty years. I moved to Memphis to be close to him after he was shot a few years ago. After he recovered, he was made Chief of Homicide. When I left the Police Department, Nolan and Briggs told me I could work here and live upstairs. They do not want this office because it would be too hard to hide from clients if their office door opened into the hall facing the lobby." Cheatham said.

"There is the matter of your fee and expenses." Vera said.

"His fees are billed through the law office. He is paid sixty dollars an hour. Fifty goes to him and ten to the firm. Expenses are forty cents a mile for his car. All bills will be paid through my office. Here is a check, an advance, for six thousand dollars. Also, you can use my firm credit card for your expenses. I know you will be reasonable and frugal, but at the same time, I want you to be as thorough as you can be." Ballard said.

"As far as reporting goes, you can report what needs reporting back to Mr. Ballard. We live in the era of e-mails. I would suggest to you that I am interested in results, not reports. If you run into a dead end, let us know and we will settle up and call it quits. But he is the last family I have. A few cousins in Hardaman County that I never see are all that is left." Vera said.

"I find him. Tell him who I am. Who my client is. Give him the letter. Tell him I will bring him home free of expense to him and leave the rest to him." Cheatham said.

Vera said, "That is the plain and simple of it. Yes."

Ballard slid an envelope over to Cheatham. "A check and a credit card. There is a letter in the file that you can show anyone who has questions about the credit card. Any expenses you incur that may require the payment of cash, keep a record. I will take your word. "

"If he does not want to come back, will you want to know where he is, anyway?" Cheatham asked.

"Never," said Vera.

"I think that is all I need to know, then. Like I said, I will start by reading the file this afternoon and tonight. Assuming I am hired." Cheatham said.

"Yes, you are hired, but I want to ask you three more questions. All are personal and you can answer all three by saying they are none of my business. I have no right to ask you any of them, but I have never met a private detective before and I am also curious about your background. I would probably be insulted if one of my patients asked me similar questions." Vera said.

"Fire away, I am curious about you and I want to ask you two questions. You get to go first. And the lawyer cannot interrupt or object. Fair?" Cheatham said. "Fair, but I get to go first. So if I think you are evasive, I can throw it back at you. First, do you have a gun? You are not wearing one of those holsters. You have on khakis and a blue golf shirt and old running shoes. No place for an ankle holster."

"I have one. A Smith and Wesson,38 revolver with a four-inch barrel. It is in a safe upstairs. I also have a permit for it. But I have only fired it at the Sheriff's pistol range. I have never pulled it on anyone. I do not expect to need it on this assignment," Cheatham said.

"Number two. Why leave the Police Department. Good benefits. Decent salary. What happened?"

"I got bored. Not with the work. The work is fine. But with the regimentation. Being at the same place five days a week and the same time every day. The constant supervision. The routine bored me. The forms. And all of the whining and complaining. The Union politics. Instant paranoia. The union mentality is that all of the officers, lieutenant and above, are out to get you, the pay is not fair; City Hall is out to screw everyone. Not a healthy atmosphere." Cheatham said.

"And last, tell me about your step-mother. No, I withdraw that. That question is beneath me. I am sorry. Forget that one."

"I will tell you this about her and you can draw your own conclusions from what I tell you. When I first met her, my father was in the hospital after being shot. I drove up from Perdido Key and when I went into his room she was there. He had been her first Lieutenant when she came on the force. She was there every night and helped me wheel him out of the hospital. She made sure his horses were fed while he was recovering and later when she was promoted to Police Director, she made him the head of Homicide. They started a personal relationship after he was promoted. Later, she ran for Sheriff and won by a comfortable margin. They are happy together and I am welcome in their house," Cheatham said. "Fair enough. Now your turn," Vera said. "Why Elton Chaney and why Yazoo County?" Cheatham asked.

"He was strong and mischievous when we first met, I knew I would not be bored with him and he was thoughtful. Yazoo County because that was him. It was all he knew. I could not get him to go to New Orleans at first. He always had something going on at the farm. He said you cannot leave the land. You have to stay close to your stock and your crops. Yazoo County was enough for him and now it is enough for me. Sick folks everywhere you go. Better money most everywhere else. But I never had a lot and now I do not need a lot.

Now I like it. The dusty roads. The plum trees in the spring. Doves on a wire. Quail running across the road. Squirrels in the trees. Flowers in the yards. Blackberry vines on a hill a few hundred yards from the house. A lot of my patients respect me and appreciate what I do. Look, the farm is paid for. My equipment is paid for. Elton mortgaged the farm so I could get the best equipment. Now, it is paid for. I need two things. My husband. That is gone forever. And my son. If I can get my son back from where ever he is, I will not be heard to complain."

"I went running this morning and only had some orange juice before you got here, so I am going to go eat a nice meal and then I will start." Cheatham said.

"You are the detective and I do not believe in micro-management but may I offer a suggestion? "Ballard asked. He had turned toward Cheatham, but now his gaze was back on the river and the lonely fields beyond the churning, brown water. The fields had been turned by a plow. You could see the fresh black earth, but the rows were still empty. No seeds had been planted this early.

"Of course," Cheatham said.

"Start down near Tutwiler. At Parchman. There is a woman down there. A counselor of sorts. I never got her title. But she is in some sort of administrative position in the prison. Her name is Essie. Essie Beard. She is from down near Natchez. Went to Alcorn State with Donald Driver. Someway she took a liking to Robert. Contact information is in the file."

"Might go down tomorrow morning early and see her." Cheatham said.

Vera got up from her chair and walked to the window and stretched. She came around behind Cheatham's desk and smiled and shook his hand. Cheatham looked into her eyes. They were big and brown and searching. Her cheekbones were high on an attractive face. Her nose was small and her lips were drawn and Cheatham wondered if she ever relaxed. Was her mind ever free of tension? He wanted to ask about the farm. Who farmed it? What had happened to the animals when Elton died? Things that had nothing to do with the case.

She still had both of her hands around his right hand when she said, "I forgot. Maybe I am a sap. But anyway. I put some copies of pictures of me when I graduated from medical school. The children. His grandchildren. Things twenty something years in Parchman may have made totally irrelevant to him. But will you show them to him anyway? And the picture of me and Elton and Big Roscoe standing under one of the big oak trees in our yard. Tell him they are for him if he should care."

She went to the window and stared across the street at the river and the fields. Gorman Ballard came away from the window and said, "Roscoe is sitting on the hood of the Escalade. Eating what I think is a tamale. Out of a big sack. Probably our lunch. He said he was going to the Blues City Café. Call me if you need anything or if you find out anything you think I should know about. Good luck and thanks for taking the case."

Cheatham followed Vera and Gorman out to the Escalade and watched as they drove away. It was almost noon and he was hungry. He looked at the hard, gray sky. No sunshine today. He went upstairs to his apartment. The brownish red file from Vera and Gorman was in his right hand. Janet, his girlfriend, was on the bed reading the Sunday paper. She looked up at him, cocked her head to the right side, and smiled. Cheatham threw the file on the bed.

"Let's go to the El Porton. Knock down one margarita. Not one each. Just one between us. Eat some food and then come on back. I want to read this file." Ethan said.

Janet was wearing blue jeans and a bulky, turquoise sweater. She was a lawyer. A brassy, short, smart Jewish woman with large breasts, a tiny waist, and freckles across her nose and chin. Her eyes were brown and large. Her hair was brown this year and out of control. She was coming up on forty faster than she wished. Just thirty-three but already worrying about forty. Janet Ruth Zeitlin. She handled personal injury, criminal, and divorce cases. She had met Ethan outside of a General Sessions Court in the basement of the Criminal Justice Center at 201 Poplar. He was a new patrolman and she was a busy, high profile, successful lawyer. He was standing against a wall and she caught him staring at her.

She walked up to him, looked up at his badge and ID and asked if he was related to Ellis Cheatham. She called his father a tough hombre and asked him how tough he was. Ethan blushed and stammered about how he was different from his dad. She thanked him for staring at her, took out one of her cards and wrote a phone number on the back. She said, "It is my private cell number. One cell number on the card is for clients and acquaintances. This number is for people I really want to talk with. Call me if you would like to take me out and buy me nice meals and expensive presents."

He took the card and put it in his shirt pocket, underneath his badge. He called her and they ate at El Porton on Highland. She had been surprised when he talked about the short stories of John Updike and fishing for cobia and grouper down in Florida just past the Alabama line at a place called Perdido Key. Things went well. The physical part took care of itself. He was in shape and liked having sex with her and, as a bonus, they had conversations. He would tell her stories about his father and fishing and John Updike and Keats. He never bought the expensive presents. He brought her books. Good books. The Warmth of Other Suns. The Unbroken. Everything he could find by Elmore Leonard. Including the Westerns. She read it all. Hoping to find out as much about Ethan as she could by reading the books and then asking him why he liked them.

Ethan was young, in his late twenties. Her clock was about to run out. She knew it. She had been single by choice. Children and a husband and children were things other women had. She had little time or energy left most days to think of these things. It was the hand she had dealt herself and she did not complain. She was in love with her life as a lawyer. She had decided to check out law school when the prospect of graduate school in the History Department of some faraway university seemed her only other alternative after completing her degree at Vanderbilt.

She had come home and lived with her parents, who owned and ran a jewelry store at Poplar and Perkins in the Laurelwood Shopping Center. She shared office space with two other women in the Morgan Keegan Building. She had a view of the River and was busy with the referrals she got from her partners. One partner handled business law. Taxes, Corporate law, and Estate work. The other partner handled Real Estate matters. The three had all bases covered. Except for Bankruptcy cases. Too tiresome and boring. Janet did not make as much money as her partners but she did not care. She was too busy to spend the money she made.

She had been in her office yelling through the phone at a Federal Prosecutor one afternoon when Ethan had walked into her office. She finished her conversation, slammed her phone down, closed her eyes, and rocked back in her chair. After a few minutes, she came around and shut her door and sat in a chair and looked into Ethan's eyes. She knew something was wrong. He usually grinned at her when they met. A big, country grin. He told her he was quitting the Police Department and opening up a private detective agency in Nolan and Briggs' office.

She bought a bottle of champagne and they celebrated at her home on Mud Island that night. They sat on her balcony and watched the dark Mississippi River roll by. The sky was clear and the stars seemed to dance across the dark river. They walked down to the bank of the River and finished the champagne after midnight. They watched stars, and a big yellow moon that hung over the busy, dark river. Barges crept by with red and green lights marking their outlines and strong searchlights scanning the water ahead.

When they were seated in a booth at the back of El Porton, Ethan ordered a margarita with salt. They each had chicken enchiladas and rice. Ethan ordered six tamales to go. Janet said, "So tell me about this new case. I saw the classy black lady from the upstairs window. She did not look happy. The other black guy and the lawyer, I could not read. But she looked sad". Ethan told her about the case and the little background information he had.

When he was through, Janet said, "Since I know you want to read that file this afternoon, will you let me read it when you are through? The Commercial Appeal is an OK newspaper. No complaints. But I am interested in Dr. Vera. To think that she would ask for help from her father, who is a convicted murderer and has spent the last twenty something years in Parchman, and has not kept up with her for all these years is, at best, a curious decision. You know she is smart. Got to be. Single practitioner in a poor county in Mississippi. Already paid her equipment off and the note on the farm."

"Maybe there are two simple answers." Ethan said. The food came. The hot plates and enticing smells turned their attention away from Vera Chaney for a few minutes. When the plates were cleared and only a small amount of ice and margarita lay at the bottom of the glass, Janet asked, "Alright, so what are the simple answers?"

"The big word. Maybe. As in I do not know or pretend to know. But it could be this. Number one, she has no one else to turn to. Number two, he is still her father and maybe she still loves him. There is a letter in the file. She asked me not to read it. But to give it to him, offer to make travel arrangements to Yazoo County from wherever it is that I wind up finding him and to walk away if he does not want to come. She also said she did not want to know where he is. Only if he wants to come back. One last try. She stressed she would not beg him or anyone else for help," Ethan said.

"She asked you not to read the letter, but she never said anything about me reading it." Janet said.

"I know that is a joke. You would not read it. You just want to get me rattled so you can tease me." Ethan said.

"Tell you what, I'll carry the tamales, you get the check. I will split it with you and then we can go back and spend the afternoon and probably a lot of the night reading the file and discussing it. Serious, I am interested in this one. You know confidentiality applies. I would never tell anyone about your clients or files. Also, on the way back, you can tell me about the little lawyer and the black guy. Roscoe." Janet said.

When they were in the car headed back west on Poplar, Janet asked, "Oh, and around six when the sun starts going down, maybe we should take a sex and tamale and Dos Equis Amber break." Ethan could not think of anything to say to that, so he just nodded his head and grinned. And drove his old, black Camaro back to Front Street and the River and home.

Gorman, Vera, and Roscoe were hungry, also, when they left Ethan's office. Roscoe cut back east and found Third Street, which would turn into Highway 61, when he got into Mississippi. It would carry them back to Clarksdale. Roscoe had eaten three tamales and a bowl of chili and drank a pitcher of iced tea, but he was still hungry. He got that way when he was nervous and unsettled. He had been sitting on the hood of the Escalade looking at the River when he had started thinking about Elton Chaney and Vera and the children.

He was not used to sadness. Turmoil. That was fine. The chaos that came with running a juke joint. That was fine. He could handle the day to day stress of his life. He was interested in people. He liked most people, but being poor as a child had taught him how to recognize weakness and evil. But he had no answers to the dilemma facing him. He wanted to protect Vera. To step in and take charge. It was not sexual. But he knew he loved her. Perhaps like a sister. How would he know? He had never had a sister. Only a brother he could never relate to. This same brother working off shore in the Gulf and living with a white woman in Port Arthur, Texas. A father and mother still live on the family farm. And that was it. He had girlfriends. But not love.

He missed his dead friend Elton. He had never thought of them being away from each other until the call up by the National Guard. They had been friends for so long and now Roscoe was swimming in an emotional river he did not like and could not escape from. He drove in silence south on Third Street. When he was almost to the overpass over the Interstate, he pulled into a parking lot next to a sprawling white building. The sign near the front door said:

"Interstate Barb-Q." He left the motor running, opened his door, and said, "I will be just a minute. They promised they would have it ready and keep it hot."

When he came back out, he had a large, white paper sack. Inside the Escalade, he turned to Gorman, reached in the sack, and took out a pulled-pork barbecue sandwich, and handed it to Gorman. He gave one to Vera and pulled away,Soon the Escalade was filled with the hearty aromas of smoked pork and heavy Memphis Barbecue Sauce. Vera said, "Bless you, Roscoe, this is great. Hard to get good barbecue anymore. But I guess if anyone would know where to find it, it would be you. Thank you. I may eat this and take a little nap if that is alright. That made me tired. All that talking about things that personal."

Roscoe said, "Doc, once we get out of Shelby County and are in our own state, unwrap one of those sandwiches for me, please. The rest of those are for you and Roscoe and Ann to eat on, tonight. Some beans and slaw at the bottom of the sack. "

Vera ate her sandwich and stayed awake until she had handed Roscoe his sandwich after they passed out of the stark and depressing South Memphis landscape. She lay back in her seat and slept until the Escalade pulled into Clarksdale. When they got to Gorman's office, she turned in her seat and said, "Let me come in and write you a check. "

"No, we will settle up when it is all through. Who knows where this is leading." Gorman said.

"Yes, but six thousand dollars is a lot of money, even for you," Vera said.

Gorman was almost out of the Escalade. He slipped back in and settled into his seat. "Doctor Chaney, you are too young to remember this. You were not quite six years old when the killing happened and your Grandmother Ann made you go to school during the trial. She was there when the verdict came in and your father, Robert Whitfield, stood up and faced the jury and heard the verdict. Ninety-Nine years. I was standing beside him. I was his lawyer. My first murder case. So, tell you what, we will go halves on this project."

Vera was going to argue, but Roscoe touched her knee and said, "Far as that is concerned, we could go thirds and that way I would have a legitimate reason to haggle and aggravate and maybe in the long run outsmart and out swap this here Delta Lawyer. Oh, and lawyer, I got cash money today in my inside coat pocket to buy into this deal, right now. And my bill for these sandwiches and per Diem and my shoe leather depreciation and gas money will come to you shortly."

"No need for folding money or checks to change hands at this time. We will let this hand play itself out and when all the cards are up and showing, and we are sure, we can talk about the money. Not today. My dad said never to think or talk about money on the Lord's Day," Gorman said.

"You interested in what I got to swap on this fee business when it is all settled?" Roscoe said.

"Sure, but I know you are going to tell me, so why should I bother to ask?" Gorman asked.

"I got a hay baler I reconditioned this winter. Collateral on a loan that went bad. A coming two year old walking horse. Stud horse with a long natural pace. One of those slender Pride heads on him. Almost sixteen hands and room to grow. And I got an old jukebox I am trying to get to work right. And a Ford tractor that runs mighty fine. Just a taste of what could be yours, Lawyer," Roscoe said.

"I been out of the horse buying business for over twenty-five years. But you give me ten percent and I might help you unload that tractor," Gorman said.

"I will call you next week after I send you some pictures. I will send you a picture of the horse, too. Just so you will know what you are missing out on. And a copy of his papers," Roscoe said.

Vera was tired. Tired of the worry and frustration. She watched in silence as Gorman walked slowly through the weak, drizzling rain. His office was dark and as the Escalade pulled away, Vera saw Gorman, his shoulders slightly stooped, walking into the lobby of his office.

The Escalade took them south, over the rickety bridge that spanned the Big Sunflower River, through the empty streets of Clarksdale, onto Highway 49 again, past all the hamlets and towns and crumbling mansions and naked pecan trees and machinery sheds and doublewides and country stores with their Bud or Miller Lite neon signs flashing in the slow persistent drizzle, and the barren fields that would soon be green and fragrant, and most of all, alive and full of promise for the brown and black and white tillers of the seemingly endless flat and for now, forlorn land of the Mississippi Delta.

It was not even four o'clock when Roscoe dropped Vera off at her home. The lights were on in the house and the babysitter had made a fire in the den fireplace. A thin ribbon of smoke snaked skyward as Vera stepped on her front door steps. Ann came out of the house laughing and met her mother at the top of the steps. She grabbed the sack of food and held onto her mother's right leg. They stood on the porch for a few minutes and looked down the winding gravel road as Big Roscoe headed home. Her son did not come out of the house. As she went into the warm den, Vera called for Roscoe and told him she had barbecue for him and beans and slaw. In a few minutes, he came out of his room and sat by the fire and ate his food, with neither curiosity nor interest, as the red and orange flames from the seasoned oak logs danced and flickered in the glowing fireplace.

CHAPTER TWO
THE DELTA LAWYER

After Roscoe and Vera left, Gorman went into his office and sat down behind his desk and shut his eyes. He needed to sort things out. His wife, Eunice, had died in the early part of 2009. A long bout with breast cancer was followed by a short fight with ovarian cancer. His father had died in the early nineties. His mother had tired of the Delta, divorced his father, and moved to St. Louis in the late seventies, then married an investment banker. Gorman had lost touch with her and she gradually became irrelevant to him. Eunice and he had married while he was in law school in Oxford. They had lived happily in a nice ranch style, five-bedroom house out Friars Point Road near Clarksdale. Gorman's father had inherited a few thousand acres of middling cropland and Gorman had built the house on the flat land. A few cedar and pine trees grew near the house and a pecan grove shaded the front lawn.

Two daughters were his remaining family. Both were grown and had moved away. The older, Ruth was in Connecticut and worked in New York City in advertising. She was divorced and had no children. Approaching thirty, she visited twice a year, in the spring and at Christmas, and sent him e-mails and called him regularly. The youngest, Sara, was in law school at Baton Rouge. She was engaged to a doctor in Shreveport. She was not as attentive as Ruth, but she did send the occasional e-mail and birthday card and came to Clarksdale either over the Thanksgiving or Christmas Holidays.

Gorman did not complain. They had been good children and his life had been full. His single regret was that he had not done more traveling with his wife. She was thoughtful and supportive and fun. He thought he and Vera had something in common. They would not love again. He felt no need for any company after the daily trials and tribulations of his daily law practice.

Gorman had decided to sell his home and move into his office. There was ample space upstairs that could be easily converted into two bedrooms with private baths. And a combination den and kitchen. Most nights he slept in the library across from his office. There was also an empty office in case Sara ever decided to come back home and practice law with him. The library had a new big screen television in it and a fireplace. A comfortable leather recliner and a small computer nook in the library were more attractive to him than going out to Friar's Point to the lonely, dark house.

He was determined to stretch his productive years out as long as he could. He was content, as he had been for decades, to traverse the Delta and listen patiently and silently to the woes and sorrows and small triumphs of judges, lawyers, witnesses, and clients. He had become a repository of the stories, confidences, frustrations, dreams, confessions, and yes, lies, of the people of not only the Delta but the contiguous hills and hollows of North and Central Mississippi. You could see him almost anywhere. At the Grove before, during, and after most Ole Miss Football games, in a Justice of the Peace Court in Horn Lake, the livestock sale in Como, every Circuit Court House in the region,, a fishing lodge near Sardis lake when the crappie and bream were biting, and an old cypress and oak hunting lodge near Mayersville, and, of course, the trusted breakfast and lunch havens in each town.

The country stores were disappearing all over the state, but he knew where the survivors were. He was still fascinated by the old stores, hardware and general mercantile, with their rough hardwood floors and seemingly endless supply of nuts and bolts and hammers and the kegs of nails and staples and the bins with the fasteners and plastic pipe couplings and joints and the galvanized and copper pipe stacked in proper lengths, and a few saddles and bridles and girths and horse shoes. The welcome smell of leather and old wood. And the proprietors and employees and customers. They all had stories and most of them had time to tell them and he took the time to listen.

He made money practicing law and he learned to endure brief periods of prosperity. He was a swapper and trader. The story most told about Gorman did not even involve the practice of law. It centered on a one-horned Brahma bull. One day , in the early eighties, when he was still a young and struggling lawyer, after attending court in Hernando, he was driving south down the Interstate on his way to Batesville. His plan was to cut east on Highway 6 and get back to his office in Clarksdale and catch up on his phone calls before going home to his wife.

But when he approached the Como exit, he saw a sign advertising a livestock sale. He had never been to a livestock sale and he was curious as to who and what would be there. He was just out of law school and he and Eunice had been married for only a few years. He went to the sale barn with a corn dog in one hand and a can of Diet Coke in the other. He sat in the stands until the auctioneer brought out a young Brahma bull. The bull lunged around the ring and the bidding started and stopped at a hundred and fifty dollars. It was a cold February day and Gorman still had his lawyer suit on. Blue with a white button down shirt, black lace up Florsheims and a green and red bowtie. Gorman left the stands and went to the edge of the ring and looked closely at the bull. He had swelling in his right front leg. Down near the hoof and you could count his bones. But Gorman liked his frame. Wide at the rear with plenty of room for growth and a short neck. Gorman bid one seventy-five. A lean man in blue coveralls bid two hundred. The bidding kept on going up until the farmer in the coveralls bid five hundred dollars. By then, the café in front of the sale barn had emptied out and the sale barn was full of farmers and cattle buyers from Memphis and Dallas. They were not interested in the bull. It was wild and hurt and skinny and who would buy a Brahma anyway except a lawyer from Clarksdale on his first trip to a sale barn?

No, the reason they left their seats in the café or crawled out of their trucks around, behind, and in front of the sale barn was to see and witness the bull and the buyer become one. Each owning the other. Shortly after the bid was at five hundred, the auctioneer asked if anyone would go five and a quarter. That was when Gorman climbed into the sale ring and started waving his arms over his head and hollering, "Wait just a minute, wait just a minute. I never been to an auction before and I just want to know something."

The bull was standing peacefully near the auctioneer's raised stand. His head was down, rocking slowly back and forth. It looked like he was studying a small sparrow that had flown into the barn and was picking through the cedar shavings on the floor of the auction ring. The ring man stood to the side with a long heavy wooden cane in his right hand.

Gorman's rival reached into his billfold and pulled a dollar out and waved it. He said, "Let him ask his question. It's worth a dollar to me to hear it and hear your answer."

The auctioneer said, "Make it fast, I got the rest of these cows to auction off and a bunch of horses for the night auction, then I got to drive to Corinth for the sale there tomorrow. "

"First question is this. My competition here in this bidding. Who is he and where is he from?" Gorman asked.

"Not that it is any of your goddamn business, but my name is Elam. Joseph Elam and I am from Nesbit"

"That brings me to my next question. And it is this, is a bid a bid or can you welch on it? And is the seller willing to take that five hundred dollars bid by Mr. Elam in front of everybody?" Gorman asked.

The auctioneer said, "I can answer that easy. The bid is acceptable to the seller. Now let's move on. "

"Just one more question. Every courthouse I go into around here seems to have an Elam or two on the docket. And them Elams is all in jail. So my question is this. Why should I bid against a man that can't even bond his own kin out of jail? I want proof he has five hundred dollars."

Elam jumped down into the ring and pulled five one hundred-dollar bills out of his wallet and waved them around. He said, "I got the money. I got more sense than to bail my worthless kin out of jail. Here is my money."

"Then you have just bought yourself a Brahma bull," Gorman said as he crawled over the top rail of the sale ring. The laughter had already started before he was out the side door. Gorman went inside the café and took a window seat. He ordered a cheeseburger and a Budweiser. Soon the café was full. Some of the older farmers came by and asked about his father's health.

A small old man in his sixties walked over to Gorman's table and said, "Elam was trying to run that bid up. That bull belongs to his brother in law from over near Holly Springs. He busted his hip a while back and couldn't keep his stock up. He's got a couple of horses he is going to sell tonight. He been letting um starve most of the winter. Out on an old stalk field. He cut the corn and sold it. Didn't have any hay, so he let his stock forage on corn stalks."

It was almost dark when Gorman saw Elam and another man leading the bull to a mud-caked stock trailer. Gorman paid his bill and asked for three Budweisers to go. The cashier put the beer in a paper sack and Gorman crossed the lot to the banged up old stock trailer. "Fellows, I hope there is no hard feelings. I did not mean for it to shake out like this, but when he bid more than two hundred dollars, I figured something was wrong. And I don't even know stock. But that bull is rank. I can see that. Now tell me where we are in this bull business? I might want back in. But way short of five hundred dollars."

He handed each of them a beer and cracked open the last can for himself. He stuck his hand out and asked Elam's his brother-in-law's name. It was Jerry Bogan.

"Well, I am out the auction barn fee which is twenty dollars and I took Elam's money but I gave it back, so I am out twenty dollars plus my gas money and time and I still got that bull. I have no way of feeding him. I been laid up and I can't go back to work at the compress for two more weeks. The company doctor finally cleared me, but set that as the date."

"Whose stock trailer and Silverado is this," Gorman asked. Elam said, "Mine."

"Here is what I think we should do. Mr. Bogan, I give you three hundred dollars for the bull and twenty dollars for your auction fee. Now you got two weeks before you can go back to work and they said you had some horses you was going to sell off. Probably going to be going to Dallas tomorrow for dog food." Gorman said.

Elam said, "Well, that is nice. But what I want to know is how you gonna get that worthless-ass bull to Clarksdale."

"Easy. You gonna take him right now. You will be back in time to get your Brother-in-law tonight before the sale is over. Oh, I forgot that halter and rope. I will need it. Fifteen dollars for both. Three hundred and thirty five dollars plus what you get for these horses will probably tide you over till you get your first pay check," Gorman said.

"How much for me? Nothing in Clarksdale I need or want." Elam said.

"Fifty for your time. Twenty for your gas," Gorman said.

When the bull was in the lot behind the barn at Gorman's place, it should have all been over. Except the bull kept breaking out of the barn and lot and when Gorman got that stopped, he noticed the bull would not put weight on. Never mind that Gorman had gotten the bull wormed and had a feeding plan in place courtesy of the County

Extension Agent.

When the bull arrived, Eunice disapproved. The bull looked dangerous. And he was ugly. Floppy skin, angry eyes, and a short stubby horn caught Eunice's attention. A month or so later, she came to the realization that the bull was there to stay unless it was sold. So when she was called upon to pray at church one bright and clear Sunday Morning, it was natural for her to include a wish that the Lord would send someone to buy this ugly and worthless bull.

Gradually, word got around and people stopped by uninvited to see the bull. The women would go inside and talk to Eunice and the men would lean on the barn fence and stare at the bull and get Gorman to tell the story of how he out traded his ownself into owning a bull he did not need and could not sell. But one day, Jamie Van Zant came by Gorman's office and gave him a large plastic bottle filled with an iron supplement. Jamie worked at the Clarksdale Country Club. He was a groundskeeper for the golf course at the country club. He planted flowers, kept the grass cut, and did any other landscaping duties that were needed. He was a man way past fifty who never was seen to stand straight. His dirty baseball cap was worn at an angle, but he knew his plants and he knew his stock. He told Gorman he had bought one of Bogan's horses that had wintered on the same stalk field as the bull Gorman bought. Gorman took the plastic jug home and sprinkled a fourth of a cup on the bull's feed twice a day and soon he started to put weight back on. That fall, Gorman sold him to a Highway Patrolman in Greenwood for sixteen hundred dollars and a beat-up, green, metal fishing boat.

Gorman napped in his leather chair until it was after dark. He knew he must go home. There would be no one there. No children. No wife. He knew he should sell the house and just move in his office. The whole top floor of his office could be converted to living quarters so easily. But it took a different kind of energy to make the transition. Leaving the house he and Eunice had raised the children in. The home of so many memories. Loud parties in his younger days. Candle light dinners with Eunice. Sundays with Eunice fussing about the bull loose in the yard. The pecans in the fall. Cleaning fish out behind the barn. The girls running through the house. So many memories. But he was tired tonight. He did not want to go home. He had clothes he kept upstairs. He knew that before the night was over he would think about Robert Whitfield.

During his thirty plus years of practicing law, he had handled so many cases. But it was only the ones he had lost or performed at a disappointing level that would come strolling across his memory on the many nights he could not sleep. The State of Mississippi vs. Robert Whitfield was his first Murder in the First Degree case. When he had set up practice after graduating from law school, he had went around to all of the circuit courts within a hundred miles of Clarksdale and signed up for appointed cases. He would sign his name on the rolls of prospective lawyers who would accept appointments from the court on indigent criminal cases or cases where ethical conflicts arose. He did this in each circuit and after signing the list and talking to the clerks of court; he would wait patiently in the courtroom until he could go back in the judge's chambers and introduce himself.

It helped that all of the judges knew his father. Either personally or by reputation. His father had been a Federal Judge. He had been sitting since the Eisenhower years. When Gorman had been admitted into the bar of the State of Mississippi, his father retired and came home to Clarksdale and reopened his old law office. His father did not practice. He had a comfortable retirement and told Gorman he would be an observer. Of the Delta. Of the nation. And of the world.

His father lived on the second floor of the office. He would come down to his office before seven, put his gray Stetson on the rack, police his desk, go back and take the Stetson back off the rack and go to a café and eat breakfast and listen to the dying breed of farmers. The older ones remembering the Depression and the World War and

Korea and Eisenhower and Jack Kennedy. They ate country ham, bacon, pork sausage, in links and patties, grits, fried eggs, biscuits, home fries, toast, pancakes with sorghum, and jams and jellies. They dressed in blue overalls or khakis and wore gray or white Stetsons with smaller brims and crowns than the Western ranchers. All had sun scarred faces. Deeply tanned and alert, they welcomed Judge Ballard. It was the early eighties and their ranks were thinning.

The Judge was silent through most of these breakfasts. He usually spoke only when asked to. He was content to listen to the stories that were told over the course of a winter breakfast. In the spring, the talk turned to the weather and planting schedules and seed prices. There were two cafes the Judge would go to. Each was in walking distance of the office. He would usually return between nine and ten and go to his office and read the Memphis Commercial Appeal, the day old New York Times, and the Jackson, Mississippi Clarion Ledger.

When the Circuit Court of Coahoma County was in session, the Judge sometimes broke his routine and sat in the first row of the jury box while the calendar was called. He would greet lawyers, talk to old friends, and stay aloof from all proceedings. He did not give advice and when asked about his son, he would smile and say, "Give him a few years. Just a few. Watch and see." He was never in a courtroom when his son had a case on the docket, but he knew his son's cases. They would discuss them in the late afternoons after the secretary had locked the front door and the Judge had read the papers and eaten his noon meal at one of the same two cafes he ate breakfast at.

The noon meals were different. Fried chicken, an occasional plate of spaghetti, pork chops lightly fried, catfish fried, hamburgers and fries, a beef patty smothered in gravy ,chicken fried steak, collard greens, spinach, fried corn, corn on the cob, green beans, lima beans, mashed potatoes, sliced tomatoes, rice, and gravy, headed the list of his favorites. And cobblers. Peach and blackberry were his favorites. And any pie known to man. And, of course, banana pudding.

When he left the bench, the Judge decided he was through with briefs and arguments and pleading. When he came home to Clarksdale, he told Gorman, "I was wrong. I thought the statutes and the pleadings and rulings were the important thing. It is the people. I want to be here for your help if you need it, but I mainly want to observe. I missed the people. Without the people, the law is just a sterile exercise in futility. I missed the people. As an appellate judge, I only saw paper. There was no depth to it."

Gorman would come in from court and his father would be in his office reading. Late in the afternoon, he would pour a small amount of bourbon or scotch into a water glass and sip it. Seldom more than one. Gorman would tell him about his day. The cases. The clients. The judges. The witnesses. The clerks. Everything he felt was important, or at least, interesting. His father would listen and offer whatever advice or knowledge he had. He was in his seventies and sometimes he rambled. When Gorman got the call from the Hardaman County Clerk's office, he was simply asked if he could appear in court the following Friday to accept an appointment on a criminal case. When Gorman got to the courthouse that Friday morning, he went to the clerk's office and spoke to the clerk who worked in the courtroom. The clerk was a large black woman, in her early fifties, with close, cropped gray hair. She was wearing a blue skirt and a blue blazer and white blouse. Her name was Marcy. She told Gorman she thought he was going to get the Robert Whitfield murder case. She asked Gorman to follow her back to her office. She moved some red docket ledgers from a green metal office chair and Robert sat down. They had almost an hour before court convened.

Marcy said, "Judge Swearingen. You met him when you come by and signed the book to get appointments. He is not happy. We got seven white lawyers in the county. Four take criminal cases. One of them, Jimmy Case, is like you. Fresh out of school. Well, none of them will take this case. Black man killing a white man. Right out in the daylight in the parking lot of the Sunflower grocery on a Friday afternoon. Fifteen or so people in that parking lot saw some of what was going on. Some claim to have seen it all. So here you are."

"You said seven white lawyers. What about black lawyers?" Gorman asked.

"Only black lawyer called me right after it happened and said for me to tell Judge Swearingen he was too busy suing railroads and school boards to fool with trash that killed people. So it is you. You got two choices. One, you can lie to the Judge and invent some excuse. He will let you off and be polite about it, but your name will come off that list of lawyers and he will remember you as a ducker. A lawyer who will not handle the hard cases. Or two. You can take the case. Take your lumps. Learn something and have a judge owe you a favor."

"I will take it. Fill me in. Tell me about Whitfield and who he killed. What led up to it? Anything else you think I need to know."

"Robert is not a bad guy. He is in his late or middle twenties. He has one child. A little girl named Vera. Vera Stepter. She is being raised by her maternal grandmother. Her mother went off somewhere up north and nobody ever heard back from her. Robert has some land. Not a lot. He left after Louise, that was Vera's mother, left him and the baby. He went to Chicago right before Christmas one year and came back in time to plant his crops. He supposed to have hated Chicago. That was the word, anyway. So Vera stays with Ann Stepter. That is Louise's mother. She retired a few years back from working in the cafeteria at the county school. Lives out a few miles from here on a gravel road. Robert's place is about a half-mile away. Robert is a worker. He can fix anything and do anything. He dropped out of school in the ninth grade. He worked on cars. Tractors. Combines. And farmed his own land some."

"Will you go down the hall and get me a coke? I like a Diet. Just for the taste. Telling all this has made me thirsty."

When Gorman came back, Marcy was on the phone. She took

the Diet Coke from Gorman and leaned back in her chair. She cradled the phone between her head and left shoulder. Finally, she said, "Look hon, I know you are right, but you still got to pay that bill. They just gonna sue you if you don't."

She listened for a few seconds more and said, "Look, I got to go. I got a Judge fixing to tear me a new ass if I don't have his docket spread out on his bench in about twenty minutes."

After she hung up, she said, "That was my cousin, Ray. He thinks cause I work in a courthouse I can make his problems go away. Like I got a law degree by sitting in the court room writing reset dates down for twenty four years."

"So where we were was Robert. He is ok. Folks know him as a good man. Strong and quiet. Not a big man. Just somebody you do not want to mess with. Now that leads us to what they call in the law the victim. In this case, it is Billy Ray Starnes. If there is one thing everybody, black or white, in this county has in common is they have been fucked over, if you will pardon me, by a Starnes. Stealing. Lying.

Cheating. There is one in Parchman right now for robbing a hardware store in Corinth. Now how low is that? His name is Ricky. That is his real name. Ricky Ricardo Starnes. But Billy Ray was just a loud drunk. Couldn't or wouldn't hold a job for long. Trash like that all over this world, I am afraid."

Gorman accepted the appointment, arraigned Robert Whitfield, and asked for a Motion Date. Judge Swearingen gave him a trial date four months off and a motion date some sixty days off. Gorman thanked the Judge and was fixing to turn to leave when the Judge said, "Mr. Ballard, dates in my court room are performance dates. You do on the date given, the task allotted. I do not take kindly to lawyers who try to delay proceedings. I am telling you this because I do not know you and I think I should give you the courtesy of knowing what is expected of you in this court. This is a Capital case. The State of Mississippi will ask the Jury to sentence your client to death by electrocution. I expect motions, but I want them disposed of in a prompt manner. In furtherance of that goal, the District Attorney will give you full discovery before you leave this county today. Next case."

It was almost noon when Gorman left the Hardaman County Courthouse and crossed the old town square with the District Attorney. Gorman knew him. Most people in North Mississippi did. His name was Richard Lee Strong. He was in his late twenties, thin, and black. He had played baseball at Mississippi State and graduated from Law School and then set up practice in nearby Corinth. This alone would never have been enough to get him elected District Attorney for a four county district that included Hardaman County. What got him elected was his mother. She was an educator. A teacher for many years, a principal for ten, and now, the Superintendent of Education for the whole state. She had called in enough favors for her son to be elected by a comfortable margin over his two rivals. He had been in his third year of Law School in Oxford when Gorman was in his first.

They ate a quiet meal in a café just off the square. Strong ate vegetable soup and a piece of grilled catfish. Gorman had fried chicken, rice and gravy, lima beans, and a bowl of banana pudding. Over coffee, Strong pulled a file from his brief case. He said, "This is your discovery. Straight up and down case. No twists or hidden dramas. Your client called Hugh Rainey on Friday night after the killing. Said he would be at his house on Saturday morning with the gun. He asked for the rest of the night off to get things straight around his place, I guess. Probably went down the road to Ann Stepter's and signed his land over to her and said good bye to his daughter, Vera. My guess. Hugh Rainey is the Sheriff. He showed up around ten the next morning and Robert was on the porch with the pistol in a paper sack. The Sheriff read him his rights and took a handwritten statement right there. Signed by Robert. No witnesses to the statement. You can ask Robert. So the questions in the case will be the grade of the

Homicide and the punishment. We can try it in a few days. One day to pick a jury. Two for my proof. One for yours. Arguments and the charge. We will work nights. So it will probably be done with middle of Thursday and then we can wait for what passes as Hardaman County Justice. Jury will probably not be out too long. Half a day or so. With the punishment taking most of the time. Call me now if you have any questions. Sheriff Rainey will talk to you. Maybe even about the case. He will want to know about your father, your mother, all your relatives, and then he will tell you about his. But he is dirt honest. So just wait him out."

Gorman crossed the square and went to the jail and asked to see his client. Robert came down wearing blue jeans and a blue jean shirt. He was lean and had alert eyes and a workman's hands. Large wrists and a prominent Adam's apple caught Gorman's attention. Gorman introduced himself to his client and showed him a copy of the indictment. Gorman explained to Robert what was before him and when he was through, Robert said, "So when do you think I will go to Parchman? Death penalty folks and folks pulling heavy time go to Parchman. Only Death Row in Mississippi. If I get it, I guess you will fight it best you can. That is all I am wanting out of. I don't want to die shackled to no old wooden chair other folks have died in. I killed him and if you put me on the stand I will say I am glad that no good bullying white trash is dead."

Gorman smiled and said, "So we know where we stand. I will try to get an offer for you. I ate lunch with the DA and he says he is going to ask for the Death Penalty. I got the file and I will study it and come back to see you. Here is one of my cards. If you need me, get in touch with Marcy in the Clerk's Office and she will let me know you need to see me. It looks to me like it is going to be a trial."

Robert got up from his chair and called for the jailer and went back upstairs while Gorman was putting papers into his file. Gorman went back over to the Clerk's Office and found Marcy in her office filing pleadings in court jackets. She said, "Glad you came back. Something I forgot to tell you. Something important. Here is your fee schedule. Seventy-five an hour court time. Sixty out of court. Thirty cents a mile travel. Twenty-one dollars a day for food. We put you up here in the old Hardaman Hotel. Not too bad. Or the Country Side Motel out on the Highway to Corinth. About two miles from the court house. Your choice. Appeal, you deal with the Supreme Court. Fee is one hundred dollars per hour office work and one fifty for actual court time."

"What I was wanting to know is would you tell me how to get to Ann Stepter's place and would you call me if Robert needs to talk to me. I would sure appreciate it."

After getting directions, Gorman left the town and drove out to Ann Stepter's house. It was a neat house set a few hundred feet off a gravel road. There were shade trees and a hen house and a small barn near the house. Ann Stepter was a sad faced woman in her sixties who, obviously, had been attractive when she was younger. Tall and lean. Dark brown skin. High, proud cheekbones, and strong brown eyes, highlighted her features. And her hands. They were long and slim with neat fingernails. Vera looked to be around five or six years old. She looked like a smaller version of her grandmother. Vera stood in the doorway while Ann Stepter came out on the porch and greeted Gorman Ballard.

Ann told Vera to go on back inside and straighten up the kitchen while she talked to Robert's lawyer. Gorman and Ann sat on the front porch in wooden rocking chairs and Gorman told her about the trial date. He also told her that Robert did not want Vera to come to the jail or come to the trial.

"Sheriff Rainey let him stay out till Saturday morning. He come by here Friday night. He had been drinking. He knew I did not want him coming around here drinking. Vera got plenty of time left to discover all about that. A child's young years should hold some pleasures for them to remember. Now I told him all that, and I was mad. He stood on the top step to my porch and told me what happened and he said he knew he was going to Parchman and he would do his time. But they was not going to kill him. He would find a way for that not to happen. He gave me some papers. The title to his truck and the title to his land. Signed over to me. Told me not to bother with no lawyer. He told me to go shares with one of the Crowder boys on his land. Said they would not cheat me. And it would pay enough for Vera to have some clothes and go to school on. Then he asked to see Vera and I called her out on the porch and she jumped up in the rocker in her daddy's lap and I started to bawling and I had to quit. So I did, and then he hugged her and said he was going away and for her to remember him and to remember he loved her and she was asking questions about where he was going and before long he just left. Walking down the gravel road to his house. We went on back in the house and I tried reading a book to her and then I turned on the television but she kept asking questions till she fell asleep."

Gorman said, "I will read the file and try to answer any questions you have." He gave her a couple of his business cards and waited for her to ask a question.

She sat and rocked back and forth in her chair for a few minutes and then said, "Do you want money? I am not so country as not to know lawyers and money go together. You sure don't work for free and we do not want charity. I am the closest to family Robert has."

"No, I am appointed by the Court. I am paid by the Court and you do not need to concern yourself with my fee at all. Do you have any other questions?"

"So the County pays your fee and then the State wants to kill him. They pay a lawyer too."

"Yes."

"Is it like that everywhere or is it just Mississippi?"

"Most civilized countries do it in some similar fashion. None as good as us."

She did not say anything for a while and then she asked if he was going back to Clarksdale that night and he said he was. She asked him to wait a minute and went back into the house. When she came back, she had a quart jar in a paper sack. She handed the sack to Gorman.

"This is red plum jelly. I pick the plums myself. Me and Vera now that she is with me. There are yellow plums too. I pick them and make cobblers out of them, but the red plums; they have a tartness about them the yellow ones don't. Only the red ones go to my jelly. Your wife make biscuits?"

"Yes ma'am she does. She is one of these women that takes to cooking real easy. She likes it but she says she is not a good cook. She is fine. She will appreciate this jelly, I know that. We will save it till it starts to get cold in the mornings. After the first frost. That is when it will be best."

"You right about that. You sure are. What is your wife's name?"

"Eunice."

"I like that name. It is one you used to hear all the time, but now it is going away. This whole county is thinning out. Not many farmers left. How about with you?"

"It is the same. My father just retired and came on back to Clarksdale full time. He says he misses the days when black people filled the streets of Clarksdale on Saturday night. Thinning. That is a good way of saying it."

In a few minutes, they ran out of things to talk about and Gorman spent the night in the old hotel reading his discovery. The next morning, he called the Sheriff's office before daylight and arranged for Sheriff Rainey to meet him for breakfast. The Sheriff was slightly overweight and in his early fifties. He stood a little less than six feet and his hair was brown and thinning. He talked slowly and was friendly to Gorman. He sat down and ordered coffee and a lot of food.

He said, "You read the file last night? "

Gorman was drinking iced tea. "Yes," he said.

"What jumped out at you? "

"The autopsy and morgue photographs of Billy Ray Starnes. No defensive wounds and the second bullet wound. The one that killed him. The one slightly above his left eyebrow. That is the one I can't get around. Yet. I got a few months to think on it. Ask my client, other lawyers, you. Or maybe think it out myself."

"You figure it out, you tell me. I knowed Robert for a long time. Hard worker. Skilled at fixing things. Never ever been arrested. Was probably going to marry that Stepter girl and raise a family, but she ran out on him. Ran off to Cleveland or Gary, Indiana. Somewhere. I run a check on her a few months ago for Miss Ann. I could find no arrests or death reports, so I guess she has just gone."

The food came. The Sheriff smiled. "Breakfast is my favorite meal. Best time to relax and visit with the voters. You know. I would tell a young lawyer. Find you a place to eat breakfast. Make some friends. Maybe some clients. Back to the case. I know you will file a motion about the statement. The way it happened is when I got there on Saturday morning, he gave me the gun in a paper sack and I read him his rights and he said he understood them and I noticed his eyes was red and I could smell just a little whiskey on his breath. Not a lot and he said he would tell me what happened and I asked him what happened and he said that Starnes was parked behind him at the Sunflower and would not move. Said Starnes told him he did not move his truck for a fucking nigger. Specially one that could not even manage his pussy no better than to let her go off and leave him with a kid to raise."

"So he told me he went back to his truck and got his pistol, that old thirty eight Smith and Wesson, and shut his door and by then Starnes had moved his truck up and came back towards Robert with a tire iron. Now right here you got a case you could argue self-defense or voluntary manslaughter, but Starnes was thirty some odd feet away when Robert shot him the first time. That old thirty-eight scaring folks that were in the grocery store. And Starnes fell on the parking lot and was rolling around and if Robert would have just left, he would be doing eleven months and twenty-nine days at the jail. Helping fix county cars in the daytime and Starnes would have lived, but Robert walked up to him, stood over him and then shot him in the head. Powder burns and stippling in that wound. So there is your murder in the first degree."

"That is what I read in the discovery. I got to talk to all the people. I hope I can get a decent offer from the Prosecutor."

"Not going to happen. You got Starnes' and their relatives all over these counties here in North and Central Mississippi and some up in Tennessee near Shiloh and Somerville. You gonna have a trial. There is something not being said, Lawyer. I been talking to folks a long time. Been lied to by every type of somebody you can think of. Robert ain't no liar but he just did not tell me the why of it all. There was something else caused this. Robert had too much sense to kill Starnes over a parking lot argument. But he would not tell me. I gave him all the chance in the world. I wrote his statement out by hand and he signed it, then the next day, Sunday, before Church, I went by the jail and read that silly little Miranda card to him again and asked him if there was something he had not told me and he just stared at me and told me I knew enough to do my job with so I stammered around some and tried some more but he was through talking. He is just waiting to take his time and go to Parchman. Robert keeps his business to his self."

"I got to file a bunch of motions. Got to challenge the statement. Advice of rights. Everything. You know better than to take it personal, I hope."

"Why sure I do. Tell me about how your father is doing. I remember him before he was a judge. I was a deputy, then a Highway Patrolman, then a retired Highway Patrolman and now the duly elected Sheriff. Tell him hello for me. He knows all my people. A lot of them dead. You have any trouble finding some folks or serving your papers you call me. Judge Swearingen wants this case off his docket the sooner the better."

They talked for a while longer and the Sheriff bought Gorman's breakfast and made his rounds in the café. Calling the men by their first name and the women by Ms. or Mrs. or Aunt. Gorman was standing out front of the café when the Sheriff came out laughing, still talking to a couple of the men who had followed him out.

He said, "Get in the car. I know you got photographs, but I can show you the crime scene. Make the trial go faster if you know what you are talking about."

They drove to the Sunflower store and the Sheriff got out and took the photos and showed Gorman where it had all happened. There was a poorly drawn sketch in the file that contained a roughly drawn outline of Starnes' body on the parking lot and the location of the vehicles. After an hour, Gorman felt comfortable with the crime scene and the Sheriff took him back to his car.

Gorman drove on back to his office in Clarksdale. He found his father reading the day old New York Times Business section. He told his father about his visit and asked about the Judge and the Sheriff and his father said they were straight up and trustworthy. Then his father asked him to sit down.

"Gorman, there is so much to learn about the practice of law. Not the law. The practice of law. You got a letter and a check and release forms from an insurance company yesterday. It is firm business so I read it and I looked at the check. Ninety four thousand dollars. Now I know what a third of that is. And I know you are young. And I know you been practicing less than three years and this is your first big settlement."

"So what I want to tell you is to learn to survive brief periods of prosperity. A common failure of lawyers. Of all ages. Get a good fee.

Spend or obligate to spend more than you should and then when lean times come and they always do, you get squeezed for money. Lawyers got enough to worry about. Money should not be one of them. Clients go elsewhere. You trust to client loyalty and you will wind up in the pore house. Save some of that money. Save most of it. You were doing fine before you got it. No need to spend it. Fill out one of those quarterly return forms for the IRS today. I got you one. Well, fill it out as soon as the client approves the settlement and the money is dispersed. Get that out of the way. And do not go around flashing money all over Clarksdale. Save all of it you can."

Gorman said, "Eunice could use a new car. But she is not complaining."

"No, and she won't. What you might do is take it and get some work done on it. New shocks. New tires. Now son, next time you go to court, look around at the lawyers. Especially on arraignment day. Lawyers looking for appointments. Looking for clients. Notice them and look at their faces. Specially the older ones. Ask yourself, who really wants to be here? Who is past sixty, maybe pushing seventy, and is still hustling cases? Most of them had a check like this in front of them. Some had bigger ones. All I am saying is you may want to do something else other than be a lawyer in your evening years. The secret is to save now. Now I am going over to the High School and watch a baseball game. Do you want me to read the discovery? I am here to help, not interfere."

His father did read the discovery. And he said the Sheriff looked to be right. Gorman filed his motions. Heard them all on schedule. The Sheriff telling Judge Swearingen the same things he had told Gorman at breakfast in the little café. He did volunteer his feeling that Robert Whitfield had fired those shots for a different reason than he gave in his statement. Robert sat quietly during the motions. He had told Gorman the statement was voluntary. He said he gave it because the Sheriff let him have that night of freedom before arresting him.

Robert said he wanted his say because he knew with all the hollering out on the parking lot after the shooting, the witnesses would get some of it right and a lot of it wrong.

Gorman went across the Square to the District Attorney's office after the motions had been heard and talked to Richard Lee Strong about an offer of settlement. Gorman wanted a second-degree plea with a sentence of twenty years. So he asked Strong for ten. Strong said he thought that was what it was worth except for that second shot. He said the family and relatives of Billy Ray Starnes, worthless and unreliable as they were, had a right to want a trial and so that was what he was going to do.

Gorman went to a café on the square and waited until almost four o'clock and went back into the courthouse. Court was adjourned and Marcy was at her desk filing and stamping papers. She smiled when she saw Gorman and waved him in. After Gorman sat down, Marcy closed the door, and smiled at him.

"A long day. Why you lawyers so long winded? Leastways, we got all them motions out of the way. Started at nine o'clock. Worked straight through lunch. Way I see it, you owe me lunch. Mr. Strong owes me lunch. Now what you need?'

"You, as a woman, see things different. Also, you probably witnessed more trials than anyone in the court, including the judge. And you live here. In this county. So you heard the whole case today. The statement of Robert Whitfield. But I sense there is something missing. I asked him. He would not add anything to his statement. No one seems to know. So tell me, based on your experience and wisdom, why did this really happen?"

"All I heard is what you all talked about today. No big secrets or rumors. Way I see it, it doesn't matter why. It just matters that he did it. Stood over him and put that second bullet in his brain. Man that is cold. Can't be no reason to justify it. I told you first day you came in here that Robert was a good man. Worked hard. Reliable. Drank a bit, but never been a problem to no one. So whatever the reason, he did it and it is time for him to pay. Starnes has a mother that loves him. Even if he is a worthless piece of crap. All you gonna be able to do is maybe keep him out of the electric chair. And do not get up there crying and blubbering about the death penalty."

"You sound like my father."

"You asked, lawyer, now you can go down the hall and get me a Diet Coke and if they are out, you can drag your ass over to one of them high priced cafes and get me a big iced tea with lemon."

"What about I go get us a cheeseburger a piece? I am hungry."

"Make it three. Two for me. I will not leave here before eight o'clock. And a lot of iced tea."

While they were eating, Marcy asked him. "You ain't one of these dipshit liberals come to help relieve the poor black man of his burden? Cause if you are, let me tell you, we don't need you. We are doing for ourselves."

Gorman laughed and said, "Naw, that is not me. But I care about my clients. Like you said, Robert is a decent man. It is just a curiosity I have. I want to know all of it. And I am learning you never know all of it. Somebody always holds something back. Or misleads you or flat out cons you by lying. You can't catch every liar. But a man like Robert, he will only tell you what he wants you to know."

"I am not saying you have discharged your debt to me with these two greasy cheeseburgers, but you are close. When the trial is over, we can sit down in one of those cafes on the square and I will tell you where you did right, where you should have shut up, and what you did wrong. "

Gorman took her up on it. The trial went off as scheduled and Gorman put on a few witnesses to show that Robert was a peaceful man until the day he shot Billy Ray Starnes. He put on Ann Stepter and she told about the baby and how Robert had come and said goodbye to his daughter on the Friday night after he killed Starnes.

Robert did not testify. He did not want to say anything that was not in his statement and he said he had no remorse. Gorman recalled Sheriff Rainey and rehashed, over objection, the facts that Robert was waiting for him on the front porch on Saturday morning with the gun and had waived his rights and answered all of the questions in a cooperative manner. But the Sheriff also added, again, that he felt Robert had more of a reason to shoot Starnes than he would admit.

During jury selection, Gorman had spent most of the time talking about voluntary manslaughter. A killing predicated upon a sudden heat of passion. The prospective jurors were a mixed group of women and men, black and white. The jury finally selected by the lawyers included a twenty one year old white welder, three black farmers in their fifties, four white farmers, ranging in age from thirty two to sixty, two white housewives in their forties, one black schoolteacher in her twenties, and a black woman in her forties who drove a school bus and told the judge she had the best garden in the county.

The testimony was predictable. Just like the Sheriff had predicted. Strong only put on four eye witnesses. There were more but their testimony was either redundant or suspect. All four witnesses saw Robert stand over Starnes and fire the last and fatal shot. There was little drama in the trial after the first eye witness. The Medical Examiner testified the muzzle to wound distance was less than two feet for the crucial head shot, that the first shot was non-fatal, and that Starnes had a blood alcohol content of,13, well above the presumptive limit of intoxication,,10.

Gorman had asked few questions. He emphasized that Robert Whitfield asked Starnes to move his truck, that Starnes had cursed him and called him a nigger several times, that Starnes had pulled a tire iron out of his truck and approached Robert with it.

There were really no disputes in the testimony. Gorman had explained the concept of remorse to Robert and Robert had looked at him with cold eyes and said he knew what remorse was and he would go to his grave without having any for killing Starnes.

Gorman kept his final argument short and focused. He emphasized the lack of premeditation, which is the key element of Murder in the First Degree. He asked the jury to bring back a verdict of Voluntary Manslaughter. He closed by emphasizing the work record and love of family Robert had shown all through his life. And the cooperation he had given Sheriff Rainey was proof of the respect for the law that Robert Whitfield had. The trial concluded with Judge Swearingen reading the jury instructions to the jury. As the jury filed out, Gorman immediately began to think of things he should have said, questions he should have asked, and questions he should have left unasked. The jury received the case on Thursday night and deliberated until mid-night. The foreman of the jury was the black woman who drove the school bus and bragged about her garden. She sent a note to Judge Swearingen asking to quit for the night and to come back in the morning after breakfast.

Gorman would always remember that night. No one to talk to. No interest in a book or magazine. No ability to sleep. He had lain in bed until after three going over everything about the case in his mind. He thought it was a good omen that the jury had picked Mrs. Scruggs, the bus driver, as the foreman. Finally, he drifted off to sleep. He woke at seven, rushed to the courthouse, checked in with the Judge, and went to the café where he and the sheriff had eaten breakfast a few months ago. The Sheriff was in the café eating with Marcy and one of his deputies. Gorman headed to the counter but the Sheriff called him over. The Sheriff did not talk about the case. They were talking about one of the girls in high school who had gotten suspended for a week for starting a fight at a school basketball game.

Gorman listened. He ate two pancakes, scrambled eggs, and bacon. He kept his mind off the case for a while, paid his bill, and went back to the courthouse and sat outside the courtroom and waited for the verdict. It was a clear Friday morning. When the jury reached a verdict, Gorman sat at the counsel table and waited for Robert Whitfield to be brought into the courtroom. Once everyone was settled and the Court was called to order, the jury came in and Mrs. Scruggs gave the trial jacket to Judge Swearingen.

The Judge read the verdict to the packed courtroom. "We, the Jury, find the defendant, Robert Lee Whitfield, guilty of Murder in the First Degree and fix his punishment at ninety-nine years in the State Penitentiary." Gorman breathed as deeply as he could and stood by Robert Whitfield while the Judge sentenced his client. He then asked for a date to hear a Motion for New Trial. He wrote the date down and thanked the Judge. He looked at the Jury and most of them were looking at something other than the participants in the trial. After the Jury was excused, and the Court was adjourned, Gorman turned to Robert and explained the next steps in the case. A Motion for New Trial and then an appeal all the way to the Mississippi Supreme Court. Robert did not appear interested. He wanted to know when he would be transferred to Parchman. The court was empty except for a jailer waiting to carry Robert back to jail.

Gorman said he would enter an order transferring him to Parchman before he left Hardaman County today if Robert was sure that was what he wanted. Robert said, "Yes, I might as well get started. I can't get no parole time or good and honor time sitting in this cell."

Gorman told him he was sorry about the verdict and Robert said, "You a lawyer, not a fucking magician. I killed the man right in front of a whole parking lot full of people. Now what you did was get me out of the electric chair. That is all I can ask. The rest, dealing with Parchman, staying alive, getting parole time. I got to do that on my own.

I ain't figured out how, but I will. So, I am obliged to you, Lawyer Ballard for what you did, but I don't have no faith in appeals and I got no money to buy a pardon with, so I got to stay alive and find a way to have a real life someday."

Robert stood up and walked away with the jailer. Before they got to the door, Robert turned and said, "Don't forget that paper you promised me. The one that gets me to Parchman." And with that, Robert left, and Gorman was alone in the courtroom. It was after noon when he walked back to the Courthouse from the café with the two cheeseburgers and the iced tea in a paper sack. Marcy was at her desk filing papers and making entries in the court docket books.

When she saw Gorman, she said, "You looked discombobulated after that verdict. I knew you was coming back, though. I got an order for you. A form to transfer Robert on to Parchman. I done heard that is what he wants. All you need to do is sign it and I will get the Judge to sign it before he leaves today. The Sheriff will send him on the first of the week."

While Gorman looked the order of transfer over, Marcy began eating one of the cheeseburgers. She said, "Lawyer Ballard, I got no criticisms of your trial performance. Cepting them bow ties but I guess that is a faint criticism of a man who been trying a case like this all week. What I need from you is some of your cards. Might give em out at my church and leave a few by the cash register at the café. Send me a mess of them next week. Now do not forget, go over and tell the Judge thank you for the appointment. Even if you don't mean it. Do it. Might pay off later. Judges like lawyers with some manners. There is so few of them."

Gorman took the order of transfer back to Judge Swearingen's chambers. The Judge was reading the current Atlantic Monthly and drinking a glass of iced tea. Gorman thanked him for the appointment and the Judge signed the order of transfer. He rocked back in his chair and asked Gorman, "Not to invade the attorney client privilege, but one thing is curious to me. Did you ever get to know your client? I say this not as a reflection on you, not by any means, but I just felt we were trying half or a third of this lawsuit. Meaning, Robert is more complex than came out in this trial. Once again, I say this as an observer. Not a critic. Hard for a lawyer to know his client nowadays. Used to we all grew up together and nobody much moved off from the county. At least not very far. And not many moved in. Now I got to go to Clarksdale, over a hundred miles away, to get a lawyer to defend this guy. No one wants to make an enemy of these Starnes folks. Nobody. I felt bad about this appointment, but I figured if you had some of your father in you, you would do fine. Now back to my question. Did you ever really feel you had some insight into your client? I am talking about something you learned on your own and not from Sheriff Rainey?"

"Well, here I am fixing to say something that may sound real stupid, but here it is anyway. I like Robert. You know, there is something there. An inner grace. What passes for dignity. This in a man that stood over a fellow human being and, oh so carefully, shot this fellow human being in the brain pan."

"Heard your father was retired. Enjoying reading and watching his son. Tell him I won't be too far behind him. I got three years left in this term and I can retire. Do some traveling. Go to New York once a year. Have a drink at an Ole Miss football game if they ever start playing better. Give him my regards and best wishes."

Gorman drove on back to Clarksdale in the fading winter light. When he got back to his office, his father was in the library reading the New York Times. There was a fire crackling in the fireplace. Gorman put a fresh log on and the flames roared up the chimney. Gorman stood in front of the hearth and felt the welcome heat warm his body. There were no glasses or bottles on his father's side table. He was wearing a coarse, blue wool sweater over a white dress shirt. After Gorman had told him about Judge Swearingen sending his regards, his father said, "So you got a verdict, but you do not want to talk about it. Is that about it?"

'I want to talk about the trial, the whole thing. But here it is Friday night. I am too tired to go home and I am hungry. I should just call

Eunice and go on home and eat a good supper. I am hungry. Hungry for a steak. Then I want to come back here and talk to you about it. I need to call Eunice, she will understand. She always does. I need to do more for her."

"I'll drive. The café down at the Holiday Inn is ok. They got a nice rib eye. We can come back here afterwards and talk or you can do it later. I do not like to talk business in a restaurant. Specially on a Friday night."

His father was right. The rib eye was good. Gorman loaded a baked potato up with sour cream and butter and bacon and passed on the salad and broccoli that came with the steak. He ate a piece of store bought cherry pie and drank some coffee. His father told him he was planning a trip in May to go to Washington and see the Museums and the cherry trees in bloom. Also, he was going to the Grand Canyon in September. Driving by himself. They did not talk about the case or anything to do with law. A few people stopped by the table and said hello.

When they returned to the office, his father put more wood on the fire and opened a desk drawer and produced a bottle of Wild Turkey. He poured each of them a small amount. Just enough to cover the bottom of the glasses. He offered no ice and no water.

"I like my scotch. Rye sometimes. And of course, bourbon. Wild Turkey is a little rough around the edges. Not as smooth as Jack Daniels but the way I see it, some nights smooth is overrated. I like the roughness. Other nights if I am reading a good Graham Greene novel or Robert Frost, smoothness is required"

Gorman took a small sip of the bourbon and sat on the hearth. He loved a fire in a fireplace.

"The verdict was ninety-nine years. Murder in the First Degree. I could not get the jury down to voluntary. Not even second."

"How did you figure on doing that? Getting it down from what it obviously was, at least to a layman, to some fairy tale verdict. How did you figure on doing all of that?"

"Manslaughter. A killing in a sudden heat. No time for Robert to form premeditation. Robert insulted in public. The time. Only a small sliver of time elapsed from when it all started until Robert was in his truck driving on back to his place. Just a very small period of time. It was manslaughter. He should be out in time for the spring plowing next year. Instead, he will be a guest of the State for ninety-nine years. Chopping cotton. Hoeing corn and cotton. Picking. Harvesting. Somebody else's crops for the rest of his life."

"But you have failed to tell me what you as a lawyer did or did not do that affected the verdict in this case. You filed and heard the motion to suppress the statement. No use challenging the eye witness identification. They all knew him by name. The Sheriff did not even bother to show them photographs or conduct a lineup. You filed motions challenging the constitutionality of the Death Penalty. You saved your man from the chair."

"I guess on a personal level, I am disappointed. I worked so hard and felt I had a shot at manslaughter. The time frame was so damn narrow and there was no proof of any prior problems. But more important, I feel I failed in not letting the jury see inside my client. He is a good man. But I could never really see inside him as close as I wanted. I feel a failure as a man. Not just as a lawyer. I thought about it all the way home. How could I have done better? In relating to my client? "

"Well, first of all, homicide is the most complex crime. We as a society choose to punish the intent of the slayer. Not the act. You can kill a man and it be ruled a justifiable act. The mind of the slayer. This is the wild card in most homicides. The hard thing for the defense attorney to convey to the jury is his client's true mental state at the precise instant the shot was fired or the knife was thrust into the body of the victim."

"And Robert Lee told me over and over. No remorse. None

whatsoever. He said he was proud Starnes was dead. But I stopped there. That was my mistake. I did not find out what really triggered his rage. I tried. And he withdrew and would not communicate and I gave up. I should have come at him a different way but I did not know how. So now, he has no hope. A life in Parchman is worse than no life at all."

"His choice. His choice to kill Starnes in the manner he did. His choice not to open up to his attorney. As for Parchman, it is better than being electrocuted some cold February morning. All you can do is try to be the best lawyer in the courtroom. And to do your best. Sometimes you do your best and the verdict goes against you. If you are going to try cases you have to have a Joe Frazier mentality. Get off the canvas when you are knocked down and keep punching. It is that simple and that complex."

"So how long did it take you to get to the point where you could be a philosopher about your trials?"

"I never did. And I am not sure you ever will. You seem more naïve than I was. You expect more than I ever did. But this is what fathers do. Try to help their sons and daughters have a better life than we had. And help them have a clearer understanding of the world we live in."

"So my reaction is not childish?"

"Of course not. But what you need to remember is that the practice of law can be a lonely grind. But sometimes when you are way, way down, a case will come along and pick you back up. Maybe because of a point of law, perhaps a client who really needs the protection of the law, or the chance of a financial bonanza. The big verdict. The important thing. Don't sell out. Do not be the ambulance chaser. Or the bankruptcy lawyer grubbing your way through futility. There are other examples, but the point is, you are doing it the right way. Now you just have to make your mind up if you are tough enough for the grind. This is not the last case you will get like this. Other judges will call on you. Wanting you to handle the case no one wants."

His father took the bottle off the side table and poured each of them another drink. Again, just enough to cover the bottom of each glass. In a few minutes his father said, "You have overlooked another important facet of the case. Or shall we call it the Hardaman County experience. And the town of Hardaman experience."

"And what is that?"

"The clerk. Marcy. She wants you to mail her some of your cards. Make that your first order of business on Monday. Write her a nice letter thanking her for her assistance while you were in her county. Remember that phrase. Her county. She can help you more than anyone. You know she comes from a big family. She told you about that. I'll bet she goes to a big church out in the county. Another mistake lawyers make. They get busy and uppity and forget to extend common courtesy to people like Marcy. Send her a card at Christmas. You ought to have a notebook with phone numbers and names for each county you go in. And never charge a law enforcement officer a fee if you can help it. They will remember it and when you have a case in their county, you will get information most defense lawyers won't."

Gorman and his father talked until after midnight. There would be other conversations. Some not as long. Some not as meaningful. But as Gorman sat in his chair and watched the dying embers in the fireplace, he remembered that night. Coming home from Hardaman County after the verdict, eating the steak with his father, the two spartan shots of Wild Turkey, and his father's voice. The slow, patient drawl.

And now, on this lonely, rainy March night, Gorman was spent. He did not have the energy to drive home to the dark and silent buildings out on Friar Point Road. The dark and empty rooms that had once been a haven for laughter and children. Their home. But now Eunice was gone. Gone before Gorman could find time to take her to Paris or Rome or Hawaii. Eunice had always been a trusting and supportive wife. But Gorman had taken her for granted. He had never even contemplated a day in his life without her. And now she was gone. He had no one to talk to at this late hour.

He thought of Vera Chaney. And Robert Lee Whitfield. Marcy had retired and moved off to one of the Western States to live with one of her widowed brothers. Judge Swearingen had died before Gorman's father. Sheriff Rainey and Marcy had both referred clients to Gorman. Judge Swearingen appointed him on other cases and never questioned his fees or expenses. His own father was dead.

Gorman doubted Roscoe would ever get out of the juke joint business. A lot of cash washed through those places. Roscoe was a good client. Paid cash. Complained about everything and referred him paying clients. There was still something missing about the day's business. Why had Vera settled on her father as a possible solution to her problems? What could have happened so many years ago that would have left such an impression on her that she would seek him out? A question Gorman had not dared to ask. Sometimes you just had to wait for a sign or a fact that would turn into an answer with some reflection.

Since the verdict, Gorman had seen Robert Lee Whitfield one time. He had visited him to tell him about the appellate process and Robert had asked him to just send him letters because a visit from a lawyer disrupted his day and he had a good job. He was working in the big shed where all the trucks and combines and planters were serviced. He thought he would be a trusty soon. Better food. Less trouble from the guards and better living conditions. Gorman honored his request and after the appellate process was completed he wrote a final letter to Robert. He advised him that he would work on commutation once he had done ten calendar years of his sentence.

The commutation had finally come through. After doing almost thirty years of his sentence, Robert Lee Whitfield had been released. He had not come to Clarksdale and Gorman had no idea where he was. It was simple luck and coincidence that had led Roscoe to recommend him to Vera to help find her father. Gorman wanted to sit down across from Robert Lee and ask him what his real motivation was that afternoon when he took the life of Billy Ray Starnes. The mind of the slayer. He just wanted to know that. The simple truth that might never be known by anyone except Robert Lee. And perhaps Billy Ray Starnes.

Gorman drifted off to sleep shortly before midnight. In the same chair he had sat in when he had come back from Hardaman and told his father about the Robert Lee Whitfield trial and verdict. Later, he woke and went upstairs and showered. While he was toweling off after his shower, he looked at himself in the long, narrow mirror on the bathroom door. It was not a sight that a woman would be drawn to. His body had little muscle definition or tone. There were bags under his eyes, but he did not have a gut and he was not losing his hair. His body was simply boring and bland. He put on a white, terrycloth robe and went back down stairs and put two more logs on the dying fire. He poured a small drink of good scotch in the bottom of his glass and sat in his chair. He thought of the bull for some unknown reason.

The bull was still alive. The Highway Patrolman in Greenwood had poked around and found that the bull had been stolen while still a calf when he was being transported in a cattle truck. The truck had broken down near Grenada and while the driver was in Grenada trying to find help, the calf and his mother had been taken off the truck. The Highway Patrolman had tried to get papers on the bull but he could not verify the pedigree and the bull remained unregistered. But that did not stop the Highway Patrolman from swapping the bull for four thousand cash dollars and two heavy duty, almost new, Poulan chain saws in 1991. The bull was still alive. There were still a few people who remembered the story of the one horned bull and Gorman had made a special trip last spring to a farm near Marks and talked to the farmer who owned the bull. They had walked out in the pasture behind the old red barn and watched the bull as he stood in a field of new grass. The one horn and the disinterested gaze were the same as what Gorman had seen in the sale barn those many years ago.

Gorman drifted back to sleep as the logs popped and sputtered in the fireplace. It was one of the last nights he would be able to justify building a fire. Soon spring would come. Plowing and planting and new growth. New seeds in the fertile soil. Flowers, honeysuckle vines, green leaves, new plants in the fields. Warmer temperatures. All designed to push away the memories and frustrations Gorman had fought with during the course of this lonely Mississippi Delta night.

CHAPTER THREE
THE FILE
ETHAN CHEATHAM

After Janet and I left the El Porton, we went to the office and spread the file on my desk. Janet took the envelope and letter from Vera Chaney to her father and laid them aside. She had let me read several of her files in the past. I had found witnesses for her and interpreted police reports at times. Confidentiality was understood. I trusted her and she trusted me. I liked for her to read my files. I liked her insights and suggestions. And, of course, her nearness helped me concentrate. Up to a point. When I lost my concentration or got tired, we would usually resort to sex as a tension breaker. And sometimes, when she was tired, she would fall asleep on my bed reading. She was usually tired from Monday through Wednesday nights. Her tough days in court.

The rain stepped up during the afternoon and the clouds were dark and the wind was from the south. Janet read to me from a transcript of a disciplinary hearing at Parchman Penitentiary. The date of the hearing was June of 1988.

"OK, it seems this is a transcript of a disciplinary hearing at the Prison on June 17, 1988. Present are Ricky Ricardo Starnes, Robert Lee Whitfield, and the Head of Maintenance, Dump Warren. The hearing is being presided over by Roosevelt Adams, assistant warden. To summarize, it seems that both Starnes and Whitfield were trustees. Whitfield was assigned to work for Warren in maintenance. I will read you Warren's narrative testimony. Listen up, big boy."

Janet had changed to a pair of cutoff blue jeans and a white sleeveless blouse. She had left her bra upstairs and I was enjoying looking at her dark nipples rise and fall under the blouse as she talked. Her knees were shiny and her thighs were silky. Her feet were tucked under her rear. She smiled mischievously as she read to me.

"So, we had the whole transmission out on the floor of the garage. Robert Lee was telling me what parts we needed and I was writing all of it down. I never saw Starnes come up. What I saw was Robert Lee stand up real fast and he grabbed a crescent wrench and he and Starnes were circling each other. Starnes had a shank. About four inches of something he had made into a knife. I saw it had a handle covered with silver duct tape. I told Starnes to drop the shank and went to the front seat of my truck to get my thirty-eight. The truck was maybe fifty yards away and when I had it in my hands; I racked a round under the hammer and told them to break it up. Starnes was close to Robert Lee and he made a lunge and Robert Lee laid that wrench upside the right side of his head and Starnes dropped straight down on the ground. He did not move. I thought he was dead."

"I told Robert Lee to sit down over by a road grader we was supposed to work on. Gonna set the blade on it true. It was loose and it would not level out. So Robert Lee went over and sat up against the front tires of the road grader and set the crescent wrench down beside him. I went to Starnes and he was not moving and his eyes was all scary looking but there was just a little blood coming out round his nose and ear. I went in my office and called the main office and told them to call you and send somebody down to cart Starnes out of my shop."

Janet said, "At this point, the Assistant Warden interrupts Dump Warren and asks some fairly probative questions."

"Such as?"

"Let me read you this and you shut the fuck up. How does that work for you, big boy?"

I got out of my chair and walked behind her and rubbed her neck.

She sort of groaned. Real soft like, so I rubbed her shoulders, right at the top. She threw her head back a little and was quiet for a few minutes. Except for a few more of the soft groans. Finally, I reached around and cupped her breasts in my hands and kissed her neck. A little more groaning and my office window rattling in the wind and rain were the only sounds. She turned around and stood up and kissed me and said, "We will get to all of that later, but you got to listen to this and finish this file so you can get up early and take a dreary drive down to Parchman tomorrow."

"Question from Mr. Adams. Mr. Warren, after listening to you, I am going to assume you were the only witness. Correct?"

"Yessir, cept for Starnes and Robert Lee. Most everybody had left the shop and was in the fields. No one had brought in anything broke that morning. We was working to get that transmission fixed. I was going to call into Indianola and get somebody at the auto parts store to run me out the parts I needed. It was about ten in the morning. Just starting to get hot."

"And the only lick passed, so to speak, was when trusty Whitfield hit Starnes with the crescent wrench. Is that correct?"

"Yessir, but Starnes tried to cut him, but he was slow on his feet and he looked like he didn't know what he was doing. Swinging that shank around off balance and Robert Lee just standing there with that big old crescent wrench waiting on him."

"And inmate Whitfield never tried to run or avoid the fray in anyway?"

"Exactly what is a fray, Mr. Adams?"

"Now let me get this straight, Mr. Warren. You are an Ole Miss graduate. Five years to get that degree in Physical Education and you never come across the word 'fray?' Last I heard they still have an English Department at the University of Mississippi."

"Yes sir, I am sure they do, but I avoided it as best I could."

"Well, a fray is a fight or a struggle. Or a physical dispute."

"Well, it is taking longer to talk about this than for it to happen. From the time Starnes come up and showed the shank to when Robert laid him out on the ground there in the shop, it was probably less than three minutes. But you are right; there was no back up in Robert Lee. His eyes was on that knife, I think."

"Just a couple of more questions. Now, was there anything said between the two that you heard, Mr. Warren?"

"No sir, not that I heard. Now I was walking to my truck real fast to get my gun. But they was no words passed that I heard."

"Now after Mr. Starnes went down, did Robert Lee approach Starnes or give you any indication that he wanted to continue the fight?"

"It wasn't much of a fight. I seen two guys get in a fight at the Phi Delt House up at Oxford years ago and there was blood all over the place but this was a one lick fight. I told Robert Lee to go over and sit down by a road grader and that is what he done."

"Alright, thank you Mr. Warren. Now do either one of you, Mr. Starnes or Mr. Whitfield, do you have something to say?"

"It says, in parentheses, that neither prisoner responded." Janet said. "Now here is Mr. Adams."

"So I will assume I have heard all the proof. Here is what I have. Robert Lee Whitfield killed Rickey Ricardo Starnes' cousin in Hardaman County a few years back. He was convicted of Murder in the First Degree and got Ninety- Nine Years. All appeals have been denied. I have his inmate file here and it appears he reached the grade of trusty real fast. He helps out Mr. Warren in the Maintenance Shop and is a good worker. Since this incident, he has been in solitary confinement with no visitors and no yard time. Two cold meals a day. Sixty-eight days in solitary. Mr. Starnes is here for the third time. Receiving stolen property. Five years. Paroled out. Got in a fight in Tupelo and came back after his parole was violated. Cut a man in that fight. Flattened that time out and was back in fourteen months after pleading guilty to robbing a hardware store in Corinth. Not eligible for parole for another six years. Achieved Trusty status two months ago. Assigned to the kitchen."

"Parchman discourages fighting and prohibits the possession and use of weapons. Mr. Starnes is the clear instigator, but Inmate Whitfield does not stand before me blameless. He could have run or tried to avoid this incident. Instead he stood his ground and struck a near fatal blow to Mr. Starnes. Now both of you inmates are lucky. Starnes, I talked to the Doctor at the Emergency Room and he said that if the blow had been an inch or two higher. Up on your temple area, say. You could very well be dead. And Mr. Whitfield, if you had killed him, you could forget about any chance of parole or pardon or clemency or trusty status."

"But life is not lived in a vacuum or a law book. Especially, here at Parchman, We got over five thousand acres of crops planted. I know what is going to happen if I do not get Mr. Whitfield back out there to that maintenance shed. I will have to listen to Mr. Warren moan till all the crops are harvested. Rice, cotton, soybeans, truck farm for the prison vegetables, and corn. Now Mr. Whitfield, you been in the hole for sixty-eight days. That is enough. But let me tell you this. Mr. Starnes has lost his hearing in his right ear. He had to have reconstructive surgery on something called his zygomatic arch. That is a bone structure right below the eye and close to the temple and the ear. He was in the hospital in Jackson under guard for fifty-one days until the Doctors let him come on back. Now he is in solitary. Mr. Rickey Ricardo Starnes, you brought this on yourself. Mr. Whitfield could very well die of natural causes right here. A ninety-nine year sentence is a long time. No matter how you slice it. We got two cemeteries here. Some folks get shanked and die here. Some we execute. Some get feeble and die of what they call natural causes. Very few leave and never come back. "

"He is being punished. Your accrued good and honor time is

hereby rescinded. You will do the remainder of your sentence day for day. You will do eleven months and twenty-nine days starting today in solitary confinement. You will receive no visitors. No mail. No time in the exercise yard. After completing the eleven months and twenty-nine days of solitary you will be removed to the maximum-security unit where you will serve the remainder of your sentence. Take him away."

"Now Mr. Robert Lee Whitfield, this is it for you. I have a long way before retirement. If you come in front of me again, you will be put in the maximum-security unit, also. So, your punishment is the sixty-eight days you spent in solitary. I am not going to take your good and honor time away at this time. I will tell you that if you had had a shank like Mr. Starnes, you would be going with him. Right now. Mr. Warren or no Mr. Warren. Now, I have looked into the Starnes situation and it looks like there are two more of them in here. One from Hardaman County and one from over in Tipton County in Tennessee that caught in a stolen car driving through Mississippi down near the Alabama line. I will have both of them in my office and impress on them the fact that this murder case is over and if they give me any problems they are going to solitary for a while. Good luck. Now you can go with Mr. Warren and do not let me see you again."

Janet laid the transcript down and said, "I have an easy day tomorrow. A prelim I will probably waive. A couple of report dates up in Criminal Court which I hope will turn into guilty pleas and a new client coming in tomorrow afternoon. You will be driving down to Parchman. Dreary roads. Rain. Dreary scenery. Looking for clues. No place to eat. All those meat and three vegetable places are drying up. None left I heard of as being worth a stop, that is for sure."

I told her I had to start someplace.

"Just curious."

"About what, babe?"

"I will look over the sexism. Just curious, see if there is such a thing, I should say, person, as a Dump Warren. Use your keen powers of observation. I will have questions. See if you can find out how and why he got that name. I am sure there is some fractured male reasoning behind his name. Subtly. Now do not offend him. I know he has another name. Says right here in the transcript. James, "Dump" Warren. "First, I am going to talk to Essie Beard. I will call on the way and be sure she is there. Hate to drive that far. Like you said, it is a dreary drive down there this time of year. You know the trees have been cleared out of most of that land. A few pecan trees and cedar trees left around people's houses and some pines and cedars growing by driveways and fence rows, but they farm that land all the way up to your back yard fence. Only other trees are around the sloughs and rivers."

I read an article from the Hardaman County Register. It was dated the Friday after Robert shot Starnes. In 1984. I read most of it to Janet. The headline read: "Local Welder Slain in Sunflower Parking Lot." The article quoted a local realtor, Holly Webster, who said, "I was in the lot putting my groceries in my car when I heard them arguing. Mr. Starnes pulled off in his truck and I thought he was leaving, but he got out of his truck with a tire iron in his hand and walked back to where the black man was. The black man shot him in the stomach and Mr. Starnes was on the ground, face up. I could see his feet twitching and the black man walked up to him and leaned over and shot Mr. Starnes in the head. The black man got back in his truck and left. I know him by face and name. His name is Robert Whitfield."

"Prosecuting that case would be like shooting fish in a barrel," Janet said.

"Yet his daughter hands over six grand to me and is clear she will pay more plus expenses and wants him back in her life. I would like to find him just to see what he is like now, some twenty-eight years later. I got some background information, but nothing that looks like a clue. I know he is not in Yazoo County or Hardaman County. That leaves the rest of the world."

"There is no mention in this file about money. How far can you get when you get out of prison without money? No car. Maybe there is a record at the prison of who picked him up. That would constitute a clue. A big one. Worth your drive down there. For sure. You ever been in a prison before, Ethan?"

"No, I transported plenty of suspects down to the Shelby County Jail but that is about all."

"I have interviewed prisoners in jails and prisons and the first thing you notice is the noise. Not much sense of time or decorum. Your clients are usually not even friendly. When you leave, you immediately want to take a shower. Parchman has a Death Row. A lot of dorms. Lot of prisoners work in the fields voluntarily. Lots of the farmland is used to grow vegetables and other food for the prisoners. Known as a hard place to do time. Once the desegregation order came down, you got a lot of gangs, all segregated by race, so social legislation is somewhat futile in prison situations. Not any safer or better in anyway. Conjugal visits started there. This was shortly after the turn of the twentieth century. The trusty system used to allow for the trustees to carry guns. That is where they got their names. Not because they were trustworthy but because they were trusty, or good, shots. "

"You know a lot of stuff about Parchman."

"And that surprises you? First, I am a lawyer. Second, I am a female. Third, I am a Jewess. And fourth, there simply are not that many people who have all of those characteristics and are not smart as hell. Couple that with the fact that I am naturally curious and this is what you get, babe."

I leaned back in my chair and looked out the window. It was hard to see across Front Street because of the heavy, dull rain. There was almost no traffic. I was ready for spring. I love the South except from January to April and April can be a tedious, long month, also. Rain and dark, dull skies. Maybe the rains would slow down. I knew the farmers were getting their equipment ready for the spring plowing and planting.

Janet closed the file and went to my computer and printed out a map to Parchman and gave it to me. She sat on my lap and we watched the rain pelting the street and my window.

"I have a plan. I have saved something from the file for last. Pictures. Pictures of Elton, Vera, the children, Ann Stepter, and the house and farm in Yazoo County. And a note from Vera to show the pictures to Robert when, not if, when, you find him. Now, you look at the pictures while I go to the Blues City Café and get some chili and crackers to go with the hot tamales."

I asked her, "Are you sure? I could go up there. Only a mile or so and be back in a few minutes. No need for you to get wet."

"No, besides my bountiful intelligence, I am resourceful and resolute and I like to drive your car. Most important, though. I want you to sit here and look at each of these photographs. Take your time. The experience will probably not yield a clue, but I just want you to see the pictures. Not just look at them, but see them. With no distractions."

There were eleven family photographs in the file. A picture of Vera as a child. Shy and uncertain in a pink dress and white shoes. She was probably eight or nine years old. She was standing at the foot of a pine tree. There were two pictures of her as a teenager. One showed her as more confident, with a shy smile, while standing in a gym wearing a basketball uniform and holding a basketball in her hands. A high school graduation picture showed a taller, more focused, Vera. There were pictures of Vera at Vanderbilt and at her graduation from Medical School in Jackson, Mississippi.

A wedding scene showed a happy and beautiful Vera. Elton was a few inches taller and was smiling. He wore a black tuxedo and Vera wore a white gown with a modest hat and veil. One picture had been taken on a houseboat in the late afternoon. Vera was flanked by Roscoe and Elton. She was wearing a black one-piece bathing suit and had a regal look. Roscoe and Elton had on bathing suits and were holding fishing rods by their sides.

Elton was posed besides his old Ford tractor in his National Guard camouflage suit. The date on the back of the photo was September, 2008. A photograph taken on Christmas Day of 2008 showed Vera, Elton, Ann, and Roscoe opening presents besides a large Christmas tree. The last two pictures were individual shots of Ann and Roscoe. They were dated on the back. February 14, 2012. Valentine's Day. Ann was growing up tall and reserved like her mother. Roscoe looked restless and unfocused.

I put the pictures out on my desk and looked at each one of them again. I wondered what Janet wanted me to see. When she came back, she took the chili upstairs and then came bounding down the stairs.

She sat down in one of my client chairs and said, "What did you see? What spoke to you?"

"Sort of sad. Vera growing up and finding happiness with Elton. Having children and then losing Elton. And now a possibility of losing the boy. You can see it in his face. A sense of disconnect. From everything. A scared retreat. And Ann, you can see will be strong like her mother."

"So we are back to where we were. No clues, but the reason I wanted you to look at them and look at them without me pointing over your shoulder is this: There seems to be no weak link. Vera is strong. The children were. Can we, therefore, assume that there is at least a remote possibility that if you find Robert Lee Whitfield, you will see some of the same strength? That perhaps Vera knows what she is doing?"

I stood up and looked out the window. The rain was coming down hard. The wind had picked up. You could see across the river into the bleak fields. The Big River was silver today from the new rain. The wind from the southwest blew small waves against the bank. My office was on Front Street, high up on the River bluff. Riverside Drive lay dark and empty near the foot of the bluff.

Janet stood beside me and watched the rain and the River. There were no birds in the air, dogs in the street, or people jogging. No ambulances or fire trucks or squad cars. Our phones had been silent all afternoon. The sky was dark and it looked like the rain and wind had settled in. It was just after five o'clock. Less than two hours of daylight left. Football season was over. Baseball would start in just a few weeks. I was one of the few people in Memphis who was ambivalent toward basketball.

"Do you think you can find him?"

"With some luck. Yes"

"Or some clues."

"Luck will probably still play a big part in it. He will not leave a computer trail. I won't be able to follow his trail by looking at his credit card charges on his bill. No paper trail."

"This morning, when they were leaving. Vera, the lawyer from Clarksdale, and big Roscoe, I was at the window upstairs looking across the River at the fields and sloughs. Hoping to see a deer come out from the trees that border the west bank of the River. Not much chance of that. Or some traffic on the River. A few barges, maybe. What I saw was Vera walking to the Escalade. And you know, women, we notice things. They, the guys, treated her with such respect. Running to open a door for her. Making sure she did not get wet. And her. She was regal. In control. Where did she get that from? Her grandmother, perhaps. Her father, perhaps. Not her mother."

"Like Katherine Hepburn? Or Lauren Bacall? Or, more to the point, Lena Horne?"

"Yes. Exactly."

We stood at the window for a few minutes more. Nothing changed. No barges on the River. Just steady rain and window rattling wind. Janet sat at my desk and arranged my file. Her black rimmed glasses were about halfway down her nose. She handed me the file and started up the stairs. I followed her. When she reached the top of the stairs, she turned to me. I was two steps behind her.

"Be nice if the next time you see Vera, she is happy and the boy is happy. "

When she was in my apartment, she went to the closet on the north wall and took her sweater off. I went to the stove and smelled the chili warming. I took the tamales from the refrigerator and put them in the oven and turned the temperature down low. I followed her into the bathroom and she helped me get my clothes off. The water was warm in the shower and she smiled at me as I pulled the shower curtain closed behind me.

CHAPTER FOUR
PARCHMAN

Janet was warring with her hair when I left the next morning to meet my father for breakfast at Harold's Donut Shop on Union. When I arrived, he was seated at the counter talking to the waitress. He was wearing a blue suit, a white shirt, a green and yellow striped tie and freshly polished black Lucchese boots. I could see some wear on him now. Not a lot. Just around his eyes and in his gait when he got up from a chair or bench. He walked stiffly and very slightly hunched over when he first got up. Within a few steps, he was erect and imposing. He was around six two and had kept his weight at less than two hundred. He worked out at the police gym when he could. His name is Ellis Cheatham. He is a Captain in the Memphis Police Department and is Head of the Homicide Division.

He turned on his stool at the counter and waved at me when I came in. I ordered iced tea and two chocolate donuts. He was drinking black coffee and eating a fried cinnamon roll. The waitress was young and black. Her name was Ilene and she was a student at the University of Memphis. Majoring in Accounting. Trying to scruff by with scholarships and jobs. When I was with the Police Department, I was on the late shift. I would get off at seven a.m. and come down to Harold's and meet my father for breakfast when I could. Ilene was almost always there. She got off at eight and beat it out to the University for Class. She was short and she had just changed her hairstyle. From corn rows to close cropped. Her eyes were big and she was easy to like. When I sat down, she already had my tea and donuts.

I had not run this morning. I was hungry for more than a donut, but this was where my father came and I wanted to spend as much time as I could with him.

We had always gotten along. The first I remember of him was when he would come to Tallahatchie County, down in Mississippi, where I lived as a child with my mother and stepfather.,He would get me for the weekend when he could. My mother had divorced him when I was two years old and married my stepfather when I was four. We would go to his parents' home and he would carry me to movies or take me fishing or turkey hunting. Or we would ride horses or work around the farm. He was living with his parents. It was always fun to go up and spend time with him. Then after his parents died, he lived alone in the farmhouse until he and Sharon decided to live together. Now he is married to her. She is the Sheriff of Shelby County. She had won the election a few years back and was virtually assured of winning reelection in two years.

When my father was shot, I was living in a high rise condominium in Perdido Key, Florida. The condo was facing the beach and the water. On the seventh floor. I was living in the condo but it was owned by Patsy Gutreau. She is in her early thirties and is a widow. She lives in Louisiana down near the gulf between Lafayette and New Orleans in a little town called Houma. It is south and west of New Orleans. When Patsy's husband died, he left her car washes, convenience stores, two welding shops, six pawnshops and five liquor stores. They were scattered all over South Louisiana. She had no trouble running the businesses or making a profit from them.

The night my father was shot I received a call from Sharon. She had gotten my name and address from his billfold while he was in the Intensive Care Unit of The Med. The Med is the hospital complex owned by the City and propped up financially by the State and County. It has one of the best trauma centers in the country. I drove up to Memphis that night and morning. The sun was just coming up when I got off the elevator and went to my father's room. I was met by a precise, tall, and striking black woman. Sharon Graham. Her skin is brown and she is in her early forties. She was an Inspector in the Memphis Police Department. My father had been her first Lieutenant when she came on the force. For the next few days, we spent a lot of time together. Waiting to see if he was going to make it. He would gain consciousness for a few hours and then the medical staff would sedate him again and force him to sleep. It worked.

A few months after he got out of the Hospital, Sharon was appointed Police Director. One of her first acts was to make my father the head of Homicide. Later they hooked up. She ran for Sheriff and I came to Memphis and joined the Memphis Police Department. I wanted to see if I could do it. I lasted fifteen months. By then Sharon and my father were married and living out on the farm near Shelby Forest. She was animated and forceful. He was quiet and resourceful. For them, the combination worked. He is in his early fifties and she is just past forty.

The rain had stopped during the night, but the sun was still hidden behind dark clouds. Water was in the streets and the temperature was in the mid-forties. I told my father about my new case. He asked a few questions about Robert Lee Whitfield and asked Ilene about her classes. Shortly before eight he got off his stool and laid a ten and a five down on the counter.

He turned to Ilene and said, "Now Ilene, you listen up. I tip you good. You being in school and all. You just be sure you ain't spending my tip money on none of them left handed cigarettes."

Ilene said, "There will be plenty of time for that when I get my CPA practice going. Won't be that long. Maybe three years before I take the test. I'll ride by in my new Lexus and honk my horn and wave at all you guys. I'll get my coffee from one of them baristas. Get on his ass if he don't make it right."

I followed him out the door. He stopped at his car door and told me baseball season was coming soon and for me not to forget the way out to the farm. I asked him about the Cardinals and he said he just didn't know how they would do with all the changes. He said he would miss LaRussa more than Pujols. He drove on off into the heavy Union Avenue traffic headed west. I left the city and drove south down Third Street all the way to the county line. It was a dismal and depressed area once you crossed the interstate going south. I turned on the radio and listened to a sports talk show for about a minute and turned the radio off and enjoyed the silence all the way past the Casinos and down to Clarksdale. I was hungry by then. Two donuts just isn't a breakfast. I switched to Highway 49 when I was in Clarksdale and when I got to Tutwiler; I took Highway 3 all the way to Sunflower County and Parchman Prison.

Before I left my office this morning, I had left a note for the firm secretary, Irene Ghormley, to call and tell Essie Heard I was on my way. I had asked Irene to call me if there was a problem. There was no problem. I showed my identification at the gate and got directions to a small two-story office building. The guard gave me a plastic visitor's pass and I pinned it on my shirt. The guard must have called Essie Heard because she waiting on the small porch when I pulled into the parking lot. When I came up to the porch, she introduced herself and asked me to come inside.

Essie Heard and I sat down in her office after she closed the door behind us. There was a computer monitor on her green metal desk and a telephone. On a file cabinet in a corner she had some family photos. No wedding ring or wedding pictures to be seen. Pictures of John Kennedy and Martin Luther King, Jr. hung side by side on the wall next to the file cabinet. Two diplomas were the only decoration on one wall. An undergraduate degree from Alcorn State and a Masters in Psychology from the University of Mississippi.

There were no rugs on the floor and no carpet. The only window was behind her desk and it was small. Essie was a little overweight. But she was almost six-foot and she carried it well. She was shy of forty by a few years and she was one of those women you knew would prevail and endure and, ultimately, triumph in life. She was well proportioned and her skin was black. Sharon Graham's skin is brown, but Essie was black. And attractive. She wore black high heels and a blue skirt and a burgundy blouse. A wide, gold belt pulled it all together for me.

She came around her desk and handed me a slim, brown file.

"You welcome to read that. That is Robert Lee Whitfield's whole history here at the Mississippi State Penitentiary. That is what we institutional types, bureaucrats to you, have to call it. But is plain and simple Parchman. One of the meanest places to do time. Especially is you are in for a long time. Also one of the first to have conjugal visits. Still got them. Parchman Farm was started right after the start of the twentieth century. Not many fences. You want to run, you could run. They would bring you back lying across a mule and bury you the next day. Or put you in solitary for a year or so and that would break your will. Now, we got a few more fences. Some folks like me. They call us counselors."

"Thank you. Can I have copies?"

"Sure, show me what you want. Most of it doesn't tell you anything. He was moved from one building to another. One disciplinary problem when he almost killed Ricky Ricardo Starnes. That was before I got here."

She took some paper clips out of top desk drawer and handed them to me and told me to mark what I need. Then she went down the hall and I read the file. As she said, there were few things of interest. Ann Stepter, Sheriff Rainey, Vera, and Gorman Ballard were his only visitors. Vera had come some ten years ago and Robert Lee had refused to see her. The commutation papers were in the file. The date was November 15, 2010. Release papers signed by Robert Lee and witnessed by Dump Warren were dated November 17, 2010.

Essie Heard came back to the office. There was an older white inmate with her. He was carrying a green aluminum serving tray, His hair was short and gray and he looked to be closing in on seventy years of age., He wore denim pants with a brown leather belt and a blue cotton shirt. Yellow letters on the back of his shirt said trusty. He put the tray down on Essie's desk and handed me a large, plastic glass of iced tea. He did not look at me. He handed Essie a Caffeine Free Diet Coke , left the room, and closed the door. There was a green plastic pitcher of iced tea , another diet coke and a pitcher of ice on the tray.

Essie leaned back in her chair and said, "I was just out of my morning shower. Around seven thirty five or so and I got this phone call from this rude old white lady."

"That would be the firm's secretary, Irene Ghormley."

"I never met her but I could pick her out of a lineup. She the type that goes to church, praises Jesus, and scorns sinners, then after the service goes out in the front yard of the church and complains about all us shiftless niggers."

"I am afraid you nailed her. She is efficient and daunting. We got two lawyers in the firm and both of them are scared of her. She is almost seventy or maybe past and you are right. Blacks are the root of all the evil in the world. Blacks and Muslims. So I am lucky to get past the first guard shed."

"No, folks like her is dying off. Fast. Sure there are more right behind them but not as many and we got the numbers. Democracy. One person. One vote. But she told me some good things and I played the Aunt Jemima role. Works most every time. She said why you were coming and when she was sure I was not going to play no rap songs or sing "We shall Overcome", she told me to watch over you while you was down here because she suspected you had a slight Attention Deficit Disorder problem and she said you would forget to eat breakfast and be hungry by the time you got here. What about that? "

"She might be close to right about all of that. Did Gorman Ballard call you this morning."

"Called on Friday. He is my lawyer. Guided me through a divorce. Charged me a hundred dollars and gave me twenty-five business cards. Said if I felt right about it, I could pass them out to any of my church members that needed legal representation in the next few years. That was right after I got here in 2003. Right about the same time I met Robert Lee."

"He one of your inmates you were assigned to counsel.?"

She laughed, "Counseling Robert Lee would be like counseling that wall. No, I met Robert Lee after my no good husband run off and left me right before I got my Masters and I came down here. I was driving a ten year old Chevy Malibu and the front end was wobbling and it was not steering right and I was living over a Chinese grocery in Indianola and paying off student loans and sweating a divorce and I was scared my car was going to die on me. One of the secretaries said to see Dump Warren and ask him if he and Robert lee could look at my car. Tell me what to do or maybe fix it. I knew it was wrong. Using an inmate to do personal labor. But I was way past stressed out and so I did it."

She was drinking her Caffeine Free Diet Coke from a glass like mine. She filled it up with ice and opened the can on the tray and poured it slowly into the plastic glass.

"I like the fizz and the foam and the smell. And the taste. So I called Dump and he came and got my car and took it down to the maintenance barn. First day, I got a ride home with another counselor and ate a pizza up stairs and worried about my car and my whole life for most of the night. It was August. I remember that. You walk ten feet out of your house and your clothes is sticking to you., Next day, close to five, Dump called and told me a guard would be up to get me and that my car was ready."

"So I go down there and I get introduced to Dump Warren and I thank him and tell him how much I appreciated it and he laughed and said he had not even made a single turn with a wrench on my car. That is when he introduced me to Robert Lee. Now Robert Lee was in his late forties or early fifties back then. Just about eight or nine years ago. But no fat and something like my brother told me about. He is older than me and sometimes he gets it. A thousand-yard stare. Looking way past you. Seeing all the way through you. My brother says he got it in the Nam. He was a Marine and he won't talk about any of it but just every once in a while he gets that stare. And that is the closest I can get to saying how Robert Lee looked that day."

Bill Nolan had told me what to say in situations like this. When he got tired during a trial or a deposition and he did not know what to say. The old reliable he called it. I tried it on Essie.

"What happened next?"

"He was uncomfortable talking to me. He said thanks and started to move away. So I asked him to come over and sit with me and have a Coke and tell me about my car. He looked at Dump and Dump nodded. The three of us went in Dump's office and Dump fished some drinks out of a refrigerator he had in his office. I remember he handed Robert Lee a Barq's Root beer."

"One of the classics."

"After Robert drank some of his root beer, he said, "I fixed the linkage. A little loose. Did not even need any parts. And I changed the oil and the oil filter and I put in a new air filter. Air filter in this Delta air needs changing a lot. All sorts of things in the air. Insecticides, fertilizer, lots of dust, trash of all sorts. Now your oil. Hadn't been changed in twelve thousand or so miles. A wonder that motor didn't freeze up on you. You would be buying a new one. Changed the oil and the filter for you. Put good oil in there. You change the oil and filter every five thousand miles and the air filter every ten thousand miles and it will run forever."

"I asked them how much I owed and Robert Lee said when I needed the oil changed again, to buy the oil and filter at one of the auto parts stores in Indianola and bring the car down and he would change it. Then he walked off. I gave Dump some money for the oil and the two filters and the next payday I went down to the shed where Dump was and gave him thirty dollars for Robert. He told me had started Robert a bank account in Cleveland at the bank his wife worked at. He gave his address as Robert Lee's address and he said Robert Lee had almost a thousand dollars in it. That was seven or eight years ago."

"So, you saw Robert Lee when you needed work done on your car."

"Not necessarily. Come November after that August I called Dump and asked him to send him up to the office when he was free. The cotton was all in by then and it was a few weeks before Thanksgiving and, gradually, my life was starting to turn around. I think I started getting my confidence back that first afternoon after I got my car fixed. It ran like a top. You know. One of my father's phrases. Smooth and strong. Jumped up to sixty right quick. The divorce started moving on along and I felt like I was going to win out over all this."

"Did you try to counsel Robert or just try to help him?"

"Both. But it was all superfluous. Wasted effort. Except I learned a very few things about him."

"Such as why he really killed Billy Ray Starnes?"

"No, he would never talk about that. I asked him why he would not see his daughter, Vera Stepter. I asked if he loved her. And if so, why not let her reach out to him?"

"He say anything?"

"Said he loved his daughter and he was glad she was going to be a doctor. He said she don't need to see me like this."

"And , of course, you tried to probe further."

"A waste of time. He would not talk about it anymore. I kept trying and finally he asked to go back to the Maintenance Shed. Said he had some tractors that needed to have the engines overhauled. So I let him go. But I saw him over the years. Him and Dump. See one. The other one was right near. He liked my car. So we could talk a little. I let him know I was grateful. He asked me one time about six years ago if he could paint my car. It was a lime green color and Robert Lee said it needed to be black. So I bought the paint and he painted it between Christmas and New Year."

Her phone rang and she held one finger up and then answered her phone. She wrote something down on a small yellow tablet and then stared at the ceiling and spun her chair around. In a few minutes the conversation was over.

"You think you got secretary problems. I asked that all my calls be held. Our secretary. She does what she wants. Three years from retirement and seventy-five to a hundred pounds overweight. Hates all us younger women."

"What did Robert say when he knew he was going to be released? I need a place to start looking. A clue is what they call it."

"What you need is some lunch. I got several clues. Around five years or so back, I was down at the Shed after work talking to Dump. Trying to find a place to fish. Dump knows em all. Robert Lee was waiting for me. He asked if he could come to my office in a couple of weeks. I told him sure and when he came, he asked me to get him some literature. His word. Literature. He said if he ever got out he was getting out of Mississippi as fast as he could and cut a trail to somewhere on an ocean. He told me he wanted to watch waves and feel a breeze from the sea. He said he had never seen an ocean before. The biggest water he seen was when he was in Chicago and he hated that lake because of the cold wind that he remembered coming down from Canada and freezing him to death."

"Did he ever narrow it down any. Like a state or a city."

"Sort of. I took him brochures and maps of California and Florida and the Carolinas. He liked the idea of San Diego, Puerto Rico, Jamaica, Hawaii, Tampa, and Miami Beach. I got him travel brochures, downloaded photos of the beaches, and one-day he asked me about aquariums and zoos. So once again I give him all the photos and pictures I thought was needed. I had called Vera before all of this started and she told me the reason she wanted to see her father back a few years ago was to tell him that her grandmother, Ann, had died. So I told Robert and he dropped his head and did not say anything. One way or the other."

"Did Robert have any friends. Inmates, or somebody besides you and Dump Warren? Somebody he might have talked to and told where he might be going?"

"You can ask Dump, but I think I know the answer. And the answer will be nobody. See after Robert was working in the Shed a few years, Dump found a little portable type building. Not a trailer. Just a little tin building. Maybe twelve by fifteen. Dump has a lot of juice around here. Keeps a lot of machinery going. We raise a lot of produce to feed the inmates. Cotton, Corn, and Beans. All that is money. And to a State like Mississippi, you need to make things run right as much as you can. So he gets this little building and puts Robert in it. It is still over at the Shed, right near Dump's office. He got a cot, put a toilet in there and soon he slipped an old refrigerator and a stove and a big window fan and a ceiling fan and a space heater in, too. Told me, Robert Lee worked round the clock during planting and harvest-time a lot. Said he needed him handy. Truth is, they was friends. Plain and simple as that."

"So what I need to do is get some lunch, ask you some more questions, and go find Dump Warren."

"I got your lunch. Not fancy, but guaranteed to keep you going. "

She reached into a lower desk drawer and pulled out a sack. It had four sandwiches and two bananas in it. The sandwiches were wrapped in wax paper and were cut in diagonal halves. The bananas were fresh. I ate my banana first and drank some tea.

"I go down to the employee cafeteria some. They post the menus a week in advance. Today is chicken and dumplings, lima beans and stewed apples. I will take a pass."

I opened one of the sandwiches. Pimento and cheese spread thick between two slices of wheat bread. It was incredibly good. I could tell she had made it. The cheese was a medium cheddar and the pimentos were sweet and she had not gone crazy with the mayonnaise.

"Nother reason I did not want to go down to that cafeteria is that I am getting restless. The new wears off of Parchman in about ten minutes. I am saving up to go back to school. Get me a doctorate in Psychology. Take me about three years."

When I was finished with the pimento and cheese sandwich, I opened the other sandwich. It was peanut butter and grape jelly. I groaned and ate the first half of the sandwich in three bites. Essie was smiling. I looked over her shoulder at the tiny patch of sunlight shining through the small window high on the wall behind her desk. When we were through eating, I helped her clean up. We put everything back in the sack and she put the sack in the green trashcan beside her desk.

"Looks like the sun finally made it back. Still not a very bright a sky, though."

"Robert Lee knows to call me or Dump if he gets in a jam. He got our numbers. He got my cell and I wrote my home address on the back of one of my cards and gave it to him. Dump did the same."

"No word at all."

"I don't blame him. I am waiting to see if some scholarship money will open up for me and I can guarantee you that once I leave, I will be steadily putting this place out of mind. If Robert was dead, I figure the police would have gotten in touch with us since he has our contact information on him. So I figure he is doing fine."

We talked for a few more minutes. I stalled around trying to think of some magic question to ask her, but I could not. Finally, I got up and asked her if she could carry me down to the maintenance shed to see Dump and Robert's room.Essie asked me to sit back down.

"Something I left out. Probably won't help you find him but if you are going to talk to Dump, you need to know this. Dump's wife passed around two years ago. They were mighty close. I snuck a look in his personnel file. He was born in the fall of 1943. Makes him sixty-eight. He looks it. Used to be laughing all the time. Talking about football. See, he is from Shaw, just a few miles from here. Went to Ole Miss on a football scholarship. His wife went to Delta State and when they was finished with their degrees, Dump did a little coaching and then landed here and his wife went into banking. She did real good. They just had one daughter. She is grown and moved off. Down to Orlando, Florida. She is like her mother. Good with figures. She is in some kind of accounting office. She has only been back one time since the funeral. I called down to the shop this morning. I figured you would want to talk to him. Well, he is off today, but I can draw you a little map to his house. His wife was named Judy. I was over there one day to pick up some tomatoes and Crowder peas. She asked me in the house and we sat and talked for a while. I liked her. She and Dump grew a big ass garden every year. We went out in the garden and picked the peas and Dump had the tomatoes all lined up on the back porch. Big old Beefsteak tomatoes."

"Dump know I am coming?"

"Yes. Told me to tell you he would be in the barn or in the tractor shed all day."

I left Parchman and followed the map Essie had drawn out for me on a piece of yellow legal paper. I crossed Highway 61 and went through Shaw and found the turnoff to Dump Warren's house. His house was a doublewide. There was no back porch to dry tomatoes on. I saw two tall brick chimneys under some tall oak trees. There had been a house there at one time. Some concrete and brick portions of a wall lay in a clump of dried out weeds. The trailer was silver with red trim. I walked about a hundred yards down to a large, pole barn. The double doors were open on both ends and I saw a large man sitting on a stool sharpening a hoe with a long , heavy file. He stood up slowly. He was probably a little over six foot one and he had wide shoulders and short red hair. His face was wide and his nose had been broken. Probably more than once. He had large sunspots and freckles on his face. His right ear looked like it was having trouble staying on his face. His teeth were white and straight. His eyes were blue. He was wearing blue overalls over a khaki shirt. He was still heavily muscled and he had large, strong hands, He got up from the stool and introduced himself.

"Name is James Warren. Only persons that ever called me that in the last fifty or so years was my wife, Judy, and Johnny Vaught. Everybody else calls me Dump. I got that name way back when we used to play football on the schoolyard at Shelby. Girl called me that in the fifth grade because she said I was big as a dump truck compared to the other boys. So I been Dump to most everybody since then. Coach Vaught up at Ole Miss recruited me and my mother asked him not to call me Dump and he called me James when he wasn't mad at me. Best I can do for a seat is a bale of hay."

He walked over and pulled a bale of hay down and sat it down near his stool. I sat down and waited a few minutes until he was through filing the hoe down. He took the hoe and ran his right thumb down the freshly filed blade. He looked satisfied. He took the hoe and hung it up on a nail on the back wall of the barn. When he came back, he had another hoe. He sat it down on the ground and looked at me.

"You see the chimneys out there?"

"Yes sir, I did. Fire or tornado?"

"Was a tornado. We went to church one clear Sunday Morning in April, three years ago and when we come back, the house was gone. Blew some trees down. Did not even touch the barn. It was a good house. Built just after my dad came home from World War Two. Tin roof. Lot of cypress in the framing and two nice porches. One in front. One in back. Fireplace in our bedroom and one in the kitchen. When my parents passed away, we sold our house in Shaw and came on out here. I got right at five hundred acres. I lease most of it out. When Judy passed away, I neglected the garden and fences. Now I think I may have turned a corner. I am going to keep my tools up better and grow me a smaller garden. And fix all my fences."

It was after two in the afternoon. I was in no hurry. I knew it would be too late to do anything else on the case when I got through with Dump Warren, so I decided to take my time and listen to his stories. A better alternative than rushing back to Memphis.

"So tell me, when were you there? At Ole Miss."

"I went there in the fall of 1961. I was a fullback and linebacker in high school, but Vaught shifted me to guard in my freshman year. Back then, freshmen could not play varsity. Had our own team. So he switched me to center in the spring and I played my three years as a guard and center. Had a nice career. Blocked a punt against LSU in 1964. Got my degree in Physical Education. Judy was two years behind me and when I graduated from Ole Miss we got married. I coached for a few years and then I caught on out at the Maintenance Shed and I been there ever since. I could have retired a few years back, but Judy wanted to work a little bit longer. Our daughter had graduated from college and she moved off to Florida. Judy and I both were happy working. No need to stop. We had drawed-up some plans for a house. Gonna keep the bricks from the fireplaces and build it back like it was. Even the tin roof. Then she found out she had a cancer. Ovarian. And it come and got her quick."

The wind picked up and rattled the barn doors. I looked outside and there were low black clouds racing across the sky. But no rain. At least not for now. Dump got up and shut the doors on the west end of the barn. There were chickens near the east doors of the barn. They were walking back inside. A large brown and white rooster with a red comb was pacing in the doorway. He would walk a few feet, then run at one of the hens, and come back to the doorway and pace some more.

"We gonna have a storm. Not a big one. Just fast and loud. That rooster knows it. I keep these hens and rooster around. Reminds me of Judy. She liked the fresh eggs. They are more trouble than they are worth. Some snake or dog or possum is always getting into my eggs. I got me two goats that keep some of that down. I leave em here in the barn and feed em and they will kill a snake right quick. And run a dog or possum out of here. Might be some thunder and lightning with this rain, but the clouds is too low and too fast to make a real storm."

"Essie said you took Robert Lee off the Prison grounds when he left. I am here on behalf of his daughter, Vera. She is a doctor down in Yazoo County. She wants him to come back and help her on the farm. Her husband got killed over in Iraq. Last October. He was one of the last ones to die"

"We worked together for over twenty five years in that Shed and out in the fields. Best man I ever seen when it come to maintaining or fixing a tractor, or combine, or truck or car. And yet, I can't tell you I knew him. We never talked about the case that got him here. I read the files up in the Warden's office when I took him to help me, but all that was said in the file was that he was doing ninety-nine years for murdering a Starnes up in Hardaman County. Then that other Starnes boy come after him and Robert bout killed him with one lick. But you know all about that."

"You know where he went?"

"West. Somewhere out west where there is an ocean he can look at. What happened is this. Robert was my main man. After a few years, when I was sure I could trust him, I found this old metal shed out by the ball fields. Twelve by fifteen or so. The Warden finally let me load it up and take it over to the Shed. Robert Lee was a trusty by then. We fixed it up so he could live in it. He had a toilet, a shower, a stove, a refrigerator, and a heater and some fans. Took me a while, but I got it all in there."

"Folks that worked here found out about Robert Lee and they

would get me to let him work on their cars from time to time. I told them to give Robert Lee a little something. He come to me one day. Had a hundred dollars in bills in his hand. Said he knew my wife was a banker. He wanted her to keep his money for him till he could get out. Well, she and I got him an account in the Farmers and Merchants Bank in Cleveland, Mississippi where she was working. I gave his address as mine and he got a statement every month. The warden let me get him a driver's license about fifteen years ago. So if I wasn't here when he needed a part, he could drive into Indianola with a guard and get it. Always a truck in the shed. So when he was told his sentence was over and he could leave, he asked me to take him to the bank and get his money. I got an old soft duffel bag I have had since college and bought him two pairs of blue jeans, some underwear, some khakis and a couple of shirts from Wal-Mart. And some shoes. A pair of good, strong walking shoes and a pair of black penny loafers. He tried to pay me, but I said no. "

He got up and walked to the east doors of the barn. There was lightning in the sky and I heard distant thunder. A hard rain was falling. The wind was from the west. I could barely see his trailer and my car.

"Give it an hour and it will have shot its wad. So Robert Lee asked me to carry him to Leland. I did not ask any questions. We was driving out of Leland and Robert Lee asked me to stop at a Sonic. He had a root beer float and a chili dog. We sat there and I was working on a cheeseburger with bacon and a pineapple milk shake. I asked him why he wanted to go to Leland and he said, 'Highway 82' and I did not ask him anything else. He paid for his own meal. He had almost thirteen hundred dollars in his billfold and a valid Mississippi Driver's License when I let him off at Leland. He was on the shoulder for the westbound lanes when I last saw him. I ain't heard from him since."

"I would like to look in the shed. Essie said you locked it up after he left. You find anybody to take his place yet?"

"I ain't even close to finding somebody that has the knowledge and the honesty. I can't find nobody that's got one of those traits, much less both."

"So I take it, he is smart."

"Yes, he can read as good as you or me. He knows figures real good. And he knows machinery. He just don't talk much."

"You think he can adapt to regular life."

"Look, you keep your mouth shut and listen like Robert, you bound to learn a lot. Most people cannot and will not do it. Judy said the word to describe Robert is detached. She meant emotionally, he had just shut it all down. Only way you can do as much time as he did and keep some sanity. He will be fine."

"Essie threw some places out to me that he could be. San Francisco. San Diego. Tampa. Miami. And others. But he wasn't in the westbound lane of Highway 82 with the intention to go to Miami or New Orleans or Tampa or Mobile. He was going west."

"You follow me up to the Maintenance Shed. After he left, I just shut it up. I never even turned the refrigerator off. He probably did before he left. I did not bother to go inside and check. I guess I was a little depressed when he left. You know after Judy died, I hung around the shed and worked more. To keep from coming home and drinking. I let the trailer go down. Dishes piled up. My daughter got her own life long before Judy passed. Sure, she loves me but there is nothing left around here for her. Jobs and money are hard to come by in the Delta. So, me and Robert would sit around and eat a sandwich after work and talk. I would do the talking, but it helped. Robert listened and he would say something from time to time. To show me he was really listening, I think."

Dump went over to a little feed room and brought out an old red Folgers can with cracked corn in it and threw it out in swift, wide arcs in front of the chickens' nests. Then he picked up a green plastic bowl from in front of the nesting area and filled it with water and sat it back down.

He went back in the feed room and came back out with the Folger's can and went and grabbed a charge of hay from an open bale and walked to a stall near the east doors. There was a brown mule standing close to the back of the stall. Robert threw the hay down in front of the mule and emptied the grain into a metal feeder in the corner of the stall. He took a water bucket out of the stall and walked to the east doors and threw the water into the rain and wind. He refilled the water, took it into the stall, and locked the door. He went back into the feed room and when he came back he had two feed sacks under his left arm.

"Way I see it, we put these sacks over our heads and you go to your car and I go to my truck. Follow me on to the Prison. I got to stop and explain who you are at the guard house and when I wave you in, follow me to the Maintenance Shed."

I was wearing a nice pair of Lucchese cowboy boots I had bought back in college. They had a good black sheen, That probably lasted about ten steps. Dump was hunkered over and running and I was lurching along in the mud and rain. When I got in my car and got strapped in, I turned on the wipers and followed Dump to the Prison. We drove slowly and most of the time I did not see much of the road. I stayed close to his brake lights. When we got to the guardhouse, Dump got out and talked to a lean, black man in a uniform and hat. Shortly, he waved me through and we drove to the Maintenance Shed. Only one of the big metal doors was open, but there was plenty of room for us to slide through.

A green John Deere tractor, a red middlebuster, and a big cotton picker were parked against the far wall of the shed. There was room for at least twenty cotton pickers or combines in the shed. There was an office in the back of the shed and I could see Robert Lee's little room near the office. Dump parked in front of his office and waved me over to Robert Lee's room. There was a hasp and small lock on the door.

Dump unlocked the door and we went inside. There was a makeshift desk in one corner of the room. His bed was made and there was a cord in the floor by the refrigerator. The door was open and there was no food or trash on the shelves or in the freezer of the refrigerator. It was as if no one had ever lived there. There was no closet. The desk consisted of a raw piece of three-quarter inch plywood that had been cut into a triangle and braced and nailed into the corner. A small metal chair was pushed under the desk.

There was a small wooden pantry near the stove. It contained a few cans of tomatoes and pineapple stacked in neat rows. Two beaten up pots and lids were on the stove. A large, black iron skillet was hanging from a nail near the stove. A faded blue dishrag lay beside the kitchen sink. There were three mismatched plates and a cracked , red and blue soup bowl on a shelf in the pantry. A blue Maxwell House coffee can held three spoons, two forks, a large wooden ladle, two knives, and a spatula.

Dump stood in the door and watched me as I walked through the little room. The bunk bed was made. A homemade quilt lay folded at the foot of the bed.

"Judy send this to him? A nice quilt. Like the ones we had at my father and his father's house. I'm partial to them, myself."

"Yes, when I told her about Robert Lee living out here in the shed, she starting sending him stuff. Warm socks. A straw hat. You see it over on the nail there by the door. When she would can vegetables or gather tomatoes in the garden, she would send things to him. She never met him."

Robert Lee's little house was up on cement blocks and there was three wooden steps leading up to the door. Dump sat in the doorway with his right leg resting on the second step and his left leg pulled up to his chin. I sat down at the desk. There was no clutter and no drawers for the desk. I sat down in the little metal chair and looked at what was around me and I saw what I hoped was a clue. There were pictures from magazines taped to the walls over the desk. Pictures of whales playing off the coast of Maui. Boats sailing off the Carolina Coast. San Francisco Bay and Bridge. Pretty girls in small, matching white bikinis strolling down Miami Beach. Gray rocks and silver water on the Oregon coast. Shrimp boats coming back to the docks in Mobile Bay. And surf scenes I took to be from the California Coast. A picture of a lobster fisherman in his boat off the Maine Coast. And a blank space. About sixteen or eighteen inches square. The blank space was in the midst of the pictures.

I asked Dump to come over and look at the pictures. He stood slightly behind me. When he was through, I said, "Mr. Waller, I want you to think for a minute. See the blank space. What used to be there? A picture of what?"

He dropped his head and closed his eyes and walked around in a small circle. One time. Then he opened his eyes and shook his head.

"I come in here probably three or four times a week. Bringing him some food or eating my lunch over at that table. But I cannot remember what was there. I will study on it some more and if I can think of it, I will call you. I need one of your cards. I got over five thousand acres of farming land here. All of it farmed by machines that are old and need repair. That is my focus most of the time. Me and Robert would come out here some during the slack season and play hearts and eat some lunch. See that old blue deck of Bicycle playing cards on the kitchen table? Right there is where we played most of the time."

"Did Essie ever come in here?"

"Sure she did, but not that much. She would come and bring Robert some banana pudding or corn bread or pork chops or spaghetti she would say she had left over. If we was out, she would lay it in the refrigerator. Did not happen every week. Not even every month. But sometimes. Yes, she has been in here. I will ask her to come down tomorrow and we will both look. Maybe something will spark me to start remembering. ”

I looked at the pictures some more and was fixing to leave when I saw some numbers scratched out in faint ink marks on the right side of the desk near the wall. 601-947-1943. I wrote the numbers down in a small blue note book I kept in my left back pocket.

“Dump, do you know anything about this number. Looks like a phone number to me.”

“Naw, you got to understand. Robert Lee ain’t somebody that feels a need to tell you much of anything about his business. He asked me a couple of times about four years ago to use the phone in the shop. He told me it was long distance. Said he would pay for it. I told him not to worry about it. We on some kind of plan where instate calls is not billed like long distance. Out of state. That is a whole new deal.”

I looked out through the door to the shed. I could see the darkness had caught up with us. When it is dark in the Mississippi Delta, it is usually black dark. The rain had stopped and the air was still. No stars. Nothing. No big yellow moon. Especially this time of year. I took my cell phone out and dialed the number. On the fourth ring a woman answered.

“Who is this, please?”

“My name is Ethan Cheatham. I am a private investigator hired to find Robert Lee Whitfield. He was released a few months back and his daughter, Vera, has asked me to find him. Your phone number is the closest thing to a clue I have so far. I found it in Robert’s room at Parchman.”

There was a pause and after a while I was afraid she had sat the phone down or we had a bad connection.

“Hello?”

“Yes, I am here. I am thinking. If you are trying to crowd me, it will not work. Tell me, where are you from?”

“I was born in Memphis, my parents divorced early, I spent my childhood in Tallahatchie County, Mississippi. Now I am back in

Memphis."

There was silence on the phone. I did not talk. I waited. The woman sounded old, but her voice was strong. Eventually, she came back on.

"If you wish to see me, go to Hardaman, Mississippi and ask for Sheriff Ike Glover. If he feels your business is worthy of my attention and if he feels I can trust you, he will bring you to the house and we will talk. I am usually home. I do not like to be bothered until after lunch. Preferably, after two but not after four."

She hung up. I did not call back. I knew I could trace the number to an address and a name. I could do that easily. On my computer in the office. I also knew if I showed up without the Sheriff, I would get nowhere. I made a few notes in my little notebook and made one last tour of Robert Lee's room. I was tired and hungry. I sat down at the kitchen table and Dump drew up a chair.

"I'm tired. With no real reason except I haven't eaten in a while. I think I will go on back to Memphis. If I need another look, can I call you and come on down?"

"Sure. I will not be moving anyone in here that I know of. I will talk to Essie tomorrow. One of us ought to remember."

When I left the shed, Dump was walking into his office. I could see the door to Robert Lee's room was closed and the lock was on the hasp. The drive back to Memphis was slow. The rain had stopped but the roads were wet and dark. When I pulled into the firm parking lot behind our offices, I saw the lights were on in my upstairs apartment. It was a few minutes after nine and I was glad there was no rain to walk through. I climbed the stairs to my apartment and Janet was standing in the kitchen. There were two pots on the stove. Each was covered and there were fires burning under each pot. She was wearing a blue and white night dress. She had no shoes on and her smile took up most of her face.

"A rare treat. I had one of those days in court. Two potential trials were averted by guilty pleas. I got a call to go over to Federal Court this afternoon. I got an appointment on a twenty three-count embezzlement case. And I was through by four. I went home, got some of my mother's spaghetti sauce out of the freezer and bought some spaghettini and French bread and here we are. About to embark on a rare Monday night feast. I hope you did not eat earlier."

I kissed her, took a shower, put on my white terrycloth bathrobe and walked back into the kitchen. Plates, silverware, dark blue napkins, and wineglasses were on the table. We had an agreement that I would not call her on Mondays. I knew she would call me when she wanted to talk to me and I was happy to wait her out. Usually, by Wednesday or Tuesday night, her week had begun to take shape. Mondays were usually bad.

"Trained detective that you are, I am sure you have noticed I have no shoes, no bra, and no panties on tonight?"

"I have."

"Do not be misled. I only want to eat a nice meal, read some, and hope that it rains and the wind blows hard against your windows tonight and that you will wake me no earlier than seven forty five in the morning."

She had left a bottle of wine on the kitchen counter. She had decanted it. I poured it back into the bottle and poured each of us a glass. Monsanto Chianti Classico Riserva, 2006. When I sat down, I took a sip. I liked it. I know nothing about wine. We ate and the wine got better. The sangiovese and the sauce were a perfect match. The sauce was heavy. Tomatoes and ground beef. Hearty fare after a day in the rainy, gloomy Delta.

Janet had showered before I got home and I could smell apples when I kissed her neck.

"Eat your pasta, compliment me on the wine pairing, and on having a thoughtful mother who can cook, and tell me about your case. What did you learn today?"

"I learned, first of all, that Robert Lee left Parchman, withdrew his money from the bank, ate a chili dog and a root beer float, and then got Dump Warren, his friend and boss at Parchman, to take him to the west bound lanes of Highway 82 in Leland, Mississippi. He was last seen standing on the shoulder of the road leading west to who knows where. And I have a phone number in Hardaman County and I may possibly get to speak to the person assigned that phone number. I will handle that tomorrow."

"So will you be off at the crack of dawn tomorrow?. And interrupt my much needed sleep?"

"No, she does not receive visitors except after two in the afternoon and before four. A two and a half-hour drive to Hardaman means I will leave here around nine thirty. I plan on fixing you a breakfast of bacon, eggs, English Muffins, and red plum jelly. I have orange juice. And coffee."

"And you will expect me to make the coffee? I suppose."

"Please."

"I will. And did you plan on getting up and going for a run before you fix my breakfast?"

I ate some more pasta and filled our wineglasses. I looked at the freckles on her cheeks and nose. One of my pleasures. I kissed her lips and found a place on her neck and bit her and kissed her again.

"I think I will forget the run. I need it, but I do not want to wake you up. Usually, you just roll over and go back to sleep, but your Tuesdays, somedays, are as bad as Mondays. Or worse."

"Or worse. Ethan, I would like to talk to you about something."

"Sure."

"Well, the subject is us. Besides being a Jewess, and a lawyer, I am, as I am sure you have noticed a woman. I fret. Not a lot. But some. So, tell me, where you want this to go."

"I think we should keep on doing what we are doing. I am just getting settled into what I hope is a career. And a new place to live. I can't see myself without you, but I cannot see us living in your beautiful house on Mud Island. There are no comfortable chairs or couches. And I don't see you stepping away from the big house and downsizing and moving in with me. My washer and dryer are down stairs in the back room of the office."

She did not say anything. I waited a minute and filled our wineglasses.

"Let's go out on the porch and watch the River and you can ask me whatever you want."

"I suppose it is my turn."

"Yes, I do not want to change anything right now. I want to find Robert Lee Whitfield. But between us, I do not want to change anything."

She still did not say anything. She opened the door to the patio and sat in one of the white plastic chairs and looked at the River. She held her wineglass in both hands near her lap. No wind and no moon were there to comfort or distract us. The River was black and empty of traffic.

"I suppose it is my turn now."

"Only if you want. I have a book for you. I bought it last month and I finished it last Wednesday night."

"A male trick. Tried and true. Change the subject. Well, I am happy. That is the problem. I am not used to being happy and fulfilled in a relationship. Resigned and accepting. Yes, I have done that several times. But happiness brings a whole new set of issues into play."

There was new light on the River. A barge passed beneath the bridge and swept its searchlight from shore to shore. It was southbound and riding low in the water. We watched it pass by in silence. After the barge passed before us, a powerful wake threw rising water on the black bank below us.

"So do you think we should say anything more? I do not want you mad because of what I said about your furniture, but I love this place.

It is not fancy. I know that. And I appreciate you not making fun of it. One of the things I like about you is that you have not tried to change me in any way. Most women try to shape a man into some vague ideal they have of what they feel a man should be."

"Men do the same thing. Men do not fret like we do."

"You said you were happy. Why not just let things evolve?"

"That will never work."

"For one thing, it makes too much sense. Another reason, I guess, is that women want promises. Assurances."

"I am not ready for promises. Until I am sure I can keep them."

"My dashing detective is a minimalist as to personal possessions and trappings. And a conflicted moralist."

"All true, perhaps. But you forgot one thing."

"And what would that be?'

"I love you. In my way. Not the way you think I should. In my way. I love the way you smell when you come out of the shower. I love the freckles across your nose. I love the way you cock your head to one side when you hear something that troubles you. I love the fact you were here tonight. Your idea. Not because it was expected of you. Problem is, I do not know where any of this leads, so I say, let it evolve and we will find out together. No deadlines and no promises and no pressuring."

"You do not like to talk about this stuff, do you?"Not really."

"Do you think I love you.?"

"I know you do. I know it."

"I have wanted to tell you but I did not want to tell you and you be embarrassed or have a feeling I was trying to trap you."

"The barge is gone and I do not see any more lights. It is starting to get cold. I feel some wind. Let's go inside."

We went inside and I made sure the porch door was closed tight. She sat at the table while I cleared the dishes and washed them by hand. I have no dishwasher. Ethan Cheatham, the minimalist. Never thought of myself that way. We went to bed and I was fixing to turn off the lamp on the dresser, when she said I had forgotten to give her the book.

I got up and went to my desk and brought the book to the bed and sat down by her. She was lying on her back and smiling.

"Name of the book is "In the Garden of Beasts." It is about Hitler and the American Ambassador and his daughter and the Gestapo and the early oppression of the Jews in Germany and how America reacted to the accounts. Set in 1933 in Berlin. Nonfiction that reads like fiction. The best kind. By Erik Larson. He wrote the one I gave you this past summer about the Chicago World's Fair and the architects and the serial killer. I liked this one better."

She sat up in bed and took the book and smiled at me. I hugged her and she held onto me for a long while. When I was in bed, she put her right elbow on my chest and looked at me for a short while and then reached over and turned the light off. She kissed me and turned over and went to sleep.

Ethan Cheatham, I woke up before six. It was still dark outside. I slipped out of bed and put on a pair of running shorts and an old purple Millsaps College T-shirt. I carried my running shoes down stairs and sat in my office and put my shoes and socks on. After I eased out the front door and locked it behind me, I ran North towards the Auction Street Bridge and Mud Island. Front Street was empty and dark, but after I had passed by the Confederate Park, I noticed the first light of the day. The old, empty buildings on Front Street and the newer, regal Morgan Keegan Building were all dark

The endorphins must have kicked in as I approached the Auction Street Bridge because I felt strong as I ran the uphill grade of the bridge. When I was at the top, I could see the River, gray and choppy, in the early morning light. There was a wind from the West, but the clouds were gone. I ran a few minutes on Mud Island. Janet's house was almost a half-mile down from the foot of the Auction Street Bridge. There was a porch light on and the rest of the house was dark. It is a pretty house. Columns and big windows. All painted white with dark blue shudders on the windows. A great view of the River from her upstairs bedroom. I turned when I was in front of her house and came on back home. The run over the bridge coming back took a little out of me, so I cut the pace back a notch until I got to the Morgan Keegan Building,

When I was even with the building I let the hammer down. That was what the track coach at Millsaps used to say. 'Hold some back until you think you need it and then let the hammer down and come on in strong.' Talking about the mile run. I never won a single time in four years but I did help on the mile relays. When I got back to the office, it was not even seven. Some traffic was on the street, Bread vans, delivery trucks, city buses, a few yellow taxicabs, and the Main Street streetcar were all stirring around. You didn't see many pedestrians. A few homeless guys standing in alleyways or at the back of restaurants going through trash bins, an occasional lawyer or secretary walking fast through the early morning light, and garbage men wrestling with large, green plastic bins were all the people I had seen.

I took a quick shower and changed into a pair of khakis and a blue golf shirt and started breakfast. I fried bacon first and then scrambled six eggs in the bacon grease. I sliced two English muffins and toasted them. Janet woke up while I was frying the bacon and sat at the table and watched me cook. I fixed her a plate of eggs and bacon, put the English muffins on a saucer and got some red plum jelly out of the refrigerator. While she was eating, I took two tomatoes from the refrigerator, sliced them and put them in the bacon grease, added some garlic salt, brought it to a boil, and then let the tomatoes simmer under a lid while I poured orange juice for both of us. I made myself a glass of iced tea and took the skillet from the stove and spooned out the tomatoes on our plates.

"Where did you learn to fix tomatoes like this?"

"My grandmother on my father's side. Good thing I did not live with them full time, the way she spoiled me."

"Ethan, did I spoil a wonderful night last night? I wish I had just shut up. You know when I talk about personal things, it always comes out weak and sappy."

"I did not think so. Like I said, let things evolve."

She took her plate and walked to the front window and looked out at the River and the early morning traffic on Riverside Drive and Front

Street. When she came back to the table, she leaned over me and kissed me and then sat in my lap and put her arms around my neck.

"Hard to be happy. I am used to conflict, uncertainty, ambiguity, and gratuitous lying."

I did not say anything and she got up and went into the bathroom. In a few minutes I heard the shower running. I was almost done with the breakfast dishes when she came out of the bathroom. She had her blue bathrobe on. The front was open. She made the bed and came over to the sink where I was drying dishes and told me one of the things she liked about me was that I liked sex in the morning as much as she did. She said her mind was the clearest and her soul the purest in the first early morning hours of her day.

I followed her to the bed. You could hear faint traffic noises but I soon blotted them out as Janet pushed me onto my back, straddled me, and guided me into her. She threw her head back and soon we found our rhythm and her hands were on my shoulders and mine were pulling on her ass and when it was over she rolled over and I pulled her to me and we lay in silence until we heard Irene Ghormley open the front door of the office.

Janet left shortly before nine. Bill Nolan and Tommy Lee Briggs were in their offices. Tommy was reading the New York Times and Bill was talking to a sad faced black woman. Her name was Ann Tisdale. She was in her early forties and Bill was telling her that her teenage son, Clyde, would be out of prison in thirteen years if he pled guilty and took the State's deal. Irene had made some strong coffee. I went back to the kitchen and poured a cup and read the Monday Commercial Appeal. After a few minutes, I lost interest and went back to my office and went through my mail from yesterday. Two checks, four letters from banks offering me credit cards, a bill from a florist for the flowers I had sent Sharon a few weeks ago on a whim, and a reminder that my subscription to the New Yorker was to expire soon, were all that I had. I took the checks to Irene and asked her to deposit them for me.

Irene is, shall we say, of indeterminate age. When Bill and Tommy Lee left their old firm and moved to Front Street, the only dispute with their former partners was over Irene. The senior partner claimed she was there before anyone could remember, She was offered a raise. She refused and came with Bill and Tommy Lee. I would guess her age as mid-seventies. She is small and her maiden name was Cianciola. She married a bright-eyed Sheriff's detective in the sixties, raised three children, and buried her husband in the late nineties.

She dotes on Bill and Tommy Lee. She often comes in on Saturdays and never leaves the office when they are in trial until they call and tell her to go home or they come back to the office and tell her all about the trial., Coffee was always brewed for Tommy Lee and Bill before they got to the office. Her hair is a curious shade of brown. It has red tints in it, and it is done up in a fifties style bouffant. Her soap opera is the Catholic Church. Her parish out in Raleigh, the local Diocese, and the Vatican are all subject to her barbs. She is not particularly fond of me, but when I need something, it gets done and it gets done right. She deems me immoral. Janet and I live in sin right above her office several days and nights a week. She smokes constantly. She has a small portable fan, which she uses to blow smoke into the air surrounding her. Bill and Tommy Lee ask her not to smoke outside her office and she complies. Except when she comes into my office. It is not a big deal to me. Janet says we should fire her. We think if the year goes right, we will give her a raise in the fall.

Irene's greatest gift is her telephone skills. She knows people in all of the clerk's offices, Federal and State, and she has an imposing voice that makes most people surrender whatever information she is seeking. I sat at her desk and told her where I was on the Robert Lee Whitfield case. Midway through my account, the phone rang and she had a seven-minute discussion with someone. It appears her priest was going to be transferred and there was a rumor his replacement was gay and , even worse, from Boston.

When she ended her conversation, she said, "So there is a vacant place about eighteen by eighteen on Mr. Whitfield's old wall and you think he took this picture, or whatever, with him and you think if you knew what it was, it would be a clue to help you find him, right?"

I said "Bingo."

She slid her glasses down her nose and looked at me. Her red lipstick was beginning to smear slightly at the corners of her mouth.

"Bingo?"

"Yes, Ms. Irene, it means you nailed it. You got it right."

"And that should not surprise you, young man. Give me the contact information on Mr. James , Dump, Warren, and I will call him mid-day if I have not heard from him."

"With Dump, be low key, please. He lost his wife a few years ago and he is a nice guy but if you piss him off, he will go into a shell. Is my guess."

"I will tell him to call you as soon as he remembers anything and if you have your cell turned off which you have a bad habit of doing, then he is to call me immediately, either at the office or on my cell, which I never turn off."

"Thanks."

"And I will call that nice Essie. The one you talked to and I will ask her if she will go down and talk to Dump. Maybe she will remember or help him remember. Women are so much better at matters of observation and detail than you men."

"Thanks again."

The phone rang again and she answered it and turned in her chair to face Front Street. I was dismissed. I went into Tommy Lee's office and told him where I was going. As I passed Bill Nolan's office, the door was closed but I could hear the soft, persistent sobbing of Ann Tisdale. She was going to spend Monday at 201 Poplar, Memphis,

Tennessee. Home of the County's Criminal Courts. And it would end with her seeing her son leave a courtroom with a sentence that could keep him away for more than thirteen years. I did not feel sorry for the son. To get a sentence requiring a minimum of thirteen years of incarceration, he had done something bad. Real bad. I felt sorry for her, though. There was no father there in Nolan's office to bear the shame and frustration. It was all hers to bear the best way she could.

Clyde Tisdale had been indigent when he was arrested for Aggravated Robbery. He had stuck up an Asian grocery in North Memphis and pistol-whipped a sixty five-year-old Vietnamese grocer. Bill had been appointed to defend him and I had done some legwork for him. The robbery detective showed me the prints lifted from the cash box that matched those of Clyde Tisdale. The detective was a short black man in his late thirties. His name is Joseph Carver. He wore a nice blue suit with a white shirt and a red and blue striped tie when I talked to him in the Robbery Office. He said he could make seven cases on Tisdale but had only submitted three. The other four were one on one identification cases. They were tough to win and hard to believe in. The three he had were solid. They had all occurred over a single weekend last September. Three weeks after Clyde had flattened a one-year sentence for stealing a big screen television in a home burglary.

Clyde had helped the Robbery Detective by confessing. Clyde was off crack cocaine by the time the detectives picked him up at his girlfriend's house. Joseph Carver let me read his file and take notes and gave me a copy of the photos and the fingerprint examination. The other two cases had at least two identifications by decent witnesses plus the confessions. I remember asking Joseph Carver how he got Clyde to confess and he said he told him he had seven cases on him but was only going to pursue the three he was sure of and Clyde told him he might as well tell him about them. Get his story in and tell why he did it. He told Carver he was high on dope and wanted more and the only way he knew to get the money to buy the dope was to rob a store.

I went and talked to the witnesses in the stores and they were all decent people with no reason to lie. They said he was easy to remember. He had a nose like Jimmy Durante on a narrow face with a shaved head and an Adam's Apple the size of a small orange. Ann Tisdale, Bill Nolan, and I had talked to Clyde the week after Valentine's Day., I went over the evidence the State had against him and Bill showed him the indictments and told him the penalties for each charge. His only comment had been to ask Bill if he could get him a nickel at the Correctional Center so he could see his mother and girlfriend some while he was doing his sentence. A nickel is a five-year sentence.

There was no nickel in the near future for Clyde. The pistol whipping of the storekeeper carried up to twenty-five, so fifteen at a hundred percent was a good deal. The way it worked, he would be able to get out in thirteen and a half. Thirteen and a half years away from Clyde would do Ann Tisdale a lot of good. But you couldn't tell her that.

I sat down in the office kitchen. There was a three-layer coconut cake in the middle of the table. It was almost half gone. Our Monday perk from Irene. I cut a slice and poured a cup of strong, black coffee. Bill was sitting across from me. The cake was still good on Tuesday. Yellow cake, white icing, and lots of coconut.

"Another day in Paradise." He said.

"I am going to Hardaman County, Mississippi. I hope to be back by dark."

"You any closer?"

"I have eliminated half of the Continental United States. The Eastern half. I am pretty sure he headed west when he left Parchman."

"You get back, if you can squeeze it in, I need you to go talk to a witness for me. It is on another appointed case. An old cop. He came to Memphis to see the Redbirds and one of my clients tried to carjack him in one of the parking lots after the game. The cop took the gun away from him and busted his skull. He probably won't talk, but it is worth a try. Reason I am bothering is that what he says could affect the charge. It could be a simple assault, Aggravated Assault, Attempted Robbery, whatever. I just need to know how far it got. His lawyer in General Sessions waived the Preliminary Hearing in exchange for a copy of the State's file, but the old cop's statement is vague. My client says he was trying to sell the guy some rip-off Viagra and the deal went bad. The old cop lives out past Collierville on a small farm."

I asked Bill to put a copy of the file on my desk and I would get to it as soon as I could. He asked me to call him when I knew when I would be back from Hardaman County. I knew why. He wanted someone to drink the night away with. I was trying to get out of the long drinking night habit. Some called it bingeing. Now I tried to quit at two drinks. It was working. Gradually. I knew I would stay straight until the Whitfield case was over. But I did want to talk to Bill about some things. So I knew if I got back before midnight I would find Bill hunkered over a glass of bourbon. Tommy usually went home to his wife, but sometimes he would take a pop or two. He said it was something to do until the traffic died down in the evening.

I left Bill to deal with Clyde and Ann Tisdale and headed north on Front until I got to Beale and took a left under the railroad bridge, I had to stop for a light before turning left on Riverside Drive. I could see the River. There was no activity and the brown water was silently gliding south toward the Gulf of Mexico. I turned left on Riverside and drove South up a long hill between the River and the Bluffs. I could see traffic high above me on Front Street. There were red and white dogwood trees just starting to bud all along the bluffs to my left. For a few weeks in April and May, the bluffs would come alive with color. Later in the year, an occasional Magnolia bloomed. After I passed Crump, I got on the Interstate and followed it to Lamar. South on

Lamar carried me past warehouses, used car lots, liquor stores, pawn shops, car repair shops, and rundown apartment buildings.

The sun was out. There was almost no wind and it appeared the temperature would hold around sixty for most of the day. The sky was clear and blue. I followed Highway 72 through peaceful farmland. Rolling hills , livestock , tall pine trees, squat cedars, and broad vistas relaxed me as I drove the speed limit in the right lane. My Camaro was like a horse fresh out of the barn after a winter of confinement. I wanted to get it up to around ninety and let it run for a few miles but I had already seen one Highway Patrol car stop a truck so I kept the speed down. I passed Holly Springs and enjoyed the sound of the car's strong engine. I turned East on Highway Thirty at New Albany and I was in Hardaman County before noon.

I went over an old bridge over the Tippah River just as I entered Hardaman County. To my right were wooden buildings with signs advertising fishing boats for rent and bait for sale. Another tin building was deeper in the woods. It had a Budweiser sign and no name. In twenty minutes, I was in downtown Hardaman. The Sheriff's office was on the Square. It was a one-story building with an attractive brick façade. There was a white Ford Explorer with a round blue and green Hardaman County Sheriff's Department decal on the driver's door. A Crown Vic with the same decal was parked next to it.

I parked and looked across the Square at the County Courthouse. There were farmers sitting on benches under barren oak trees. Two lawyers were standing on the courthouse steps arguing. The four tall columns in the front of the Courthouse had been painted white recently and the grass was just starting to grow on the lawn. Everything was neat and no one was hurrying. In Memphis, the lawns surrounding 201 Poplar where the Criminal Courts were housed was never neat. People walked across the grass and the trees were mostly anemic. The old oaks on the Hardaman County Courthouse lawn were tall and serene. I could imagine Gorman Ballard sitting on a bench under one of these trees listening to an old farmer tell him a story.

An inmate was in the front yard. He had a rake in his hand and a black plastic trash bag sticking out of his left back pocket. He was wearing khakis, brown work boots, and a blue denim long sleeve shirt. INMATE was written in yellow on the back of the shirt. He was in his sixties and his white face was wrinkled. He was a little over six foot tall and his hair was gone except for a short, small gray border. He may have weighed one hundred and fifty pounds. His eyes were brown and alert. He did not have the long stare I had seen yesterday at Parchman.

I was almost past him when he said, "You from Memphis? The detective wants to see the Sheriff?"

I said yes and he laughed. He said I might be in more trouble than he was. I didn't say anything else because a small black man was standing in the doorway with his hands on his hips. He wore a holster with a big handled revolver in it. Fresh pressed khakis and black boots with a spit shine polish went well with his erect posture and neat mustache. He was in his middle to late thirties and was probably five seven. He did not weigh as much as the inmate.

"I can see you are from Memphis. You in deep, deep shit with me. I might have to make you buy me some lunch because I had no breakfast, thanks to you ,and my supper was cold last night. All because of your sorry ass. Come on in here and sit down."

I started past him and he walked out into the yard and looked around.

"Jake, get this looking nice, then go on across the street to the Square and police it up Judge is coming next week and we will be having court all day long every day. You want me to buy you a cheeseburger and bring it on back to you? I'm thinking this here city boy is going to wind up doing the buying in exchange for me not letting him be the guest of the county tonight."

Jake said, "If he is buying, get him to throw in some fries and one of them Baby Ruth candy bars."

We went into the Sheriff's office, there were autographed pictures of the last three governors on the wall behind his neat, oak desk. A computer monitor and printer were on a small desk near a window. He asked to see my identification and when he had checked it, he handed it back to me and motioned for me to sit down.

"Mr. Cheatham, I was just sitting down to eat when Nora Deen Barksdale called me all upset about some private investigator from Memphis wanting to stick his nose in her business. This being Hardaman County business. Well, in a few minutes, I got her calmed down and she said you told her you were working for Vera Chaney. So I said I would check it out and get back to her. She said you would probably show up this morning. She also said you sounded too young to be a real private detective. She thought you are some kind of scam artist."

I told him about finding the phone number in Robert Lee Whitfield's office and he laughed.

"Well, Miss Nora Deen left that part out. Now where is your piece? I am particular about people bringing guns in my county to interview people. Specially when they are not the real law."

"My gun is back in the safe in my apartment. I didn't figure I would need it talking to an old woman. Especially with you tagging along."

"So then, I tried to get ahold of Dr. Vera Chaney. When I knew her, she was Vera Stepter. I am a few years older than her and I tried to take her out a few times and she never said yes. As they say, I was smitten with her. Just like the rest of the boys around here."

"I got a number from the Sheriff's Department down in Yazoo County and left a number for her and she woke me up before six this morning and told me you were working for her and I could trust you. Then when I got in this morning, I call Miss Nora Deen before eight and she chewed on my ass for a while about calling her so early but when I explained the reason for your call, she said for me to send you out there around two and she would see you. No need for me to go. I made you a copy of part of the County map that will show you how to get there. About a fifteen-minute drive for me. For you, make sure it takes twenty."

There was a round clock on the wall to the right of his desk. It was twenty five past twelve. A map of the county covered most of the wall to the left of his desk. It had eleven red thumbtacks stuck in it. There were seven green tacks stuck next to seven of the red tacks. Six blue tacks were pinned to the map. I noticed a green, red, and blue tack stuck on the map near where I had crossed the Tippah River.

"What are the tacks for, Sheriff."

He walked to the map and picked up a short wooden pointer from the floor. He held the pointer close to his right side.

"First, I been Sheriff just a few months shy of two years. Had to stand for election last year and won. Got the job from Governor Barbour. An appointment after the old Sheriff died. Not Sheriff Rainey. He has been dead a long while. Anyway, those green tacks was put in to show where we had semi-confirmed meth houses while I was a deputy before I was Sheriff. The old Sheriff was sick for a year or so before he died and we had no direction. So when I got in, we started to up our intelligence on those eleven places. I call them meth houses. Just a phrase. Some were labs. Most were just places you could buy the stuff. Some were both. Three years ago, the principal of the school said some of the seniors said they had tried meth and they had bought it right here in the County. I went around to all the churches talking about the meth problem and folks started calling in and telling me stuff and we have got it down to four now. Four suspected. I think two of them are for real and they just cook it here in the county. Principal of the school is mighty pleased."

"What about the blue pins."

"Blue pins is for farms I think are growing Marijuana. I tell the State drug boys what I know and let them handle it. The Marijuana is harmless lest it be sold to high-schoolers. I think I got that business about shut down, but they can go over the County line into Tupelo and get it. We are about half way between Corinth and Tupelo."

"Meth scares the hell out of me. I was a policeman for a little over a year in Memphis and that stuff tears a person down fast. A psychologist told me it was harder to rehab someone on Meth than cocaine."

"Jake, the inmate outside. He is one of those guys you can't rehabilitate. I can't keep him out of here. He cashes his Social Security check and when it is gone, I find him passed out somewhere. Usually up on one of the benches by the Courthouse. I arrest him for public drunkenness and littering and take care of him for a few weeks at a time."

"So my sentence is lunch?"

"Only one decent choice left unless you want fast food. We got a Sonic, a KFC, and a Wendy's. Little restaurant one street over is fine if you like turnip greens and chicken fried steak or hamburger steak."

The restaurant was really a diner. A counter with red stools. Four red leather booths against a window facing the street and six tables in the middle of the floor. The floor was wooden and the booths were tall. We sat in a booth by a window and I had a hamburger steak, rice and gravy, and turnip greens. The Sheriff ate roasted chicken, green beans, and turnip greens. A brown plastic bowl with yeast rolls and cornbread sticks sat between us. I drank iced tea and he drank water. Dessert was lemon meringue pie.

Sheriff Glover ordered coffee after we finished lunch. I had a refill of iced tea and sat back in the booth and relaxed. It had been a good meal. The kind I remembered from my childhood. Hard to find in Memphis, nowadays.

"So, tell me about Nora Deen Barksdale."

"White lady. In her seventies. Native to our county. Got a Doctorate in Education up at Oxford and came back home and started teaching history and English in the white high school in the early sixties. Married a young doctor came here a year or so after she got to teaching. His name was Harrison Barksdale. Now, this is all before I was born in seventy seven. What I was told by my folks."

He called the waitress over. She was tall and her red hair hung in a ponytail down to her skinny rear. She was about the same age as the Sheriff.

"You want me to put in an order for Jake. A cheeseburger, some fries, and a candy bar. Baby Ruth and Snickers is the freshest. I can tell you that. And some tea with a lot of ice and sugar in it."

"That's right. And put it all on one check. Give it to this fellow from Memphis."

She laughed and went to the order window and gave the ticket to one of the cooks and leaned against the counter and talked to one of her customers.

"You too young to remember this, too. What I was told is that when the State of Mississippi finally got around to integrating the public schools, it was in the seventies in some counties. Hardaman being one. By this time Nora Deen Barksdale was principal of the white high school. She and Dr. Harrison, they fought the idea of a white academy school. Happened all over the Delta. Whites made their own private schools before they would come and sit and learn and eat with us. Hill folks, like in Hardaman County were more prone to at least give it a try. Anyway, they made Nora Deen Barksdale the County Superintendent of Education and it all worked out. She stayed on as the Principal of the high school and she and some more folks with some sense held it all together. Now the schools in the city and county are pretty stable. No blacks raped any precious little white girls. No white thugs used the N word in the halls and got away with it. Least in Nora Deen Barksdale's high school, anyway. Once they was home, things was different, I know. But at least you didn't hear of it in the schools."

"You know anything about Robert Lee Whitfield?"

"Seen him one time in my life. At Parchman. Back in the fall. One thing I do is keep up with our fine citizens who have been doing time at Parchman. I get a printout every week of the inmates being released. I give em a visit. Try to nip any bullshit in the bud. They get up one morning and they are brought in to see me in an interview room. I got a file on em from here and what I can get at Parchman. I ask them if they are coming home. What their plans are if they do come home. Find out where they going to live. Who their folks are. Let em know I will be on their ass if need be, but also tell em I will try to help em find work if there is any here that the Parole Board has overlooked. Works out sometimes. Sometimes it doesn't. You still got to have a plan and try to implement it."

The waitress brought a white paper sack over to the table and gave me the check. We had refills on our coffee and iced tea. The diner was empty now except for a farmer in overalls who was bent over a coffee cup and was talking to the red headed waitress.

"Way it was with Robert was different. I got a call from Essie Beard at Parchman. She said the word came down from the Governor that Robert's sentence was commuted. So I drove down the next morning. They would not bring him out to me in an interview room. Nah, I had to ride out there with Essie Beard. Out to the Maintenance Shed. Robert was under a tractor when I got there and I sat in the office with Dump Warren for almost an hour before Robert came out from under that tractor. I told him who I was and he just stared and would not answer me except to say he needed to be left alone and he would go where he wanted to go and do what he wanted to do when he was released but I could damn well bet that none of it would happen in Mississippi. I gave him my card and asked him to call me if he changed his mind and came back to Hardaman County. Still some of them Starnes' left in our county. He just turned around and walked back. Last I saw of him was when I walked out of the shed. He was sitting on the tractor he had been working on. His head was down close to the steering wheel and he was listening to the tractor idle. Was a green John Deere."

"You ask him where he was planning on going."

"Sure. He said that wasn't the law's business. His papers were going to say he was free. His phrase was, 'My debt will be paid and marked cancelled., The law's hold on me is gone day after tomorrow."

"No news of him coming back here?"

"None. Now, let me tell you just a little bit more about Nora Deen Barksdale. I liked her. We all did. Looked up to her. She was in our churches. The white churches, too., Trying to get the schools and the community to working together. Her husband was there for her all this time up to about three years ago. He came down to this diner one Wednesday in the late spring when everything was blooming up on the square. The Dogwoods and the jonquils and the geraniums up by the courthouse steps and the petunias. Just a great day. I got a call. I come down to the café and he was in the alley on the ground. His glasses was broke and laying off in the gravel by his right hand. He was deader than a hammer. A heart attack. I was still a deputy but no one bothered the Sheriff. He was home waiting to die. So I went up to the High School and she was in the auditorium. It was some kind of musical contest with each class performing and it was noisy and carefree. You know how kids are in the Springtime."

"I sat in the front row and let everything in the program finish out and then I went and told her. Well, she bore up under it good. Until after the funeral. She sent a letter to the school board saying she was taking her pension and resigning. She never came back to the school. She comes to town some. Mainly for groceries and to get her hair and nails done down at Gloria's Beauty Shop. You passed it coming into town. I go to see her when I can. I forget, though. I got my own life. When I go, we sit outside on the porch and we talk."

The Sheriff was staring through the window at some blue jays fighting over some red berries in a flowering green bush across the street from the diner., He didn't want to talk anymore. I paid the check at the noisy, metallic gray cash register. The red headed waitress had a nice smile. When she gave me my change I gave her a five-dollar bill and she asked if I needed any change back and I said no. The Sheriff followed me out of the diner.

When we got back to his office, I thanked the Sheriff for his help and gave him one of my cards.

He followed me out to my car and before I opened the door, he said, "She has a broken heart. She and her husband, they was something else. Older you get, harder it is to get a broken heart to mend. Together all the time and they seemed to be happy. Once he died, she started going down. Fragile. That is what my wife says she is. Fragile. They don't list a broken heart as an official cause of death. I hope something will jumpstart her and get her back to where she enjoys her life. You can grieve yourself right into the grave."

As I drove out of the Square, I saw Sheriff Glover with the white paper sack. He was walking up the steps from the street to the Court House lawn. Jake was on his knees in a flowerbed. He was planting purple petunias. The Court House steps were empty but the doors to the courthouse were open. Three farmers sat on a bench beneath a tall oak. Two were playing checkers and the third was watching and smoking a black pipe.

Sheriff Glover gave me good directions and I had no trouble finding Nora Deen Barksdale's home. I drove up a long gravel driveway and parked in front of a large Southern Mansion. It had a well-kept yard with cedar and oak trees providing shade for the long, front porch. An ornate iron gate and fence surrounded the front yard. I opened the gate and walked up the stone path to the white wooden steps leading to the porch. It was a few minutes after two. A male and female Cardinal were in a cedar tree. The female was building a nest. The male was just hopping around on one of the top branches. There

was no one on the porch. I rang the doorbell and waited. The front
door was open, but the screen door was shut.

I rang again and a small Hispanic woman came to the door. She
did not open it, but spoke through the screen.

"Wait on the porch. Ms. Barksdale will receive you shortly."

I waited on the porch for at least fifteen minutes. I sat on the top
of the porch steps and looked out at the empty fields. There was a red
barn off to the right. A gray Ford tractor was parked in front of it. It
had a bush hog attached. A small brown man was pumping gas from a
white farm tank into the tractor. The house was at the top of a long hill.
On my left as I sat on the steps, I could see a long pond near the
entrance to the driveway. The sun was still high in the sky and the
pond was silver and inviting. A few trees leaned over the pond near the
dam. There were no boats or docks.

I heard the screen door slam and I got up and turned around. A
once beautiful woman stood before me with a stiff and uncertain smile.
I introduced myself and gave her one of my cards. She looked at it and
turned and walked to a wooden rocker. She motioned for me to
follow. I sat in a rocker beside her. Her hair was gray but neatly
combed. She was around five eight. Her eyes were a beautiful shade of
blue. Blue like the sky in the springtime when there are no clouds. Her
face was lean. She had a small nose and high cheekbones. Her mouth
was small and her lips were thin and seductive. Even at her age, you
could tell. She had been a looker. A woman you would look at and
write off as unattainable. Her posture was still erect.

After we sat down, the maid came on the porch with a silver
serving tray, On the tray was a pitcher of iced tea and two glasses.
Napkins for each of us. Lemon slices. And a small glass container with
sweeteners in it. And a sugar bowl with a silver spoon. The china sugar
bowl was blue and white. Some macaroons were stacked neatly on a
blue napkin.

"Thank you, Sylvia. Thank you. The detective will not be staying for dinner. I will be content if you will make me two tuna salad sandwiches and leave them on the table for me. You can go on home when you are finished. I see Ramon down at the barn. Tell him I want this whole front down to the road neat and trim as soon as that old Ford tractor decides to run."

She poured some tea for me and I sat and slowly rocked. Not a bad way to spend a few hours on a Spring or Fall day. Or a Summer night.

"Thank you for seeing me. Your phone number was on the wall of the room Robert Lee Whitfield stayed in. It was not a cell. It was a room they fixed up for him in the Maintenance Shop. I am trying to find him and deliver a letter to him from his daughter, Dr. Vera Chaney."

"I asked Robert to call me a few years ago. A few years before I lost Harrison. What happened was so sad. Ann Stepter, Vera's grandmother. Died. So I called the Governor and he was tied up with the damn fool legislature so one of his aides took my number and in a few days Robert Lee called me from Parchman Farm and I told him. She passed quickly with little suffering. Robert thanked me and that was that."

"You were around when Robert Lee shot Billy Ray Starnes up in the parking lot in Hardaman?"

"Well, if you mean, was I there, no. I did not see it but I knew it happened and I can tell you about it. Boy, where did you get your education?"

"High School at East Tallahatchie and college at Millsaps College."

"I can tell by looking at you. You majored in girls and liquor. Now what was your official excuse for being there?"

"I majored in English. Supposed to have gone to Law School, but I didn't. I went to Perdido Key and stayed for almost five years. Living the good life. Sun and girls and margaritas and fishing. I was a fishing guide after I worked a summer and learned where the fish were and how to catch them."

"But now you are in Memphis. Where is your gun?"

"Locked in my safe at the office."

"The short version of how you got off a fishing boat in Perdido Key and got to where you are right now. "

"A few years back, my father, a Memphis policeman, got shot. I went home and tried to be a good son. I joined the force and I lasted fifteen months. I just got restless and fed up with all the regimentation. So I took out my own license last fall and Dr. Vera came to see me last Sunday."

She looked off into the bright, blue sky. There were no clouds but a restless breeze blew across the yard and rustled the limbs of the still barren shade trees. A mockingbird was singing somewhere behind the house. Spring was near. The temperature on the porch was in the low sixties. Nora Deen Barksdale was wearing a pair of blue cotton slacks and a white blouse. She wore matching blue heels. She sat back in her rocker and closed her eyes.

"I am surmising there was a divorce by your parents and a change of location for you. Perhaps not as much time with your father in your childhood as you would have liked."

"You would be right. But we are close now. He has remarried in the last year. He did not even care when I left the Memphis Police Department. And I like his wife."

"I will tell you about Robert Lee. But in my own way and at my own speed. It could have been a nice story but as often times happens, Fate , or in this case, Evil steps in and things get ruined quickly. "

"Take your time. I am in no hurry."

"Soon, this whole place will be alive. I usually walk at four. Sylvia and I. She has got me up to four miles. It is keeping me alive. When Harrison died I lost the will to go on. Now, it is coming back. I am still trying to figure out why I am here. What I can do with these remaining years. I guess I am looking for a sign. Won't be long now and this impatient time of the year will pass. The birds will nest, the flowers will bloom, the tractors will break the ground and seeds will be planted and the children will be out of school and into mischief. I grew up in this county and in 1954, I went to Oxford to get my college. I was a Chi Omega and a cheerleader. Football, boys, and school. Trips to Memphis and the Peabody Hotel and the Ducks. Trips to New Orleans. Not hardly a care in the world. A great time to grow up, I taught a few years and I was like you to a point. I wanted my own school so I went back and got my Doctorate in Education and came on back home. My father was a doctor and I was an only child."

She drank some tea and shifted in her rocking chair and looked down at the barn. The male cardinal had left and there were some doves on a wire down near the main road. I took a macaroon from the tray and took a bite. Lots of fresh coconut in it. The sun was hanging low in the blue sky. We had a good three hours of day light left.

"I am getting to Robert Lee real soon, be patient. Well, it was 1971 before they made me the principal of the High School. I was still single and my father was getting on. He took in a new doctor. Harrison Barksdale. Harrison was from a farm town in western Pennsylvania. Went to school at Purdue and then Med School down here in Jackson, Mississippi. He was an orthopedic man, like my father. Dad lived here in the county but did most of his work in the hospitals in Corinth and Tupelo. When he wasn't in surgery or making the rounds at the hospitals, he saw patients in Hardaman. Harrison followed right behind him.

"Of course, we got put together at dinner parties all over the county. I detested him. He had a back East smugness about him that made me so mad I could have eaten a burnt biscuit. And he was shorter than me. But he was a good listener. And gradually, we got to be friends. I told him he was exasperating and that I did not appreciate his smugness but I did not tell him how much I admired his mind. I got to where I relied so much on him. Those were troubling times. Both JFK and Robert and Martin Luther King, Jr. were killed in the sixties and there was Vietnam and I did not have anyone to talk to about any of it. No one I trusted. Till I met Harrison and then all of that was over and we had Nixon to worry over."

"One night in the spring when he first got here, we were in Memphis together. Sitting in the bar at the Peabody. Drinking Vodka Martinis. He told me the trouble with our educational system at the high school and college level was that it taught us to take tests. Not think. And when he said that I felt small. That was me. Taking tests and doing great, but not thinking. Not understanding why things went awry in Viet Nam. Why was a question I never concerned myself with."

"Later that night, I asked him when he was going to get around to marrying me. He had a round face and unremarkable brown hair and he wore round metal-framed glasses. He had small lips and soft brown eyes. He laughed and asked me right there in the lobby of the Peabody Hotel to marry him. So I suggested we go ahead and do it while we were in Memphis and we could plan a hone moon later. So we scandalized the county by showing up for work on Monday with wedding rings on our hands. We bought this place and fixed the house up. New hardwood floors, walk in cedar closets, new bathrooms, a bigger kitchen and then he started on the outside. Had the pond drained and cleaned. Restocked it with bass and bream and catfish. Bought a Case tractor used. It wouldn't run half the time."

"One April Saturday morning in, I think it was eighty one, we were lying in bed right after the sun had come up. Half asleep, half awake. You know how it is. And Harrison set up in bed. He asked me if I heard something. I listened and I heard that old red Case tractor. Purring away. Strong and regular like a healthy animal breathes. So Harrison gets up, throws on some clothes, and goes down to the barn. I was out here on the porch with a green wrapper on over my gown. I saw Robert Lee up on the tractor. His head was cocked and he was listening to the motor run. Robert Lee was young back then. He had dropped out of school to work. No family to speak of and he lived on a little farm not too far from here. He and his Uncle, Leon., Robert Lee told Harrison he had heard some folks at the Davis Feed Store up in town say that Harrison was looking for some help on the farm. "

"Ann Stepter lived about a mile east of here and she worked in the cafeteria at the grammar school. But I knew her. So Robert and Harrison were together most Saturdays or Sundays. Robert was independent. Harrison would tell him he needed him to do this or that and Robert would nod his head but he did things his way on his own time. He would see things needed to be done and he would do them without being asked or told. He would tell Harrison he was going off for a while and we would see him when he got back. Harrison followed him around like a child when he came and worked on the place. Robert knowing everything about a farm. When to prune the fruit trees. When to cut a tree down. Where to make the cut when you pruned a rose bush. All that. And a car or truck or lawn mower or tractor. Anything with an engine he could handle."

"He told Harrison he had spent some time in Chicago but did not like it. When he met Vera's mother, Louise, it wasn't long till she moved in with him and Vera was on the way. Louise had a cousin named Mardine. She went bad and hung out down in the joints down on the bottoms on the Tippah River. Always some joints there. Used to be just whiskey and beer and a few girls but by the time Robert Lee killed that worthless Starnes boy, there was supposed to be cocaine and marijuana to be found down there. Sheriff Rainey would catch some body and close one joint down and six months later some body new would be down there running it again full blast. One of the joints let Mardine work there."

"Now Mardine was a few years older than Louise. Louise confided in her and looked up to her. Louise was a good-looking woman, but she fell behind in school early and dropped out when she met Robert Lee. Here is what led up to the killing. Least this is the way Harrison told it and I believe him because he was careful with his facts and slow to trust people."

"One night Mardine took Louise to the Bottoms with her. Whites and blacks went to some of the same places. Billy Ray Starnes was there and saw Louise and made a play for her and Louise didn't want anything to do with him. So Billy Ray started driving by the house a lot when he thought Robert Lee was not there. Louise told Robert Lee about it and Robert Lee caught him somewhere off in the county and told him to stay away. Then Louise left. Didn't have nothing to do with Billy Ray. She knew she was pretty. She was tired of being a mother and she took Vera up to Ann Stepter's one night and lit out for the Tupelo bus station."

"It crushed Robert. Mardine said Louise bought a ticket all the way to Cleveland. Ohio. Wasn't true. She went to Atlanta. But all that came out later when Mardine settled down and got off dope and tried to make peace with Ann. Nobody ever heard anything back from Louise. Harrison tried to find her but the law in Atlanta could not or would not help. So that was why Robert Lee shot Billy Ray Starnes. He had all he could take of bad luck, betrayal, and lying. See Billy Ray put it down at the joints that he took Louise to Memphis to catch a train and she gave him some in a motel on Lamar Avenue before she left. You know all that got back to Robert Lee. Truth was Mardine drove her to the Tupelo bus station. So, I can tell you the why of it all, but that part of the past never got to Vera."

A phone rang inside the house. Nora Dean let it ring. When it was through ringing, she got up and went into the house. I watched some doves fly into a tree down by the pond. The male cardinal had returned to the cedar tree and was watching his mate building the nest. When Nora Dean came back, she had half a tuna fish sandwich on a napkin. She gave it to me. It was on wheat bread and Sylvia had mixed in some boiled eggs and sweet pickles. I took a bite.

"How long did it take you to piece all of this about Robert Lee together?"

"It was a while, maybe six or seven years. Mardine moved back to Hardaman and got on with the high school in the cafeteria. She was on probation out of Hinds County for drugs, but I gave her a chance and she did alright. But she just switched off to alcohol. She handled that okay. She never missed work enough to where I noticed it and she liked Harrison and told him all about it. I never asked. "

"I was already home when the shooting happened. When Harrison got home that day, it was almost sundown and he told me what he had heard. Round ten that night, we heard Robert Lee knocking on the front door. Harrison sat out here on the porch with him. I was not invited out. I brought some food out to Robert Lee and Harrison asked me to bring a bottle of Jim Beam out with some ice and two glasses. It was after two in the morning when Harrison came to bed. Then he sat on the edge of the bed with his head in his hands. I got up and we talked for a while and he finally slept. Harrison said he offered to hire a lawyer for Robert Lee but Robert Lee said he did not want that. Later, we learned he left here and sat up and waited until morning when Sheriff Rainey came and got him."

"Harrison went to see him some here in this jail before he went to Parchman. Finally he came home one day and told me at dinner he was tired of being in a dither about the murder. And he never talked about it again except to tell me what Mardine finally told him. All Robert Lee ever told Harrison or anybody was that Billy Ray Starnes had it coming, which nobody could argue with, and that he was not sorry. And that you can always argue with. "

"You up to one more question?"

"Of course."

"Tell me about Vera. Now I see her in my office just one time and I would take her case for nothing. Where did that class and regal bearing come from?"

"It came from Ann Stepter. And Robert Lee. Robert Lee was somebody you could look at and know you could trust his word. Ann had the high cheekbones, the long legs, the flashing brown eyes, and a way about her. The way she walked. She didn't talk much, but she was smart. And resolute."

"Three or four years after Robert Lee went to the penitentiary down at Parchman, I was shelling purple hull peas out here and I saw Ann driving her old black two door Plymouth up the road. She got out and went and got Vera out of the passenger side and walked up and asked for Harrison. He was down at the barn tearing some piece of machinery apart so we walked down there and he got up out from under the same old Case tractor Robert Lee had kept running and wiped his hands and smiled that thin shy smile."

" Ann said Vera wanted to be a doctor and she had no doctor type books to read and she wanted to know if Harrison would help her. She was just eight or maybe nine. Well, that started it. Vera might as well have moved in. Harrison had someone he could talk to about medicine. The history of it. The new procedures. The diseases. The human body. He started out by giving her a big old poster of the human body. It had all the major bones, the glands, the organs, the muscles. Not all of them. But most of them. She took it home and put it on her wall and it was like putting a match to kindling. Harrison said it was exciting to have someone to talk to about medicine. They would sit out on the porch in the late afternoon and talk about diseases and fractures and Dr. Jonas Salk and Dr. Michael Debakey, the heart man down in Houston, Texas."

"She got a scholarship to Vanderbilt for undergraduate study then came back to Mississippi and finished Med School and her residency in Surgery down in Jackson. We assumed she was coming back here, but one time when she came home in the spring of her last year of residency, she told Harrison she had met a man and fell in love. Down in Yazoo County. He was a hill farmer with some cattle, too. Harrison was hurt. I know that. He was counting on her to come back here and let him teach her some of the practical things a doctor has to learn about setting up a practice."

"When she set her practice up, Harrison went down a lot of weekends and helped her set up her billing and appointment procedures."

She got up and walked down the driveway and opened her mailbox and came on back and sat on the porch. She laid the mail on the porch beside her chair and rocked some more. I finished my sandwich and ate another macaroon. She laughed. A soft, bitter laugh. The kind we all have in us when we recognize we have just come up short. Or missed out on something. Or lost something incapable of being recaptured. A laugh of disappointment. She got up from her rocker and looked at the blue sky and the soon to set sun and she listened to the trees as the soft wind ran slowly through the branches.

"Do you believe in God, young man?"

"Never found a reason not to. I do not pretend to understand how it all fits together, but yes, I do."

"See, when Harrison was here, I assumed it all had a meaning. Some things like Robert Lee shooting that Starnes boy, you have to accept and go on with your own life. Harrison always had a good answer. Sometimes he would exasperate the living hell out of me. Taking so long to answer a question, but he was just careful. Now he is gone and I am looking for a sign. Anything to help me live with a purpose."

"Do you want to give up and die?"

"No, I don't. Ramon and Sylvia came last fall. I need a man around to help with the place. Sylvia is my friend. Once a week she cooks their native food and we three eat together. I look forward to it. Posole or chicken enchiladas or brisket with a red sauce on it. New smells in the kitchen. I look forward to it. It is for Friday night. Our time together. But I am scared. They could leave. Like Vera left. I know I want to live, though. I wish Spring would just get here. I am tired and want to see flowers and leaves and crops and fruit on the trees and the pecans in the fall."

"You got any idea where Robert Lee might have gone? Maybe a place he and Harrison talked about?"

"No. If I remember anything, I will call you."

I could not think of a reason to stay. Ramon was bush hogging down by the fence near the road. Old brown grass and weeds from last year. The doves were gone, but the Cardinals were still in the cedar tree. I had finished the half sandwich. I stood up to leave and Nora Deen Barksdale brushed my right forearm with her left hand. Her smile was still something to remember. Just a tinge of sadness set it apart. I knew I would remember it.

"Will you call me if you find Robert Lee Whitfield. Tell him Harrison has passed if you find him. He might like to know. Also, you can tell him the Starnes' have just about cleared out of the County. The ones that are left are right decent folks."

"I sure will."

She stood on the front steps and waved as I backed my car out of the driveway and turned around and headed out the gravel road. Ramon had his head down watching the track the tractor was making in last year's grass and weeds. I still had plenty of time to get back to Memphis and have dinner and a belt or two with Bill Nolan.

CHAPTER SIX
IRENE GHORMLEY

I was traveling North on Highway 78 when my phone rang. I was past New Albany and Hickory Flat and I was coming up to the Potts Camp Exit. I waited until I got to the exit and pulled over in front of a boarded up cotton gin and checked my phone. It was Irene Ghormley. I called her. The sun had started to sink in the west over the pines.

"Mister Cheatham."

"Yes, Ms. Ghormley."

"How far away from the office are you.? I mean in normal driving time. "

"I will be there in about ninety minutes or so."

"I will wait on you. The traffic is bad, anyway. I have some good news for you. We have now not eliminated every State except one. We have eliminated every city except one. I have your first real clue."

"And you are going to make me wait till I get there to tell me. Get my curiosity all up in the air. "

"Yes, I will tell you that you got the correct side of the Mississippi River. You did narrow it down that much."

"And you did the rest. Right?"

"Yes. That is exactly right. Now come on back to the office wearing a humble and grateful smile so I can brief you and you can go eat with Mr. Nolan and I can go home."

She hung up and I turned around and got back on 78 and drove on back to Memphis through the twilight and early dark. When I walked into the office, Irene Ghormley was on the phone and had just started smoking a very long and thin cigarette. The fan was not on. I sat down and waited. When she was through talking, she sat the phone down and took a long drag from her cigarette.

"I have written you a memorandum recounting my efforts on your behalf today. It is lying in your chair. I also straightened your office up. Would you like for me to tell you where you should go to find Robert Lee Whitfield?"

"Please, but before you tell me, let me thank you for your help."

She had her cigarette in her right hand. She took it and waved it across her face in a theatrical gesture and leaned back in her chair.

"Well, I called Mr. James " Dump" Warren shortly after you left and as is usually the case with the male mind, he drew a blank. I asked him to go into the room and just sit there and try to think and if that did not work, to call Essie Beard and ask her to come down to the Maintenance Shed and help him remember."

"I then called Essie Beard and she is so nice. Obviously a lot smarter than Dump Warren. She went down at noon and they ate their lunch in the room and finally it came to Dump. The missing paper was not a picture. It was a map."

She took another drag from her cigarette and I knew I would just have to sit there and let her torment me for a few minutes before she would tell me about the map. She went back into the kitchen, I could hear her rattling plates and silverware. She came back shortly. She had a cup of black coffee in one hand and a glass of iced tea in the other. She handed me the glass of tea and looked at her computer screen.

"This Dump Warren. I would like to meet him. He sounds like the most country person I have ever met. There's probably not a lot like him around anymore."

"Probably not. He never abandoned the land. Most of us do. Grow up on a farm or ranch and then leave. He stayed. He probably has never left the State of Mississippi except to play in football games when he was in college. Still lives on a small farm down near Shaw."

"Well, I think the traffic has probably died down enough so I can have a peaceful drive home. Dump finally remembered. Before Essie. That surprised me. The San Diego Zoo. A place I have always wanted to see. I have just not gotten around to it."

"That fits. San Diego has an ocean. Plenty of beaches. Weather is the same most all year long. The Zoo is famous. I should hop a plane and go out there tomorrow."

"No, you should board a plane on Thursday. Tomorrow is Wednesday. You can go and talk to Mr. Nolan's witness tomorrow and send out some bills for that Arkansas business you finished last week."

"Yes, you are right. "

"I have your tickets ordered. You can get your boarding pass tomorrow. You will leave on Thursday morning. Early for you. Eight forty five. You will get to San Diego in the middle of the afternoon and you are booked at the Holiday Inn down on the Bay. Oceanside View. On the eighth floor. About fifteen minutes from the Zoo."

"Thanks again."

She was gathering up her pens and putting them in a round ceramic stein. She did not answer me. Once again, I was being dismissed. I went into my office and read the memorandum Irene Ghormley had prepared for me. It had been a good day. I sat in my office for a few minutes and I heard Irene lock the back door. I took a quick shower and called Bill Nolan.

He was at Texas de Brazil. A Brazilian steak house. I walked the few blocks to the Restaurant on Third Street. Bill was at the bar watching Sports Center. The sun had just gone down and the bar was almost full. I ordered a Mojito. Bill was drinking Scotch. His face was red, as it always is, and his eyes were tired.

"What about the Tisdale case?"

"He entered his plea. Took his fifteen years that will really be thirteen and a half. He has done around six months, so he will be out in thirteen years. He barely acknowledged his mother's presence in the courtroom when he came in. They brought him in at the first recess and I had the papers ready and I was out of there before eleven. He walked out and never even looked back at his mother."

"I had an interesting day. Down in Hardaman County. Found out some things. None of which got me any closer to finding Robert Lee Whitfield, but Irene took care of that for me. I am going after your witness tomorrow. Drive out and surprise him in the morning. If I call beforehand, I bet he won't talk to me."

"He may not talk anyway. Sounds like the same old pissed off retired cops we run into all the time. If he won't talk, just write it up and come on back. We have to make the effort. No way I want to try this. Sixty something year old man taking my client down. Jury would love it."

I nursed my Mojito and watched the women walk by on the street. Headed for Beale Street a few blocks away. The bar was getting noisy. Lots of pretty girls in their early thirties or late twenties. Outnumbered three to one by young and old lawyers and bankers. I was hungry but I did not want to eat at Texas De Brazil. I liked to save it for special occasions. Bill and I drove out to El Porton. I ate two chicken enchiladas and drank iced tea. Bill ate beef fajitas. I told Bill about Dump Warren and Essie Beard and Sheriff Ike Glover and Nora Deen Barksdale.

Then, after the plates were cleared, I ordered black coffee and Bill had another Scotch and water. I told Bill about telling Janet I loved her. He asked me if I meant it and I said I did but I wasn't ready to settle down and start a family or just get married and he asked if I had told her that and I said no. He leaned back in the booth and said I should tell her. I owed her the truth. She could handle it. She would have to. She had no choice. She did have a choice about what to do after I told her. She could drop me and find a husband or we could let things evolve. My word. Evolve. A natural progression.

Bill said there was no order or natural progressions between most men and women in romantic relationships. It was all crazy, irrational, and counterproductive. Bill is in his mid-fifties and is divorced. His usual relationship bottoms out after six or seven months. Afterwards, he always entertains Tommy Lee and I with tales of his misadventures.

Sometimes I would see Bill jogging or walking down Front Street in the early morning hours. He lives in a nice row house near the River bluffs and is content to practice law and have the occasional affair. He and Tommy Lee have season tickets for the Red Birds and Bill has season tickets for the Grizzlies and the Memphis Tigers.

He is generous with his advice and my father and some of his friends in Homicide often join Bill and Tommy Lee at the Red Birds games. He represented my father in his divorce from my mother. I like to sit in the stands with them and listen to their stories about old ball players and the women and lawyers and criminals they have known. The summer nights and the immaculate green ball field with the brown dirt infield and the long white stripes marking the infield and outfield boundaries are relaxing. The park is clean. The barbecued chicken nachos and beer and peanuts are all first rate. The season would start soon. There were no articles in the Commercial Appeal about the team yet. That would come in April.

I leaned back in the booth and ordered another cup of hot black coffee. Bill was nursing his scotch.

"So Mrs. Tisdale sees her son walk out of the Courtroom without even looking back at her. Then you go out of the courtroom with Mrs. Tisdale a step or two behind. What do you tell her? What soothing words can you give her. She is not even your client."

"I could not think of anything to say, so I took her to the Madison Hotel and bought her lunch. We talked about her daughter who is a nurse at the Trauma Center of the Med. Positive stuff. Then she asked for one of my cards and I gave her a few. She said someone at church might need a good lawyer some day and then we walked outside and talked about the fact that it was not raining today and it might not the rest of the week and she thanked me and walked down the Mall to get her car and I came on back to the office and ate some more coconut cake and drank some more coffee and procrastinated the rest of the day away."

The waiter brought the check and Bill threw two twenties and a ten on the table and I told him about Dump Warren living off by himself in the Delta near Shaw, Mississippi.

"Where we all wind up. Alone. Without the energy or inclination to get back into the flow of life."

I thought about that for a minute. Dump probably would never really connect with the world again. Nora Deen had a chance. She was trying. Vera Chaney had her career. Little Roscoe needed to get back into his child hood. Ball games. Field trips. State fairs. Fishing. Playing with his friends at school. Church. Mrs. Tisdale had her church and daughter.

Bill had the practice of law and sports and the occasional interlude with a woman. Bill preferred the exotic. A Korean woman who owned two restaurants, a black woman who was a ghetto dentist, and a brown eyed Costa Rican beauty who worked for the county in Hispanic Relations, and several strippers were all in his recent past.

Bill had divorced in his thirties and survived a brief period of alcoholism. He loved the company of women. But Janet said he had a commitment phobia. He was content now to be a rambler and an observer. He was efficient and valued his time away from the practice of law. He always had clients and made money, but he tried to finish his business before lunch, so he could meet up with Tommy Lee Briggs or me and eat a leisurely lunch. He usually had a scotch or bourbon with his lunch. Tommy Lee is the book man. Any motions or responses that need to be filed, Tommy Lee is content to research and file the appropriate papers. Bill handles the negotiations with insurance companies and the criminal trials. Bill likes to reserve the afternoons for reading the local papers, Sports Illustrated, The Atlantic, and during baseball season, The Sporting News.

I stopped on the way back down town at Harold's Donuts on Union and bought me a half dozen chocolate donuts for tomorrow. I offered to take Bill home. He lives less than a mile from the office. He asked me to drop him off at Earnestine and Hazel's. It is a late nightspot for the serious drinker. The juke box alone makes the stop-in for a late night drink worthwhile. Memphis artists dating back to the fifties, Etta James, Isaac Hayes, and the Stones all share the nights with the drinkers.

When I was home, I looked at the bottles on the little wooden bar I had made for my apartment. I had plenty of bourbon, some rum, and scotch. I poured a shot of Elijah Craig Bourbon into a glass and poured some water over ice in another glass and sat on my patio and watched the traffic on Front and Riverside and the occasional barge on the River. I felt good. The day had been productive and I was stopping my liquor intake at two drinks.

I paced myself and sipped the smooth bourbon. When it was gone, I definitely wanted another one. At least one. But I stopped. When I turned and went inside, the river was dark and there was no moon and no rain and a very slight breeze from the southwest.

On Wednesday morning, March 20, I woke up before sunrise and ran my usual route down Front to the Auction Street bridge and over to Mud Island and back. I called my Dad and he met me downtown at the Arcade and we ate breakfast. The Arcade is the oldest restaurant in Memphis. It started in 1919 as a diner and moved to its present location on South Main in the 1950s. It is a typical fifties diner with a brick and glass front, The teal and gray naugahyde booths, the country ham breakfasts, the sweet potato pancakes and the lunch specials have all helped sustain the legend. I do not go on the weekend. Too crowded and the service can be spotty. On a week day morning, it is perfect for an early breakfast. The Arcade is located on

South Main, near the end of the trolley line. Earnestine and Hazel's is just up the street. The train depot is across the street. A number of art galleries and condos are nearby. On the weekends, the whole area can be lively. It is just a few blocks south and west of Beale Street.

I told my father about the case and my upcoming trip to San Diego. Then I asked him about Roy Hamers. The retired policeman who had disarmed Bill's client after a Red Birds game last year.

"Roy Hamers was a good cop. A no bullshit guy. He worked for me a while when I was in charge of the South Precinct in the late nineties. He was one of my lieutenants on the night shift. Not a guy you would think was strong, but he was. Had a chip on his shoulder. Did not trust the brass. I was part of the brass. He did not like the idea of community policing. Sharon was big into that. One of the first. Sharon and I were not even in touch back then. Roy did his job but you knew he wanted to lash out at the whole system. Suspects, fellow officers, the Union, the City Council and the Brass. But he kept it to himself and never even had a write up that I heard about. He is a loner. Widower., Children grown and moved off. Lives out near Eads. Raises horses and farms a little. I saw him at Costco a few years back. He looked trim and mean. Same as ever. He would be in his sixties by now. Me and him. We never had any trouble. He stayed with me at the South Precinct and retired the day he got his thirty years of service. What have you got to see him about?"

"Seems Mr. Hamers was leaving a Red Birds game last August and when he got to the parking lot, somebody tried to put a gun on him and rob him and he took the gun away and laid it upside the would be robbers head. Question is, what is the offense? Statement he gave the police is vague as to what, if anything, Bill's client said or did to indicate a robbery. But he had his gun out. So I suppose there cannot be much of an issue. One of Bill Nolan's cases."

"He'll give you some trouble. Don't bother to tell him you are my son. He probably doesn't approve of Sharon and I was brass, his boss, and in his opinion, he did not need a boss. Don't take it to heart if he won't talk to you and do not crowd him. I always gave him a loose rein and backed him up on any problems. He did his job the right way. But remember, you will be on his place and he will pull a gun on you if you get into it with him. I can promise you that. If he says no, back off and come on back to the office and write it up. Bill will understand."

"How is Sharon?"

"Fine. But the new is wearing off on her being the first female black Sheriff of Shelby County. She says she may hang it up after two terms. She wants me to retire. Says I work too hard and put in too many hours. A lot to do around the place. I need you to come out and see my new heifers I bought. Maybe walk the fences with me a couple of days and make sure they are cow proof. The heifers are all Hereford. I bought them with the money I got from selling my other cattle after I got shot. I only bought twenty. I had over fifty head when I got shot a couple of years back."

"I got to go to San Diego to find Robert Lee Whitfield and when I get back, I will take some time off and we can fix the fences and maybe go fishing before the crappie season is over."

"Robert Lee the guy from Parchman who got out last fall and now his daughter wants you to find him and deliver a letter to him?"

"That is him."

The waiter came by and my father ordered some orange juice and asked for a refill on his coffee. "Hard to get a simple hot cup of strong black coffee anymore."

"Starbucks is good."

"I feel out of place there, you know. Sharon makes good coffee. She is telling me she may hang it up after two terms and make me take her to see the world. That would be less than seven years from now. I would be in my early sixties and she would be in her early fifties. Last night she said, 'I finally got my man problem fixed and now I don't have time to enjoy you.'. Tell me, when will you be in San Diego?"

"I will get there tomorrow, I know he likes the ocean and the San Diego Zoo. I can start there. I figure he is down town by the Bay. Somewhere. He doesn't have money to commute and that is all he talked about when he talked to people at Parchman, The ocean. Did not say which one. Just said he had never seen one and he wanted to live by one before he died. Wanted to hear the surf and watch the birds and look at the boats."

My father drank the orange juice and I looked at my watch. It was almost eight o'clock. I took the check and my father threw some bills down on the table. Outside on the sidewalk, I stood and watched my father walk to his big Crown Vic. It was an unmarked police car, but everyone with any sense knew it was a cop car. He stood tall as he walked to the car. The sun was already shining and the sky was clear. He walked a little slower and he was still a little tentative. Being shot does that to you. Most people would not have even noticed his limp. Sons notice that sort of thing as their parents grow older.

The drive out to Roy Hamer's farm took almost forty-five minutes. He lived out past the city limits of Memphis near the eastern boundary of Shelby County. The nearest settlement is Eads, Tennessee. It is a small town composed of a few older stores and a couple of churches. The Hamer Farm was a few miles from Eads. I drove up a short gravel driveway to his red brick home. It had white wooden shutters and a small porch. There were no chairs on the porch. The yard was neat and a barn was about a hundred yards behind the house. Large Azalea bushes were just starting to bloom on either side of the porch.

There was a garage and the door was up. A blue Ford Focus was parked in one of the two spaces in the garage. There were a few oak trees in front of the house and some pine trees in the back yard. I rang the front door bell and waited. In a few minutes, a round-faced older woman came to the door. She opened the door and smiled at me. I told her who I was and what I wanted and she invited me in.

She asked to see my badge and when I showed it to her, she took it out of my hand and reached into her apron pocket and pulled a pair of glasses out. She took a long time looking at my badge and then she handed it back to me and smiled.

"Mr. Cheatham, forgive me if I am cautious. I am eighty-four years old and people try to take advantage of us older citizens. Especially women. I am Roy's mother. Lurleen Hamer. He is up in Eads, but he will be back a little after nine. He goes up to the Country Market and sits in the back room with some friends. They drink coffee and eat ham or sausage and biscuits and talk about things. Things I tell Roy he should not trouble himself with anymore. You know, politics and Obama and Memphis."

"You mind if I wait here for him? Or I can wait in the car. I just need to see him for a few minutes."

"We can pass the time here in the living room. It is almost nine now. He gets up and feeds the stock and is up at the Country Market way before eight. Do you know Roy?"

"No, I just know he used to be a Memphis policeman before he retired. Had a good reputation as a policeman."

"Yes, but you know he got so bitter toward the end. Disturbed me. He hated Memphis. Said it was not worth saving anymore. All the dope and the crime. This farm has been in the family since before World War One and he is at peace here. He just gets upset about politics and the way things are in Memphis. He is a widower and his daughter has moved off and doesn't come back very often. He goes up to that old store and sits around and gets all stirred up. I say we should support our President and try to help him."

I did not say anything. Soon, I heard a pickup truck pull into the garage and a truck door slam. Roy Hamer came into the house through the kitchen and when he saw me, he was definitely not happy.

"So, who the hell are you? You trying to sell my mother something, you can get your ass on up and out of here right now."

He was not a big man. I am five or six inches taller than him and his hair is gray. His eyes were a hard and angry blue. He was strong, and on a compact frame, he advanced on me and I thought he might try to hit me.

His mother said, "Now Roy, you sit down. I am too old for any foolishness. Did you bring me a country ham and biscuit?"

"You know I did. I never forget you, mom."

"No, you don't. I like this young man. He does not want to sell me anything. He wants to see you."

"What about?"

"Well, I did not get around to asking him. Now why don't you calm down and put my ham and biscuit in the microwave for just thirty seconds and pour this young man a cup of coffee and come on back in here and we can get this business out of the way and you can go on and get those soy beans planted in that back field."

Roy went in the kitchen. He soon returned. He gave his mother a ham and biscuit on a small plate and handed me a cup of black coffee. When he sat down, I told him why I was there.

He said, "Ain't gonna sit here half the morning answering questions. I do not have to tell you nothing. I know that much about the law. What I will do is tell you what happened and you can make do with that. Take it or leave it. Like Mom said, I got soybeans to plant. Let me tell you this. I figure you are Cheatham's kid. He was fair to me. Never pressed me or crowded me. Now I see where he is married to that black woman. You go back to Memphis, ask him for me if all the white women was taken. Was that the reason he married a black woman? Memphis. That place has gradually been going to hell since the seventies."

"I keep tabs on the department a little. Heard how you came and busted out after a year or so. I do not hold that against you. If you had come in the seventies or sixties, you might have stayed. Now, the City Council is taking benefits away from the police every chance they can.

No money for raises. More chances of being shot."

His mother sat back on the couch and said, "Now Roy, you are out of all of that and you get a nice check each month. From the city. You need to show some respect and gratitude. Just be grateful for what you have and go on with your life. This young man is not going to try to trip you up. He just wants you to tell him what happened. So tell him and be done with it. Today is a good day. I have got some of those quail you shot last fall thawing out on the drain board. I am going to fry them up real nice and make some gravy and rice and some of those little lima beans you like. And if I have time, a rice pudding. So it is a good day. Looks like the weather is going to be clear through the weekend."

"Alright, well here is the way it was. I went up to see a ball game. I had been to St. Louis to see the Cardinals back in July. I wanted to see Pujols one more time. Everybody knew he was leaving. No way the Cards could tote the freight on him any longer. Not for no nine or ten years without us having a designated hitter. Which I am opposed to, but you know in time, that is coming, The Players Union will eventually push it through. More players making more money late in their careers"

"So this was in late August. Too early to pull the corn. Beans weren't ready and the hay was all cut. I was hoping for a big rain so I could get some more grass for hay, but it wasn't coming. So one night, I just decided I would go to the Red Birds game. Momma wanted to stay home and watch her shows on television, so I went by myself."

"The game was good. I already forgot who we played. I sat on the third base side down near the Red Birds dugout and had a draft beer and a bunch of peanuts. Lot of pretty girls walking around. Anyway, the game was over and I was walking to my car. I saw this guy out to my side, coming up fast. Not a big guy. Black. Maybe my size. He gets up to me and I see him raising the gun up and I went for it and rolled him over my hip and the gun came out. I had both hands on his wrist, the right wrist and he was on the ground cussing me. Saying I had broke his back and I had just flipped him. Not even hard. I did not smell any liquor on him but he was talking goofy like he was sprung on dope. So I brought his arm with the gun behind his back and he dropped it and I picked it up and he got loose and started to stand up and I laid him out. I had the gun in my hand and I hit him upside the head and he went down."

"By then there were a few people around and I put my foot on the guy's head and one of the black guys in the crowd was starting some shit with me but the Uniforms got there in a few minutes and I gave them the gun and they took him to the Med. The gun was loaded. One of those cheap old Taurus thirty-eights. I thought they were all discarded or blown up. They were a sorry lot of guns, I can tell you that."

"Did he ever ask you for your money or say something to indicate it was a robbery?"

"No, we wasn't having a dialogue, I saw the gun and he started up with it and I grabbed it and moved inside him and did a hip roll on him and that was it."

"Were you scared or frightened."

"Police training kicked in. I was scared when I was driving home. I got home and got momma out of bed and we sat up for three hours. Just trying to get calm enough to go to bed and get some sleep. But there wasn't no time to be scared. It didn't last a whole minute, I bet. Not even a minute."

"Well, I will write this up and let you read it and sign it. You know how it is.":

"Yes, I do know how it is. I never even knew the guy's name and I do not want to know it. He sure wasn't very stout for a young man. I rolled him over my hip real easy. Usually when those guys are sprung on cocaine, they are hard to take down. He might have been high, but hungry. That is my guess."

I wrote out the statement on the kitchen table. He sat on one side of me and his mother sat on the other side. I could see the package of quail thawing out on the drain board. The kitchen was neat.

"Young man, where in Memphis do you live.? Lurleen asked.

"Up on Front Street in an apartment over my office. I have a balcony and sit out on it at night and watch the River and the barges and other traffic on the water."

"I haven't been down there in so many years. Used to on a Saturday, we would go down to Goldsmith's on Main and shop and go to a movie. At one time there were four nice theatres on Main Street. This was after the big war. Main Street Memphis on the weekend was busy. Now I hear they have made a mall out of it and planted trees and got a streetcar running down the middle of the mall."

"That's right. There are some good things down town, but not a lot of shopping. Most of that is in the malls."

Roy said, "You don't want to go down there, mom. It would just make you sick. Most of the old buildings are gone. The ones that are still around are either boarded up or half-empty. Alright, I have signed this. But before you go, let me tell you something."

He handed the statement back to me. He had initialed and dated all three pages and signed and dated the last page. He drank some coffee and leaned back on the couch and shut his eyes. In a minute, he leaned forward and put his coffee cup down.

"Momma keeps telling me to stop talking to all of those guys at the Country Market. Just get some biscuits with ham and sausage and come on home. I guess I just need some folks to be around. Most of the guys are fine. But the frustrations are there. We remember when Memphis was one of the cleanest cities and one of the safest. Now look at it."

He poured some more coffee and stood up and looked out the side window of the living room. He blew into the coffee cup and turned back to face me.

"Something about that whole thing. The attempt robbery was all wrong. You know one thing no one noticed except me and I thought of it a day or two later?"

"What was that."

"I only got a glimpse of his face but I swear he was wearing lipstick. Not a lot but some. He bled when I hit him upside the head with the gun, but I know I saw it. The lipstick. Like he had tried to wipe it off or something. I mean the whole thing made no sense. After I left the game, I walked by two police cars. One was less than a hundred yards away from where this happened. Now you tell me. Maybe the guy is mental or some kind of a weirdo. I never in my thirty years of being a policeman had that many physical confrontations with people, but most people would have kneed me in the kidneys before I got that hip roll going. I probably arrested two or three thousand suspects. Some I had to wrestle down. But this guy was weak ,man, weak. The hip roll was a sloppy move. And usually, if someone is high, then they are harder to bring down. This guy was too easy."

Lurleen said, "Son, you are lucky. He could have shot you or hurt you."

"I can handle myself but you are right. It was a gamble, but it was just a split second decision I made."

I stalled around and thanked Lurleen for the coffee. I was out of questions and I thought Roy Hamer was going to think of something else. I was almost to the door when he told me he would walk me to the car.

When I was opening my car door, he said, "Look, do me a favor and let that pass. What I said about your dad marrying a nigger. That is his business. He was always square with me. Just when you are a policeman and you put in thirty years and drive out of town the last day and see things are worse than when you started on the force, it makes you bitter. Look, I was you, I would tell his lawyer to get somebody out at the firing range to look at that gun. What a piece of shit. It was loaded, I know that. But I wonder with what. Have it checked out The cylinder had rust on it."

I did not like him calling Sharon that name but it wasn't worth arguing with him. I let it go. I cut on down to Poplar Avenue and drove on through Germantown and got off on Park and then cut through the University of Memphis campus and followed Central Avenue on into Central Gardens. The houses are old and set back from the street. Majestic oaks and neat yards line each street. This was the first day I had noticed the Azaleas blooming. Petunias and yellow marigolds had already been planted in most yards, along with impatiens. Bright colors and quiet streets relaxed me and took my mind off the bitterness of Roy Hamer.

When I got back to the office, Irene offered me a tuna sandwich, I went back in my office and ate the sandwich and wrote out a report on my visit with Roy Hamer. Shortly after two o'clock, Janet called. I told her about San Diego and we agreed to go out after work. She sounded tired.

I thought about Roy Hamer. Thirty years of being a good police officer and driving out of town on your last day and thinking things were worse now than when he started on the force. I had the feeling that Roy Hamer was like that for many years before he even thought about retiring. It mystifies me. People work for thirty year, get a good pension with benefits and wind up not enjoying their lives.

I looked at Bill's file he had copied for me. The client's name was Nathaniel Groves. He was just past nineteen years old. The arrest ticket listed his height as six foot even and his weight at one hundred and thirty pounds. Roy Hamer's statement to the police did not mention how easy it had been to throw Nathaniel Groves down and disarm him. Nothing about the lipstick. No booking photo. Something for Bill to get. The statement from Hamer to the robbery detective had been taken shortly after eight a.m. on the morning after the attempted robbery. Hamer probably did not get home until after midnight, got up early and fed his stock, and drove on down town. He said he had stayed up until three a.m. when he got home after this had happened. So not many details. Just going through the motions. An easy case. Solved at the scene. The why of it all would have to come from the suspect and he had refused to give a statement.

It was almost three o'clock when I finished up with my report on Roy Hamer's interview. I had just finished printing the report out and stapling it together when I noticed Sharon standing in my doorway, smiling. Her hands and arms were folded across her chest. She was wearing a dark blue suit, a white blouse, and black high heels., She is almost as tall as me and only slightly shorter than my father. She is slender with long, shapely legs. Her hair is short this year. Cut close and sculpted. Large brown eyes and a small narrow nose.

"Your father told me about your case over lunch. We met at the El Porton. We had only forty-five minutes and it was warm enough to sit on the patio. I wanted a margarita so bad but I could not have one while I am on duty. All those people sneaking looks at us. You are leaving tomorrow?"

"Yes, I think I have a good chance of finding him. "

"Where are you staying?"

"Holiday Inn down by the bay. Got an ocean view, according to Irene."

"Good, I heard you went to see Roy Hamer this morning?. How did that go?"

"Got some good stuff from him, but the facts are the same. He had a gun and pulled it on him. But he was really weak. Bill's client, I mean. And the guy may have had a little lipstick on."

"Where is he now."

"Jail."

"One thing we try to do. Check on prisoners to see if they are HIV positive. Sounds like that could be the answer. If so, he will be isolated. What is his name?"

"Nathaniel Groves."

She took a cell phone from her purse and dialed a number. Someone picked up after a few rings.

"Nathaniel Groves."

She waited a minute and motioned for me to give her a pen. She tore a sheet out of a yellow legal pad on the desk and waited. She wrote a few things down on the paper and said thanks and hung up.

"What I thought. In isolation. HIV positive. Was wearing a dress and high heels the second night in custody. They jerked him off the cellblock and tested him and there you go. Twenty years old by just a few months. Bill Nolan can get him a time served offer and get him out of my jail. Not enough cells for the healthy. Much less the ones with problems."

"Did you know Roy Hamer when you were on the force."

"Sure, he was a lieutenant a few years after I came on. He stayed one till he retired as a thirty-year captain. Way it goes. Or the way it used to be. It is changed now. But used to be if you survived thirty years, you retired as a Captain and drew a nice paycheck for the rest of your life. Guys retiring in their early fifties was the norm."

"He is a widower now. Lives with his mother out near Eads."

"Don't tell your father this. I worked a concert back in the late eighties at the old Mid-South Coliseum. One of those deals where you had a lot of local and regional acts and then the headliner comes on around ten thirty and works out for forty five minutes. Headliner at this one was Chuck Berry. Well, you know, it was in August and I am sweaty and tired. I had to go to work at midnight down at the South Precinct. Anyway, I am standing there at the top of one of the aisles watching the crowd. I feel this hand on my back. Way lower back and then when I turn around, it is starting to go lower and I stepped out of the way. It was Roy Hamer."

"Not unusual for that to happen back then. Most of it was innocent, but Hamer gave me a look that said it was different. He scared me. I could tell he wanted to press it, but I just walked away. I asked around about him and found that he had a reputation for wandering hands, but he wasn't my Lieutenant so I didn't worry about it. Then he started calling and leaving messages at my house. Calling at the precinct and one time when I got off he was parked behind my car and I got my Lieutenant to walk out with me to the car and after he got him to move his car, I went over to his car window and told him to leave me alone. In front of my Lieutenant. And he did. "

"You did not file a sexual harassment charge against him?"

"No, now I tell the female recruits to let me know if something like that happens, but back then, in the eighties , it was not a good career move. And I wasn't worrying about the other females on the force. I was a patrolman. You know how it is. You worry about your own self. Not a good career move. Say you file a complaint and you win. The other officers don't want to ride with you because they are scared you are looking to sue them. If you do not get beat up or raped, most of the other officers will say, what's the harm and brand you a troublemaker. If you lose, then you are made out to be a liar. I knew back then I had a chance to advance. Your dad was my first lieutenant and he told me I had a bright future and I was ambitious"

"He is living out near Eads with his mother. His only daughter has moved off and doesn't come around much and his mother is in her eighties. Roy doesn't strike me as someone who places or answers personal ads on the internet or the newspaper. No personal life. Just a sour guy in a permanent rut. With a nice pension. But you know, he helped me. Didn't want to. Like my dad said, he did his job the right way. Except for the wandering hands. Dad did not mention that."

"He probably had not heard it. Plus the guy probably cleaned his act up when he started working for your father. In fairness to Hamer, he was not the worst. Not by a longshot. Did your father tell you about his new heifers?"

"Sure did. When I get back from San Diego, I am going to take some time off and help him run the fence lines and get things straight. Maybe go down to Tunica Cutoff and catch some crappie before the season is gone."

"Give me a Janet update."

I got up and shut the door. When I sat back down, she was smiling. She took out a Virginia Slim , lit it, took a deep drag, and said, "I am waiting. I think I sense some hemming and hawing coming."

"The long and short of it is this. I am happy with her. She is fun. Genuine. A good brain. Considerate. Well, the other night, I told her I loved her and since then I have been miserable. I do not want to get married. I do not want to see anyone else, but if I meet someone else I am interested in, I want to be able to make a move. Without guilt."

"What has she asked of you?"

"Nothing."

"What else did you tell her?"

"Just to let things evolve. Progress naturally."

"And she made no demands on you?"

She took another long drag on her cigarette and leaned back in her chair. One of her three cell phones chimed in her purse. She looked at the number on the screen and turned the phone off.

"My staff is determined. They want to be sure I do not have a waking moment to myself. I have to be at a meeting at four. It is just a few minutes after three. They can wait. Back to Janet. Do you think you are the first somebody on the face of this earth to honestly tell a woman that you love her and then have second thoughts? Quit feeling guilty. It is a natural reaction. She may be feeling the same way. Sounds like she has a boatload of sense."

"She does."

"Then follow your own advice and let it evolve and worry about finding this guy. Robert Lee Whitfield. Your dad told me his name. All about the case. Call me from San Diego if you need any help. And call your father. He wants you to find this guy. You know what he asked me?"

"No, what?"

"What are you going to do with him once you find him. Hard to just read him the letter and not get involved."

"I will bring him back with me if he wants to come."

"What if he says he doesn't want to come back to Mississippi?"

"If I try to talk him into it, that would be like Janet trying to crowd me into doing something I am not ready for. The answer is, I do not know what I will say, but I will leave it up to him. Then walk away if he says for me to. No hard sell."

"You are right. He comes back. Doesn't like it. Leaves. The boy will go further into his shell. Two people in his life leaving unexpectedly. You will just have to walk away."

"Sharon, is anybody normal?. Just having a nice happy life?"

"Nobody I know. Why do you ask."

"The people I am meeting. Older people. Most of them are not really happy. Playing out the last few years grieving over a dead spouse or just in an inescapable rut."

"Well, you know, some people never find happiness or find it and don't take advantage of the time and the experience."

"You think I should tell Robert Lee Whitfield that. Take advantage of this opportunity, Robert. It may be your last one. Seeing the ocean is a nice dream. Living in solitude for the rest of your life, I don't know about that."

"I would do what Vera Chaney said. Give him the letter and let him do what he wants to do."

"Only way to do it. Her life. Her consequences."

She walked to the window and looked out across the street. The sun was shining and there was no traffic on the River and very little on the streets. She stood up and I got up and followed her out to her car. There was a large, muscular, white Deputy Sheriff with a Glock on his right hip leaning against the hood of Sharon's car. He looked at me and did not smile. He opened the front passenger door for Sharon and they drove away North on Front towards Poplar and the Criminal Justice Center.

At five o'clock, I went into the lunchroom in the back of the office. Tommy and Bill were seated at the table. I pulled up a chair and put the sack of day old donuts on the table. They both took one and I told Bill about Roy Hamer and Nathaniel Groves. I handed Bill a copy of the report of my investigation that I had just finished.

"Twenty years old. Just barely. Well, I can get him a time served offer. The DA's office will call Hamer and talk to him, but he won't care. He will understand. I am not even going to bother with the gun unless I get some grief from the prosecutor. Don't see that happening."

Tommy said, "You better have some sort of plan in place for him. Some place for him to go. Medicine. Treatment. Something. The judge will crawl over your ass if you don't have something. Get Irene to call tomorrow morning. She will find something out. Something we can do for him. Probably get a guilty plea for say three years, then file a petition to suspend the remainder of his sentence he has not already served. Get in touch with probation and get it all expedited."

"I should have already been over to the jail to see him, but I wanted to wait to get the discovery and our investigation completed first, then get an offer of settlement from the DA and then see him so we would have something concrete to talk about." Bill said.

"I am going to San Diego tomorrow. I will be at the Holiday Inn on the Bay. "

We sat and ate donuts and talked about the upcoming baseball season for a while until Irene came in with a folder. She handed it to me.

"Mister Cheatham, your boarding passes are in this folder along with confirmation of your reservations for your rental car and hotel room. I heard you talking about that boy with AIDS. It is God's curse. You know that, don't you.? "

None of us answered and she left the room. I told her thank you as she walked down the hall to her office, but she did not turn around or say anything. Bill got up and went to his office. He was back in a minute with a bottle of bourbon. He got three water glasses out of the cabinet and poured a shot into each glass. He gave me some ice and water in separate glasses. Tommy took his straight and Bill put three cubes of ice in his glass and added another shot.

"Russell's Reserve. Another in an increasingly impressive line of smooth bourbons. Here's to life's small treasures."

We sipped our bourbon until six and Bill and Tommy left shortly afterwards. I went upstairs and called Janet. She was tired and had changed her mind about going out. She wanted to come to my apartment and relax. She said she would order a pizza from her house after she had time to change clothes and rest a minute. It was after seven when she got to my apartment. The sun had set before she got there. I had seen it from my balcony window. Today it was a great shining orange ball that had lingered long enough to spread calming evening shades of orange and red and purple across the horizon.

Janet was wearing blue jeans and a soft red tee shirt. Her hair was in a ponytail. We sat on the balcony and when the pizza came I went downstairs and paid for it and brought it up stairs. We sat on the balcony in the warm spring air and drank wine and ate pizza. We were almost finished eating when Janet said, "You do not want to change everything and get married and have children and be domesticated, now do you?"

"No, but I do not want to keep you from having those things."

"These are things my mother wants for me because it would be fun for her and because she thinks it is best for us. But I like this. I am not ready for all of that. I am worried that I have scared you off. I just wanted to know how you feel and where you wanted to take this."

"Hard to beat what we have right here, right now."

She got up and walked to the balcony railing and looked across the street and past the trees on the River bank at a barge that was lumbering southward in the soft spring night.

"I wish I was going to San Diego with you. Let's take a trip sometime this spring. Somewhere nice with water and a beach."

I pulled her to me and kissed her and she broke away from the kiss and sighed and put her head on my chest and held me tight. We went inside after a few minutes and I gave her a book to read while I was gone. Long, Last, Happy by Barry Hannah. She took the book and laid it on her side of the bed and pushed me back on my couch and went into the bathroom and soon I heard the shower running and I joined her and when we were through we came to bed and made love. When I rolled over and went to sleep, she had her glasses down on her nose, sitting up very straight in the bed with two pillows behind her back , and was reading the first few pages of Long, Lost, Happy. She had a glass of red wine in one hand and she was smiling a thin smile of satisfaction. I hoped it was me who was responsible for that satisfied and content look, but I sure would not have been surprised if it was Barry who was putting that smile on her face.

CHAPTER SEVEN
LIFE AFTER PARCHMAN
ROBERT LEE WHITFIELD
NOVEMBER 8, 2011

I thought it would all be about leaving and smelling the earth and seeing the sky and feeling the wind blow on me differently. But it wasn't that way at first. First I wanted my free black ass out of Mississippi. Just to get outside the borders of Mississippi where I had been penned up all these years. I know I brought it on myself. Killing that worthless-ass Billy Ray Starnes. Sitting up in my room at the maintenance shed all these years thinking. If you had just waited, somebody else would have done it for you. Probably his own kin or one of his friends down at some juke joint on a Friday or Saturday night. Maybe his wife or one of his own kids when they growed up a bit. But I didn't. I shot him and to make sure he was dead I shot him again.

No, what I was studying and studying hard when Dump let me out of his truck and wished me luck was just how long it would be until I would be on my way. I was out on the highway. Highway 82 West. Right there on the sign. That one word giving me hope and making me stir again. What you learn doing time is to put hope on a shelf. Don't let nothing stir you up. But looking at that sign. Highway 82 West. I knew what I wanted to do. Catch a ride out of this state and get up past Oklahoma and past Amarillo and then over to New Mexico and follow the Interstate 40 all the way to Flagstaff and then cut south past Phoenix and get down to another Interstate Highway I could not call right then. I had it on the map all highlighted out. The map was in my bag.

Then a straight shot to San Diego. And the water and the weather always around 72 degrees and not much rain. First thing was the Ocean. Just find a comfortable place to sit and then take my clothes off and finally for good wash the whole State of Mississippi out of my system in the blue waters of the Pacific Ocean. Fuck Mississippi and the horses and mules the white people had rode in on and the black folks it had made slaves and fools and drunks and hopeless losers. And I still got my good attitude. Just let me get that said and out of my system.

See what we black folks do to survive is to pretend in front of white folks that we do not know or remember or care about any of the past,. This is the New South. Sure it is. For some maybe. For most it is not that much different. Same old stupid red necks like Billy Ray Starnes. Same old hard knocks and low paying jobs and second hand cars and too many children to raise and failing crops and cheap liquor killing you slow but sure. I stayed up in the shop away from the other inmates but I still heard them and studied them when I saw them. Some driving tractors or combines. Coming up to the Maintenance Shed to work and looking to steal sometimes. Get my ass in trouble. Morons mostly. That would be what Ann Stepter would call them. Morons.

So that was the way I was feeling when I first got out of Dump's old truck. Me standing on the side of the highway with my thumb out and my bag at my feet. I waited until midafternoon before an old black woman in a red Dodge Dart came up and stopped. She had grey hair and was missing some teeth but her eyes were soft and friendly and she leaned over the seat and opened the door. She said she was just going to Leland and then turn south but she could leave me at the crossroads there where old Highway 61 and Highway 82 come together.

She did not ask me anything and in a few minutes she was there.

All that traffic coming down both highways I should get a ride and be well on my way by dark. I took two dollars out of my billfold and handed it to her and she laughed and said no that she had not had to go out of her way and so I got out and watched her turn on South on Sixty-One. She told me she was going down to Hollandale and see her new grandbaby. She never asked me my name and I forgot to ask her what her name was. I do remember the inside of that old car smelled like vanilla and the dashboard was wiped down clean. And the rest of the car was clean on the inside.

So there I was not thirty easy driving minutes out of Greenville and across the River Bridge and into Arkansas. What I knew from years past and what I had heard from other inmates, Arkansas wasn't much different from Mississippi until you got west and north of Little Rock and then it was mountains and a pretty countryside. The sun was still not too low in the sky and the wind was not blowing and for the first time I checked the sky and it was all blue except for a few clouds. None of them looked like they had any rain in them so I put my mind on getting a ride.

Was a while before anyone stopped. Man that stopped was driving a banged up pulp wood truck. The racks for the logs were set up but the truck was empty of logs. The cab was red. It was an old snub-nosed Ford. The driver stopped and rolled down the window and asked where I was going and I said San Diego, California and he laughed and told me to get in.

The seat was full of ropes and wrenches and screwdrivers. A short handled shovel lay across the whole mess. I moved the shovel and laid it in the floorboard and sat down. There was no seat belt. The driver was a small white man in his late twenties or early thirties. He had bad teeth and told me his name was Royce. When we got across the River Bridge and out of Mississippi, the sun was starting to fall behind the distant pines. Royce let me off on Highway 65 in Lake Village, Arkansas. He said for me to go on through Pine Bluff into Little Rock.

From Little Rock I knew to take the Interstate through Fort Smith and into Oklahoma. All the way into Phoenix. Interstate 40. I remembered that. I just wanted to let Royce think he was helping me out. Black man always wants the white man to underestimate him.

Royce talked all the way. Said he wanted to go out west and ride a horse in the mountains. But not in California. He said what he had read and seen on TV and heard on the radio was that California was fucked up and expensive to live in. Then Royce got to talking about women. He was living with one in a double wide outside of Monticello, Arkansas and getting all he could handle. Man that talks that much about pussy don't know anything about it. Way I see it. Royce was in serious need of dental work but he was harmless. I knew one thing. Living in California would really have to be bad to be worse than driving a pulp wood truck in Eastern Arkansas.

I could smell new cut wood in the cab of his truck. There were chips and shavings in the floor of the truck. I loved the smell of new lumber. But I had cut some wood back in the day. Even with a chain saw, it is hard and the pay is poor. Even for white men.

Royce had taken a load of wood all the way to a sawmill in Grenada for some reason and he was on his way back to Monticello. When he let me out I offered him the same two dollars I had offered the black lady and he waved it away and smiled. I remember his hair was scraggly and he seemed happy to be where he was. In a few hours I caught my last ride that day. A black family picked me up and carried me as far as Grady. I was still an hour south of Pine Bluff. The family was in one of those king cab trucks. I rode hunched down and happy in the bed. Every once in a while, a little girl with big eyes and pigtails would open the back window a little ways and make a face at me. She had lost a couple of her front teeth. I figured she was just barely starting school. One time when she opened the little window, she gave me a chocolate chip cookie and a few Doritos. The sky was dark and the wind had picked up. I could not see any stars or the moon out.

There were dark black clouds drifting across the trees that crowded the twisting road., When we were a few miles from Grady, the truck pulled over and the driver got out. A nice looking woman in her late thirties. She had pulled off the highway onto a county blacktop road. There was an overpass a hundred yards or so up the road. She told me to get under the overpass because there was a big storm coming. I thanked her and walked up to the shelter of the overpass. Her husband stayed in the truck and never turned around. There were only a few cars and trucks that passed in the next few hours. I figured it was just a little past midnight when the storm came.

You could smell it on the way before you felt the cold rain or the strong wind out of the west. I hunkered down as far as I could get away from the rain and listened to the thunder and saw the lightning all just south and north from where I was crouched. I wasn't really cold but I did get my shirt wet some. Later that morning I saw a white law car of some kind go by heading south. I guessed it was around two in the morning. The car went a few hundred yards on down the road and came back north and stopped under the overpass where I was. A large black man got out. He had his pistol drawn. He was in a brown uniform. He was in his forties and had his hair done in a permanent. He left his hat in the car. I could hear a radio squawking in his car. The rain was shining like silver in his cruiser's lights.

He threw me up against the back of his car and searched me. He told me to stay quiet and he searched my bag. He emptied everything out on the trunk of his car and one of my new shirts Dump had bought me fell on the wet ground. He did not pick it up. I still had my head down but I was watching him. My arms were stretched out across the back of his car. Straight out past my head.

When he was finished looking through my clothes he told me to stand up. I asked if I could pick my shirt up off the ground. He said yes. I did and repacked my stuff and stood at the back of his car. I looked at his nameplate. He was a deputy sheriff. His name was

Luther. Luther Wages. He told me there was no place for niggers with nothing to do but cause trouble in his county. I told him I was sick and tired of hearing black people calling each other niggers. I told him I was as free as he was and I was wanting out of his fucking county as soon as I could get out. He told me he wanted to know where I came from and I told him to take my name off my driver's license and run me on his radio and he would find that nothing would show up and then he could leave me alone and go on and arrest somebody that was breaking the law.

He opened the back door and shoved me inside and took my bag with him. He went to the front and got into the big cruiser and called my information off my driver's license in to somebody and we sat in the rain for a few minutes and finally a young white female voice came on and said there was nothing outstanding on me from Mississippi or the Feds or the State of Arkansas.

He started the car up but did not pull off. He told me that in the old days I would be run in and then taken before a magistrate and sentenced to six months for loitering and put on the county work gang. I did not say anything. I knew he was right and I knew he was waiting for me to give him an excuse to run me in. I did not say anything. He said I could say what I wanted but he was tired of worthless ass niggers in his county. Making it hard for the black folk that was trying to get ahead by working and raising a family.

I asked him what made him think I wanted to steal something in his county. I was under an overpass looking for a ride and not hotwiring a car in a used car lot. That made him mad. But he didn't say anything for a few minutes. Cars and trucks were passing us in the rain. The dome light was on and folks slowed down when they saw someone was in the back seat. I knew I should have just shut up. If it had been a white deputy I would have but he pissed me off calling me a nigger and throwing me up against the back of his car when all I wanted to do was get out of the rain and get on to San Diego. He asked me where I was going and I told him.

He asked me if I had relatives there and I told him no. He asked me what kind of trade or skill I had and I said I worked on cars and trucks and combines and tractors and cotton pickers. He said he bet he knew where I had been working for the last few years and I shut it down. I did not say anything else. He asked me some more questions and I sat silent in the back of his car. I was hungry and my stomach growled.

He asked me when was the last time I had eaten a decent meal and I told him this morning and that it was at the Sonic and he shook his head and turned the dome light off and pulled into traffic. When we were in Grady, he pulled off at a truck stop and told me to come inside, There were diesel pumps off to the side and I could see a dozen or so tractor-trailers parked off in the dark behind the truck stop. Some were dull colors and some were silver and glistened in the steady rain.

He parked in front and opened my door and told me to come on. He gave me my bag and told me to keep my mouth shut and let him do all of the talking. We sat at the counter. I saw a sign saying showers and there were eight or nine men sitting in the restaurant. A nervous white lady just past forty came over and Luther ordered coffee black for both of us and asked me was I one of those sissified black men of culture who was allergic to everything and I told him no and he ordered two plates of fried whole catfish and some slaw and macaroni and cheese.

I drank my coffee and looked around the room. There was a large white man in his thirties seated in a booth near the front windows. He looked nervous. Luther looked at him and asked him to come over. The man got up and he had this hard stare right on Luther. I had seen it before. For thirty years I been looking at it. Some get it naturally and some practice it to fool you into thinking they are for real. I could not tell about the big white man. He had on dirty tan coveralls and a blue denim shirt under the coveralls. A red ball cap sat high on his head. His dirty blonde hair hung long over his ears and the back of his neck. He was taller than Luther but his edges were round and Luther's were angled and sharp.

Luther told him Andrew I have told you not to bring them whores down here to my county and here you are again. Not six months later after I told you. You think I was going to forget or something. Andrew opened his mouth to say something and Luther hit him hard in the stomach and when Andrew bent over, Luther turned him towards the front door and kicked him hard in the ass. Nobody laughed. I started to but it was not over and I had no business saying or doing anything. Prison rule. Stay out of other people's fights. Specially don't look at them after the fight. Never mind who wins or loses. And do not say anything. Move away and act like you never seen nothing. That goes as far as even talking about them days or months later.

Andrew stayed down for a minute and when he got up he stumbled towards the door. Luther told him to go get his whores out of the trucks and get out of the county. Andrew looked like he was going to say something for a minute then he moved on out the door. Luther made him come back in and lay some money at the cash register and then Luther shoved him back towards the door. Luther took his pistol out of the holster on his right side. It was one of those new guns. Automatic with a big handle. The whole gun looked like it was made out of some hard plastic. He held it down by his side and walked a few feet behind Andrew.

In a few minutes I saw a ratty looking old blue van leaving the main parking lot and heading north. Luther came back in and sat down at the counter. A couple of truck drivers were at the cash register paying their tabs. Luther stood up and said before anyone left he was trying to help this country looking free black man get a ride. He told them I was going to San Diego. By way of Interstate 40 from Little Rock on to Flagstaff and then down to Phoenix and across to San

Diego. No one said anything. Luther sat down and soon our catfish came. There was some hushpuppies. Little old pieces of corn dough fried so hard the flavor was long gone. But the fish were good and the slaw did not have too much mayonnaise in it and the macaroni and cheese was so good I got another helping of it.

The café emptied out soon and the waitress came over and told Luther he was bad for business but she was laughing when she said it. She had a nametag on that said Chloe. I told her I thought that name was pretty and she smiled. Luther said Chloe was pretty a few years ago but she had run afoul of some bad luck and Chloe laughed and said he was right but her bad luck had run off to St. Louis right before Christmas and she was making out fine now.

Her hair was black and her eyes blue. She was not very tall but she had a nice ass and I thought about it. Here I was not even out a whole day shed of Parchman and Mississippi and my belly was full of catfish and I was admiring some high grade white pussy with a black Deputy Sheriff in the State of Arkansas. But this was not the time nor the place. Chloe was friendly but that was going to be it. I could tell. She told us she was the night manager and her brother ran the truck stop during the day and the place was owned by her uncle James on her mother's side.

Chloe told Luther she told Andrew that Luther was working tonight and that he would probably come in for something to eat but Andrew said Luther wasn't shit to him and he could not go into any of the cabs of the tractor trailers without a search warrant and he would set Luther straight on that. Luther said he was straight on that. That Andrew was right but he could knock on any door in the county and ask folks how they was passing the time. Didn't mean he could go in.

Luther got the bill and I reached for my billfold and he told me he knew I was released from Parchman today and he could help a man get a new start. Specially a free black man content to pass through his county and not come back unless he had a decent reason. He paid the bill and ordered a warm up on his coffee. He walked to the door of the café and looked out across the lot. You could hardly see the road for the hard rain.

Luther told Chloe to let me stay until it quit raining. It was right about three in the morning. Chloe said the trucks would be pulling in for breakfast after five and she could scare me up a ride to I-40 in Little Rock or beyond. I had not even noticed but I was sleepy. The coffee was hot but I had gotten soft. Sleeping off in that quiet shed. Quiet most of the time. Cepting when the Spring plowing and the Fall gathering time came.

Luther sat and drank his coffee. A few trucks came in and Chloe drifted off to serve the drivers in the tables and booths. I saw her nod to a dark-complected guy a little shorter than me and maybe a little older. It was hard to tell. He came over and asked me my name. I told him and he said his name was Ramon Silva and he had dumped a trailer of tomatoes off in Baton Rouge and he was going to pick a load of steel rods up in Oklahoma City and then cut down to Houston and dump the steel rods then go on back to Brownsville and rest up with his wife and kids for a few days. I asked if I could ride to Oklahoma City and he said yes. He said I should go on to Flagstaff and cut south to Phoenix. That was the way I planned all the time.

I told Luther thank you and got up to leave and Ramon said he was going to get about four hours of sleep and he would be ready. I told him I would be right here unless someone else came along. Luther left and Ramon went outside and I saw him climb in a big Peterbilt rig. Chloe kept coming on back and telling me things about the other drivers and her brother and her uncle who owned the place but I was tired and finally I went over to a booth and put my head down and slept for a few hours. Chloe woke me up around seven.

The place was filling up so I went to the counter and sat on the far end and ordered me some eggs fried hard and some fried country ham and grits and biscuits. Ramon came in and sat down and ate some cereal and drank some coffee and we left around eight. The cab of his truck was black and he had an open trailer with a bunch of chains and wooden pallets stacked neatly on it. There was red lettering on the cab that said Silva Trucking. When he got out of the lot and onto Highway 65 going to Little Rock I asked him if this was his rig and he said no, it was his son's. He said his son had went to school and learned how to read and write and keep figures and had bought some trucks and trailers and ran the company. Ramon lived in Brownsville. He said it was tricky down there. You had to watch. People would put some cocaine in your load and then call the cops and you would get stopped and your load confiscated and you would be charged and whoever set you up would use that to get his brother or son out of trouble. He told me that his son told him he felt stupid running a real business when the money was to be made in drugs and guns not tomatoes and long hauls.

I was sleepy and before we got to Little Rock I drifted off to sleep and slept until we were passing by Fort Smith and going into Oklahoma. I asked Ramon what was the prettiest country he had seen and he said he liked the Texas Hill Country and that when Lyndon Johnson was President he would see the pictures on TV and in magazines of his ranch and that was what he always wanted to have but he could never make that kind of money to buy the land. There was a picture of a woman taped to the dash. Had to be his wife. Big smile. Lot of black hair and a red skirt and white blouse and silver Concho belt. A pretty woman. Ramon looked to be my age. Late fifties. The woman maybe late forties.

Ramon was wearing a straw cowboy hat, blue jeans with a belt and a big silver buckle, and a blue and red cowboy short sleeve shirt. His hair was turning gray but there was still a lot of black showing. He was content to drive and we drove over a hundred miles into Oklahoma before he asked me had I ever seen the hills down near San Antonio. I said no and he said in the late afternoons when the sun was setting the hills turned a color of green that was close to being blue and he could not describe it but I should see them and put my own words to them.

I asked him if he had ever seen an Ocean and he said he lived right close to Padre Island and he could go to Corpus or Galveston and fish anytime he wanted. He liked the Gulf of Mexico but said he did not care that much for the Atlantic and that was because the water he had seen was all gray and there was so much building on the beaches nothing looked relaxing to him. He said I was smart to go to San Diego. He had been all the way up to Vancouver with his wife on vacation and they had driven down to San Diego and then back to Texas. He liked the Pacific. The water was prettier and everything. The houses, the streets, the beaches and even the people were cleaner on the Pacific side.

I told him I had been in Parchman Prison for a very long time and I wanted to see the Ocean before I died. I asked him about the zoo in San Diego and he said he and his wife were saving that for another time. He said it was getting harder and harder to make a living. His wife had been laid off from her job at the school. She was not a teacher. She worked in the office and helped keep records. And she had been let go just because times got hard. Not because of her work. Both he and his wife were born in the United States. His parents worked on a cattle ranch just south of San Antonio and raised him all his growing-up years on that ranch in Atascosa County. His wife had grown up in Harlingen.

We quit talking and the peace and quiet was nice. The Oklahoma countryside looked like a good place to live if you had some land and liked to raise cattle but there were no big trees like back home in Hardaman County or in the Delta, The land was open. You could see for a long way and all there was to see was a few cows and fences and a tree here and there. We were pulling into Oklahoma City when Ramon told me if I was ever in Texas the best drive for him was to take 281 out of San Antonio and drive north through the Hill Country past Marble Falls and the lakes on the Colorado River and just follow it all the way north on up to Lampassas. I was not studying going to Texas but I did not tell him. Way he talked about catching small mouth out of Lake Buchanan and drinking Lone Star beer and eating fried fish up at the dam sounded good. Lots of places to go but I would see my ocean and the zoo first and go from there.

I laid back and closed my eyes and the first thing I thought about was Chloe. Nice easy smile and pretty hair and a nice ass. A long time to do without a woman and I wanted one bad now that I seen some out in the free world. No use looking at the women you see in prison. Women like Essie Beard they looked mighty fine but if you thought about them all you did was antagonize your own self. Be nice to run up on a nice settled age woman in San Diego. One with some sense that liked sex and kept a neat house.

Ramon let me off at a truck stop on I-40. He told me to look for a ride in the café or back where the drivers was gassing up but not to go knocking on the cab doors of the ones that was parked out back of the café. This was a big truck stop with a big restaurant. Not a café. And a couple of other shops right in the truck stop. A Taco Bell and a Subway Shop were side by side. There was a gift shop where they sold stupid looking Indian stuff that anybody could see was fake. Me on my second day out of Parchman Prison deep in the Mississippi Delta could see it. Tomahawks with lots of feathers on the handles. Pots with crazy loud colors. Moccasins you knew were made in China. And row after row of little trinkets. Gave me a headache and I went in the restaurant and ordered some coffee and the bony ass waitress brought it and left without asking me if I wanted any food but that was alright. I would wait and eat tonight.

I looked down the counter and saw some drivers seated at the far end of the counter and there were some others seated at some of the tables and booths. I asked one at the counter if he was going west. He was wearing a Detroit Tigers baseball cap low over his forehead. He was a young white guy wearing a yellow tee shirt with the sleeves cut out. I told him where I was going and he did not look up and said he did not give rides to shiftless ass niggers and I knew I could take him. Just like I knew I could take Billy Ray Starnes but I moved on down the counter and was going to ask a man of color for a ride when I heard someone say he was going to LA to drop a load of tires and pick up a load of televisions to carry back to Ohio. He said he could carry me to Flag and let me out there. He had this electronic thing that looked like a large metal book in front of him. It had pictures on it. He asked me to sit down. I got my coffee and came back to his booth and sat down.

I mean I seen some ugly white men in my life. Even before I went to Parchman. I mean some ignorant looking trailer trash and of course right recently Royce the pulpwood truck driver and cock hound. But this guy. He would probably load out at over three hundred pounds and he was probably six foot six. His head looked like it belonged on a hog. He wore a green John Deere baseball cap and a clean blue denim shirt. Big forehead and chin and little blue eyes that were set way back in his head. His face looked like somebody had taken one of those scour brushes you see in the prison kitchen to him. He stood up when I came back to the table.

He said his name was Ott. I didn't ask if that was his first or last name. Didn't matter. I felt I could trust him and Flagstaff was a long ass haul from Oklahoma City. No way I was going to start culling my choices. I sat down and he said I would like San Diego. Pretty women on the beaches and lots of stuff to do.

He told me it would be easier to go straight to LA and then get a ride south. I told him LA was too big for me. I asked him what that was he was looking at. He told me it was a laptop computer. Something you could use to get on the Internet with and send e-mails back home with. He closed the top down on the laptop and drank some coffee.

I told him I was from Mississippi and I just wanted to see an ocean. He was from Spanish Fort, Alabama. Down near Mobile. He was raised up on a farm like me and said he had been driving almost thirty years and had his own rig. He was living in Columbus, Ohio. His wife, Laurie, taught biology at Ohio State. She had tenure and they could retire back to his home place a few miles from Spanish Fort in about ten years. I made Ott to be in his middle forties.

Ott reached in his back pocket and pulled out his billfold and showed me a picture of his wife. She was a pleasant faced white lady in her mid-forties. Blond hair and a nice smile. A long face and hair all down her back. The picture had been taken on a lake and she was wearing blue jeans and a white tee shirt and she was standing in the front of a boat that was tied to a dock. She was holding a string of fish. A couple of nice bass and some big bream. She was smiling to the camera and you could tell she was somebody who enjoyed the water and the wind and sun. Her cheeks were tan and her hair was mainly under a blue handkerchief.,

I thought at first he might be lying. She looked smart and classy but the boat and the dock and the lake looked like a place you would find Ott and he showed so much pride when he showed the picture to me I just could not see him as a liar. Least about that, anyways. I handed the picture back to him and he looked at it and smiled and put it back in his billfold.

Ott said they met in junior high school when she moved down to Alabama from Connecticut. He said he was the biggest boy in school. Junior high or high school both. She had helped him in his science class so he could be eligible to play football. He followed her around all winter then took her fishing in the spring down off Bon Secour and they drank cokes and ate goose liver sandwiches in the boat and caught some nice speckled trout and it just worked out. He said she liked him because he did not rush her and she could not take rushing from a boy because she knew she wanted to go to college and she was scared and did not want to get pregnant and be poor all of her life and spend all of her good years raising kids,

He was quiet after telling me all of that and in a few minutes a waitress came to the table with a greasy rib eye steak and some grits and three eggs all fried up together and a side plate of two blueberry pancakes. Her name was Lola and she was crabby and old and white. Silver hair and squatty, Flesh hanging off her short arms , wide thick hips, and too much make up on a puffy face. An old bitch was what she was. Probably in her late sixties. She looked at me and asked me if I wanted something to eat and I said I would like a warm up on my coffee and some orange juice and some bacon and eggs. Three eggs fried. She acted like it was putting her in pain. Just talking to me. I looked at her nametag and it said Lola. Wasting a sexy ass name like that on an old bitch like her. A face like a wet cardboard box and a head of dirty gray hair that made you want to cry. She had a smoker's voice and I thought to myself that all the trash had not made it to prison. Some was still out and doing fine.

Only thing I knew to talk to Ott about was fishing and I told him about going fishing with my uncle and catching a bunch of slab crappie over at Sardis Reservoir in the spring one year. I did not tell him anything about Billy Ray Starnes or Parchman Prison. My food came and the eggs was runny and cold. Ott told her to take the goddamn food back and bring it back right. Breakfast needs to be hot. He was right about that. Lola went off in a huff with my food but when she come back in a few minutes the eggs was nice and the bacon was warm and crisp.

I was almost through with my eggs and bacon and she come back with my juice and gave Ott a mean look and did not even look at me. Ott asked her why she didn't bring me some biscuits or toast and she asked me which one I wanted and I said biscuits and she brought them back and I sliced them while they was hot and poured some syrup over them and dipped the bacon in the syrup and thought to myself it was sure nice to be out of prison. Sure was.

We got ready to go and I laid two dollar bills down on the table for ignorant ass Lola and when we left I noticed the red neck with the Detroit Tigers hat was hunched over his coffee talking to Lola about Detroit. I followed Ott on out to his truck. The driver's door had Melvin Ott Trucking Company in white letters stenciled on it. The cab was painted black We moved easily into traffic and soon were on the broad, almost treeless, plains of Oklahoma. I did not know whether to call him Ott or Melvin so I said nothing and he was content to drive in silence for an hour or so.

There were pictures of his wife and a grown boy taped to the dash. After a while he told me he and his wife had a son and he still lived on the home place near Spanish Fort. He taught history at a local community college. He told me his wife called him Melvin and when they were in high school a guy named Bob Rutledge hung the name of Oink on him when he was in the ninth grade. Rutledge was a senior and the starting quarterback. He said it was not long until everyone on the team called him that. He didn't mind unless you weren't a football player. Then he took care of it. He and Laurie dated all through high school and she went up East to college to the University of Connecticut and he went over to Hattiesburg and played three years for Southern Miss. She always called him Melvin and wrote him nice letters from college and they talked about getting married when the time was right.

After his junior year he came back home. He had been redshirted his freshman year and had two years of eligibility left. He was a starter at right tackle and he knew he had a chance to go pro because he was right at three hundred and was six foot six. This was twenty something years ago. But he told his coaches he had to go back home and help his family. His father had just went through a heart attack and was laid up for almost a year. Melvin took over most of his jobs at the truck line and when his daddy came back to work he could only stay until noon and run the office. So Melvin drove and filled in everywhere he could and the rest of college didn't happen.

Laurie came back to Spanish Fort in the summers and after she graduated from Connecticut, she got some more schooling over at LSU and then came back and married Melvin. She had taught at South Alabama for a while but then she got the chance to go to Ohio State and they packed up and went on up to Columbus. By the time he was through telling me all of this we were out of Oklahoma and into the Panhandle of Texas. I nodded off to sleep and when I woke up, Melvin said I had missed Amarillo but I was going to get a jolt in a few minutes. And he was right. We passed a couple of feed lots and the smell came right in the cab and stayed a while. Thousands of cattle standing quietly in wet, black filth. Put out a smell that made me sad and I love beef. Waiting for the trucks to come and get them and take them to the slaughterhouse. Not knowing what was going on. Just standing there and eating and getting fat.

But the land was changing. More washes and rolling hills and a few canyons and not much water. The grass was dead and there were no buildings or people for miles. The trees you saw did not look very healthy and were twisted and scrawny and set low to the ground. You would see an occasional wad of cows or a few strung out on a hillside but it was mainly miles and miles of blue skies. I looked for rain clouds and there were none. The clouds hung high in the sky and were not moving. So this is the West.

We stopped in Tucumcari right after we crossed into New Mexico and ate a hamburger and fries at a truck stop way up on a windy hill. After we fueled up, Melvin was back at it. The sunset when we started down the long mountain trail going into Albuquerque. All the night-lights started flickering on before we settled down and started the swing around the town. Later, we pulled off at the Acoma exit and pulled behind a truck stop. Melvin told me he was going to go into the Casino and do a little gambling and I could come with him but if I stayed to watch out for the whores who knocked on the cab doors. I remember him saying pussy is too dangerous to fool with on the road.

I followed him on into the Casino. It is owned by the people of the Acoma Pueblo. You could see a lot of them working at the tables and in the restaurants. I had never been around many Indians. There was just a few at Parchman and they stayed off to themselves and nobody bothered them. They was known to be good fighters. I saw Melvin sitting at a quarter slot machine. I had my money in my boots except for a couple of twenties and a few singles. I went to a bar and drank a margarita and ate some guacamole and a chicken enchilada they brought in from the kitchen. This woman comes up to me. Little past forty and hard to tell what she is. A broad nose and dark skin but the nose is not too broad and the skin is real brown and she does not look like the folks working in the Casino. Her features are rougher.

She asked me to buy her a drink and so I did. She was wearing a tight blue tee shirt and white blue jeans that showed her ass and legs off nicely. Her hair was black and set up nice in a ponytail. She smelled good and wore gold rings on her fingers and silver bracelets on her wrists and one of those greenish blue necklaces they wear out west. Turquoise. She told me it was turquoise and she took the necklace in her fingers and ran one of the stones from my hand up to my forearm and cocked her head. She was wearing a heavy perfume and told me she was Mexican and was from Albuquerque. She said her name was Estelle and she was lonely and mad and I asked her why she was mad.

She told me she was supposed to meet a man here at the Casino and he was going to sell her some grass and she was going to take it back home and smoke some and sell most of it. She told me it was easy to make money selling grass. You just had to have a decent connection and not get too ambitious and keep it quiet and watch your customers to be sure they were straight and would not come back and rip you off or turn you in. I figured Estelle for a whore at first but she did too much talking and did not seem to be concerned about me that much. Her ass was nice and big and her breasts were big enough to keep me interested. I remembered what Melvin said but I was wanting some real honest good pussy real bad. You trained yourself in prison to do without or you went fucking crazy or turned to boys and that was not of any interest to me.

The waitress came back around in a few minutes and I was just finished with my margarita. I could already feel it. Estelle told me the next round was on her. She was drinking margaritas like me and when the waitress left she put her hand on my knee and ran her long fingernails up my thigh. Estelle told me she had never done a black man and she was thinking on it but for me not to crowd her since she had some things on her mind. I told her we had just got there and I pointed out Melvin to her. He was still playing the quarter slots but he had moved to another machine. A Bud Light was in his left hand and he was sitting on a stool with his John Deere hat cocked back on his head. There were a lot of people playing the slots. They all looked like truck drivers but some looked like they come from the Pueblo. The cocktail waitresses were mostly young pretty girls from the Pueblo but there were a couple of tough looking older blondes, also.

I thought to myself that I would play it like it came to me. Estelle was even on the drinks so she was not acting like money was part of the scene. Her eyes were brown and I could see a lime green bra strap on her shoulder. I put my hand on her knee and she did not move it. I left it there a minute and squeezed her knee and moved my hand back to the bar. There were three big televisions on behind the bar. No sound. One was on a football channel. One was on a golf channel and the middle set was on ESPN and they was showing a lot of highlights from football games. Estelle asked me what I was doing and where was I from.

I told her I was from Mississippi and I worked on cars and trucks and tractors but I was going to San Diego and she asked how and I told her I was riding with Melvin Ott. In his truck. At least to Flagstaff. She said she envied me because by rights she should be able to go. Just pick up and go where you wanted to. But she couldn't. She had a daughter with a baby and no husband and no job so she had to keep working and staying in the rut she was in. She sold jewelry and pots at a trading post in a place called Old Town in Albuquerque. The money was ok but it had been better but the tourists were starting to come back and she made some on the side selling grass. She asked me where I was going to live in San Diego and I told her by the Ocean and she shook her head and said I was in for a surprise. The land was all snatched up by the swells. All over California. I did not tell her I could sleep on a park bench or under a tree. I would worry about all that after I saw the Ocean. The surf and the birds dipping down to the water and catching fish in their beaks. All this I had been dreaming of for so long. And the wind off the water and the beach at sunset and sunrise. I heard you could walk for as long as you wanted to on the beach.

No use telling her any of this. We was just going to be together for a few minutes or a few hours. Her choice and I was just going to have to wait and see which it would be. I thought I might help the situation along some by buying her another margarita but she nursed it along and when she finished it, she slid off the red bar stool and asked me if I wanted to see her van and I said to let me tell Melvin and she laughed and went to the ladies room and I went over to Melvin and told him where I was going and he laughed and said he did not blame me. He told me to look at the clock. It was twenty minutes until two a.m. He said he was going to get back in the truck at two thirty and sleep till seven thirty and his tires would be on gravel coming out of the parking lot at eight and if I wanted a ride on in to Flagstaff I was welcome but not to wake him up in the truck.

I went in the bathroom and washed my face. I needed a shave but all my stuff was in Melvin's truck except my money so I had to be there when he got up to leave. Most of my money was under the innersoles of my boots. I bought a couple of gloves out of the machine in the bathroom. Good old lubricated Trojans. A three pack. Hope I could use two tonight and keep the third for down the road. Maybe in two feet of surf in the future. I went back out into the Casino and I did not see her. I sat at the bar and in a few minutes she came out of the bathroom and I followed her out the front door. We stood under the entrance and stared across at the lights from the trucks on the Interstate. There were a few stars and a distant moon. The wind was blowing hard and I put my hand around Estelle's waist and she pulled me to her and kissed me right there in the light with people coming and going all around us.

We got to her van and she opened the doors and we crawled in and she took my shirt off and ran her fingers across my chest and I took her tee shirt off and she helped me slide her blue jeans off and she had on one of those thongs that I had heard about. It was lime green like her bra and she helped me off with my clothes and she turned to me and ran her fingers up from my knees real slow all the way up my thighs and when she grabbed me I was already sitting on ready and we did not do much talking and I forgot how her thong came off but I know I took her bra off and her breasts were beautiful and round and brown and the nipples were stubby and black and her breasts did not sag and I pushed her on her back and took her and she talked to me in soft Spanish while we were doing it and I did not understand any of the words but the softness of her voice excited me even more than when she ran her fingers up the insides of my thighs. She took her hair down sometime or another when we were taking our clothes off and some of it was down her back and some was over her left breast and when it was over and I rolled over and she rolled against me and I was holding her ass close to me and listening to her long content breaths I could see the light coming in from a street light near the van and I listened to her breathe and the wind gently brushing the van.

I thought she might put the arm on me for some money or be

withdrawn after the sex. Lots of women give it up and then wish they hadn't but she was happy and she talked to me in English and asked me if I would call her once I got settled and ask her to come to San Diego and she told me while we were doing it she was thinking of doing it on a beach like she had seen Burt Lancaster and some pretty girl do it in a black and white World War Two movie she had seen on late night television.

She fired up a joint and I thought why not and took a few drags off it and it felt good to be with Estelle and smell her womanness and her perfume and listen to her talk. I loved her ass. Nice and big without being fat. Something to warm up with in the cold winter. It was not fat. It was muscular and fun to hold onto. We sat there and talked. She said she was going to have to go back home soon. She told me the bastard who had stood her up drove an old yellow Cadillac and lived down near the Zuni reservation just south of Gallup. She said I would probably see his sorry ass broke down on the Interstate tomorrow. I told her I would take her number and call her when I got settled and she turned on a light in the van and wrote two phone numbers down. One was a cell phone and one a home number.

She asked me if I had a cell and I told her I did not and that I was traveling light and I might get one in San Diego and she asked me laughing as she turned the light off if I had been living under a fucking rock. She said I must be the only adult in the whole big ass United States without a cell phone and I told her I had not been living under a rock and she looked at me and stroked my stomach with the nails of her left hand and told me that she was kidding and she would not ever disrespect me if I was nice to her and I pulled her to me and it was on again and this time she took charge and pushed me back onto the floor of the van and straddled me and guided me into her and threw her head back and my hands found her breasts and I shut my eyes and when it was over I was totally spent. I did not want to move. She was sweating across the tops of her shoulders and as she lay by me she held my head between her breasts and I could hear her heart beating and her breath in her chest. Short and fast.

We lay together for a long time and she finally moved and put her clothes back on except her bra and panties and told me she had to go on back home. She did not have to go into work until ten when the shop opened but it was still a long drive back. She said I could come with her and stay and I told her it would probably be best if I went on and called her after I got to San Diego. She said I was right. As I crawled over the seat, I saw the handle of another gun like the Sheriff's deputy in Arkansas had. I could see the black hard plastic of the square gun. It was between the seats. I asked her about it and she told me it was a Glock and she had paid almost five hundred dollars for it and two clips of ammunition. She told me she had never fired it with a round in it but had loaded it and unloaded it and knew how to use it. She said a woman living by herself needed protection. She got into the driver's seat and started the engine. She said a Glock was the way to go if I wanted a pistol but it would be jail time if I got caught with a stolen gun or an unregistered gun in California and I told her I would try to do without one if at all possible but if I got one it would just be an old fashioned Smith and Wesson,38 revolver since if you hit somebody with it they would go down and stay down. You did not need no eleven or thirteen shot pistol. She said I was probably right but she like the feel of the Glock and the idea that she could fire a lot of shots in a short period of time.

She handed it to me and she was right. It did feel good but I just did not see the sense in it but I did not say anything else about it and handed the Glock back to her butt first and she put it between the seats and turned the defroster and the heat on. We sat there and let the van heat up and we held each other and when the van was warm and the windshield was clear she took me to the front of the casino. She said she was going to take one last look for the yellow Cadillac. I watched her as the old black van crawled through the parking lot. She left and crossed under the Interstate and got on the frontage road and she was gone. I went back inside the Casino. It was almost five o'clock. The sun would be up soon. I walked out back and saw Melvin Ott's big rig. It was dark and silent. There were other trucks with their running lights on just warming up and getting ready to head on out.

I saw a young girl in a short red skirt and a white sweater and black high heels stepping out of the cab of a tanker truck. She walked on toward me and when she got close to me she put on the stroll walk. The hip swing, the long steps and the come on look but it was wasted on me. She was too young. If she was eighteen I would be surprised and all of the make up in the world could not hide the fact that she was white trash all the way. Nice body but a dumb face and eyes that belonged on a snake. She said do you want a bump, pops and I did not say anything. She went on into the coffee shop and sat by herself in a corner booth.

I sat at the counter and ate a beef and bean burrito and some fried eggs and drank iced tea. I was hoping I could see the sun rise but I was inside on the west side of the casino and all I could see was first light and a bunch of trucks growling in the early morning rush to get back on the highway. In an hour or so when I was through with my meal and had switched to black coffee a tall white guy in his thirties came in with a dark headed girl. Looked like she was wearing a wig. He looked like he had done time before and she was fighting her weight but she had nice breasts and decent legs and she was wearing a black skirt and a white sweater. I figured her for her early thirties. The sat down in the booth with the first girl and ordered coffee. Around seven a third girl showed up and she looked bad. Short, overweight, with a blond wig, and she looked sprung. High on something. She sat down and ordered coffee and pancakes.

They did not talk much and the last girl definitely had the shakes. The girl in the black skirt and red sweater laughed from time to time. A smoker's harsh throaty laugh. She was laughing at her own jokes and no one else was smiling. The tall man had steady hands and a low deep voice and the girls bent over and listened to him when he talked. The last girl in. The short one with the blond wig got up and walked into the bathroom and then the other two followed her. It was a long time before they all three came out together. The short blond was wobbling when she walked and when they got back to the booth, the girl in the black skirt was behind the short blond. She was looking at the tall man and shaking her head. She looked disgusted.

Before seven thirty they were gone. I saw them load into a black SUV and pull out. At seven thirty or so, Melvin Ott opened his cab door and walked across the gravel to the coffee shop. He ordered some bacon and eggs and coffee and asked if I wanted to go on with him and I said please and he laughed and he never asked me what I had done. He told me he was looking forward to the day he could get off the road and go on back to Spanish Fort with Laurie. His son was watching after the place for them and he was starting a family up and Melvin would be a grandfather soon.

He told me he liked the drive on into Flag. That's what he called Flagstaff. Flag. All the way into Gallup he was quiet except to tell me his son was not anything like he or his wife. He stayed on the computer all the time. He kept the fences up and the yard was neat but he and his wife were always on their computers. Each had one set up next to each other in a converted bedroom. Just a different world. The boy hated fishing and hunting but he liked a neat yard with flowers and clipped grass.

He said the boy was good. Solid with his feet on the ground. Worked hard and had a predictable, sensible wife and he and Laurie could not talk to either one of them. They would visit and after the first thirty minutes it was hard to carry on a conversation and their visits were for Christmas usually and that was about all. Melvin said it was strange how you could raise a boy and take care of him and feed him and stay under the same roof with him all that time he was growing up and he could grow up to be somebody you did not really know.

There was nothing I knowed to say so I just shut up and watched the road and the flat, hard land pass by. Mountains and buttes were in the distance but not much of anything was green. Hardly any cattle anywhere. I saw an Indian on a skinny white horse herding sheep with a brown and white dog when we got past Gallup and into Arizona. Melvin Ott said that the Navajo Reservation was north of the Interstate and he had cut through it one time going up to Moab, Utah and it was pretty grim country. Not much water and grass and taxing on the folks that lived there and tried to grub a living off the land. But to me, it was pretty. The red rocks and tall buttes rising out of the land. You could see for a long way.

I dropped off to sleep after a while and I dreamed about Estelle and me and the ocean. We were walking along the beach and you could not see any houses on the land and there were boats off in the distance with tall white sails and birds dipping into the surf. I woke up when Melvin Ott pulled off the Interstate and told me we were in Flagstaff, Arizona. It was along in the late afternoon and he took me to a truck stop where he said I could get a ride down Interstate 17 all the way to Phoenix and there I had to hook up with someone going South on Interstate 10 until I passed through Casa Grande and I got to Interstate Eight and that would carry me right on into San Diego. He told me to try to get a ride with someone heading to Tucson or the Border at Nogales. They would go right past the junction with Interstate Eight.

I thanked him for the ride and he said 'down the road' and pulled on off and I went into the truck stop and ate another hamburger and then tried to scare up another ride. It was cold outside and when I went outside the truck stop I could smell the pines and the clean air. A wind was whistling down from the North and some pine trees on the edge of the lot were bending in the steady wind. I spent the whole night there wishing I could have rode all the way down to San Diego with

Melvin Ott. I sat at the counter in the restaurant for hours. I finally got bored and walked outside and walked around the whole truck stop and got cold and come back in and drank more coffee.

Around four in the morning a short, skinny , white man wearing a dusty straw cowboy hat came up to me and said that the night hostess had told him I needed a ride and that I could be of a help to him. I told him where I was going and he said he was carrying four new horses down to Tubac. Horses his boss had bought in Utah just north of Salt Lake City at a ranch.

He worked for a ranch off in the hills east of Tubac. Down in Arizona. South of Tucson and just north of the Border. It was really a horse farm and there was some thirty horses. All American Quarter Horses except for three Appaloosas and definitely no cows or sheep. He wanted to know if I knew anything about horses and I laughed and said I had ridden a little but I was a car and tractor man. He laughed and stuck out his hand and told me his name was Lim Couch. He was wearing blue jeans and a white one-pocket tee shirt and a pair of broken down brown cowboy boots. I followed him on out to his truck and trailer. We drove on out of Flagstaff and after a few miles he turned off the Interstate and drove a few hundred yards to an open grassy area. We got out and walked the horses around for almost an hour. There were two sorrels, a grey, and a horse he called an Appaloosa. The horse was solid black except for a white blanket on his rump.

Lim said the App was a coming three year old his boss, Ms. Lakey, had bought on a whim. Not to show, but just to ride around up in the mountains. After we put them back in the trailer, Lim went back to the truck and came back with two cans of Budweiser. They were cold and it was just past sun up and I was hungry again. We both drank a beer and then we got back in the truck.

I liked the country we were driving through. The air was crisp and clean and the pine trees were way taller than the ones back home.

There were a lot of valleys with horses and cows in the still green meadows. There were mountains all around and Lim told me we were lucky we were not caught in a snow blizzard.

After a while we passed out of the tall pine country and drove through some red rock country and then went down a long steep road and passed a town called Camp Verde and then we came back up on the climb out of the Verde Valley over a tall mountain and then things leveled out for a while and then we made a long descent into the Phoenix area.

Lim told me he worked for a woman named Susan Lakey. She was just getting into her forties and she was divorced from a plastic surgeon from somewhere off in Oregon. She had inherited the ranch from her folks and turned it into strictly a horse operation. She had a trainer who was from Texas named Roy Stutts who had got half of his left leg blown off in Iraq. He had some medals and all the judges at the Quarter Horse shows liked him and he had a plastic thing he put on his stub and he could walk real good. When he wasn't taking pills and mixing them up with beer or tequila.

Lim said he was kind of a assistant trainer and stall-cleaner and in charge of everything else on the place that Roy and Susan wanted done. The fences, feed, hay, and the long haul driving to the big shows. The Houston and Fort Worth Shows were probably the biggest. He would get to the shows ahead of time and ride the horses and groom them until Roy and Susan showed up.

Roy and he drank together sometime but Lim did not like to drink with Roy because he drank too much and drove too crazy and sometimes he mixed the drinking with pills. Lim had sat down a rule. We drink. I drive. Lim had got eased out of his job one dry and windy day a few years back when Susan had come down to the barn and told him she was going to let Jody try her hand at his job. Jody was a girl Susan had met at a show in California. She smoked a lot of grass and cussed too much for Lim's liking. Jody and Susan slept up in the nice adobe ranch house and Jody did not like Lim or Roy either one.

Jody was not the first girl to wind up sleeping up at the house with Susan. There had been two others. Both in their twenties and both lookers. Lim said he went on back to his parent's home in Marana, right outside Tucson and banked the two thousand dollars Susan gave him as severance pay. He said it was almost two years later, sometime in 2010, when Susan came into the Guadalajara Grill over in Tucson and asked Lim if he would come back and he asked her if he had to give the severance pay back because he had used a couple of hundred dollars of it to buy a better truck and she had laughed and bought him one of those big margaritas and he had come on back and they had all gotten along just fine up to now.

Roy never talked about Jody and told Lim to keep his fucking mouth shut about it. Lim said that now there was a lawyer out of Tucson came down some Friday nights and stayed and dressed up like a cowboy and rode around on the weekends with Susan. His name was Johnson Raines and Lim said he did not have any business around a good horse. Especially the ones Miss Susan kept.

Lim told me he and Susan would go to the Amado Steak House on most Thursdays right at sundown when all the stock was fed and he would drink a Dos Equis Amber with his porterhouse and she would eat a filet and drink margaritas. They sat in the bar and talked to the other ranchers and hands that came in. Lim said before they went to Utah, she told him they were going to pick up three horses. The sorrels were mares to be bred soon and the Grey was a coming two-year-old that she was going to try to get some points on. AQHA points. That's how the shows worked, Lim said. You win and you get so many points depending on how many horses were in the class. She had not mentioned the black app with the white blanket.

She and Roy rode up with him to the ranch near Bear Lake right close to the Idaho state line. Once she was settled on the mares and the grey, she and the main wrangler at the Bear Wallow Ranch took

Lim back down to the barn and Susan asked Lim to ride the App. His name was Tony. Lim said Tony had a nice handle especially when you took into account he was so young and he was easy to work with opening gates and backing up and making side passes and Lim told Susan he was nice but he had not been cut yet and he did not know what she could do with him.

Susan was leaning against the rail of the corral Lim had been working the horse in and she told Lim if he liked him the horse was his to keep and ride for as long as he wanted and Lim was embarrassed and asked her why she was doing it and she said it was an atonement and he asked her what that was but she was already walking away from the corral with the head wrangler and he would wait till he went back to Marana and he would ask his little sister who taught school what that was. An atonement.

Lim said he slept in the trailer that night and then unhooked the trailer and took Roy and Susan to the Logan airport the next morning and then came back and stayed around the ranch for a few hours riding the App up in the nearby mountain meadows. When we hit Phoenix, Lim was quiet except to cuss the drivers pulling in and out of traffic in front of him. We made it through Phoenix and past Chandler Road and Lim pulled off at a drive in. It was a Carl's Junior. Lim bought me a couple of hamburgers and some fries and a strawberry milkshake and when we got back on the road after finding a vacant lot to walk the horses in. After we had the horses settled down in the trailer and was out of town, he cracked open two more cold Budweisers and we headed south.

We had driven out of all the city traffic when Lim asked me where I had done time and I told him Parchman in Mississippi and he told me we was going to pass close by where he did two years in a hot hell hole called Florence. I asked him what he did to get the deuce and he said it was a bar fight down in Nogales, Arizona when he was twenty three and he had torn the bar up worse than the guy he was fighting.

The other guy got his jaw broke but Lim said he did not think he hit him that hard., He figured his wife did it when he got home broke and drunk and a little beat up. It didn't matter. He got the two years and did all but four months.

He said he watched his drinking ever since. He asked me what I did to get in prison and I told him I killed a man back around the time he was born. Back in Mississippi. After that Lim did not ask me anything about myself. He was quiet until we got to the exit for Interstate Eight. He told me good luck and dropped me off on a frontage road after we found a place to walk the horses. It was in the middle of the afternoon and the wind was blowing hard and cold. Lim told me good luck and gave me another cold Budweiser in a brown paper sack and pulled on off.

I sure wanted a ride before dark. Lim had told me I was just around five easy hours from the beach. But it was not to be. It was morning again and I was standing in the cold wind with no ride all night when an old green and tan Subaru Outback pulled off the Frontage Road and stopped about fifty yards ahead of me. I ran to the car. When I was about twenty feet away, the driver's door opened and a tall, thin white lady got out. She was wearing a blue, long dress with lots of pleats in the skirt and a silver Concho belt and a big turquoise necklace. She wore reddish brown cowboy boots and her hair was white. She looked to be a few years older than me. The sun had not been kind to her. Wrinkles and creases were everywhere but her eyes were a real bright and alert blue.

She asked me where I was from and I told her Mississippi and she asked me where I was going and I told her I wanted to see the Pacific Ocean and the Zoo in San Diego and she told me to come along. She had been raised in North Carolina. Up in the mountains near the Blue Ridge Parkway but her husband had been in the Air Force and he had not come back from the first fight in Iraq back in the day when Bush senior was the president of our country.

Her name was Helen. She said folks nowadays would tell you their first name and not tell you their last name till they were comfortable with you and she said she was not like that. She still had those mountains in North Carolina in her. She laughed and said Helen Hatch. Like it was one word. She had lived in Denver when her husband was alive. She had been back to North Carolina to bury her husband in his family plot and nothing fit right there anymore and she had not been back since even though she truly cherished his memory and she had not made any real effort to hook up with any men since her husband went down in flames near Kuwait when the war was already won and it was all just a bunch of macho posturing in her eyes.

Now, she lived out from Silver City in the southwest part of New Mexico. She skied all over the west in the winter and hiked and rode motorcycles the rest of the time. She said something told her it was the right thing to do. Picking me up and trusting me and giving me a ride. She said the girls in her church group would all be horrified to know she picked a black man up on a lonely frontage road in Arizona.

She asked me when the last time I had eaten was and I told her it was yesterday and she said it was a long way to Yuma and laughed. There was some tuna fish in a cooler in the back seat and I crawled over the seat and made us each two sandwiches and fished out two apples from the ice. We drank A and W root beer from the can and ate in silence. She asked me what I did and I told her the truth and she drove on for a few miles then pulled off at an exit and looked in my eyes for a few minutes and then asked me if I felt any remorse for killing somebody and I said not the somebody I killed. She asked me to tell her what happened and I did. I told her I did not have any weapons and she was safe but if she was scared I would get out of the car and go on back down to the highway and catch another ride. She sat there a few minutes with her hands on the steering wheel without asking me anything else or saying anything.

There were tears in her eyes for a minute and she wiped them away and got back on the Interstate and in a few minutes she laughed and she said did I want to know what was funny and I said yes and she said that she felt safer with me than she did with her minister who dropped by without calling first and asked questions about her financial situation and had put his hand on her knee once but not ever again. Not since she set him straight on that sort of thing.

I asked her where she was going and she told me she was going to a place called Del Mar that was not far from San Diego. Just up the road from La Jolla and La Jolla was just up the road from San Diego. She was going to see her daughter and her two grandchildren who were still not teenagers and were nice to her. She said her son in law was a piece of work. He made a lot of money in the high tech scene but she thought he was boring and he was polite to her but was clearly not interested in anything about her. Past, present, or future. Her words. She would stay for four or five days, see the ocean, and maybe drive on to San Francisco for a few days. Everybody in Del Mar had too much money and no soul and they were too crisp in their speech patterns and a lot of them were rude.

Because she was old and from the South. People nowadays did not think anyone old like her from the South had the brains to do anything except get in the way and bore people. But she loved her daughter and she had a fantasy that her daughter would divorce this pompous bore and bring the children and live with her out in the mountains and trees near Silver City right on the edge of the Gila Wilderness area., She could buy the kids horses and teach them to fish for trout and go camping with them in the mountains and take them skiing.

Now all the kids did was sit in front of computers and argue with their parents and slam the doors to their rooms and talk all day on the phone with their friends. Some of whom lived on the same street a few houses away. When she was through with all of this I thought I saw her chin quiver but she took some deep breaths and asked me to put a

Lyle Lovett CD in the player and I figured out how to do it and the music calmed her down. She really liked one song about a rodeo cowboy who had missed his ride and would have to go on to the next town and try again.

I told her about Lim Couch and the black Appaloosa with the white blanket and how Susan Lakey said the horse was an atonement and I told her me and Lim did not either one know what that was and she did not laugh and told me in a low voice that an atonement could be a payback. An attempt to right an old wrong. Or heal a fresh emotional wound. She asked me if I went back to Hardaman County when I got out and I said no and she asked if I felt I should make an atonement to anyone and I said almost thirty years in Parchman paid a lot of debts and she said I was right about that and we drove through the gray morning to Yuma.

We were driving through country that was flat with squatty cactus and sorry looking trees and gray mountains way off in the distance. There were a few farms with green truck crops growing every few miles. You could see the irrigation water running in ditches between the fields. There were signs on the Interstate that said this and that river but there was no water under the bridges and Helen said there had not been any water in them for a long time because the water level was so low.

In Yuma, she gassed up and I bought some more root beers and some new ice for the cooler. She asked me to get her a candy bar while she was in the rest room and I bought us both a Baby Ruth. A big one and we were eating Baby Ruth's and listening to Lyle Lovett as we passed into California. Soon we passed through some sand dunes and then into part of the Imperial Valley. There was a lot of water in irrigation ditches and plenty of green crops growing.

I liked Helen. She had an easy way of talking to me and when she told me about atonement and what it meant she was like my lawyer from my murder case. Gorman Ballard. Slow and easy talking. And

Dump. Easy people to talk to. Helen I figured was one of those one-man women. Now her man was dead and she would just not go to the trouble of finding another one.

Helen said that once I had seen the Pacific I should see the rest of the West. New Mexico, Arizona, Utah, Oregon, Wyoming, Idaho, and Montana. And the Dakotas. She told me to see it before it got too cluttered up with people and tall buildings. Then she added Colorado. She laughed and said it was just like her to leave out what might be the prettiest state of them all.

She told me she would take me to Balboa Park and show me where the Zoo was and then she would carry me down to the Bay because it was close to the Zoo and there were plenty of piers and benches for me to sit on down by the Bay. I wondered if she was dreading getting out of her car in Del Mar and facing her family but I did not ask. She told me the ocean was beautiful there and there were some inlets that had marinas. She said I would like to watch the pretty sail boats with the sails down as they bobbed up and down in the calm blue water and big white sea gulls with black on top of their wings and nervous feet swooped down and stole scraps of food off the boats. Also pelicans. I should watch for them diving after fish.

She and the grandchildren liked to eat at a café in Del Mar near the water where they could eat outside and watch the birds and the boats and the water. I was ready for some of that. After a while we left the Imperial Valley and went through some more boring desert country until we climbed a tall mountain range and we were in San Diego County and still had a long way to go. Once we hit the top of the mountains, Helen said we had passed over to the wet side of the range and there were green fields and meadows and a lot of houses started showing up. Houses on tops of big hills and lots of pretty green valleys.

Soon, it was just Interstate and other big highways and houses and Helen said for me to relax. We were going to see the Ocean soon. She took a bunch of roads and then pulled off Interstate 5 to Los Angeles and we drove through Balboa Park and she showed me where the Zoo is located and then in about fifteen minutes she had me right on the Ocean. She said it was the Bay area.

We turned right on Harbor Drive and drove past a Holiday Inn and there was a big cruise ship docked across the street. She slowed down in front of a restaurant right in front of the Holiday Inn and told me to remember the name of it. Anthony's. She said it was her husband's favorite place to eat in San Diego and I should go there and eat and have a drink and watch the sail boats in the harbor at sunset.

She kept driving and went on past the airport and turned on a road by a big city park and found a parking place and said come on I will show you the real ocean and I asked where we were and she said Mission Beach. We walked a few blocks up a hill and there it was. All silver and blue in the late afternoon sun. Ocean. As far as you could see. We stood at the top of the boardwalk and I did not say anything. And she was right. There were sea gulls drifting over the water and some were even walking on the beach and the wind was blowing in my face and it was a little cold but the sun was bright in the low blue dying sky.

We walked out on the beach and I listened to the wind and the gulls calling and there were a few sailboats off in the silvery distance. Helen said that this time of the year, there was a fog in the morning but by noon the sun burned it off and the afternoons were clear. I told her the least I could do was buy her a drink and she said that was an excellent idea and we walked until the sun ducked behind some low clouds on the horizon and the beach was almost empty.

Off to the north I could see some brightly colored gliders with people guiding them in the wind. They were a long way off and the gliders were soaring and swooping as the day's light softened and dimmed. We saw a restaurant with two floors on it and walked up to the second floor and I ordered a shot of Jack Daniels with water and ice on the side and she asked for a martini with extra olives.

Everyone else had on shorts or bathing suits but no one paid attention to us. There were red and pink streaks in the clouds near the edge of the horizon and the windows were open across the front of the top floor of the restaurant. Helen ordered oysters on the half shell and we shared them and she said she should not have said anything bad about her son-in-law but now that she had said it, it was out of her craw and she could drive on up to Del Mar and act like an adult. We were through with the oysters and were waiting on another dozen when her phone rang. It was her daughter and Helen said she would be on directly because she had stopped at Mission Beach and watched the sunset with a friend.

She did not order another drink and I did not either and she picked the check up and would not let me pay. She slid a credit card over the bill and the young waitress took it. After she returned with the receipt, Helen and I finished our drinks and watched the night slowly come down over the Pacific Ocean. She asked me where I was going to sleep tonight and I told her I did not know. I would worry about that when I got tired of walking on the beach.

She told me I needed a blanket and I said I would make do with what I had and she smiled at me and said she kind of thought that was what I would say. We walked on out to the car and I got my bag from the back seat and she held out her hand and it had a bunch of twenties in it and I told her no, that I had money and something would come up and she said she could not see me begging on the boardwalk like some people. I told her I was not afraid of work and I could lay off the booze and I was scared of dope and she laughed and gave me a card with her name and phone number on it.

She wanted me to call her collect when I got settled down and I took the card and she gave me the wad of twenties and told me to go on to the Bay after a few days and eat a meal at Anthony's at sunset for her. She said try the oysters on the half shell and the crab cakes. I took the money and thanked her and she started to get in the car and turned to me and told me to call her sooner if I got in a jam and I laughed and told her I was through being in jams and she told me to enjoy my walk and she pulled off in the busy night traffic and headed north to Del Mar.

CHAPTER EIGHT
FREE BLACK MAN IN SAN DIEGO

When Helen left, I went on back to the beach and walked until I was tired and then I put my bag down and watched the surf and listened to the waves break on the beach. There were a few people who walked by but there was no law-boys out hassling me and I felt relaxed and tired. The air was cold but it refreshed and calmed me. I could see lights on ships a long way off and there were some sailboats that cruised by. I could see women in sweaters and jeans on the sailboats drinking and looking into the night. There was light from a silver moon and lights from the bars and restaurants on the boardwalk.

I slept on and off and Helen was right. A blanket would have been nice but all I had was a light jacket I pulled over me. I was awake before first light. I was hungry and walked back to the boardwalk and found a convenience store down on the street and bought me a hot dog and a big drink and walked back on the boardwalk and found a bench and sat and ate. I never wanted to move off from the ocean. I liked the smells and the wind and the sound of the surf on the beach. There was a morning fog and I walked the beach for a long time and finally the sun burned the fog off and the afternoon was clear and warm. The gulls came back and I saw some small fishing boats drifting in the calm sea.

For a few days, I just wandered around the beach and enjoyed myself. I needed a ride to the zoo and a waitress at a little Vietnamese restaurant told me where to go to take the bus. I finally found my way to the Zoo and I did not see all of it the first day so I hid when they closed it. I hid behind some ferns near a bench and I slept there until the next morning and by the end of the second day I had seen it all. The birds, the monkeys, the big apes, the big cats, the sad old elephants, and the pandas. I left the zoo on the second day when they closed.

I walked on down to the Bay and I saw Anthony's and it was night time and it looked to be full and I was not very clean so I wandered around and went south on past the cruise ship and the aircraft carrier, Midway, and through Seaport Village and I came back up and found a bench across from the Midway. No one had claimed it. There were homeless guys all up and down the streets. I was new and did not want to be homeless and a bum. I had to get things straight in my mind and find something to do and some place to stay. It was getting cooler at night and it even rained some but I was so busy seeing things I had only dreamed about for so long that I was not bothered. I found a pawnshop and it had a nice green sleeping bag in it and I bought it for twenty-five dollars.

I knew I did not want to live like this forever but my money was going down slowly. I still had the wad of twenties Helen Hatch had given me stuffed under the soles of my shoes. I counted my money and figured I could last at least a month like this and still have some left over. I usually ate just twice a day and I picked up a little money here and there.

I split my time between the San Diego Bay area and Mission Beach, but one morning I got a ride with a bread delivery truck and I helped him carry in racks of rolls and bread in La Jolla and Del Mar and then the next day we went all the way up to Ocean Side, He bought me a cheeseburger at Carl's Jr. each day and he dropped me off back at Mission Beach late in the afternoon and gave me a ten. He said I could count on him every week on Monday and Tuesday. The other days he worked other routes and did not come by Mission Beach.

One Tuesday, I caught a ride on in with him all the way to Harbor Drive and went back to the Bay area. I usually hung out down near the Midway carrier and in the park by Seaport Village. I wasn't wanting to meet friends. Guys to steal my money after we got drunk. Guys who wanted to fight if you went in with them on a quart of wine and didn't share right. I stuck to myself. Most of the homeless guys were harmless.

The police left us alone. They would ride by on bikes. Two abreast wearing some girlie looking blue shorts with white shirts and white helmets on. Usually young guys that looked like they had spent most of their time in the gym. They was content to give directions to the pretty tourist women as long as nobody did a lot of cussing or threw bottles on the concrete or left stuff in a mess on the grass. Or harassed the tourists. I never asked nobody for nothing except the delivery drivers. All I asked for was a ride and when I got one I wound up doing some work. Usually helping to load or unload the truck.

In a short time, I started to recognize some of the guys. Some slept all day and some roamed all day and slept at night like normal folk. There was two brothers from Nebraska that had staked out a bench near where I slept. They was both in their twenties. One about five years older than the other one. They were both stocky and had reddish brown hair. I heard the oldest one call the youngest one James. The oldest told me his name was Harold. Harold said he was tasked to look after his brother. Way it was. I never heard no one say that before. They was tasked to do something.,

James did not talk to anyone but his brother. Way his brother explained it to me was that James went in the Army right out of high school and lasted almost three years. He was supposed to be on his way to Afghanistan when the Army sent him home. James got on heroin over in Germany before the Army could even get him into the war. James's brother said they were living in Lebanon right near the Kansas line and there was not much there in the way of jobs. Harold was living in a trailer behind a truck stop there in Lebanon and took his brother in and when James got his last check from the Army, they lit out for San Diego.

Their family was down to one sister that lived in Denver and their father who was disabled and was in his late sixties. He lived on a small farm out from Lebanon. Well, the plan Harold had was to let James relax for a while near the Ocean and then go to North Dakota and get one of those twenty five dollar an hour jobs roughnecking in the oil fields but it had not worked out that way. Way I saw it, Harold was alright. Both body wise and head wise. Pretty close to normal.

But James. No. He was always trying to score some dope and he would panhandle the tourists. Sometimes a little too hard. And they would get scared and sure enough there would be police all over the place for a day or so. None of them ever bothered me. I would just go on up to Mission Beach until everything got quiet again. Up on Mission Beach, I hardly ever saw any law. Not many panhandlers at all and no trouble on the beach.

Harold said they had been there over six months and he knew what he should do and that was to put his brother in some rehab joint or a mental health facility and then he could hitch hike to North Dakota and get a job. One thing I did not understand was how in the hell James ever got in the Army in the first place but this was something you would not ask Harold. He thought that one day James was just going to change. Just out of the blue sky.

James and Harold had some restaurants that they had staked out. The restaurants or fast food joints would empty their trash in a dumpster and there would be enough food in them to keep them going. One was a pizza place. James loved pizza and so he liked pulling cold pizza out of the dumpster. This was a place up in Little Italy. Just a few blocks north and east of the Midway and the cruise ships. I was proud I did not have to do that but I knew it was coming and coming in a few months. I could not count on a few cheeseburgers and ten dollars a day twice a week from a bread man.

The bread man was Hector Reyna. Guy with a big weight problem. Almost three hundred big ones on a five ten frame. We had fun on the bread truck, though. Hector had been driving for close to twenty-five years and had raised his kids up good. None of them in any trouble. Hector said he was a native American. None of his folks had ever been down to Mexico except to fish in Ensenada and Cabo. Maybe buy some Talavera pots in Tijuana. That's it.

Hector was always on the lookout for good-looking women. Any store we went into. He was all business but the man had good eyes. He would say, hey Robert, be cool but check the black sweater and white pants out over by the coffee displays. He never said anything to any of them but he liked to get back in the truck and drive up the PCH talking about how he loved his job. Never had to stay in one place too long and never got involved with anyone long enough to have a real dispute.

Most days he would get bread back from some of the stores to carry on back to the bakery. Stale rolls or donuts or loaves of bread. He always let me pick something out to carry with me at the end of the day. He liked to sit and watch me bring the bread in and stack it. Sometimes we got a few things from the meat markets. People Hector knew would slip him some pork chops or chorizo and one day we got three slabs of good pork ribs that had been laying under the heat lamp for a few days. From a Frys in Del Mar.

Hector stopped at a Circle K and got us both a Dos Equis and we parked out on the lot by the Torrey Pines Beach and ate ribs and drank a beer and Hector asked me about when I was a kid in Mississippi and I told him it was fine as long as I had something to eat and a clean place to sleep. Just no ocean and no pretty girls on the beach. Lots of farm work and sweat and low wages.

Hector said he could retire soon but he would not even be fifty-five and he wondered what he would do with his time. His words. If you step off the bus, you may not be able to ever get back on. Meaning to me he would keep on working. He loved Circle K. Women always in there and more cheap good things to eat like hot dogs and burritos, Hector would help stack the bread and then grab us a hot dog and a drink. Sometimes he had to pay full price but most of the times, he either got waved by for nothing or he had to pay for the dogs and not for the drinks.

I had another place I could stop in and get a meal. The White Lotus off a side street in Mission Beach. Vietnamese people ran the place and I went in one morning while I was just waiting for the sun to cut a hole in the fog and there was this little man sweeping and moving tables and talking to himself. He was real small and slender and I told him I would sweep and help him clean up for a meal and he gave me the broom and I got started and when I was about through, I looked up and he was standing by the kitchen with a mop and a bucket.

I stood up and groaned a little and we both laughed. His name was Mr. Minh. All I ever knew. He called me Robert Lee and I would come in a couple of days a week and clean things up and straighten the tables all out. The place was cool. Man, it had this pictures of lions and tigers and trees with white blossoms all over the walls and red tablecloths. Mr. Minh was up in his fifties and looked every day of it but now his wife, she was something else.

Mr. Minh had this sort of dark brown complexion and a long face but his wife, she had a light complexion and told me she never went in the sun without a big hat because she did not want to look like a peasant. She had all this jewelry. Gold earrings and a couple of big watches with diamonds on them. I never knew her name. Just Mrs. Minh.

There was a couple of white girls worked the tables and some more Viets in the kitchen. There were about thirty tables in the place and they did a good take out business. I would clean the place up and sit in the back of the restaurant and drink tea out of these little fragile white cups with blue and yellow flowers painted on the sides.

Mr. Minh told me I could come in and bus tables and wash some dishes if I would just get on a schedule so he could depend on me and I told him I had been penned up for so long I just wanted to do what I felt like doing for a while longer and he said he understood that because he had been on a boat for a long time many years ago coming over from Viet Nam to America. He had wound up near Port Arthur, Texas and worked on a fishing boat and stayed when he was young. He had saved up enough money to come to San Diego in the early eighties and now he was a citizen.

The Minhs had a son. They called him Tommy and Tommy was my idea of an asshole. He came by in the mornings some days and he and his mother and father would sit off by themselves in a corner and Tommy would look all put out while he was drinking his tea and looking out front at his shiny, black BMW. One of the big ones. Tommy was in sales and was taller than his parents and dressed in suits and blue or white button down shirts and red and yellow ties like you see lawyers wear. He had cut his hair real short and twirled his sunglasses while he was in the restaurant and he would look around like he was disgusted and I wanted to slap the shit out of him for the way he talked to his folks.

And I could not even tell what they were saying. They talked in what I figured was Vietnamese. Neither Mr. Minh or his wife were ever happy after Tommy left. I would stay until it was almost eleven and when the first lunch customers started coming in I would go on in the back and they would fix me some lunch. Wonton soup with shrimp in the wontons was my favorite. I never asked for anything. I just ate what they gave me. I would sit at a little table next to a door the deliverymen used in the back. Off from the kitchen.

Mr. Minh would bring me my food like I was a real customer. First the soup. Always hot and always good. Then an egg roll and then chicken or pork or beef over rice with vegetables all stirred in or sometimes just rice with shrimp and chicken stirred in. Whatever they brought out, it was good. One day, Mrs. Minh bought me half a duck. Best meal I had since I got to San Diego. I remembered when I was in Parchman and Dump's wife would send me a plate of food a couple of days a week. Usually greens with corn bread and some fried chicken but sometimes it was spaghetti or meat loaf. Something good.

And Essie would bring me a bunch of turkey and dressing with real cranberries in a sauce after the holidays. On Easter, I usually got some ham from one of them and Essie would make me a cobbler with peaches or cherries sometimes. Rest of the time, it was sort of grim. But those days are gone. Never to be repeated. Funny how when I think back on it I remember more of the few good things I have had happen to me than the many bad things that have happened.

One thing I liked about the Minhs. They were patient with me. Mr. Minh told me he was not in a hurry. One thing you knew in the restaurant business was that bus boys and dishwashers come and go. So, I was happy. Me and Hector in the bread truck stopping in at a bunch of stores. Looking at the pretty girls and pulling off the road and drinking a Dos Equis from time to time. Like Hector said. Best to wash a hot dog down with a beer. And the Minhs. They let me come and go and when I showed up early in the mornings, Mr. Minh would give me the broom and then run back and bring the mop and the bucket back with a big smile on his bony face.

I would go back to the Bay some. I just liked the change but I got tired of the bums all around. And I did not want anyone thinking I was one of them. I never had to ask anybody for money. I still had more than seven hundred dollars because the Minhs had given me some money when they needed something done with one of their cars or at their house. Mainly, though, I was drifting. I liked sleeping up on the beach better than sleeping near the bay on the ground or on a park bench because there were people around.

People I did not care about being around and I did not want any of that bum mentality to become any part of me. I was free for the first time in a long time and I felt good and had energy and sure I liked to take a pop whenever a good time came about. Like on a day me and Hector was fixing to have us something to eat or when I dropped by a bar and I felt the need for a shot of bourbon but I could not stand the idea of getting up in the morning and having nothing to look forward to but some pills or a quart of Gallo burgundy.

I liked being able to walk where I wanted to. San Diego has parks all over the place. Mission Bay, San Diego Bay, and Balboa Park were the ones I found but I heard of a lot more. I mean big parks. Big enough for family groups to come out and play volleyball and stretch out wherever they wanted to. I would walk around the Mission Bay Park sometimes on Sunday or Saturday and watch the people and one Sunday there were some black folks having a picnic and I could smell the hamburgers cooking so just on a spur of the moment I walked up and said hey, this is nice but no one was friendly and I did not bother them.

Looking back, I guess it was stupid to even walk up, but in Mississippi if I had done that, someone would have said something nice to me and I could have sat down and eaten a hamburger and watched the children play. That's all the fuck I wanted. It is all the difference in the world. Your Southern blacks got a lot more class dealing with folks on the down and out than these other blacks we got scattered all over this country. Least ways, the ones I have seen.

Way it is, lots of blacks got this fuck you I made it now why haven't you and if you haven't don't expect anything from me. Well, I did not want anything from them except I thought it would be good to talk to some black people for a change. But fuck them. And their success. I was doing fine and I look back on it and that was the only thing happened to me since I been out of Parchman that I have even come close to regretting. Just the look some of them folks gave me when I walked up. I was clean, Not very stylish, but my clothes was clean and I had washed up that morning in the Minhs so it was just I was poor and getting old. That was what they could not take, I guess. Soul Brothers my ass.

I remember I walked on off and no one said anything and when I got back to the Beach the sun was almost down and the water was gray and a wind was blowing from the South and I did not know what that meant. Something else I needed to learn. A South wind. And little clouds way up high in a clear blue sky. This is the kind of thing my uncle down in Mississippi knew and I should have learned. Signs nature gives you as to the coming weather. He told me a lot of it but I forgot it and did not care while I was in prison.

One of the problems of being young is not learning things that could be useful. I remember Dump would watch the clouds and feel the wind and tell you whether it was just a shower coming or some big rain or a storm. I could do it most of the time by simply looking at the clouds, but there are some folks got a real knack for the weather. Telling you what is coming and why.

I remember walking out of the park that day and heading on back to the beach. I wondered if I needed to be in Mississippi again. I mean for the long run. It was just a thought that came to me and I thought about it but I could not see a way for me to live back there. So the way to go was to make the best of what I could here. Took me about twenty steps walking back to the beach to figure that one out.

After that day in the park, I went on the route up the PCH with Hector Reyna the next day and when I told him he got real serious which is not the usual thing for Hector and he told me that was the way things were nowadays. Crime and fragile family relationships was what was doing it. He told me had a brother name of Luis who he played with all the way up through grade school. Luis being a year younger and then Luis still his main friend all the way up through high school but Luis went in the Marines and married this scrawny Anglo bitch from back east that analyzed everything to death and now he and Luis never even talked because he could not stand to be in the same room with Ruth. Ruth the Anglo bitch that married Luis. Luis was out of the Marines now and owned a convenience store down in Florida and he had seen Luis and the Anglo bitch at his mother's funeral two years ago and his brother Luis had said to him Hector come on down to Florida and we will go fishing for a few days.

And Hector said he smiled and said sure knowing all the time he would not go because of Ruth the scrawny-assed Anglo bitch who had given Luis only the two daughters and no sons. Sons he knew Luis wanted and he had told Hector she said after two she was through having kids like Luis had no say in it and she could not even cook anything. Luis did most of the cooking and she was an accountant and Luis said she was good in her own way but Hector said he could not handle her and his own wife had told him he was wrong but time was going on and he had not been to see Luis and he guessed he should.

The rest of the day was quiet and Hector did not even notice the twins in the grocery store. Blond with big breasts and just short of fifty. I wished I could talk to them. Still friends and doing stuff all these years. I did not bother Hector about the twins because I could tell he was thinking about his brother, Luis, and I started to tell him what the fuck, just get on a plane and go to Florida and catch some fish and tell some stories and maybe go see the Rays since Luis lived near Tampa but I shut the fuck up.

One thing you learn in Parchman. When to shut the fuck up. I figured Hector would wind up doing it because he was smart and I could not see him letting some bony assed white woman screw his life up. One day, had to been on a Tuesday, Hector let me out near the Minhs and gave me my ten dollars and I stopped by the Minhs and went in the back door and Mr. Minh was in the kitchen and I asked if could clean up and then come in the front door and eat and he laughed and said yes. I went in the employee's bathroom and cleaned up. Mr. Minh let me keep my bag in his store room and that way I could do what I wanted during the day and come on back at night and get it and go to the beach without having to lug it all over everywhere with me.

I walked around the building and came out to the front door. There were some tables out front but no one was sitting in them because the wind had started blowing hard out of the West and I did not notice it at the time. I walked in and ordered the shrimp wonton soup, an egg roll, and the special fried rice, which had onions, shrimp, beef, pork, and chicken in it. I drank iced tea and when I was through eating I drank coffee for a while and thought about Hector and his brother, Luis. I wished that I had had a brother to grow up with.

I got up and paid and left through the back with my duffel bag and sleeping bag over my shoulder. I walked a few blocks and turned into a bar and sat and watched Sports Center and drank a shot of bourbon. When I left, the rain had not started but I could hear it out on the Ocean and you could smell it right there in the front door of the bar. I knew there was some rain and maybe a storm coming so I stopped at a little store and bought me a pint of tequila. Might as well drink a little and watch the storm come in.

CHAPTER NINE
THE STORM

I walked south through the rising wind and saw a pier off in the distance. It would have made sense to have camped under the pier and rode the coming storm out. But I was afraid I would not be able to see the whole storm from under the pier. When I had been in Parchman, I loved storms. I would sit in the doorway to the maintenance shed and watch the lightning and the rain and listen to the thunder crashing. I could always walk under the pier later tonight and play it safe.

I found a few pieces of driftwood and went to a place on the sea wall and pushed my bag behind me after getting a couple of matches out of a pocket in the duffel. I had some little twigs and a couple of sheets of paper I had picked up on the beach and I started a small fire with the second match I used and I was busting the driftwood up into smaller pieces when the first rain came up the beach and passed over me and headed east over Mission Bay.

The surf was not very high yet and you could still see boats in the water but most of them were going parallel to the shore. Like they was headed to a place to tie up or anchor to ride the storm out. I popped open the tequila and took a slow pull. It was warm in my throat and stomach. I could see some low black clouds coming hard with rain falling beneath them. It wasn't even midnight yet and the ocean was getting empty. There was one big liner you could see way out in the water. Red and blue lights flashed off the hull. A bunch of swells going down to Cabo. Buy some trinkets and eat some fish in Mazatlan and Puerto Vallarta then go to Acapulco and watch the cliff divers. Maybe go all the way down to the Canal and cross over and sail on back to Miami Beach.

But tonight it would be rough seas and drinks at the bar for the swells. They were heading right into the storm. The wind coming up at an odd angle from the south and west. I thought about the bums down on the Bay near Seaport Village. All of them living for a drink or a pill or a hit of some kind from some drug and here I was just sitting and enjoying the night with a small fire and a pint of tequila that I knew I would finish before I went to sleep.

Something had to change soon. I could always work a deal with the Minhs. Sleep in the back of the restaurant and work in the restaurant and do handyman work around their house and fix their cars. But maybe something better would come along. Mr. Minh was not crowding me and I was liking being able to do what I wanted to without no one hassling me. I looked around. All up and down the beach for as far as I could see there were no birds squawking and diving for food or walking along looking for food on the beach. They were gone. Probably laying up in some trees riding the storm out.

A patrol boat came by heading south. One man at the back steering and another one with field glasses looking at the beach. They did not notice me or if they did they did not care. They were probably going on in for the night. The hull of the boat was slapping down hard on the water and it looked like it was running wide open. The wind was picking up and bringing that salty smell off the water. The rain was cold and steady but I had my sleeping bag pulled up over my head and I was protecting my little fire with part of the sleeping bag and my bag was against the seawall.

After an hour or so, I could not see the lights off the big liner anymore and it started getting a lot darker and the rain picked up as the wind got stronger and stronger. Soon, I gave up on the fire and pulled the bag tight against my body and enjoyed the lightning way off shore to the south and the thunder sounding loud and deep off in the distance. Everything was gray and black. No more boats came by and I kept looking off into the south and west to see if there was a sign to show me the storm was fixing to quit. But it kept rolling in and I took a long pull off my bottle and soon I was thinking about things way back in my life. Things I had thought were forgotten but it looks like your memory never leaves you. My past came thundering into my mind just like this storm.

First thing I could remember was when my mother and a man with a big green coat and a big brown pimp hat bought me up to Hardaman County., His name was Odell and he come down from Milwaukee to see his folks and he and my momma must have took up together real fast because there she was. Going with him and not knowing him for much over a month. Odell had gold in his teeth and was a big man with a deep voice. It was the summer before I was to start to school. Odell never talked to me but I remember him telling my mother that as soon as they had some money they would send for me and bring me up to Milwaukee. We had been living in a little town in the Delta. Ruleville. Not much there and my mother worked a lot at some white folks house. Cleaning and washing and cooking and I guess she got tired of it because she told me she could make more money in Milwaukee and if that did not work out she could go to Detroit and get a job on the line at some automobile plant. Odell would work it out for her.

Odell, the big man with the big hat, had an old banged up green Oldsmobile 98 that would run and run hard, What I remembered is we passed through Hardaman and I saw a hamburger joint and I asked my mother if we could stop and Odell made a turn and parked and went inside and came back out with some fries and hamburgers all wrapped in wax paper and a bottle Coke for me and Miller High Lifes for my mother and him. It took a long time to find my Uncle's place and when we did, we went up a long gravel road and there was a house sitting up on a little rise that was black dark. No lights on at all and it was still not ten o'clock my mother said.

When the Oldsmobile got in the yard a little yellow light came on and my Uncle Leon came out on the porch of the old country house I was to live in until Sheriff Rainey drove out that Saturday morning and took me on into Hardaman to answer for killing Billy Ray Starnes. My mind jumped on back to that first night and I took a real small pull on the tequila and breathed in deep and smelled the Pacific Ocean right there on top of me. The waves getting bigger and crashing harder. I could hear windows rattling and the wind whipping around the buildings behind me and the seawall. I looked for as far as I could see both ways and there were no lights on the water. My mind drifted back to when my mother and I walked up on the porch and Uncle Leon was standing just outside the screen door looking out at us.

My mother said she wanted Uncle Leon to take care of me for just a little while. She said she had some papers in my suitcase that showed it was time for me to go to school. Uncle Leon was a tall and rangy man with brown eyes sunk back in his head. He lived alone. His wife had died a few years back and his kids was all grown and moved off. Mother said she wanted to get settled in Milwaukee and she would send some money as soon as she could. Odell was in the car and I remembered the deep growl of the big Detroit engine idling in the yard while we was on the porch.

Uncle Leon did not say much. He took my bag and asked if Mother wanted to stay the night and she said no because they could make Memphis by midnight and then St. Louis before daybreak and they were going to rest there for a day at a friend of Odell's and when she said that Uncle Leon kind of smirked and said something to himself that I could not hear and it was mighty quiet on the porch for a few minutes and I could hear a whippoorwill way off in the woods behind the house.

Finally, Uncle Leon said come on in the house boy and we walked in and he never said anything else to my mother and he left her on the porch and she did not come inside and hug me or give me some money or anything nice like that. I looked back through a window in the living room and the last I saw of my mother was when Odell was turning around in the yard to leave and my mother was sitting in the front seat looking back at the house and I waved out the window but she must have not seen me because she never waved back.

There was a little single bed in a side room of the old farm house and Uncle Leon told me to help him make the bed up and when we had tucked a sheet in and put a case on a little pillow, he gave me a nice quilt and he told me I was to mind him and respect his house and his property and help him around the place. He said you are never too young to learn to work and he meant it and he did not have a lot of rules. He got a lot of work done and never was I to see him in a hurry. He was not slow. Just steady. He showed me the barn out behind the house. I could barely see it in the dark and he told me that was where he kept an old horse he should have sold years ago and a red Farmall tractor he used to farm his land.

When school started he carried me up to the school and showed them my birth certificate and left me in a room with a bunch of other kids. My teacher put me on the bus that afternoon and I stayed in school till I was ready to work full time and Uncle Leon and I never had a big fight or much of a cross word. I tried to do what he told me to and he was patient and when I took the fuel filter off the tractor and cleaned it up one day when I was ten years old, he said he thought I was somebody who could learn about motors and I said it looked like fun and from then on when something needed working on, I would do it while he told me what to take off and when to put it back on and what screw to tighten and why and which one to loosen and why and then when I joined the National Guard and went down to Camp Shelby down near Hattiesburg that was the first time we was apart for more than a night for all those many years.

My Guard unit was at Camp Shelby for a month and there was a sergeant there from some place down near Mendenhall that showed me a lot of things about tools and listening to an engine and when I came back I started working on other people's cars and trucks when I could and I got enough spending money to buy me a used red Ford 150 truck and things was going along real good and I was still in my twenties and one day I had been to Hardaman all day and came home and Uncle Leon was not back from the fields and it was looking like rain so I thought maybe he was just getting all the plowing in he could and I did not think anything about it until it was almost dark and I said I might as well walk on down to the field and see if everything was alright and I got down to the field and I remember the smell of the freshly plowed red dirt and I could not see good because the sun had just crashed down behind the pines west of the field but I saw the tractor but I could not hear it and so I got scared and ran as hard as I could across the neatly plowed rows and he was slumped over the wheel and passed out and I got on the tractor and drove it on in to the barn with him on the seat and me behind him holding him and listening to his breathing and I was crying and I had not cried hardly any in my life and I took him on into the hospital in Hardaman and they sent to Tupelo for an ambulance and when it came they put an oxygen mask on his face and I followed the ambulance on in to the big red brick hospital in Tupelo and after a while a serious young white man in a white coat and wearing a blue and red tie came out and found me and told me Uncle Leon had had a heart attack and it was no wonder since he was almost eighty years old and it had been over ninety in the field. Hot even for Mississippi in the springtime.

I brought him on home a few weeks later and got a lady down the road to come in and do the cooking and I took care of the fields and worked on cars at night and we made it fine and he would tell me what needed to be done and the woman, her name was Miss Alma, was on social security and was lonely so she did not mind helping us. She could cook some food, clean the house, and sit on the porch with

Uncle Leon and read to him out of the National Geographic or the Reader's Digest and still be gone by the middle of the afternoon.

One day in the last dying days of the fall I was sitting out on the porch with Uncle Leon. He was rambling a little. He asked me not to judge my mother. He said she had sent money and he had put that money in the bank and I could have it. It was not much. Just a few hundred dollars and he said the last check she had sent had been drawed on a bank in Omaha, Nebraska and it had bounced and that had been around ten years ago and she had not written since but Uncle Leon said not to judge other people too hard. Sometimes things just would not work out right for people. Nothing they did was the right thing at the right time. He looked off at some jay birds fighting in a fig tree out by the front fence and was quiet for a while and then he said it looked like women with some schooling was making it big in the world but the women without it was stuck in hard times just like always.

Miss Alma had left some lemonade in the refrigerator and he was drinking that and I was drinking me a High Life and I had poured a little salt around the top of the can and the sun was starting to dip behind the trees and there was already some yellow and red in some low clouds back in the west. Uncle Leon rocked in his chair for a while and he told me I needed to carry him into Hardaman so he could give the clerk in the courthouse his will he had drawed up a few years back.

I took him into Hardaman the next day. It was a Friday and there was people all over town shopping and going in and out of the courthouse. All in a hurry. I wasn't in a hurry or even paying a lot of attention to time,

I parked my truck up close to the courthouse as I could and helped him up the courthouse steps and he gave the will to the clerk and asked if he owed anybody some money for filing it and the clerk asked for a filing fee and Uncle Leon reached for his old brown bill fold and counted the twenty seven dollar fee out for the clerk and then he asked for a receipt and he asked me to carry him to one of the cafes

on the square and he ate a hamburger and french fries and dipped the
fries in ketchup and smiled and had a big piece of lemon meringue pie
and when we were waiting for the check he looked at me and said
Robert Lee it is time for me to lay my hammer down and for you to
take over. Like the old people used to say it is time for me to cross
over to Jordan and I did not have an answer for that but I felt my
throat tighten and I was afraid I was going to cry right there in the café
but I didn't.

We got on home and was sitting on the porch and I told him we
was doing alright. The cotton was in the gin all baled up and I had put
the money in the bank just two weeks ago and the cribs was full of corn
and there was plenty of hay for the few cows we kept and he smiled
and said you are right but son I will not make it through a hard winter.
I just know that. It is my time. And I did not argue with him.

I just told him to get stronger and we would go rabbit hunting after
it got just a little colder and he did not answer me and I hoped we
would not have much of a winter, but right after Christmas everything
in the whole county froze up and we lost all our power and the schools
was closed just about the whole of January and I kept the house warm
with wood in the fire places as best I could and Miss Alma cooked up
some good food but it was no use. He walked slower and slower and
would get out of bed in the morning and put on his old brown sweater
and sit by the fireplace and tend to the fire all day and he would not
even go into town with me to get the groceries on Saturday but I
bought him a big piece of that lemon meringue pie he loved home
from the café in Hardaman and he ate it by the fire but he would not
read the newspapers I bought him. He said he was not studying the
world anymore.

One clear day, a friend of mine. One of the Hixon boys came up.
Johnny Hixon. My age, We had went to school together. He had a
couple of decent rabbit dogs. One was a brown and white beagle called
Toby and the other one was smaller than the beagle and he was just a

mixed breed dog Johnny called Stevie. Stevie did not have much of a nose but once Toby found the scent Stevie was on it and would stay on it. We killed three rabbits that day all down in the bottomland by the little sandy-banked creek that ran through our land and cut down to the river. Rainey Creek after the Sheriff's people way back before I was born. And Johnny Hixon let me bring two of them home with me even though he shot two and me one and he had the dogs and I went in the house and showed them to Uncle Leon.

I laid em out on the hearth and Uncle Leon smiled and the next day, Miss Alma fried them up and made some candied sweet potatoes and some rice with good rabbit gravy and we all three sat at the table in the kitchen and Uncle Leon looked like he was happy and he ate most of the food and I thought he was going to pull through. I told him about the hunt and we drank a shot of bourbon each in front of the fireplace after the sun went down and the cold started creeping in the house and Miss Alma had been gone for a while.

He told me to look in his dresser when he was gone because he had his Army uniform in there and he wanted to be buried in it and I told him I wasn't studying any burying because he was gonna help me in the spring and we was going to plow some new ground in a bottom we had let alone for a few years to let the soil come back to what it needed to be. He smiled at me and said he had been in World War Two and had seen General Patton and General Ike when he was in France after the invasion of Normandy Beach in 44 and he told me blacks did most of the heavy truck moving and loading of supplies and one day he was helping load a truck and here comes Patton riding hard down the muddy road in a jeep with new tires and he stopped and thanked all the black soldiers for helping and then jumped back in the jeep and the other black soldiers had stopped what they were doing and watched Patton and his jeep slide down the road and one of the boys from South Carolina said he would hate to see what would happen if the driver let that jeep slide off the road and they all laughed and got back to loading trucks.

He stopped talking for a few minutes, then got up and put a nice oak log on the fire and punched at the other logs and then sat down and in a few minutes he told me he saw Ike after they got to Berlin and for me not to ever believe there was a chance the Russians and us was going to fight. Everybody was bone tired and the Russians was out of food. He said a lot of the boys never came back home. They just went straight to LA or Detroit or New York or Kansas City or somewhere else. Away from all the little Southern towns and the hard farming life.

But he said he missed the place. That's what he called the farm. He got back home and farmed the land and raised a family and lost a wife and now he was ready to cross on over to Jordan and see all the boys he served with in the Big War and his wife and parents and friends. He talked like that for a long time that night and I helped him to bed and made sure the little gas heater in his room was putting out enough heat to keep him warm and I went back to the living room and sat down on the hearth and put logs on the fire and thought about my mother and I was worried for her and I saw what Uncle Leon was saying. She was weak and things just did not fall her way. She did not know how to handle a situation and I knew I was lucky because I had Uncle Leon to watch after me all these good years. I hoped she had found some part of a good life but I did not believe it because I think she would have called us or written or maybe even come to see us. I figured she might be on the bottle or worse or dead now.

From then on, he would talk about how it was going to be when he died and got to see all his friends again and I did not argue with him but I figured when you died, you died and that was the sorry ass end of it. He kept to the fire every day and Miss Alma and I started carrying his food into the living room and he stopped eating much and I asked the Doctor up in Hardaman that lived up the street to come and see him and this was Doctor Harrison Barksdale and he had just moved into Hardaman and married Nora Deen and he came by that same afternoon I called and sat in the living room with Uncle Leon and they talked for a long time and he came down to the barn and gave me a bottle of something and told me there was nothing he could do because Uncle Leon was doing what old people do sometimes and that was gradually pulling out of life and stopping eating and not moving and just waiting.

Doctor Barksdale said he did not know how to make someone want to live but for me to call if he got worse and we walked out of the cold barn on up to the house together and I followed him to his car and he asked me to come up on a Saturday soon if I had time to help him get his tractor going. I went on back in the house and sat with Uncle Leon by the fire and he told me about when he was young and went down to the State Fair in Jackson. This was when they had a separate day for black folks. One day out of seven we could go to the fair. Back then Uncle Leon said we was niggers or coloreds or nigras but he knew once they let us in the Army and we showed we could be good soldiers that things would change but he said he never thought he would see the day in Hardaman County when the black kids and the white kids played on the same playground and went to the same schools and studied in the same classes with the same books and teachers.

He told me back in those days you would leave Hardaman on Fair Day early in the morning and the way it was somebody would get a dollar from you for gas and let you ride and you would get to Jackson and ride down State Street and Capitol Street and see the big buildings and maybe stop by the big Sears store and buy something and circle back by the Governor's mansion set back in some pretty oak trees and then drive down a hill to the Fairgrounds.

And folks that worked in the fair talked funny and fast and was not kind to the black folks. Tried to rook them out of their money and charged them too much money for the rides but it was fun being there with black people and black people only from all over the state and he laughed and said that was when you saw the pretty girls walking up and down the midway in their fall dresses and sweaters and there was always at least one knife fight and it was always over a fellow drinking too much and trying to crowd in on somebody's woman.

Uncle Leon said when he got back from the Big War, he liked going to the Fair and one time he went and there was a tall pretty woman with gold in her teeth and a yellow dress with light blue bra and panties and red high heel shoes that took him out in the big parking lot and gave him some right in the back seat of his new black Buick for not much cash. He said he saved him some fair money every year and hung around the livestock barns early in the afternoon and then ate Philly Cheese Steak Sandwiches and big old German sausages in a bun with sauerkraut and mustard and drank lemonade that was so cold it made your teeth hurt and he would sit in the tent where he bought the food and watch the women stroll by and then he said they started letting the whites and blacks all go together and he did not like it as much then as when the blacks had it all to themselves one day.

He got his call to glory. Got it on a cold but clear February afternoon and Miss Alma and I were on the porch with him, I was telling him about a green Malibu I was going to fix for the Hixon up the road and I looked at him and he was gone and Miss Alma said Lewd, Lewd and I did not cry till he was buried in the church cemetery three days later and I was back home with a fire built in the fireplace and I had a plate of deviled eggs by my side and everyone from the church had left and I remember the food on the little table in the kitchen. Fried chicken, some pork chops, sweet potatoes and two pies and macaroni and cheese and deviled eggs and banana pudding with vanilla wafers all around the top of the bowl.

My mind drifted in and out from the storm right on top of me on out as far as I could see and the good things I had had back in

Hardaman County, Mississippi. I thought about the place I inherited and how I let it go just so I could make things right with Billy Ray Starnes. There was no call for him to do what he did in the way he did it. Louise was my wife. We was getting around to a ceremony and then things got wrong and she was gone and she was like my mother. No reason to ever expect her to stay there in Hardaman She was convinced there was a better life somewhere and somehow and maybe she found it and I know she left but I think in her mind she was going to come back and get Vera and make a good life for her just like my mother was intending to do the same for me years before Louise went off.

Billy Ray wanted some of Louise which I could not blame him for. Every man that ever saw her had to either want her or be bent the other way. She had a way about her that would get you unsettled and wanting her. Just the way she moved. Not cheap. Just a graceful glide that I ain't seen since and how she come to pick me out was just luck. That is all. She was below me in school by a few years and I remember us talking on the school bus when she was little and I would look after her and then when I was out of school I would see her up on the streets in Ackerman or at the little store at the crossroads down the road from where I lived and when she got up in high school she asked me to carry her to Tupelo to see a blues revue.

Percy Sledge, Jerry Butler, Fats Domino and some others all supposed to be there but when we got there it was just Jerry Butler and some locals they scared up and Louise said they was none of the real blues folks and she named off a bunch of real blues singers she liked like Mr. John Lee Hooker who I had seen on the same show as Chuck Berry and we went to a restaurant out by 78 Highway after the show and ate fried shrimp and she had a banana split and I drank me just one cold High Life and she fiddled with the radio dial on the way home and I kept my hands to myself and left her alone.

I got her home about two in the morning and Ann Stepter was out on the porch fighting mad and she came out to the car and said Robert Lee Whitfield, I done called Sheriff Rainey and he is coming to see you tomorrow and he said if he saw you tonight he would bring this girl on home and give you a good talking to. You wait till Leon hears about this and Louise was laughing and saying Grandma he is too shy to even try to kiss me and if I want to get kissed I guess I will have to have to hook up with one of them Graham boys in Hardaman County.

So then Ann swatted Louise on the butt and told her to not be studying no Graham boys and to get inside because she had a lot of peas to shell tomorrow and you could hear Louise laughing all the way through the front door and then Ann Stepter told me to get on home and thank you for not bothering this girl. She too young and too smart to be ruined so early when she does not know how to make any choices. So I drove on home and lay in bed till it was almost light thinking about Louise and how pretty she looked in her little white dress with blue lace on the sleeves and a shiny blue barrette in her hair.

So we went on and hung around together. She would call me and I would take her places and when I would go to pick her up Ann would always say You be a gentleman tonight Robert Lee and I was for a long time but when she out of high school and was working the summer before she was supposed to go to Jackson State on a scholarship we started doing it and once we started that was all we did and she got pregnant with Vera and stayed around Hardaman and had Vera in the hospital in Tupelo and she stayed with her momma and wanted to come and live with me and Uncle Leon but Vera was sick the first year and Louise did not know nothing about taking care of babies so she stayed with Ann and I was over there all the time and sometimes she and Vera stayed with me and Uncle Leon and when they did, Uncle Leon made over Vera and Louise and told Louise there was plenty of room and if things got crowded I could sleep in the barn and we were happy like that for over two years and then Louise got it in her head she wanted to go and see some of the world and she knew I was not game for that and she knew that Vera would be safe and be taken care of in a proper way as long as I was around and Ann was around.

Billy Ray Starnes run his mouth down at the joints on the river when you first come in the county that he was going to try him some dark meat and Louise was the one and he would try to talk to her when he saw her and she would just ignore him and I kept hearing from folks how he was using my wife's name in the gutter and I told him to shut up but he just sneered and laughed and then after Louise left he put it out all over the county that he had taken her to Memphis to catch a bus and she had given him a blowjob in a parking lot over behind the Peabody Hotel and I knew that was all wrong. Mardine took her to the bus station in Tupelo so when he asked for it in the Sunflower parking lot that day, I gave it all to him. More than he could take.

And when I was standing over him, I could hear him grunting a little bit and he was clutching his stomach where I had shot him and his feet were moving and I figured he was fixing to go into shock and for just a moment I remembered what Uncle Leon had told me about soldiers he had passed on the road that had been gut shot and how some of them would try to hold their guts in their bodies and that thought left me in just a moment and I stood over him and capped him and I was not sorry and I am not sorry as I sit here and look out at the night and the angry sea and feel the rain pelting me and the wind slashing across the water and the sand. Sorry is for somebody else at some other time.

I was sitting out on the porch the next morning when Sheriff Rainey came up the road driving real slow with no lights on and no backup and no deputy and he sat down beside me and put his glasses on and then took out a notepad and a pen from the inside of his coat and made no move to handcuff me and I think he understood the feeling I had about the whole thing because he never raised his voice to me and he started out by telling me how he had shot some Chinese soldiers years ago in Korea and he had no feeling about it now one way or the other. Not something he was proud of and certainly not something he was ashamed of and he talked to me about how folks who had never been put in a position to kill somebody could never understand and he knew there were cowards that poisoned people and some that used a knife and some that slipped up behind somebody and shot them or some that could not do it themselves so they hired it out and paid a half down before the killing and the rest after the killing but when you are in a war or a fight things is different so he did not want me to think he was judging me because he knew those Chinese boys he had shot and watched die in the snow had folks that wanted them to come home alive just like Billy Ray's folks was sorry he was dead.

He said all that and took his time telling it and then I got up and went in the house and came back with the thirty eight wrapped in a rag and gave it to him and he pulled this card out and handed it to me and I looked at it and I had seen it before up in a movie I had gone to in Corinth a few years back. He asked if I knew what it was and I said yes it was a Miranda card and he asked me to read it and when I was through he read it to me again and so I knew I did not have to talk and he put the card up and gave me a sheet of mimeographed paper that had the same words on it and I signed it and he put it back in his folder and told me how he did not know so many people could all be in the same parking lot and see a killing and get things so balled up and he told me I could give him the truth if I wanted to and I told him what happened and when he had it all written down he asked me why, why did I do it and I said that was between me and Billy Ray and he knew when he was laying on the ground with his feet jerking around and his hands over his guts why I did it and why I shot him the second time and the why was because that was the only way I could make sure it was really all evened up.

If they had got him to Tupelo one of those doctors in the hospital up there might have stopped all of that bleeding and he could have come on back and sicced his whole family on me and now it was over and there was no chance of him running his mouth again. And Sheriff Rainey asked me if he could put that in the statement and I said no. All that was between the two of us and what was on the paper was all I wanted said in court by me and now I did not even have to testify and I signed the paper and initialed the pages before the last page and we went on into Hardaman and when we was almost into town, he handcuffed me and got me into the jail real fast and I saw some of the Starnes trash and their friends across the street from the jail and they hollered at me and called me a murdering nigger and Sheriff Raines told them to shut up or he would put them in a cell down the hall from me.

I began to wonder about what time it was but I could not tell but after another hour or so the rain turned into a slow and steady drizzle and the sky lightened up a lot and I was warm and had some tequila in the pint bottle. Bout a third left and I was taking it down just a little at a time. I was warm. Warm inside and the wind quieted down and I was ready to wait for first light and I lay down on my bag and pulled the sleeping bag over me and held the tequila bottle up close to me and tried to drift off to sleep.

I got to thinking about the friends I had in my life. There was Johnny Hixon. He was still in Hardaman County. Slowly buying up small farms and running a lot of nice cattle and making some money off of growing and selling soy beans. That is what I was told about ten years ago by Rocky, A white boy from Hardaman County I run into at Parchman. He had lit out for the coast after high school and got into trouble down at a redneck bar in Pascagoula. A frame job he said. He had broke a guy's jaw and stomped his elbow to where it was all messed up so they sent him up to Parchman for three years. He told me Johnny was doing great and had some kids and grandkids strung out all over the country.

Johnny was the best friend I had. All the way through school. I quit school and Johnny kept going and was just finishing up at Jackson State when I got in trouble. He had a little brother name of Tommy Lee used to follow us when we went rabbit hunting and he would bring some old shoe strings and tie the dead rabbits feet together when we killed any and sling them over his shoulder. He was a little fat kid and Johnny would never stop and wait when Tommy Lee got tired. And Tommy Lee would keep on coming after he rested a little. His head would rock side to side as he followed us and Johnny would not let him carry a gun or even walk close to us.

Tommy Lee would be in his thirties now. I wonder if he ever got to the point he could go hunting with Johnny. Johnny probably taught him how to handle a shotgun. I never had no brothers or sisters. My early memories are of living with my mother in some little shack in the Delta and once we lived in a red and white little trailer down by a river somewhere up in Desoto County. I always will think of Hardaman County as my home. And I lost the farm Uncle Leon left me. I do not regret shooting Billy Ray Starnes. I regret losing the farm.

That old farmhouse with the tin roof and the long porch across the front was a nice place to live. The ceilings were high and the fireplace was warm in the winter when there was ice in the pond down the hill behind the house. Cedar trees in the side yards were thick enough to keep the wind down and there was always some blue jays or cardinals sitting on the branches. There was doves that watered late in the evening down at the pond. Quail was all around. Mocking birds would fight in the big oaks out in the front yard.

We never killed much of anything. Just some rabbits me and Johnny would scare up in the bottoms down near Rainey Creek. But Uncle Leon and I caught bream and white perch and catfish out of our pond and the ponds in the neighborhood. Dr. Barksdale had a big spring fed pond on his land and I showed him where to catch bass with minnows or crawdads.

That was another friend I had. Dr. Harrison Barksdale. He was something. A man of science. A doctor who knew every bone in a man's body and every ailment you could have and how to cure you and he could not keep his tractors or lawnmowers or cars or hay baler working. I was at his house most every Saturday fixing something and him standing there beside me in the barn handing me wrenches and asking me what and why I was doing something.

We baled hay, planted corn, pulled corn, stacked hay, wormed cows, went into town and bought feed, fixed fence, built a small pole tractor shed , fixed the roof on the old red barn he refused to tear down, painted the old barn, seined his pond and took out the trash fish and the stunted little bass and bream, cut firewood, picked blackberries and plums, gathered up figs and apples off the trees back behind his house, planted the garden, shelled peas one day when a sudden rain caught us in the middle of the afternoon, and drank some whiskey in the late afternoons. Dr. Barksdale knew his whiskey. Never drank any of that rank stuff at his place. He had Wild Turkey for when it was cold. Hard and raw. Jack Daniels for the soft Fall afternoons when we would sit in the den late and catch a football game. Nora Deen serving us ham sandwiches and potato chips while we watched the games.,Smooth whisky, and relaxing , that is what I like about Jack Daniels. Both whiskies straight up with some ice and water on the side.

Sometimes I would be up there almost the whole weekend. During football season, he would take a few trips and leave me with some jobs on his farm, He and Nora Deen never missed an LSU and Ole Miss game and usually they would leave a few days early when the game was in Baton Rouge and stay in a fancy hotel in New Orleans and then drive up to Baton Rouge for the game. He used to tell me that one thing I needed to do was go to New Orleans and eat shrimp and oysters and chase the food with champagne. When Ole Miss played at Oxford, he and Nora Deen would be out of the house before eight so they could get a decent place in the Grove. Nora Deen would come home from the game and tell me about all her sorority sisters and other friends she had known at Ole Miss and how they had fucked their lives up with abortions and divorces and pills and alcohol and some was just bored and trapped in their lives. She would tell me about them on Sunday after she got back from church and was feeding me and the Doc some lunch, usually tuna fish sandwiches with the bread crusts cut off, out on the front porch with the mocking birds or jay birds off fighting in the trees.

Doc, he would just smile that thin lipped smile of his and let Nora Deen rattle on and when she slowed down, he would say, now tell Robert Lee about the game and she would and she would always talk about how the coeds were not dressing as nice as when she was in school but that the cheerleaders were better trained and how she wished they had had cheerleader schools and competitions when she was in school.

And the Doc would say, now Robert Lee I want you to know I looked at every pretty girl at that ball game and I brought the prettiest girl to the game and left with her too and he would laugh and Nora Deen would say she was shore fighting hard to stay in the ring with all these young girls coming up and it was a pleasure to be married to a man that respected beauty the way the Doc did and then we would sit on the porch and let our lunch settle down and Nora Dean would fuss at us when we left and say supper would be at six and was I staying and I always said yes ma'am and we would always be a few minutes late and I would take Sunday supper with them and carry some home to Uncle Leon while he was alive.

When I was in jail, the Doc came to see me one time and I told him to just let things play out because I did what they said I did and I remember he put his hand on my right shoulder and squeezed it and called for the deputy and when he left he looked tired and he was bent over a little and his blue suit needed pressing. I wonder if he and Nora

Deen are still alive. Be nice to walk up on that porch again and hear them talk about New Orleans and the football games and maybe go down and drain the fuel tank on the old, stubborn tractor and bleed the lines out and clean the carburetor up and get it to running again. I know the Doc never would remember to burn all the gas out of his lawn mower and tractor when the winter was coming on without me being there to tell him.

Doc was forgetful about things. Always forgetting to put his tools up, change the oil in his tractor, leaving his chainsaw laying on the ground outside the barn, and where he laid his glasses down. But he was a friend. A hard to beat friend.

I took another long swallow out of the tequila bottle and raised it up and I could see it was almost gone so I said well, what the hell and finished it off and soon I was drifting off to sleep thinking how Dump Warren was my friend, too. Lots of time Dump would be grumpy. Not to me. We hardly talked. He would usually start the day by saying now Robert Lee you know what needs to be done so let's get started and me and him would work side by side or close by each other for most of the day. Every day and some days when it was slack and that was not many. Usually in the real cold months. Then we would talk and I asked him one time why he never drove on up to Oxford and watched the games since he had been a good player and there would some friends there for him to see and he looked off and smiled and said he never felt at home at Ole Miss because he came from poor stock and most of the fellows on his team got caught up in that drinking and fraternity life and he never had enough money to buy that many nice clothes and he had trouble dancing and he was scared of drinking and he did not really know how to act at fraternity and sorority parties, so he came home a lot on Friday afternoons when the season was over and helping his daddy around the place was fun to him and sitting around on Saturday night and Sunday eating his mother's cooking was just fine with him.

No way I saw it playing out nice and easy for Dump. Just no way. Not a chance of him meeting a nice woman, Especially with him just about spending his whole time at Parchman in that shed or at home fixing up his place. I bet he never will build that house back up. Probably just live there in that old trailer. I wondered how it would be if I went back. Back to Mississippi with some money in my pockets. Nobody would know me. Maybe see my daughter the doctor. But for now I was content. Sitting and watching the first light of a new day. The light not bright but just a soft and gray early morning light. The sun nowhere to be seen.

I went on up to the White Lotus around eight in the morning. Mr. Minh let me in the back door. He was moving slow and did not look at me. I grabbed up the broom and dustpan and started cleaning. Mrs. Minh was at the cash register talking on the phone. She turned and I could see she had been crying and she looked scared. Her eyes darting around and swollen up.

I didn't let on anything was different and I tried not to look at either one of them. Mr. Minh was talking to his wife in a loud and nervous voice when I had everything straightened up and I went in the back and got the mop and bucket and filled it with hot water and put some soap in it and came out and mopped the floor in long, patient strokes. When I put the mop up and squeezed out the mop, they was still talking loud at each other. He was sitting down behind the cash register with his head in his hands and she was in the doorway looking out at the early morning traffic.

Usually when I got through, Mr. Minh and I would sit in the back in the kitchen and he would bring me some good hot food. He forgot about all of that so I just shut the back door and took my stuff with me and went back to the beach. I wondered if I would ever find a place out here where I would belong. It was getting close to Christmas and I wanted it to be over. Just like in prison. I knew it would not be anything that special so I would just get through it and go on with life.

No different this year even if I was a free black man.

The next day when I went in to clean up, Mr. and Mrs. Minh made over me like I was something special. They told me they were sorry and I said it was nothing and I could tell they was busy talking about something so I had just eased on out and Mrs. Minh dropped her head a little and then went on back to the front of the restaurant and started straightening things out on the tables and setting the silver and napkins out.

When I had things all cleaned up, Mr. Minh had some hot chicken soup set out for me at the little table in the back. It had a lot of that bok choy and big pieces of white meat in it and some onions and when I was through with that, he brought me a plate of brown rice with half a duck laid on top. Lots of spices on the duck. When I was almost through he told me Tommy had married an Anglo girl. A blonde they thought was already pregnant. They had went to Vegas and tied the knot and Tommy had not told them till it was a done deal and she was moved into Tommy's house up near La Jolla.

Mr. Minh said he could live with it alright but his wife did not like the idea of a quick marriage and did not like the idea of her already being pregnant. Mr. Minh said Tommy's wife was quiet and restrained and he could see why Tommy would like her but he was hearing nothing but bad things from his wife. Tommy's wife was just learning to cook and her parents were retired military living in Florida on something Tommy's wife called the Redneck Riviera.

I asked if Tommy's wife had a name and Mr. Minh said it was Beth and I said that was a nice name and for some reason that was funny to Mr. Minh and he sounded the name out a couple of times and we laughed and he told me that after February First the weather got better and by April every day was beautiful and he would welcome the good weather this year.

When I left the restaurant that day, you could feel a soft, cool breeze from the south. The birds were back on the beach and in the air looking for food and the sea was almost calm,I spent the rest of the day walking on the beach and watching the birds and the boats and the gray sky and the blue water as it lapped at my feet as I walked south and thought about Beth and Tommy and the new baby coming in a few months. Nice to think about other people and their predicaments sometimes. Nice to wonder how it will all shake out for the Minhs. And I thought about that soup and that half a duck. The duck was cooked just right. The meat was tender but the skin had some crackle to it and it had some chili spice on it. I could have eaten another one but I knew better than to ask.

There wasn't much sun out but when the sunset, it left behind a lot of orange and red on the horizon. I stood out on the beach and watched the orange and red horizon and the dark blue water and the white surf and listened to the surf break on the beach until it was completely dark. The only sound was the heavy surf breaking on the beach. Enough company for me any night.

CHAPTER TEN
MARCI

Robert Lee Whitfield - One day after Christmas and just right before New Year I was walking up on Fifth Street in the Gas Lamp District. I was down to about six hundred dollars but I was not worried. I knew Mr. Minh had a job waiting with my name on it. Low wages and lots of good free food and no strain and right on Mission Beach. I was not studying any of that. It was around ten o'clock in the morning and I was just walking and enjoying the sunlight and the little breeze that came up the hill from the Ocean,

I walked past the Blue Point, a nice seafood place, in the Gas lamp. I hoped someday to have enough money to go in there and sit at the bar and eat raw oysters and drink a tequila shot or two and watch the world go by. I had seen some fine looking women coming into and leaving the Blue Point. I was wearing some nice pressed khaki slacks and a blue and green island shirt with parrots on it that Mrs. Minh found for me at Goodwill. I was also sporting some decent black loafers and a genuine Panama Hat someone had left in the White Lotus. Not too bad for a fellow who lived on the beach at night and caught rides with deliverymen and stashed his whole belongings in a closet in the White Lotus when he was off the beach.

There was a sign in a window of the business right next door to the Blue Point that said Help Wanted. I had been in about fifty places looking for jobs not a fucking handout and it had always been the same deal. No permanent address. No California driver's license. No employment history. No phone. No references. No job. But I stepped back and looked the joint over anyway. It was a bar. A small red and green neon sign over the doorway said Marci's Beer Joint and Bar. Two large wooden doors were open and I could hear Sam and Dave blasting out "Hold on, I'm coming" from inside the bar. I walked in and saw a white woman with a cleaning rag in her hands.

She looked to be crowding forty. She wore her hair in a long black ponytail. She was wearing blue jeans and a blue Charger tee shirt. She was my height and her eyes were brown. She filled out her clothes in a nice easy way. She told me the bar opened at eleven but I could have a beer now if I would let her straighten up the place in peace.

I told her I was interested in a job and she asked me what could I do and I told her just about anything and she cocked her head at me and told me it was too early in the morning for her to put up with a smart ass and I told her my name and where I had come from and why I made the trip out here and she asked where I lived and I told her I slept on the beach most nights and she laughed and said she had always had bad judgment when it came to men and she would give me a chance because I had an honest face even if I had just got out of prison and besides there was no one else busting their ass to work in her bar so what the hell. She would give me a chance but for not to think she was some kind of a fool and she could fire me just as fast as she hired me. I didn't ask about money.

She came up to the bar and we sat down. Sam and Dave were off and Isaac Hayes was singing that long assed song about Phoenix. The sun was shining and there were no rain clouds in the sky. The breeze from the ocean was rustling some leaves on the trees on Fifth Avenue. A nice gentle, sunny morning. Temperature in the mid-sixties and me fixing to have a full time paying job.

She opened a pack of Marlboros and offered me one and I said no thanks and she said she smoked three a day at most and sometimes none. She lit her cigarette and told me how she and her ex-husband had bought this bar the year after 9-11. Him with the money and her the brains and elbow grease. He had lost interest in her and left her the bar and went to San Francisco to open a bookstore and coffee shop. The main concept behind the bar was to keep it simple. Food was limited to salted peanuts, ham sandwiches, hamburgers, and potato chips. I could hear the cook back in the kitchen scraping the grill clean.

She went behind the bar and showed me what she called the spirits. Jack Daniels Bourbon, Jim Beam Bourbon, two kinds of scotch, gin, and vodka, and about five kinds of Tequila. She stocked some bottled beer from local breweries. Mission Amber, Blonde and IPA. Karl Strauss Full Suit and Stone IPA. She also had Blue Moon, Dos Equis Amber, Negra Modelo, Corona, Alaskan Amber, Fat Tire, Sam Adams, Sierra Nevada Pale Ale, and Bud and Miller Light and regular Bud and Miller Highlife. She showed me how to pour the draft beer and told me not to worry with anything more complicated than bourbon and water or bourbon and coke.

She showed me how to run the credit cards and to figure the tax and she gave me a sheet with the prices of everything and by then it was eleven and in a few minutes the customers started in. I made it the whole day until we closed at two in the morning without any bad things happening and when she locked the doors we sat down and ate a ham sandwich and drank a bottle of Mission Amber and she broke out the cigarette pack again and looked at me and said I would do as long as I showed up on time and did not show up high or hungover or plain drunk.

She leaned her head back and closed her eyes and said twelve dollars an hour and we split the bar tips. The wait staff takes care of themselves. You do not split tips with them. Just me. Because I am back there with you serving the bar most of the time. I told her that was a deal and she asked me where I was going to sleep tonight and I told her I was going back to Mission Bay and sleep on the beach and I would be back by ten in the morning. My routine went on like that until the middle of January when we cleared a space out in the back of the store room behind the kitchen and she put a mattress and some bed linens down and I got my stuff from Mr. Minh one morning and moved on in. I had a bed on the floor, a few little shelves for my stuff and a metal rod to hang my clothes on. And cash. I was clearing up to five hundred a week and I had a day off. On Tuesdays.

She did not close on Mondays. She said there was Monday Night Football and a lot of college sports on TV Monday but Tuesday was just slow. So one Tuesday morning close to the first of February, I got up and cleaned up and went into the bar and Marci was sitting at a table with an adding machine and one of those hand held computer things working on the books. I asked her if she liked Asian food and she said yes. She was wearing a nice blue skirt and a white blouse and her hair was mighty pretty in the early morning light and there was a pleasant bulge in her blouse.

I told her I wanted to go see Mr. and Mrs. Minh and eat some lunch and walk on the beach and then go down on the bay and eat raw oysters and shrimp and crab cakes at Anthony's and I would buy if she would drive. Marci took a drag off her cigarette and did not say anything so I got up and went back in the kitchen and straightened up some. Marci came in the kitchen a few minutes later and told me we had a deal except for me not to think we were on a date and as far as she was concerned she would be happy not to ever get hooked up with a worthless man again. She told me to use worthless and man in the same sentence was a redundancy and I told her I knew what that was and she laughed and asked me to wait an hour and she went back into the bar and sat back down and wrote a few checks and then went upstairs to her place and I waited for her in the bar and watched ESPN. Commentators talking about Tom Coughlin and Bill Belichick since the Super Bowl was coming up soon.

Marci lived upstairs and had a nice and neat apartment. She said she was a minimalist in a lot of things. Furniture and clothes and jewelry being some. She had asked me to fix some things around her apartment and I had done it. Nothing much. A cranky light switch. A loose knob on her bedroom door and a window that would not open because the outside paint had sealed it shut. Not a hard job to be had. Nothing like a combine breaking down in a bean field at two in the morning and having to call Dump and then meet him in the field and try to get it going so as the beans would not be lost to the rain you knew was coming in just a few days.

I was doing fine. After cabs and the little bit of food I bought and the clothes I found at Goodwill, I was still bringing in five or six and sometimes seven or eight hundred cash dollars. I was thinking on getting a bank account and keeping my money there. Because I wasn't spending anything. Living off ham or bacon and eggs and store-bought biscuits for breakfast and ham sandwiches and hamburgers and potato chips and peanuts was fine with me. Sometimes Marci and I would eat a pizza at closing time.

The folks that came in the place was fine. Most of them white guys who just wanted some good beer and a sandwich with lots of meat on it. No dumb ass fools like Billy Ray Starnes. Sometimes a guy would get loud or slur his words and try to act tough but I would just tell them to keep it straight or move it down the street and that had worked so far. Lot of tourists would stop in and listen to the music and drink a beer and eat a sandwich before turning in at night. Last place they stopped. One guy said we had the best beer selection in the whole Gaslamp Quarter so I asked Marci about that and she laughed and said there were some more good places but none of them called themselves beer joints and played as good a music as she did. And served as good food as her.

In an hour or so Marci came down the stairs and walked into the bar. She smelled good and I could tell she had just washed her hair. A few strands were still wet and she was wearing some nice pressed blue jeans with a red leather belt and a white blouse with lace on the cuffs.

We locked up ,set the alarm, and went out the back door. Marci had a black Honda Accord. She drove us down to Mission Beach and we walked into the White Lotus just a few minutes after eleven and Mr. Minh came out of the kitchen and was laughing and I asked him what was funny and he said it was his wife and we all three sat down and he said something in Vietnamese to the kitchen and soon we were all three eating shrimp wonton soup and he asked Marci about business in the Gaslamp. I told him I was prepared to pay retail now and he laughed and told me his new daughter in law was nice.

She was shy and walked around the house barefoot and kept a smile on Tommy's face and was coming down to the restaurant and helping some on her own without wanting money and he and his wife were helping her learn to cook and she blushed a lot and he and his wife had talked about that and said that a wife that blushed and was shy and made Tommy smile must be the right one and she had asked them what they wanted to name the baby who they had found out was going to be a boy. She had told them she and Tommy would pick the baby's first name and they could pick his middle name. Now all his wife studied was buying baby stuff. Clothes, a bed for the baby's room, and, of course, toys. Toys for a baby still a few months away from being born. Something new to me.

We ate General Tao's chicken over white rice. It was spicy and I could tell Marci was having a good time. She told Mr. Minh she did not have his skills. Her beer joint had hamburgers, cheeseburgers, and ham sandwiches and that was it. She said if she kept things simple she could stay in control and not get overwhelmed. If the cook did not show up either she or I could cook and tend bar both. I was glad that had not happened yet. Our cook worked till midnight and we filled in after that but we were usually not too slammed so as not to able to handle the late night food orders.

After the meal, we drank some hot tea and Mr. Minh said Marci was right. Tuesday, not Monday, was his slowest day of the week.

Neither one of them could explain it. I asked for the check and Mr. Minh told Marci to call him and tell him when she was coming and he would have the spicy duck ready for us. We walked on the beach for a long time. When we finally turned around the sun was hanging low in the sky and the breeze was a little cold. Birds called off in the distance and Marci told me she was not gay but she was burnt out on men for now and it was something she had to work through.

We stopped and watched a young Mexican family packing everything up and Marci lit up a cigarette and took a long drag and I stayed quiet and listened to the Mexicans talking to each other in that rapid Spanish lingo I have a hard time picking up on. We walked on slowly. Nice to be able to set your own pace in life. At least for part of the time.

Dalton was her husband. He was a spoiled pretty boy. Marci's words. Spoiled by his parents and his teachers and everybody. Marci said he had a nice build and straight, pretty teeth and natural blonde hair and of course she had fell in love with him when she was in the tenth grade and he was a freshman at Cal-Riverside and he came back home to Oceanside and wooed and screwed her during the summer between his freshman and sophomore years. And then they had grown apart until she had finished college at San Diego State and they hooked up again and got married and she said she was so dumb. They bought the bar with some of his inheritance after his grandparents died and it had made good money from the start but she had trouble with Dalton going in and getting money and spending it on stupid stuff they did not need.

Dalton was a dreamer and could not keep focused on the daily needs of the bar. But he had a great personality and they were successful but not the way she wanted it to be. He stocked a lot of wine and tried to woo the upscale wine and martinis crowds. All sorts of expensive single malt scotch. Marci though their overhead was way too high and they began to bicker and after a few years he lost interest in her and the bar.

One day he told her they needed to talk and he got this real serious look on his face and began to tell Marci all these dopey things about her thwarting his journey towards self-realization and after a few minutes he said it was best for them to divorce and Marci told him to leave but not to expect to keep the bar and as soon as she left she changed the name of the bar from Dalton's to Marci's and sold the wine and expensive scotch and changed the menu to hamburgers, cheeseburgers, and ham sandwiches and stocked the best beers she could find. She hired waitresses from the local colleges and played the music she liked. Old Country, blues, and soul music. The classics from Sinatra and Dave Brubeck and Etta James and Louis Armstrong. Sheryl Crow and Bonnie Raitt were about as modern as she chose to be. And some Springsteen. She said he was timeless and had a great sax man.

Her clientele changed, her stress level went down, and she started loving living alone. She said she was happy and was having fun walking on the beach with me but for me not to get my hopes up because that feeling would not translate into an invitation to me to come up to her room and spend the night. We both laughed and I said darn or something stupid like that but the truth was I sure wanted to go up those stairs with her one night after work.

I asked her if I could have a tryout or audition and she laughed and said no, she was just not attracted to the idea of a man and all this time we were joking and laughing and then we walked in silence for a few minutes and she started telling me about how to open a bank account and how the bank would mail me a credit card within a few months and I could build my credit up that way and I told her that was nice but why did I need credit when I did not need anything except a new pair of pants or a shirt or some good shoes and she said it was always good to have. I asked her if she was going to stay in San Diego forever and she said Maui and I told her I had seen pictures of it and she said that was where she would retire to. Live on the beach and go snorkeling most days.

The sun was not all the way down when we got back to the car. We drove back to the bar and walked down to the waterfront on the bay. We were waiting to cross North Harbor Drive and go to Anthony's when the sun dipped down below the horizon. Orange and red clouds hung over the sea on the horizon and Marci put her left hand on my shoulder and her long fingers dug into me for just a moment and then we were jaywalking across the street.

We got into the bar in Anthony's at just the right time. It was quieting down as the after work crowd slowly left for the drive home. We got seats at a table right by the water and I drank a High Life and she had a mojito. We ate oysters on the half shell and shrimp scampi and crab cakes and watched the sailboats on the bay, I stopped at two beers and tried to talk her into taking a cab back but she wanted to walk and so we went all the way past the Midway and Seaport Village and cut up the long hill to the bar. There were not many people on the street and even The Blue Point seemed to be dragging.

We went in The Blue Point and I had a Jack Daniels and she drank a margarita on the rocks. When we went home to the bar, Marci flipped on a few lights behind the bar and we sipped some bourbon and listened to some real old country music. Gene Autry, Johnny Cash, Marty Robbins, Tex Ritter, Bob Wills , Earnest Tubb and Ray Price were the ones I remembered. There were others but I did not know them. The songs were mostly sad but they reminded me of when I was a boy and I would go to Hardaman on Saturday with Uncle Leon. We would walk around the square for a while. Seldom did we buy much. But we saw friends and talked and when you went into the hardware store or Western Auto, that was the music you heard.

We would go in the Sunflower store after we left the square and buy groceries. The butcher stayed in the back of the store behind the meat counter. He was a big man name of Rufus. He was a black man with that old fashioned marcelled hair. All shiny and wavy., He never had but one expression on his face. The expression that told you he was listening to you and wanted you to tell him what you wanted in clear tones. Least that is the way I saw it. Rufus would see Uncle Leon and even if he was waiting on a white lady he would holler out. Leon, I got the pork chops cut just the way you like em. Thin for breakfast and thick for dinner. And all the time, that proud soul music I liked coming through his little radio he kept behind his scales.

I told Marci all of this and she listened and when I was through she said that sounds like a hard place to leave and I dropped my head and I was missing Uncle Leon and the farm and I felt like some weak-assed fool And here he was dead all these years and a couple of drinks would bring back those memories. So I told her the rest. Talking low with my head down and her leaning over with her hand on my knees and me looking at a nice turquoise ring she was wearing. It was her right hand. I remember that and the hand never went up my leg like I willed it to but that was ok and when I got through telling her about killing Billy Ray Starnes and not being sorry about it she asked me if I ever thought about Louise and I told her just about every day.

She asked me what I felt towards Louise and I said I loved the memories I had of her but that was all it was. Memories. They just never go away. But the only ones I have of Louise are good. But tonight I wasn't studying Louise. I was enjoying Marci. She went upstairs and took a shower and came back wearing a pair of cutoff blue jeans and a white tee shirt and I could see she had no bra on because I could see her nipples bulging., And those cut off blue jeans showed off her long legs right nice there in the shadows behind the bar. And best of all, she had let her hair down and it was streaming down her back. All wavy and black. Reaching almost down to her ass, but not quite. We was both drinking Jack Daniels now. Just a last shot apiece in a heavy shot glass. Sipping it and holding off the end of the night as long as we could,

I did not make a move on her. I was just waiting to see if anything would happen. I did not want to get put out on the street and lose my job. We were in the rainy period in San Diego. People said it would slacken up after Christmas. Rains came hard out of the South and West now.

Not every day, but a lot of days, you would see the sky blacken and the wind pick up and the rain would come in heavy sheets. The sky would get so black over the Pacific, and the wind would be so powerful and swift, it made you scared to be outside. It had not taken me long to get spoiled by a steady job, some money, a roof over my head, and a comfortable, warm bed. Even if the bed was in a storeroom. It was working out fine.

I wasn't about to make a move on Marci. Nice round, dark nipples almost coming through the fabric of that tee shirt and those long pretty legs and strong thighs right there across from me. We were both leaning on the bar and watching the folks out on Fifth and sipping our bourbon. Finally, she asked me if I would make sure all the doors was locked and for me to set the alarm and turn out the lights behind the bar. I set the alarm after I had checked the doors to be sure they was locked and I went back behind the bar and took up my glass to finish the last shot of the night and I heard her walking back into the bar and she stood at the end of the bar and looked at me and said Bring the bottle and come on upstairs.

When I got up stairs, I put the bottle and two fresh glasses on the dresser close to her bed and sat on the bed and waited on her to come out of the bathroom and when she came out, she had changed into a white, cotton gown with blue and red flowers embroidered across the top. It reached down almost to her knees and when she got to me, she reached down and pulled her gown over her head and by the time it hit the floor I was kissing her neck and she turned her face to me and held my face in her hands and said, I am ready for it now, we can fool around later and when I got out of my clothes she already had a hold of me and was guiding me onto the bed and she never let me go until I was inside of her and then she grabbed my ass and it was not long until we were through and she was lying on her back and I started to tell her I could have stretched it out for a lot longer but she was smiling and still breathing hard, deep breaths, so I shut up and went to the dresser and poured a little whisky in the shot glass and went on back to the bed.

The wind was blowing off the ocean and the windows was rattling and I said it was coming up a rain and she laughed and pulled me to her and my head was between her breasts and she asked me if I had anymore bullets in my gun and I said sure and we lay there quiet like for a few more minutes and then she got me hard and rolled on top and guided me in and this time I held off as long as I could and tried to keep it hard for her and she rolled over again and went in the shower and when she came back out, she had the pretty gown on and we got under the covers and slept for a long time.

I woke up when I heard some pounding on the back door and I looked out the window and it was one of the beer trucks and I hustled on down stairs and let them in and stayed and helped them stack the cases and change out the kegs and then I signed the bill after I checked to be sure we wasn't being shorted, I let the beer men out the back door and went in my room and changed and brushed my teeth and shaved and went back to the back door to let the cook and one of the busboys in and when I opened the front door right at eleven, I had not seen Marci.

She came on down right before twelve and she was wearing those cutoff blue jeans again with a pair of red high heels and a fresh white tee shirt. This time she had on a bra and the white straps were showing and her hair was in a ponytail again. By now there were some customers, two waitresses, the cook in the back, and a busboy in the bar. And me. Behind the bar. The place started to fill up after eleven thirty and we were both so busy, we never had a chance to say more than a few words to each other until after two o'clock. Lunch music had been the Eagles and some of those old, good Linda Ronstadt tunes.

When we were down to a few customers, she came down to my end of the bar and said, I want you to think about something. Think about it slow. I cleared room in a closet for you. No use in you staying down here when I got a nice flat screen and some loose joints and my bed and my shower and bathroom upstairs. Only thing, just roll with the flow. I do not know what this will turn out to be, but if you make that trip up my stairs tonight, I will assume you are not going to fuck things up. You can stay as long as you are a do right man. I heard that in a song. A do right man. So think about it. She had her right hand on my left shoulder and she moved it up to my chin and looked at me and kissed me, well barely, it was just a brush of her lips and then she walked away and I was loving the way she looked walking around the bar in her cutoff blue jeans and her red high heels and her long pretty pony tail.

She left around three o'clock and said she would be back by five when the crowd from the tall buildings started coming in. I was busy straightening up behind the bar and putting beer in the cooler when she got back and the night moved along fast. I can not say we was slammed. It was just a Wednesday night but folks came in steady and they seemed to be staying longer. Marci put on a CD she made up with Bob Dylan, Sheryl Crow, Johnny Cash , Ray Charles, and Allison Kraus all singing some fine songs. When the last customer was gone, me and the bus- boy and the dishwasher put all the chairs up on the table and the bar and I stood and watched as they mopped the floor.

When the cook had left, I checked everything and locked up and set the alarm. I did not have an awful lot of clothes. Marci had bought me a nice Nat Nast solid white dress shirt. I had bought me some things, but I got it all upstairs in two trips. When I got upstairs with the first load, Marci showed me a closet I could use. She was sitting in a nice brown leather chair reading a magazine called The Yorker that had pencil drawing on the front. Three pretty young girls in shorts and cut off tee shirts jogging through a park while leaves was falling off a tree and an old man was sitting on a park bench watching the girls jog on by.

So when I had my clothes straightened out and my shaving stuff in the bathroom, I sat on the bed and asked Marci if she was bossy. I said I should have told her that I could not handle much of that and she told me Dalton never said she was bossy but he used fancy words and phrases and they all come down to that. Yes I am bossy. Even in bed, I guess. I told her she could be the boss in bed if she wanted to and we laughed and she said we will see how it plays out. She pulled a loose joint out of her bedside table and lit it up. She offered me one but I said whisky or a Miller High Life was all I needed and she took a long, heavy hit off the joint and closed her eyes and held her head back.

The bottle of Jack Daniels was still on her dresser and I washed the glasses out and poured me a little in the bottom of my glass. There were two dark blue leather recliners in the little den and we sat there and I read the USA TODAY and she smoked most of her joint and then asked me would I think she was bossy if she asked me to turn the lights off and take her to bed and I said no and when I got to bed, the pretty blue gown she had been wearing was on the floor and she was turning and reaching for me.

And it kept getting better. She did not boss me around. She gave me more to do around the bar. I fired a bus boy and interviewed and hired his replacement. I ordered all the beer and checked it in and when a liquor rep came around it was me that told him what we needed, Marci did the paper work. I ran everything behind the bar. She spent more time walking around talking to the customers. More time getting her nails done and other stuff they do around beauty shops. I asked her not to cut her hair and she teased me and came home from the beauty shop with a bunch of pictures of hairstyles. A lot of that punk stuff. And when I told her I liked it long, she laughed but she kept it that away.

Tuesdays was our day. Lots of time we would get up and walk. Walk up the hill to the Zoo. Spend a lot of time there and walk on back to Little Italy and eat pasta. And one day we were eating in Little Italy at a trendy little restaurant and I told her Little Italy was not what I wanted it to be. I wanted it to be red and white checked table cloths and lots of waiters and waitresses with accents and lots of pasta items on the menu with red sauce and meat and it looked to me like it was just getting trendy and touristy. And she agreed.

Or we would walk down to the bay and watch the boats go by in the harbor and then walk on back and get her car and go to Mission Beach and eat lunch at the White Lotus with Mr. Minh, Then long walks on Mission Beach. Watching the gulls and the boats and the surf. I liked the gulls riding the air currents and Marci liked the old grumpy looking brown pelicans, Most times we would drive back to the harbor and watch the sunset and eat raw oysters and shrimp and crab cakes and drink Miller High Life or Mojitos or Margaritas at Anthony's after.

Sometimes we would go up to Pacific Beach and watch the surfers and then walk the beach, but we liked Mission Beach best. Maybe because of the White Lotus and Mr. Minh. La Jolla was alright but I never felt at ease there. Way too rich for me. But the beach and the seals on the wet dark rocks made it worth the trip.

We did not have any arguments. Nothing to fight about. Just fun. I could not have been happier. I had a checking account, a credit card I paid off each month in full, and a savings account. All things Marci showed me how to do. I liked the times we had after work. Up in her room, taking a shower together, then her helping me dry off and saying, out, out, let me have my bathroom and I would go into the den and read for a while and sip Jack Daniels and then she would make her entrance into the den. She had a black silk gown, a red cotton gown, a mint green gown and bras and panties to match all of them and she would put on this perfume that had a faint citrus smell. Like a lime. And when she came into the den, I always grabbed her and pulled her to me and kissed her on the neck and held her as tight as I could. We were happy.

It was a different kind of happiness from what I had with Louise. Louise was my first love and that is something that can not be replaced or duplicated. Me and Louise. Everything uncertain and complicated. But new. Now, this is different. I think, well, I know, I appreciate Marci more and show her more thought and consideration. With me and Louise, I had the farm to worry with. Uncle Leon took care of me for so long, and I had no idea about banks and loans and being a husband. I never saw my dad and I never saw Uncle Leon as a father and husband. That was all in the past when he took me to raise. All in the past.

So how can I hold anything against Louise for leaving when I was not strong? I never gave her a lot of choices or any real direction. I was worrying about making a living out of that farm and fixing cars. We were both young and she was bored to hell with Hardaman and the rest of the County and she knew I would not leave that old farm. I was tied to the land and truth is I miss it right now sitting here with Marci in beautiful San Diego, California.

Marci says the only places she has ever seen that will match San Diego are the little towns up the coast. Laguna Beach, Monterrey, Venice Beach, and Maui. She called Maui the last best place in Hawaii. We talked about training one of the waitresses to run the place for a week or so and going to Maui next January and watching the whales and going snorkeling off some island near Maui. She said Dalton had carried her there and even he could not ruin the trip.

So, I was settling in. enjoying the days and nights with Marci. I gave Marci two hundred dollars every Monday and she put it in my savings account. My regular check I never saw. It went right into my checking. The two hundred was from my tip money, Soon I was packing a wad of cash around and by the middle of February, I put another two grand in my savings. I liked my work. Mainly just pulling a stick and pouring a draft or opening a bottle of beer. Got to be where I had regular customers, People I was comfortable serving and talking to. Folks that was in your life from thirty minutes to two hours. And then out the door and gone.

After a while I stopped thinking much about my life back home in Mississippi. I was figuring on riding this good set up for as long as it lasted and I figured that would be a good while. Marci was a good woman. No way around that. If she had a bad side, I only saw it once and that was when this black woman came into the bar one slow Monday night. She was tall and her skin was a shade lighter than I like. And she was not what I would call pretty or even attractive. Too damn hard and business like. In her late twenties and already got a cold look about her. Anyway, after she sat down at the bar and I took her order, she asked me was I from Texas or Mississippi and I told her Mississippi and she laughed and said she had a trained ear and she was from Chicago but her parents were from Grenada, down in Mississippi.

We talked a little and she finished her Bud Light and left. Never to return, I guess. Marci came down to my end of the bar when she left and gave me a hard look and I thought she was going to say something, but she let some air out of her chest and then breathed in some more in a long breath like she was taking a drag off a joint then turned and went back to the cash register.

That night after we went upstairs, she took a long time in the bathroom and when she came out, she was wearing a white tee shirt and that was all. She came and sat in my lap and we held each other for a while and then she broke away and pulled an ottoman up and said she knew it was stupid but she was jealous of the black woman who came in. Marci said when the woman walked in the door something went off inside her and she was jealous. There was women in the bar all the time and most of them are nice. Specially after that first drink has gone down. And not nice in a sexual way. Just nice in a natural way. What a bar is supposed to do. Relax you after a rough day or for some folks after a rough or boring morning.

I told Marci I was glad she was jealous but there was no reason and she said it was because the woman was black and white women most all figured black women had something on the rest of the women in the world when it came to sex. So I told her she was wrong and she sighed and took her hair down and said how all this worrying and being jealous had made her tired. She called it negative energy. She took me by the hand and we went and sat down on the side of the bed and she pulled a joint out and fired it up. She took a long and deep drag and we sat and talked for a long time before we went to bed. She always was asking me questions about Hardaman County and I was asking her about beaches she had seen.

After about the second hit on a joint, Marci would be ready for me. One thing I liked is how she would stretch and pull her dress or nightgown or tee shirt or negligee up over her head. Way she did it all slow and easy always made me harder than an anvil. And then she would look at me with them big brown eyes and smile, then turn the lamp off, and come back to me and kiss me and then bite me on the chest and push me down on the bed and climb on top of my chest and move my hands up to her breasts and throw her head back. After that, things took care of themselves. Once I learned that when she took her top off, she was ready for the real thing. Not no fooling around necessary.

Everything I could want out of my life was right there for me and I was enjoying it. Every day. Best thing about Marci. She took me for what I was and never tried to change me other than upgrading my cheap ass wardrobe. Just about every week, she would buy me some little something. Nat Nast shirts, most of them black, some Island

Shirts she found at a thrift shop, nice pleated khakis, a couple of belts, socks, and some plain white shirts. And a watch. It was a silver watch with a silver and gold band, Had Citizen on the face.

Something around the bar would bother Marci, she would stay off to herself and work it out. Only thing, she liked for me to fire people. And hire people. She hated dealing with that. Once they was hired, Marci would spend all the time in the world just training them and encouraging them. Her rule was show up on time , leave your attitude at home, and things will work out fine. I was the one that told the new waitresses, bus boys, and the cook's helpers this. Me, I was getting used to Marci and I knew it was love, but we didn't talk about that part but I figured it would come up and I was hoping I would not say something stupid when it did.

March 29, this year, 2012, a little after two in the afternoon, it all changed. It was a Thursday and some of the lunch crowd was still hanging around and there was two nice white ladies down at the end of the bar with me. They wore business suits and were talking about business. They had been in a lot of times before, usually after work. Today, they both wanted a cheeseburger and a Fat Tire, which is a pretty good way to go. They told me they were going to make an afternoon of it here in the bar. One was in her twenties and she was wearing a beige suit and a blue blouse and a red scarf tied up at her throat like an ascot. The older one was close to fifty and she had on a black suit, a yellow blouse and an open collar. They was asking me about cars. The younger one told me she had a knock and a shimmy and she had been told I knew about cars. So I told her to bring it around early one morning and park it in the alley behind the bar , tell me the day before you come, and we can line it up. She liked that idea. She was afraid of getting ripped off by a shop. Lot of that going around, according to her.

I looked past the women at the bar and I saw this guy coming in. Sort of a grin on his face and I could tell he was some kind of law dog.

See, when a normal person walks in a bar, they look at things differently than a law dog. The law walks in, they looking for trouble. Looking to see who might do something stupid. Who is drunk. Who might be packing. Who is on the nod. Maybe somebody selling some dope at one of the booths or tables. They see all that.

This guy was over six foot tall, white, young, in his late twenties probably, and wearing some blue jeans and a white island shirt outside his pants. He wasn't carrying and he had no badge. He walked up to the bar and leaned across it and offered his right hand out to me. I let it stand there out in the open and he said, Mr. Robert Lee Whitfield, I am glad to see you. A friend of yours down at the White Lotus on Mission Beach told me you was working and living up here. My name is Ethan Cheatham. I am a private investigator from Memphis, Tennessee. I was sent to find you and deliver a letter to you and some photographs if you want them.

Marci was down by me now and the two nice white women at the bar was right there listening and pretending not to be watching us. I asked him if this was some kind of scam and he said there is no scam. I forgot to tell you. The letter is from your daughter, Dr. Vera Chaney. Her husband was one of the last ones killed in Iraq. He was in the National Guard Unit out of Yazoo County, Mississippi. She is raising two kids by herself and she wants you to come home if you feel it is the right thing to do. I do not know what is in the letter. She asked me not to read it. Just to find you and put it in your hand. I did look at the photographs. Some nice kids.

But she told me not to try to persuade you either way. You come back, fine. You don't, she will work through this phase in her life by herself. You got a strong daughter, I can tell you that, Mister Whitfield. A strong daughter. Way I plan to work it now that I found you is to go to the Zoo tomorrow and catch a plane out Saturday morning. You want to leave with me, come on. Meet me at the American desk at six, Plane leaves out at eight. Ticket is on us. I will drive you down to

Yazoo County. She lives on a farm and practices medicine up on the main street there in Yazoo City.

He handed me a brown folder. It had some pictures in it and an unsealed envelope with a letter in it. There was writing on the back of the pictures. Marci put her hand on my shoulder and said, Robert Lee, I got the bar. You go on upstairs and read the letter from your daughter and look at those pictures.

Marci said all that in a soft and gentle voice I had not heard from her ever before. My chest was thick and I was having trouble swallowing. The older woman at the bar said Robert Lee, shake the man's hand. And Marci said, "And tell him thank you."

I shook his hand and he grinned and asked Marci for a Fat Tire and a cheeseburger with no mayonnaise. I did not say thank you. I did not say anything. I had kept all the emotions I down in my heart while I was in prison. You got to if you want to make it out. And now I felt all of that for all those years, my feelings on losing Louise, losing Uncle Leon, spending all that time in Parchman, and losing touch with my only child, Vera, all of that was coming back in one big wad right between my chest and my mouth and I wanted to get upstairs.

So I didn't say thank you to Elton Cheatham. I just nodded at him and he smiled and said you bet and before I was at the end of the bar he was asking the two nice white women and Marci about the beaches.

I was upstairs before my chest stopped pounding. I sat down in my chair in the den and laid the brown folder down and then went into the kitchen and found a bottle of tequila and poured myself a shot , went back and sat down and tried breathing real deep an there was just a little moisture in the corner of each one of my eyes. I stared at the folder in my lap for a few minutes and then opened it up. It was time for me to step into the next part of my life.

CHAPTER ELEVEN
A DAUGHTER'S CALL FOR HELP

Robert Lee Whitfield- I sat in the leather chair for a few minutes before I picked up the letter and read it. It was written in my daughter Vera's own handwriting in black ink on some nice white paper that smelled of old roses. The way roses smell when they are about to fall off the stem when summer is ending. Here is what it said:

Dear Dad, I was so glad when I found out you were being released from Parchman. The plan was for me to be there with a friend of the family, Roscoe, and pick you up and bring you down to my home in Yazoo County.

My husband, Elton, was killed last year in Iraq by one of those roadside explosive devices. I am practicing medicine in Yazoo City. I have two children, a girl , age 7, named Ann and a boy, age 5, named Roscoe. I named my daughter after my grandmother Ann who raised me. As you know, she died a while back. Roscoe is named after my husband's childhood friend Big Roscoe helps look after me and the place as best he can but he has several businesses and has to give them his time.

We live on a farm that was passed down to Elton by his parents. It is not quite two thousand acres. It is mostly hills and hollows and good hardwood timber that I will never sell. But we have a nice seven-acre pond that is full of fish. There is also plenty of bottomland and meadows to sustain crops. The house is an old rambling, wooden structure with big shady porches in front and back. Oak and pecan trees give us plenty of shade during the summer months. Plenty of bedrooms in the house. Also, Elton had a big tool shed where he kept his tractor, his tools, and his Ford 150 and his hay baler and plows and a couple of gas generators we use if the power goes out. There is a big pole barn about a hundred yards behind the house with a red tin roof and cypress siding Big Roscoe and Elton trailered up from a sawmill near Mayersville in the Delta a few years ago.

You have your plans for your life, I know , but I need you.

I need you to come back and help me raise this boy. I am afraid I have lost him. He is not a bad child at all. He has withdrawn and his mind lives some place I can not find. I took him to a psychiatrist down in New Orleans and he told me not to crowd the boy and just try to wait him out. Easy to say and hard to do.

My grandmother Ann told me to never lose faith in you, Dad. And I haven't. We did not have much time together, I know that.

But I remember you taking me for long walks in the woods behind your house and showing me trees and telling me what kind they were and showing me a squirrel's nest. Roscoe needs that. Somebody to tie the land, the weather, the crops, the seasons, the flora and the fauna all together. Someone to show him an appreciation of farm life.

You knew all the names of the trees and bushes and birds and you would tell me all about the animals that lived around Hardaman County. You took me to the pond on your place once right before all the trouble started and we caught a nice catfish we brought home and you cooked it for Ann and me.

You skinned that fish out in the back yard and told me what all the organs were. Those early times we had together helped shape my curiosity about anatomy and plants and led me to being a doctor.

When Elton was here, Roscoe followed him all over the place. Getting into everything. Chasing chickens in the back yard. Throwing dirt clods at an old sow Elton kept up down near the barn. Picking plums and blackberries with his dad and bringing them home for me to make cobblers.

Now, he stays in his room after he does his chores and reads some. Dad, it is like he is waiting on something or somebody. I have already had men come around the office and call me. I refuse to go looking for a substitute father and husband. I am never going to leave this place. I had planned on settling down in Hardaman County on the home place. Ann left that to me and, also, Uncle Leon's old place you left to Ann before you went off to Parchman. I wanted to come see you and show you my report cards and pictures I had drawn for you but Grandma said you had told her no. You told her Parchman was no place for a child to come to. Didn't matter why.

What you can give my son is what you gave me in the few years I knew you. And more. You can teach him how to use a saw. What snakes to watch out for and which ones are good for the environment. How to fish. How to drive a nail and which hammer to use and why. Things a boy needs to know. And cars. When he gets older, you can help him understand how and why a car works and how to maintain one and how to fix one when it doesn't work right. You can take him out in the woods and show him the trees and name them for him and show him how to tell one tree from another. You can show him how to work with his hands.

Lot of things to do to keep the farm up. I would like to buy some yearlings and get him a horse and let him be in charge of keeping the fences up and managing the cows.

Not a lot. Just enough to keep him busy and learn some responsibility.

If you want to plant some crops, that would be fine. The tractor is one of those big old green John Deere.

And we have a garden tiller you can ride. That is something else. He and Elton used to get out in our garden in the summer and early fall and stay past dark some days. He likes to plant seeds and Elton cut the handle down on a hoe and Roscoe tried to help with the weeds. We grew Crowder and purple hull peas, Beefsteak tomatoes, okra, squash, a little field corn for roasting ears, bell peppers, and those long yellow peppers, butterbeans, and green beans. I asked Roscoe if he wanted a garden this year and he sort of got sad and nodded but he had no enthusiasm about the idea. Ann, my daughter, is strong. She is introspective and reads a lot and stays on the computer most of the time.

I keep the television off most of the time. Ann has been to my office a few times and she is interested in science so who knows what she will wind up doing. She is good for Roscoe but I think she and I are too protective of him. Somebody is going to have to show him how to throw and hit a baseball. Things you can do.

The way I see it, that psychiatrist is probably right. Roscoe is waiting on something. Something he does not know. Some direction. Something and that something might just be you. I want you to think it over and if you come, I want you to be dead sure and be committed to helping this boy grow into a man we can all be proud of. If you can not make that commitment, stay where you are and live your life the way you want to. The worst thing you can do is to come and then go away again. I won't have this boy hurt again like that.

So just do what you feel is best and remember that I love you and am proud to be the daughter of Robert Lee Whitfield.

Your loving daughter,

Vera Chaney

I read the letter twice and folded it back up and put it in the envelope. I thought on it a few minutes. I needed to ask Marci what flora and fauna meant. She would know. I looked at the pictures. Roscoe was slender with big eyes and long arms and legs for a boy his age. Ann looked a lot like her namesake. Roscoe was always smiling in the pictures taken before his father died. The Christmas pictures taken after his father was dead and buried showed a withdrawn and sad little boy.

I sat there for a while. I could hear the music from downstairs. The Eagles. Marci said she loved to listen to the Eagles in the middle of the afternoon. I shut my eyes and thought it through and when I was sure I knew what I was going to do, I thought about it some more and then I stopped thinking about the possibilities and choices I had and I went down stairs and told Marci we needed to talk and she left one of the waitresses in charge of the bar and came on upstairs with me and I let her read the letter and look at the pictures and when she was through she looked at me and asked me if I was going to go back with Elton Cheatham on Saturday and I told her no, I was leaving tomorrow.

I did not need no white boy to help me go home to my own daughter and she laughed and leaned over and kissed me and held me and I could fell a tear on her left cheek but she did not say anything else. She just held me tight for a long time. I asked her what flora and fauna were and she explained it to me in a sad, slow voice I had not heard from her before.

She stood up and went over to the computer and told me she was going to get me my airline ticket and print me out a boarding pass and I asked her what a boarding pass was and she asked me if I had ever ridden on an airplane before and I said no, I had never wanted to and she laughed again. I went downstairs and helped run the bar and after an hour or so, right when the crowd starting coming in, she came back down and told me it was all taken care of and I would leave in the morning around eight and she would have to get me to the airport before seven and for me not to worry because she would walk me through it. I asked how much I owed her for the ticket and she said we could settle up when I came back to see her. She told me the beaches were not going anywhere and Anthony's and the White Lotus and the pier and the seagulls and the old brown pelicans and the sea would all be here when I came back to see her and I told her I loved her right there in the bar and a couple of the customers pounded the bar and said nice stuff and we was both embarrassed and we went back to work but my mind, my heart, and my soul was already back in Mississippi with my daughter.

After we closed the bar, we went upstairs and packed my bags. She had bought me a nice suitcase and we filled it full with most of the clothes she had bought me and the ones I had that I had bought for myself plus the shirts and pants that Dump Warren had bought me. We sat on the edge of the bed and talked until it was almost sunup and she explained how the trip on the plane would work. I had two boarding passes. I would use one to get to Dallas and the other one would get me from Dallas to Memphis. The planes to Jackson, Mississippi were hard to schedule and kept me waiting in the Houston Airport for nine hours so Marci had me going to Memphis.

She told me about security and how it worked and how it all came about because of the 9/11 attacks. I went and took a shower and she came in behind me and we stood in the shower with the water running over us and held each other and kissed and then we went and dried off and made love for what I hoped was not the last time.

We finally went to bed with the idea of sleeping until five thirty but we wound up lying in bed and talking about all of the good times we had and how we was so busy having fun and working we never even had time for any fights and she told me I was doing the right thing, but I should come back and bring the two kids and my daughter, the Doctor, and we would go to the zoo and the beach and the harbor and over to Coronado Island and I told her I would do it and then the sun came up and we went down the long hill to North Harbor Drive and we were at the Airport before seven We went inside and since I just had the one bag, it did not take long to get through the security line. The folks were nice to me and I told one of the security people this was my first time to fly and she made sure I got everything out of my pockets and into the little containers and when I was through, I turned around and Marci was gone.

I had an aisle seat to Dallas and I slept most of the way once we was off the ground. Flying is ok, but I like to drive and see the country. In Dallas, I had just enough time to eat a barbecue brisket sandwich and drink a Miller High Life and then get in the line to board the plane. When the plane landed in Memphis, it was raining a hard, steady cold rain. It was Friday afternoon and the airport was full and I finally found the taxi stands and I asked the taxi driver to carry me to Third Street and then go South out of Memphis to the state line. I was going to hitch hike the rest of the way.

I had the letter Vera had written me and it had a rural address in Yazoo County but I figured if I got to Yazoo City, everybody would know where the lady Doctor lived. The rain was coming down real hard and when we got to the sign that said State Line of Mississippi, I asked the cab driver to let me out under an overpass so I could stay out of the rain until I could catch a ride. I paid the driver and he left and there I was, back in Mississippi again.

Highway 61 was three lanes going south and three coming back north into Memphis. It was Friday night and the southbound lanes were bumper to bumper in all three lanes. I could not understand why all those folks was leaving Memphis and going into Mississippi. It was just past six and the sun was starting to go down. Soon, there was no light except for the headlights of the fast, passing cars.

CHAPTER TWELEVE
DOWN TO YAZOO COUNTY
Robert Lee Whitfield

Friday Night. The rain was coming down hard. I stood under the overpass and watched the traffic going south on 61. It was coming down a long hill for as far as I could see. Most people had their headlights on as the sky was almost black even though it was not time for the sun to go down. I had a watch and I had set it in the Memphis Airport back to Mississippi time. It was not even six o'clock. I waited under the overpass till the sun had gone down and still, there was nobody slowing down to pick me up. It was past seven o'clock and dark and I was standing and waiting for a ride. No need to panic. One thing prison teaches you is to wait. Sometimes it is all you can do. The traffic had not slowed down and I could not figure that out. A few minutes passed and I saw flashing blue and red lights headed my way. When the big grey car saw me, he changed lanes and stopped in front of me. It was a Mississippi Highway Patrol car. One of those big Fords they like. A grey car with the map of the State of Mississippi and a Magnolia in the middle on the driver's door.

A tall, tan white man got out of the car. He was wearing one of those flat-brimmed gray hats they been wearing forever. His shirt was starched and his pants was creased and he had a big forty-five in a black holster on his hip. He looked to be in his late fifties or early sixties. He had big hands and he was slender and had a big Adam's apple. He stuck his hand out and grinned.

He said, "You are Robert Lee Whitfield. My name is Johnny Ray

Sykes and some say I am in charge of the North Mississippi Division of the Mississippi Highway Patrol. I live down in Clarksdale. Ever since you was released from Parchman, I have been getting calls from everyone from the Governor and some of his flunkies to your daughter, Dr. Vera Chaney and , of course, from the Delta Lawyer, Gorman Ballard."

I did not say a thing. It was his show. Man with a big forty-five on his hip always is head of the show. He picked my bag up and said, "Come on, I am taking you to Yazoo County if that is where you want to go. "

I nodded my head and started to get in the back seat and he laughed and said, "You a guest, Mr. Whitfield. Come on and sit up front. We got a long drive and you ain't done nothing wrong. Besides I do not want to get a crick in my neck while turning around and talking to you." He opened the front passenger door for me and I sat down and put my seat belt on. When we got back into traffic, he got on his radio and called in and told the dispatcher, he called her Miss Rose, he was heading on to Yazoo County and for her to call his wife and tell her that he would be late and to keep his supper warm for him but not to wait up because of the rain and the traffic.

I asked him about the traffic. Where could everybody be going? He said they were all going down to the Casinos in Tunica. He then told me how the Casinos all came into Mississippi in the nineties and now they was coming off some down times. All the big money had already been made. Selling off good cropland for a Casino, the construction costs, and the land speculation. That was all over. Nobody dumb enough to build another casino in this economy, so some people got caught holding the bag since they paid big, big money for land thinking there would be more casinos and other businesses being built. But that was not the way it worked out. The recession come and the gambling industry got stung like everybody else. Maybe not as bad, but bad enough to discourage any growth around Tunica.

All that Memphis money going down to the casinos at sixty-five miles an hour.

The traffic thinned down some and I could see some lights from the casinos. We kept on rolling through the dark, rainy night. Johnny Ray said he was against the casinos and all the trash that came with them but he said he was married to a smart woman and he listened to her and she said he was wrong. She said fools were going to act like fools no matter what the law was so why not get some tax money and some good shows and some high paying jobs out of it? He said he guessed she was right but then the world was changing too fast for him now. He told me he was lucky he got along with the last Governor and he had picked right again during the last election and the new Governor had left him alone and not made him fire anybody or hire any fools or dullards.

He asked me if I minded telling him where I had been and I told him San Diego and the Pacific Ocean and he laughed again and said he had gotten a memo from the old Governor back when I was let out of Parchman and he had put out an all-points bulletin to every law enforcement officer in Mississippi and Arkansas and Tennessee to be on the lookout for me. He said it was hardly a week went by since I left without him hearing something from somebody. He told me Gorman Ballard was doing fine but he had lost his wife a few years back and his kids had both moved off and were living their own lives. I asked him if he knew my daughter and he said no but he could find her place and take me home tonight without me having to show up all wet and tired.

We drove on to Clarksdale and he circled by the Courthouse and there was a two-story house right on the square with a light on in one of the back rooms. It was nigh onto nine o'clock. He stopped in front and said, "Come on in. I want your lawyer to see you and then maybe he will leave me alone for a few weeks."

We walked up to the front porch in a hurry because it was still raining. Not quite as hard as when I got under the overpass but still hard. Lucky, though, there was not much wind blowing. Johnny Ray tried the door and it opened and he said, come on, he is probably asleep back in his library. Sure enough, we walked into the library and there was just one little lamp on and he was asleep in his leather chair. He had a red leather bound book in his lap and I saw a cocktail glass with just a little brown liquid in the bottom. I figured it was bourbon.

Johnny Ray said, "Least you could do is wake your ass up and tell me thank you. Here he is, Mr. Robert Lee Whitfield, late of San Diego, California, and fixing to be a fine citizen of Yazoo County, Mississippi."

Gorman Ballard woke up and Johnny Ray started in on him again and Gorman stood up and he had a big smile on his face and he said, "Mr. Whitfield, welcome back to Mississippi. I hope you decide to make Yazoo County your home. You got a fine daughter waiting to see you." I could some age in his eyes and some sadness, too. But he was still the same. He had fell asleep with his blue dress shirt on and his nice blue suit pants on and freshly shined black wingtips and a red and yellow polka dotted bow tie. He had some gray in his hair now but he looked good. No weight on him to speak of. Still slender and fidgety.

He said, "Robert Lee, thank you for coming back. I will not call your daughter. I think she is due a happy surprise in her life. The best kind. And so few and far between. Give her my regards. Now what sort of detective work did you do to find him, Johnny Ray."

"The best kind of detective work there is, Lawyer Ballard. Luck. Works better than anything. I was in Memphis for one of those tiresome interagency meetings the Governor insists I go to and I stopped at Neely's afterwards and had a barbecue sandwich and came on down Third and when it turned to 61, I topped a hill and saw him standing there and the thought came to me that maybe it was Robert Lee Whitfield under that underpass and sure enough, it was."

There wasn't a lot more to say and we were all three tired so Gorman Ballard walked us to the door and we ran to the car and drove on South to Yazoo County through the dark and gloomy , rainy Delta Night. Johnny Ray Sykes talked some on his radio but usually the only noise was the big motor carrying us through the night. When we got to Yazoo City, he pulled up to the police station and went inside and got directions out to my daughter's place. When he got back in the car, he said it wasn't hard to find out where the only black doctor in the county lived. He laughed and headed the car north up 49. When we got to a little place he called Little Yazoo, he turned west on a narrow blacktop road. He told me it wasn't far and then he crossed the railroad bridge in Anding and in a few minutes took a right on a gravel road that wound up a dark hill.

At the top of the hill, a house sat back in some tall trees. There was a porch light on and a security light out front of the house. Johnny Ray pulled up in the driveway and stopped at the front steps and turned his rack of lights on and hit his siren once and told me to go on. I got out of the car and went up the front steps. I had one foot on the porch when another light came on right at the front door and then my daughter was out the door and had her arms around me and she was crying and saying Daddy over and over again and I held her tight and she kept on crying and she was shaking in her shoulders and I told myself be strong, be strong, and I did not cry but I kept holding her and I heard something go thump right behind me and I knew it was Johnny Ray Sykes leaving my bag on the porch and I meant to turn around and say thank you, sir but my daughter was still shaking and crying and there was a little girl in the doorway and she was looking at her mother and you could tell she did not know what to make of all of this. I heard the big Law car drive down the driveway to the long gravel road.

Ann said, " Momma, are you alright?" and Vera slowed down her crying and shaking and pulled Ann to her and said, "Why sure, I am alright. Sure I am." I knelt down and looked at Ann and said, "I am your grandfather. My name is Robert Lee Whitfield. That is what I want you to call me. Robert Lee."

Vera knelt down also, and she said, "Ann, this is my father, he is going to stay with us and help us." Ann smiled and looked at me and did not say anything right then. We started to walk in the house and I picked up my bag and Vera and Ann were standing in the door waiting for me. About five feet behind them in the dark hallway was Roscoe. He was small. He had good height alright, but he was frail and his eyes were nervous and scared. I went in the house and Vera had Roscoe by the hand and I knelt down and told him who I was and Vera told him I was her father and he looked at me and turned and walked back to his bedroom and shut the door.

From what Vera had said in her letter, I knew Roscoe was grieving hard over the death of his father. Hard not to understand his feelings given the facts Vera put in her letter. Vera said, "He is just confused and tired." I said I understood and I stepped back and looked at her. She was as tall as me and slender. You could see some stress in her face. But there was plenty of strength, too. Ann was like her mother. Just a smaller version. Ann asked me, "Mr. Robert Lee, are you hungry? We got some left over fried chicken and two pieces of lemon meringue pie left from supper."

I laughed and said, "You do not have to call me Mister. Robert Lee is fine. Just don't call me Grandpa or Gramps or any of those names. And yes, I am hungry."

I ate three pieces of good fried chicken and some green beans and I had been talking to Ann and Vera and had not noticed but Roscoe was standing over by the refrigerator listening to us talk and he was looking square at me. Ann got me a little plate and I ate a piece of the lemon meringue pie then I got up and went over and found a fork in a drawer and came back and sat down and gave the pie and the pie plate and fork to Roscoe and he said ' thank you' real low and came over and sat down by his mother and looked at her and she said , "go ahead and eat a piece of pie, son, go ahead and eat it."

Vera is a good-looking woman. She takes pride in her hair and the way she looks. Her cheekbones are high up on her face and her eyes are brown and bright and alert. She smiles easily but sadness will bull its way in sometimes. I was there to help keep some of that away.

When Roscoe finished the pie, Vera told them to go on to bed and Ann smiled at me and said "Good night, Robert Lee." And then she was gone. Down the hall to her room. Roscoe took the pie plate and his fork over to the sink and laid them up on the counter. Then he turned and went to his mother and said good night and looked at me and I could tell he was confused so I just told him good night and he left. I heard the door to his room close softly.

Vera still had on a skirt and blouse. She said she had not had time to change once she got home. She had put the kids to bed and fell asleep in the den reading yesterday's New York Times. We sat there in the kitchen and talked for a long time. I told her about San Diego, the Pacific Ocean , the gulls ,Mission Bay , the White Lotus and Mr. Minh and, finally, about Marci and the detective from Memphis bringing the letter and me catching the plane to Memphis and getting caught in the rain and being rescued by Johnny Ray Sykes.

I asked her about the farm. The land. What needed to be done and what she wanted from me." She said, "I left out some things in my letter. One thing I need is to have some adult conversation. With someone I can trust. Both for judgment and for discretion. I got friends at Church and friends at the Hospital. Other doctors, too. But I do not want my business out on the street. I say something in confidence and it gets out. I know this county and these people. Even with satellite TV, the major pastime is gossip. A doctor stands alone in a small community setting. You have to."

I said I understood and she drank some iced tea and said, "I left out some other things. Things about the garden. We had cantaloupes and watermelons. Two kinds of watermelons. The big round green ones and the long green and black striped kind. And cucumbers. Elton liked cucumbers in a vinegar and pepper brine. And I put up bread and butter pickles like Ann used to do."

"And you forgot radishes. And eggplants. You gently fry up some eggplant or slice it up and bake it with cheese and onions and tomatoes and you got yourself some good eating," I said.

"And I forgot onions. Little green onions and big white onions. We always gave away more food than we grew. One of Elton's pleasures."

We sat in the quiet of the kitchen and listened to the fading storm. There was some lightning and thunder off behind the barn. Flashes of silver and yellow across the black sky.

Vera said, "I take comfort in the rain. And the storms. Now that Elton is gone, I listen close to the sounds and smells that come with the rain. And the storms. Lightning and thunder. For some reason, they comfort me. The morning after a storm. I like to go outside and smell the land. The wetness makes for a fresh smell. A new beginning in an old world."

We sat there and just listened to the rain. Slacking off some. Almost no wind. The storm losing its force. Moving on east at a slow pace. I told Vera about the storm I sat through out on Mission Beach. I left out the part about the pint of tequila. I told her how I met Marci and I left out the parts about the sex and the loose joints. She liked the part about the zoo. I saw her eyes dart to something behind me and I looked and there Roscoe was. Standing in the door with a little blue blanket pulled up on his shoulders.

"They got lions and tigers and big old elephants in that zoo, Robert Lee?"

"They shore do and they got parrots and other birds. All sorts of colors. Red and yellow macaws and blue and yellow macaws. Macaw is a lot like a parrot. Your momma knows science. She can tell you the difference between a parrot and a macaw if there is one. They look alike to me and then they got these white birds with big yellow beaks. I forgot their names. Best thing is this zoo is only a few minutes from the Pacific Ocean. Sail boats and gulls diving for fish. And ugly old brown pelicans. I'll take you all someday. "

Vera said, "Now, Roscoe, go on back to bed. Plenty of time for talk tomorrow."

"OK. I'm going." He turned to leave and then turned back around to me and said, "You her daddy, for real?"

I said, "Yes, I am."

He looked at me and he did not say anything else but I knew the day was coming when I would have to tell him about my life and hope he would understand. Way off from now. Way off. I would face that day and I would tell him the truth. He turned around again and we heard his door close and the house was silent except for a gentle rain outside. The wind was picking up but the rain was slacking off and I knew sleep would come easy tonight.

Vera went and got some coffee going and then came back and sat down at the kitchen table. We sat in silence and waited on the coffee. She remembered I liked it black and strong and she took it the same way. She poured me some coffee in a heavy white mug. It was hot and it relaxed me. I looked at the big round clock on the wall. It was just a few minutes past two in the morning. Vera looked at me and smiled.

"Elton was a fascinating man. I was just getting used to him when the National Guard came and took him away. To a war I have never understood. Now, Afghanistan, I get it. But Iraq. We missed on that one. Big time. But enough of that. Me and Elton had talked it out. He agreed with me. The man read a lot and not like a lot of people, he could cut to the chase and come up with the right answer. He told me he had to go. Had to. He joined to serve and now it was his time. I worried about him. Even before he left."

Night before he left, we had a nice supper. Collards and chicken fried steak and rice and gravy and a coconut cake with yellow cake and white icing and lots of coconut all up in the icing. I made it for him the way Ann showed me years ago.

When we was through eating, he asked us to go into the den with him and he got down on his knees and he asked us all to get close to him. We did and then he said we were all strong because the four of us made a tight circle and as long as we stayed together and looked after each other, we would be alright. He told Ann to help me in the kitchen and around the house. He told Roscoe to quit chasing the chickens and to feed them first thing every day and last thing right before the sunset. He told Roscoe to feed the old brindle jersey cow and the mule and to stop aggravating his sister and not to be a strain on me while he was gone. They both said they would do as he said and they have. The next day I took him to Yazoo City and he stepped out of the car, gave me a kiss and went on in the armory. I never saw him alive again."

I didn't say anything. I knew she wanted to say more so I just shut up and looked at the black, steaming coffee in my white mug. The house was quiet. The wind had picked up and it rattled the windows some but the rain was gentle and steady now.

"So you see, Dad, where I am. The circle is broken. I need you to help me mend it and get it back strong. This is a mean-ass world. You know it better than me. I want these children to see the good of it. I need you for that. So many things you can help with. Teach the boy to respect and love the land. When Elton asked me to marry him, we were sitting out on the balcony of our room in the French Quarter in New Orleans. We had eaten dinner at Commander's Palace out in the Garden District and Elton had ordered some good French wine to go with our meal and we were in love. No way around it."

" He takes this ring, the one I am wearing now, out of his blazer pocket and says to me, 'I want you to marry me but you got to know I am already married. To the land. It can be our land. The trees, the hollows, the bottom land, the thickets, all of it. But you got to know. That land is part of me and I can not give it up or leave it ever.' And I said yes, but then in a few minutes I asked him to get me a satellite dish so I could watch the Discovery Channel and A and E and he laughed and I put aside my thoughts about coming back to Hardaman County and helping Dr. Barksdale. I turned my back on him after all he had done for me. I went back and told him and he laughed and said there was roads that went from Yazoo County to Hardaman County and he came on Saturdays or Sundays after I sat my practice up and helped me. So it all worked out. Till Elton went off to Iraq."

I did not know what to say for a while and all you could hear in the kitchen was the faint rattling of the windowpanes. I told her I would start getting things in shape tomorrow and she said thank you and told me to be patient with Roscoe. It was going to take time. A lot of time. For the second time she told me he had not laughed since his father died. Not a lot of crying and no whining. Just a withdrawal.

We got up to go check on the kids and then go to bed. Ann was asleep with the covers drawn up to her chin and a little teddy bear lying close by. We went into Roscoe's room. He was sitting in a chair, looking out the window at the slow rain and the distant lightning. He looked at us and smiled. Vera picked him up and put him to bed and told him to close his eyes and rest and sleep would come soon. We left the room and Vera took me to the guestroom. I started to take off my shoes and Vera kissed me on the forehead and said she was glad I was back and she turned and left the room. Well, here I was. Back in Mississippi. Maybe this time I could get it right.

CHAPTER THIRTEEN
VERA'S FARM
ROBERT LEE WHITFIELD
SATURDAY, MARCH 31, 2012

Yazoo County, Mississippi. I got up with the sun the next morning. The house was silent and I went in the kitchen and the boy was sitting at the table cutting a banana up with an old brown ,wooden handled, kitchen knife. The banana was on the kitchen table right by a big box of corn flakes. I sat down opposite him and asked him, "Roscoe, you got some time this morning? Some time to help me?"

He nodded his head and said, "I guess so."

I went to the refrigerator and found some eggs and bacon and Roscoe showed me where the pans and skillets were. He waited to pour the milk on his cereal until I sat down across from him with my eggs and bacon. He got up and took some white bread out of a silver breadbox on the counter and put two pieces in a toaster and fixed them for me. He went in the refrigerator and got a white butter dish out and put it next to my plate. I had started some coffee but it was not ready and I was drinking a glass of iced tea.

I waited him out and ate in silence until he asked, "What we gonna do.?"

"Walk around all over the place. Check on the fences. Check on the tractor and that truck your daddy drove and check on the barn and the shop, or tool shed, whatever you call it. And the hen house. And I want to look at the garden. See where you planted last year and get an idea of where we are going to put everything."

He did not say anything. His face was down close to his cereal bowl and when he was through eating his cereal, he tipped the bowl up and drank his milk. He said, "I already fed the chickens. I do that right after I put my shoes on. That way I don't forget it."

He watched me eat my eggs and when I picked up my toast, he went back to the refrigerator and came back with a jar of fig preserves. He sat them down besides my plate and watched me eat. I was almost through when Vera came in. She was smiling and said, "The Weather Channel says it is going to be a cloud free day today all the way from Memphis past Jackson to the south. Temperatures in the low seventies later today but in the sixties for the morning hours. The main part of that storm stayed in the Delta and never climbed up into the hills. We got that to be thankful for."

By then the coffee was ready and she poured us each a cup. Roscoe went to the cupboard and got a cup and sat down and asked for some coffee but Vera said no and he looked at me and said, "Hurry up if you want me to help you."

I drank about half a cup of coffee and we left out the back door. It was my first chance to get a good look at the farm. I could see the house was set in among a good stand of pecan and oak trees. There was a nice white washed fence across the front yard and a rail fence around the other sides of the yard. The grass in the yard had not started greening up much and I had plenty of time to get the lawn mower ready to run before any grass was ready to be cut. There were yellow daffodils on both sides of the walkway from the front gate to the front porch steps. A few yellow crocuses were in the flowerbeds lining the front of the house. There were rose bushes next to the porch and some small cedar bushes around the house.

I saw I would need to prune the roses a little. Take the dead canes off the bushes and cut some of the long stems back. All of it easy enough to do. I had forgot about roses. All those years in prison I had not seen or thought a lot about flowers. There was some at Parchman.

Around the office where Essie Heard worked and when I would go out into the fields with Dump I would see some wild roses growing by the side of the road. Most of the time the little white flowers would be covered in Delta dust but after a rain they were pretty. But I can just remember a glimpse here or there. I looked at the roses and thought about Ann. Vera had told me she was good on a computer. Maybe she could get me some pages on how to care for roses.

Roscoe bent over one of the rose bushes and said, "Daddy cut them all back a day or so before he left. All that is left is healthy canes. Look, Robert Lee, every bush has got this little wire leading to a tag and the tag tells you what kind of rose they are." He was right. I read the names on the tags. Tropicana. Queen Elizabeth. Mr. Lincoln. Names I remembered from the past. I wanted to see them grow and watch Ann and Vera cut them and put them in vases and set them on the kitchen table. I wanted to walk out of the house and smell them in the summer when they were blooming and the sun did not go down till eight o'clock.

There were empty flowerbeds all along the front of the porch and empty baskets hanging down from the porch ceiling. The flowerbeds would need to be hoed out and just a little manure worked in the soil before planting., And that all needed to be done soon. The baskets would need to be taken down and soaked with water and fresh soil worked in with a little manure. And once again, that needed to be done soon. But it was fun work. And not that taxing on you if you took your time and started out early in the morning when things were still and it was cool.

I asked about the cow and the mule and Roscoe said they was down in the back pasture and he fed them in the afternoon after school. First thing when he got home. We walked on out of the yard through a gate in the back fence and I turned and looked at the back porch. It did not get as much sun as the front. You could tell easy enough because of all the trees in the back yard. There were still a few pecans on the ground.

There was a hen house about fifty yards down a path leading to the barn. There was a six-foot high fence around the yard where the chickens stayed. It was a good tight fence but I knew with chickens, they was always finding a way out of their yard. We went through a little gate and Roscoe showed me the inside of the chicken house. There was a light bulb inside hanging from a wire that ran from a rafter. A switch for the light was right inside the door.

There was wooden boxes for nests set up about three feet off the ground. Narrow wooden walkways led to the nests. I counted a dozen nests and eight chickens sitting on eggs and a nervous looking red and yellow rooster. The rooster was on the ground circling me and Roscoe and clucking loudly at us. I told Roscoe, " We need to shovel this coop out. Won't take long." He did not say anything and we left and walked down to the barn. It was a sturdy pole barn with stalls for a few horses or cows and a hayloft. A feed room was in the back. It had two barrels in it. One was almost full of oats and the other was full of shelled corn.

"I give that old brindle cow and that worthless mule four parts oats and one part corn. My daddy said they did not need a lot of high-powered food like corn or pellets. Oats and hay were plenty and just once a day. I give them enough hay at night so they can have some to eat the next day. Soon as the grass is up, I will cut the hay out. I feed them out back. There is a wooden trough. They eat together and they don't fight. They both too old for that was what my daddy told me. "

I looked around the barn. Elton had been neat and organized. Hay was stacked high and neat in the loft. I could smell the lespedeza grass in the hay. We went out back where Roscoe fed the cow and the mule. There was hay under a small, wood covered rack, A water trough was turned over on its side. Roscoe saw me looking at it. It was a silver barrel cut down the middle.

Roscoe said, " Daddy said they could drink out of the pond during the winter and he cut the water off in the barn before he left. I will show you where to turn it back on. He gives them water in the trough when it gets hot and the pond gets low in late July and August.".

We had passed a big tool shed and equipment barn on the way to the pole barn. I turned and walked back to it and the boy followed. He told me about all the farm equipment and tools in the barn. The bush hog, the big John Deere tractor, the Yazoo lawn mower, the hay baler, the plows and little green lawn tractor. Most of the hand tools were hung on nails on the old cypress walls of the shed. There was cans of oil and transmission fluid and anti-freeze all stacked neatly on shelves above the long cypress workbench along one wall. There was a shorter workbench, maybe three feet tall at the end of the shed. There were two short handled hammers lying on the smaller bench. One was a claw hammer and the other one was a ball peen. A wood saw , a square and a level were hanging on the wall behind the small workbench. A short handled shovel was leaning against the end of the bench.

"This yours?" I asked.

"Yes, but I am going to grow out of those short handled shovels and hammers pretty soon. My dad said I would catch my growth soon. Soon. And then I will have muscles. You still got muscles, Robert Lee. I seen some men at church your age can not even hardly walk around. They let their wives drive them around everywhere they go."

"They might be losing some of their sight. That happens to all of us. Some sooner than the rest."

"How you keep your muscles, Robert Lee? You been working all these years you were gone. You never even come to see me and my sister or my daddy when he was alive. Why is that?"

"I was working at a place would not let you up and leave. No matter how you felt about it."

That did not satisfy him, I could tell, but he let it drop. I knew it would be coming up again. I would talk to Vera about what to say. You lie to a child and they will not forget or forgive you., He showed me everything in the shop. All the tools. Where the nails and nuts and bolts and spare parts were kept. There was plenty of light in the shed, so I knew I could work there as long as I needed. A big fan was in the wall in the back of the shed. I asked Roscoe where the keys to the tractor and truck were and he pulled out a key chain from his right front jeans pocket. He said, "These are my keys. My daddy gave them to me and told me to take care of them in case he lost his. His are hanging up in the kitchen by the refrigerator. But they won't do you no good. Daddy drained all the gas out of the truck and tractor. Even the lawn mower and that little lawn tractor and his edger. Told me to always make sure not to leave fuel in something you was not going to use over the winter."

We left the tool shed and I thought about Elton as we walked down the fence line around the farm. He took care of his property and his machinery and his stock. Just like Uncle Leon. The fences were all in good shape and Elton had fenced the farm into four separate parcels. It took us a long time to walk over the land. There was a nice pond where a little creek had been damned up. Some willows had grown up at the shallow end of the pond and I could see where Elton had thrown some old treetops in part of the shallow end. A good place for bream and bass to bed up in the spring.

We walked down to the pond dam and I looked out over the pale green water. The pond looked to be over ten acres. I did not see any boats pulled up under the trees. There was a nice dock that had been built on one side of the pond. I asked Roscoe, "You got bream and catfish in this pond?"

"And bass. I caught one last year weighed almost two pounds. Caught him on a red worm. The bream bite red worms early when they spawn and later we use crickets. Dad piled the grass from the yard cuttings in a pile down at the barn and you can always get crickets from under that grass pile in the summer and early in June there is grass hoppers but I did not have much luck with them."

We walked out on the dock, The board and the pilings were all treated wood and I could not see anything that need replacing. I asked about a boat and Roscoe said, "Big Roscoe got an old bass boat with a trolling motor he brings over here but Daddy said the best fishing was from the bank or the dock. But I know what it was. He did not want to get a boat until me and Ann knew how to swim and he could trust us in a boat. That's why he did not have a boat. Because of us."

We walked over all four parcels of the land. In one parcel, corn stalks still stood brown and bent in a field. Just the one field for corn. The other fields were all cut low with no weeds at all. Hay cuttings and cows had kept the fields all clean of weeds and saplings. I saw cow piles in all four parcels. The cows had been sold but Vera wanted to buy some more now that I was here to take care of them. And trees. Hardwoods mostly, but there was some tall pines and cedars around the place. The land was mostly rolling hills and Elton had only cut hay in some of the meadows. A clear creek ran across the land.

The pond had a little, narrow spillway and the creek picked up right below the dam and ran into the trees below the dam. The spillway was not very big but the water was cold and tasted good. Roscoe kept up with me all this time. It was after noon when we got back to the tool shed. There was a refrigerator in the back of the big shed and I pulled a couple of diet Dr. Peppers out of the top shelf and Roscoe and I sat around and rested for a few minutes. I had seen some deer tracks down at the pond. Roscoe said his Daddy killed one deer a year. He and Big Roscoe would go hunting and the first one to kill a deer would get the backstrap and then they would split the rest of the meat up. He said his Daddy died last year before he could get back home and go deer hunting with Big Roscoe and that he had heard his mother ask Big Roscoe about going deer hunting and he had told her he did not think he would go no more for a while.

There wasn't much to say to that. I asked about the cattle on the land and Roscoe said his Daddy had way over a hundred head of Black Angus he had sold to a cattle buyer out of Canton who had come to the house and backed a couple of trucks up to the barn and unloaded some horses and loaded the cows in. He said it took several trips to get them all loaded and after it was done, the cattle buyer came into the house and drank some iced tea and ran the figures by his daddy and wrote him a check.

Roscoe said after the big white man left. The cattle buyer. Said his daddy sat there at the table and looked at the check and bowed his head and looked sad. In a few days, his dad went to Iraq and his mother finally took the check off the drain board and put it in the bank.

I asked Roscoe how his dad had taken care of the cattle. He said he had a nice little sorrel cutting horse he had bought in Texas but after he sold the cattle he gave the little horse to Big Roscoe to care for until he got back from Iraq. Roscoe said he wanted to keep the horse here on the place but his dad said he was too much horse for him. I could tell from the way the boy talked, he wanted a horse. I asked him if he wanted a horse in a few years and he told me he wanted one now.

One like his Daddy's. That would turn quick if you just gave him a little pressure with your knee and one that had some cow sense. A sorrel with a blaze in his face and a couple of white stockings on the back feet.

We sat and talked for a while about the place. Roscoe showed me where his dad had stored the fishing poles and tackle in a big wooden cabinet in the tool shed. Everything was arranged neat on shelves except for four or five cane poles that were leaning against the side of the cabinet. Corks and hooks and line and sinkers all neat. A few flies, some popping bugs, and spinning lures hung on a board at the back of the cabinet. There were two little short rods with open faced spinning reels on them lying on the bottom shelf. One was Ann's and one was Roscoe's. A long Sage fly rod had been broken down and put in its case. A single action fly reel lay on one of the shelves. A Shakespeare open faced spinning reel lay next to another rod case. I opened it and it had a spinning rod in it.

Roscoe said his daddy and Big Roscoe fished a lot and they had let him go with them last spring and summer and he showed me a freezer in the back of the shop by the refrigerator. It had fish and venison and beefsteak wrapped in white paper and labeled in Elton's handwriting with a black pen. A lot of the venison had been ground up like hamburger. Roscoe said his mother and daddy used it to make spaghetti sauce and meatloaf. Roscoe showed me a package he said was chili meat his daddy had ground up rougher than the other meat. He had mixed venison and beef for the chili.

I was hungry and I knew Roscoe was, too. But he had never said anything about being hungry or tired. Here I was on my first day here and I was already getting attached to this boy. My legs were sore from walking up some of those short, but steep, hills. His had to be. We walked up to the house and his head was drooping and I knew he was tired. We got in the house and there was a big pan on the stove with some aluminum foil covering the top. It smelled good so I raised the top and it was meat loaf with a tomato sauce all over it.

Vera had left a note. It said she and Ann had gone to Yazoo City to buy some groceries and would be back soon. There was a pot of rice and pot of green beans on the stove. I warmed everything up and fixed some iced tea and Roscoe and I ate. He was tired and did not say much. Another thing to like about him.

It was later in the afternoon when Vera and Ann came home. Roscoe and I helped them unload the groceries and then I walked down to the barn with Roscoe and we fed the old mule and the brindle cow. Roscoe said he used to throw corncobs at the cow but his dad saw him one day and told not to do that. That the animals on your place got treated right even if you did not like them. He said he still liked to throw dirt clods at the rooster just to hear him squawk.

When the kids were in bed, Vera and I went and sat in the den. She asked me about the place and I said I thought I would plant a garden soon and get ready to plant the seed corn out in the fields. She said that Elton rotated the fields for the corn. She would show me the ones he was going to use this year. She said on the few days she could get home before dark, they would walk around the place or go fishing down at the pond. Vera said she was lucky. Getting the chance to live out here and not having to fool with no big city and all its problems.

She told me that Yazoo City and Yazoo County had problems, too. Drugs. Meth and marijuana mostly. But not like in the big cities. I told her Roscoe wanted a horse but his daddy had told him to wait until he got a little bigger. Vera said he was the smallest boy in his kindergarten class and she fretted about it. He ate a lot and had energy. He had a touch of asthma every year in late April through June until the first real hot spell came and burnt off some of the bad pollen bearing weeds that sprung up in the late spring and early summer months.

Vera told me that Elton taught Roscoe to read last summer with seed catalogs and old seed packages from the garden, The packages and the catalogs had pictures showing the vegetables and flowers in color. He kept the seed packages for the vegetables he planted every year and he and Roscoe sat at the kitchen table and read the labels and the instructions. She told me Roscoe had gathered up all the little packages from the garden after Elton left for Iraq. They had been tacked on sticks at the head of the rows or where one vegetable planting stopped in a row and another one started.

I told her we would get the garden tilled next week as soon as the ground dried up enough. I asked about the cattle and she said we ought to get some in the fall after the crops were in so I would not have to fool with crops and cattle this first summer. She wanted Black Angus. I was always partial to Herefords but I did not say anything. It did not matter.

Vera said Elton had close to two hundred head but she wanted to stay at less than one hundred. Less strain on me and less strain on the grass I started to tell her that there was enough land for four hundred or more cattle but if we did that, we would have to buy feed in the winter. So one hundred would work fine. We could raise plenty of feed for them right here on the place. Big Roscoe would bring the little cutting horse back for me to use with the cattle. I had not ridden a horse in a long time but I knew I could do it without any problems.

Vera told me the man to see when we got ready to buy the cattle was my friend, Johnny Hixon. She said he owned a lot of land back in Hardaman. He was leasing Uncle Leon's old place I had given to Ann when I went to jail. And he was leasing Ann's old place. Vera said she was using that money to add to the children's college fund.

Johnny Hixon had lost his little brother to Memphis and drugs, Vera said. He rarely smiled and lived alone and was probably the richest man in Hardaman County. That did not stop him from grieving for Tommie Lee. He leased land and farmed it or ran cattle on it and had a reputation for being honest. His little brother had went up to Memphis and fell in with the cocaine crowd and got shot to death in a drug dispute over two grams of crack. Vera said I should go see Johnny in a few weeks and let him help us buy some cattle in the fall.

It was past ten o'clock and I was fixing to go to bed. Vera was in the den reading and the phone rang. She answered it and I could tell she was talking to Big Roscoe. When she hung up, she laughed and told me he had called to see if he could come over tomorrow and cook for all of us. Vera said he and Elton would cook on Saturday or Sunday when the weather was good. They would stand around the big grill Elton had made out of a silver barrel. Big Roscoe was at his juke joint tonight but he would be over in the middle of the morning tomorrow. He told Vera he was going to cook some ribs and chickens.

When I went to bed, Vera was sitting on the nice brown leather couch in the den reading a book. I looked at her and regretted all the years I had been away. But I was right when I told her grandmother, Ann, not to bring her to Parchman. Nothing good would have come of it. It would have just confused her. I had done the right thing. I knew that. But that didn't mean I couldn't miss all those years we were apart.

CHAPTER FOURTEEN
ETHAN IN SAN DIEGO AND YAZOO COUNTY

When I checked into the Holiday Inn on North Harbor, I sat outside on my ninth floor balcony and looked out at the harbor. Sail boats anchored in the calm water, a cruise ship docked almost directly across from my window, a Navy carrier slowly pulling out into the ocean, and countless small fishing boats returning with the day's catch caught my eye. After I put my clothes away and got settled in my room, I went back out on the balcony with my Robert Lee Whitfield file and began to focus on finding him for Vera Chaney.

I had thought about the situation on the flight out to San Diego but I can not concentrate very well on airplanes. As I sat on the balcony, I thought about Robert Lee. Not much money. Object of the trip out here was to see the Ocean and the Zoo. The Zoo was less than two miles from where I sat. The Ocean was across the street. No beach, but a convenient harbor area with lots of boat activity. And park benches to sleep on at night if you had no money. A place to start. At least. For some reason I wanted a drink. It was still late afternoon in Memphis and barely four o'clock here in San Diego.

I crossed North Harbor and began walking along the spacious concourses alongside the harbor. I talked to some homeless dudes. Most wanted to hustle me for money. I showed the picture I had of Robert Lee Whitfield that was taken at Parchman before he was released. Finally, I found a young black man who remembered Robert Lee. He said Robert Lee slept there a few times back before Christmas and was real quiet and did not steal or drink or fight or panhandle.

The young man said his name was Edgar and he was from Detroit and came out here to get away from the crime and the gangs and try to get off drugs. I asked him when was the last time he had seen Robert Lee and he smiled and said, "I saw his lucky ass coming out of Anthony's a few weeks ago, late at night. He had a white lady with long black hair and big tits hanging all over him. Robert Lee looked sober and she was talking loud and I thought she was drunk. I got a little money off Robert. A ten-dollar bill. I saw his billfold when he took the ten out. It was full of bills., We had talked some before when he was down here. All he told me was he was just out of Parchman Prison. I did not ask what for. I can tell you, everybody heard of that place knows they got some bad dudes down there. Robert is quiet but you best not fuck with him. Everybody could see that."

Edgar's hands were shaking a little bit and we sat down on a bench and he looked at the picture of Robert Lee some more. He asked, "So you just want to deliver some letter from his daughter to him? He ain't in no trouble? You look young to be the law, but you still got the look. You ain't even thirty yet, are you.? One thing, I want you to tell me. That is what did Robert Lee do? I don't see him as a burglar or a stickup man nor a paper man or a sex offender. That just leaves one thing. Quiet as he is, I figured he killed somebody. But I got more sense than to ask him."

"Where did they go after they left Anthony's? You see a car or which direction they went?"

He looked out at the boats in the harbor. The sun was low in the blue sky. A few clouds were way out on the horizon. The temperature was in the low seventies and a lot of people were walking or jogging on the waterfront.

"No, see, he gave me the ten. I was thinking vodka then. A half-pint is all. So I got me some. I drink Popov. Not too bad and the price is right. That was what was on my mind. I went up to the grocery store. About a ten-minute walk and got a half-pint right before they closed. I never looked. They was just walking away. Which way, I never noticed."

"So you are off the hard stuff and just drinking to keep you going?"

"I think I am just about ready to get back into life. You know. A little job. Some place to stay. Just a few months. Half pint of vodka a day is just enough to keep your nerves in line. Way I see it. Lots of bankers and doctors and lawyers. All them fine folks. I bet most of them drank at least this much. But I am off the hard stuff. I can tell you that. Most guys down here like me. On pills prescribed for their nerves and paying for it and a little wine with a government check. Me, you come down here in ninety days and I will be somewhere else. I just need a little more time."

"You got a trade?"

"Carpenter work. Construction. About anything to do in a restaurant. Got no computer skills though. I got to learn something about a computer and get me one of those fancy phones. I was in jail some. Never long enough to enroll in a school or anything. You know, do ninety days to work off a fine or a weekend for fighting. That was me. That kind of little stuff. I will be thirty in six years. By then, I will be somebody. I just hope it is here. Wish I could find a job right here close to the Ocean. Ocean helps keep me away from drugs. Sit on a bench and watch the boats in the harbor and the pretty girls walking by and all the time the weather is in the seventies. All of us you see sleeping on these benches or under a tree or in an alley. We got one thing in common. That is, we better off here than where we was before we came here. I never want to leave this town. Never."

We sat in the warm afternoon sun and I could see just what Edgar was saying. Same way I felt when I was on the pier or the beach or the Gulf when I lived in Perdido Key. Different Ocean. Different fish. Same breeze and same salt water smell to the air. I gave Edgar one of my cards and wrote my cell number on it and put my room number at the Holiday Inn on the back. I gave him a twenty and asked him to buy himself a nice meal and not blow it all on vodka. He laughed and put the twenty in his right front pocket of his wrinkled khakis. He was wearing a Detroit Tigers ball cap and a white tee shirt.

I got up to leave and asked him, "Anything else you remember about Robert Lee I should know? Something he said? Somebody you saw him with other than the white woman with the black hair? Any friends down here among the homeless dudes?"

Edgar shut his eyes and thought for a few minutes and then opened his eyes. One thing I heard him say to the woman. "Mission Beach." He was talking when I first saw him and when I walked up I heard him saying stuff to her and she was laughing and holding on to him but the only two words I can remember him saying was Mission Beach. I can not remember nothing else. Except one more thing. A little thing. He had nice clothes. Pressed khakis and an Island shirt. A blue one with some parrots on it and palm trees. And he was wearing this nice hat. Panama. Hat like that goes for a hundred dollars or more. So he is doing alright. He ain't sleeping here at night no more. I can tell you that."

"Prosperous. You saying he looked prosperous, to you?"

"Say this. If he is buying vodka, it ain't by the half pint."

Edgar got up and started walking toward North Harbor. Probably going to spend my money on vodka. Ethan the Enabler. But he earned the twenty. And I could see his point. Alcohol will kill you just as dead as the hard stuff, but you can manage alcohol, or at least control it somewhat. Addictive personalities. All over the world. And me with no real answers. Just find Robert Lee Whitfield and bring some hope into Vera Chaney's life. Maybe. I knew I could not solve society's problems out here on a bench late in the afternoon but it sure would be nice to see a smile on Vera Chaney's face.

What I could do is watch the sun when it set over the horizon. I knew it would be an explosion of red and orange and purple with all of it on top of blue water with a backdrop of beautiful blue sky. I was not going to miss it. I went back to the hotel and bought a Fat Tire in the bar and walked to the elevators. I punched the up button and looked up. The elevator was on the tenth floor. A pretty Hispanic woman came up to the elevator and folded her arms and asked me if I was the private investigator from Memphis with the funny sounding biblical name.

She was wearing a white blouse and a tan skirt and blue blazer. The badge was pinned to the left front pocket of the blazer. San Diego Police. She had beautiful brown eyes and long black hair and her skirt fell just above her knees. Nice legs. She said, "Look, hillbilly, when you get through scoping my body parts out, we need to talk and don't you know better than to walk through a lobby of a nice hotel like this with an open beer in your hand?"

I said, "Look, I just got into town and I am working. I want to get up to my room and watch the sunset, get something to eat, and plan out how I am going to spend my day tomorrow. Come on up to my room with me. I figure you got one of those scaled down Glocks in your purse, You want half this beer?"

She shook her head and frowned. The elevator came down and we rode to my floor in silence. When we were in my room, she threw her blazer on the bed and called room service and ordered a vodka martini and told them to get it up fast because she wanted it in her hands before the sun set. We walked out on the balcony and she turned to me and said, "Name is Elena Garcia. Lieutenant, San Diego Police Department. I was supposed to meet you at the airport but I got hung up on a real call. You know. A crime. A stickup where somebody working in a real store got a real gun stuck in her face. I told my boss I was too busy to chauffeur some hick private investigator around and so I missed you at the airport. Sheriff Sharon Graham out of Memphis called this morning and asked us to give you whatever assistance we can in finding your way around town and also in finding Robert Lee

Whitfield."

"Far as I am concerned, you can go home or wherever it is you want to go. I did not ask for your help and as far as looking at you, I'll bet you been getting a full dose of that all your life and it probably won't stop for a few more years."

"Well, I got a son playing his first year of competitive soccer and I was planning on being there about now so I am not in the best of moods. My husband will be there, though, so I guess it is not the end of the world."

She wanted to know how come the Sheriff of Shelby County cared about finding a former convict from Mississippi. She said there was no record of him being arrested or detained for a traffic stop. But one of the bicycle patrolmen had stopped him and talked to him before Thanksgiving. Had gotten his name and where he was from and found out he did not have a job and was planning to stay in San Diego and find a job. The officer had stalled around and run a record check on him and found nothing outstanding and rode off without saying anything else to Robert Lee The officer had written a report on his interview with Robert Lee and had noted that he was clear eyed and sober and he appeared to be in good physical shape.

She said, "He has not been in our jails and has not showed up as a witness, victim, or person of interest in any investigation of a crime. He could have moved on up the coast and be in LA or San Francisco or Tijuana now or he could be in an alley within a mile of where we are sitting keeping company with a bottle of strawberry wine."

While we were waiting on her martini to come up, I told her about my father and Sharon and me leaving the Memphis Police Department and my new career and living on the second floor of a law office and watching the barges going up and down the Mississippi River. Her martini came and I signed for it and tipped the waiter in cash.

The sunset was what I had hoped for and more. Lots of reds and oranges and purples all mixed in together and the sun dancing on the horizon for a few seconds and then gently sliding away. Elena relaxed a little. She put her bare feet up on the balcony rail, leaned back in her chair and slowly sipped her martini.

I told her about Vera Chaney and Elton dying in Iraq. I showed her pictures of Ann and Roscoe and she smiled and kept them in her lap for a while. I told her about Robert Lee and the murder and Parchman and the equipment shed and Dump Warren and Essie Beard. When I was through, she told me to call her if I needed her. She said her guess was he was somewhere inside the 5. I asked her what she meant by inside the 5.

"The 5 is the Interstate right by the Zoo. It goes all the way to LA. Inside the 5 is the phrase we use for the Gas Lamp District, the beaches, the Harbor, and Little Italy. La Jolla. Coronado Island. He won't go out in suburbia. You watch. You find him, he will be inside the 5. West of Interstate 5. Do not bother going to the Zoo to look for him. Probably, he has been there but there is no place up there for him to stay. Costs a lot to spend a day at the Zoo. Least for a guy like him with no job, it will be a lot. You ought to go, though. Make that your reward for finding him. If you find him. He isn't in the morgue. The officer who saw him said he was sober and the guy you talked to. Edgar. The black kid from Detroit. He said he was sober. He will be around here and working. Like Edgar said, those Panama hats cost a bunch He didn't bring it with him from Parchman."

When she was through with her martini, the sun was behind the horizon but purples and faint oranges and reds lingered in the darkening sky and the shimmering water., There were few boats moving in the harbor. Some sailboats were coming back into the harbor and there were lots of lights on in the cruise ship at the dock in front of us. She gave me one of her cards and told me to call her if something came up she could help me with. She left and I went outside and crossed North Harbor and went into the bar at Anthony's.

I sat down and ordered another Fat Tire and some oysters on the half shell.

The bartender was a sour little guy with a back east accent. New Jersey, Philly, or Brooklyn, probably. He was around fifty, short, and not very helpful. I told him who I was and showed him the picture of Robert Lee and he said he had seen him in the bar a few times with a nice looking woman. Drank Jack Daniels real slow. I asked him when the last time they had been in and he said a few weeks ago and drifted down to the end of the bar.

When he came back and asked if I wanted another beer, I asked him if he could give me a line on either one of them. Something they had said. Anything to help me find them. He said he had long ago passed the point where he had any curiosity about people who came in the bar. He said you could go nuts listening to the customers talk. Just serve them and hope they left you a decent tip. That was his motto. I left him a decent tip and left and walked up the pier to Sea Port Village. I had no luck in any of the bars and the homeless dudes were all looking for a drink or a handout and nobody gave me any help

I went on back to my room and sat on the balcony and watched the lights and the boats in the harbor. The crowd on the pier thinned out after ten o'clock and I went to bed and tried to read but I fell asleep within minutes and did not wake up until the sun was up. I ran for an hour in the early morning quiet and read the paper and ate some oat meal and raisin toast in the hotel restaurant.

After breakfast, I showered and put on some blue jeans and a blue polo shirt and went to Mission Beach. I got there around ten and spent part of the day walking on the beach and looking at the ocean. The water was calm and there were just a few white caps. The surf made a soft and lonely sound as it hit the beach. There were not many people in the water or on the beach.

It was Tuesday and I wanted to find Robert Lee in the next few days. I knew I would get paid for my expenses but I did not like the idea of running up a bunch of bills and going back empty handed when I knew he was here. Inside the 5. West of the 5. A lot of people in that area. I burned the rest of Tuesday showing pictures to shop keepers and bar tenders up and down the beach area. I went home Tuesday night tired and discouraged. I felt dumb. Where should I be looking?

I went back to Anthony's on the off chance he might be there with his girl but I had no luck. There was a new bartender working but he was no more helpful than the first one. This one was friendly and he had seen them come in but he said he did not remember anything from their conversation. He said he did not know the woman's name but he knew she was a local. He had seen her before but did not remember where.

When I got back to the room, I did not even turn a light on except in the bathroom. I went out on the balcony and watched the lights and the water and the sailboats in the harbor.

I tried to clear my head and think of a plan for tomorrow. It would be Wednesday. Not many days until I would have to make a decision to stay and keep looking or go home empty handed or r try to call in some local help. I decided to go back to Mission Beach. Wednesday was no better. But Thursday, I went into the White Lotus and sat down and ordered some iced tea and shrimp fried rice. I showed the picture of Robert Lee to the waitress and she looked at it and went in the back and in a few minutes Mr. Minh came out.

It took me a few minutes to convince him I was not going to arrest Robert Lee. When I showed him the envelope with the letter in it and the family pictures, he caved in. He told me Robert Lee worked as a bartender at a place that started with an M. He said the bar was named after the nice woman that came around with Robert on most Tuesdays. He said the place was next to the Blue Point in the Gas Lamp District.

I walked in Marci's and there they both were. Robert Lee looked healthy and alert and happy. I laid it out to him and told him to meet me at the airport on Saturday morning at seven o'clock and I would take him back to Memphis and them drive him down to Yazoo County. I wanted to wait a day before I left. I wanted to spend a day at the Zoo and that would give Robert Lee some time to sort his thoughts out.

I handled it just like Dr. Chaney had asked me to handle it and yet, when I walked out of Marci's I did not feel right. There was something else I should have said. But it was his choice. I had earned my money. I could file my report and close my file. So why did I feel like a jerk and a failure.? I ate that night in the little restaurant in the hotel. A cheeseburger and a Fat Tire. Then I went upstairs to my room and tried to sleep. Janet called and that did not do much for me. I told her what had happened and she told me she was impressed and for me not to worry. I had done my job and there was nothing else I could do. If he did not want to come, he did not want to come. Nothing I could say or do would change his mind., She told me to quit worrying and get a good night's sleep.

And of course I agreed with her and as soon as she hung up, I tried to sleep but it did not work. I ordered two beers and some ice from room service and sat out on the balcony until I nodded off to sleep. I woke up asleep on the balcony and got up and slept until dawn.

I ran up the long hill past Little Italy and through Balboa Park to the Zoo the next morning and sat outside the gates until it opened. The day was beautiful. Sun drenched, a clear sky, temperatures in the seventies, and a slight breeze. It was Friday and the Zoo was crowded but the crowd was nice. No rude people. No loudmouths. Clean. No paper or soft drink cans on the ground. Great animals. Should have been a perfect day but it wasn't. Most of the time I was looking in the cages, my mind was back at Marci's replaying my conversation with Robert Lee Whitfield. I should have done something different.

One thing kept nagging at me the whole day. When Robert Lee

gave me that hard stare, it threw my mind off balance and I could not keep my focused. Some tough private detective. My dad would have handled it better. I know that. I walked on back to the room late in the afternoon and then took a cab to the airport and explained my situation to a kindly ticket agent who got everything fixed up for me.

I felt a little better when the cab dropped me off in front of Anthony's. It was Friday night and the bar was crowded. I ate some shrimp and oysters and drank a mojito and went back to my room. I was tired and slept until five. I packed and called a cab and was at the airport at six thirty. No Robert Lee or Marci.

I had forgotten to even get a phone number for the bar. Not the time to call anyway. If he was going to show, Marci would have him here and have him here on time. Well, he did not show and I got on the plane and came home. It was late Saturday night when the taxi let me out in front of my place. There was a light on in my apartment. Janet was waiting at the door for me when I came upstairs. She was smiling and telling me how proud she was of me and I told her Robert Lee had not come back and she said for me not to be worrying about things I could not control. That never helps. No matter how right it is.

It would be hard for Robert Lee Whitfield to leave San Diego and Marci. Hard for anybody. Real hard for someone who had been in Parchman for over twenty-five years. Plus the San Diego Detective, Estelle, she got it right. Why would anyone leave that area inside the 5? Beaches bars, great weather, laid back cops, and pretty girls. Awful hard. But I was not thinking about that. I was thinking about letting Dr. Chaney down. I told Janet I was going down to Yazoo County tomorrow and tell Dr. Chaney in person what had happened. I just could not see sending her an e-mail or a letter or calling her on the phone with this news. She might have some questions. I owed her that much. And more.

I dreaded the drive. But it was something I had to do. I thought now I knew a little bit of what my father felt when he had to tell the family of a homicide victim that his squad could not solve the case. At least with a murder case, you could keep it open forever. Not the same with Robert Lee. There would be no new developments. He had made his choice and now it was final. I had the lingering feeling that there had to have been something I could have said that would have helped change his mind. Janet offered to ride down with me but I told her it was something I should do by myself. She understood and said she would make lasagna for me tomorrow so I would have something to look forward to when I got back home. I was restless and we walked down to Beale Street and sat in some bar and drank for an hour or so. When we were walking home, I was thinking about what I should tell Dr. Chaney tomorrow.

I ate breakfast with my father on Sunday at the Arcade before I went to Yazoo County. He was walking slower and he was tired at nine o'clock in the morning when we met. He had come down to meet me after roll call in the Homicide Squad. He had been out until four A.M. on Saturday and had answered a call last night at ten o'clock that he could not get away from until after three A.M. He had slept in his office for a few hours. He said he was living on coffee until he could get back home and get a decent night's sleep.

I did not feel like bothering him with my frustrations but he asked so I told him. He said he understood my frustrations. Handling homicides meant not catching anyone sometime, not catching all of the culprits sometimes, and hardly ever being satisfied with the court results. He said you never really accepted it. You just learned to keep it to yourself and move on.

He agreed with me. Go see Dr. Chaney, look her in the eye and tell her what happened and tell her I was frustrated because I could not think of anything more compelling and convincing to tell Robert Lee. We ate in silence for a while. He drank three cups of coffee and ate a piece of country ham, two scrambled eggs, and a biscuit. I had a Denver Omelets and whole grain toast and iced tea.

When we got up to leave, I reached for the check but he got it first. He told me he was proud of me for finding Robert Lee. After we went outside and were standing and watching the early morning traffic drift by, he told me I had to learn that sometimes when you did your best, there were still disappointments. I told him I knew he was right. He then told me it was good to have me close by. I had forgotten to ask him about the fishing trip to Tunica Cutoff I knew he wanted to take. Sharon had told me he wanted to go while the crappie were still biting.

As he walked to the car, it was easy to see he was exhausted. His gait was slower than usual and he was bent over just a little. Not much but a little. His puffy eyes were tired and sad. I stood and watched as he eased his big Ford away from the curb and slowly headed back to the Criminal Justice Center. He wanted to work ten more years and then retire and travel with Sharon. I had no idea where I would be in ten years. Probably right where I am today.

But I could not see marriage, children, and suburbia in my future. And I knew that someday, if I had the money, I would be leaving Memphis and going back to Perdido Key and a life of fishing and private investigations.

But today, my focus had to be on Dr. Chaney. I had typed up a report this morning instead of going for a run and I laid it in the passenger's seat in my Camaro and headed south. I wanted to get there around one or two. Give her enough time to get home from church. The drive down was fun once you got past the Sunday morning traffic headed to the Tunica casinos. Some roadside fields had been plowed but most had not. That would come soon. The fields always looked dark and depressing after the fall harvest and before the spring plowing. Today was no exception even though the sun was shining and the temperature was in the seventies. A nice calm Delta spring day.

Unlike the hills, there were no flowers or trees to be seen except in a few yards that were near the highway. When I turned into the bluff much of Yazoo City was built upon, it was just past one. I stopped in an empty store lot and looked at the map Janis had made for me. I drove on south on 49 and almost missed the turn off at Little Yazoo. Soon I found the turnoff to Vera's farm. No Sherlock Holmes deductive reasoning needed. A gleaming silver mailbox with the black lettered name, Chaney, was a convincing clue. I turned up the gravel road at the mailbox and drove a few hundred yards up a hill until I came to the house.

There were a few cars and trucks in the driveway. I parked and walked toward the house. A lot of pecan and oak trees were in the big yard surrounding the house. The house was a sturdy, wooden frame house with a tin roof. A long porch ran across the front of the house. I saw three young girls on the porch. One I recognized as Ann. She still had her white church dress on. She saw me and went in the house and when I got to the first porch step, Dr. Chaney came out of the front door.

She was wearing jeans and a white blouse. She was smiling. Big time. When I was on the porch, she hugged me and said Thank you and I felt like a fool. What was there to thank me for? I was going to ask if we could go in the house and talk but before I could say anything, she said, "Robert Lee told me you found him and gave him the letter and the pictures. Thanks for coming down. Stay and eat something. Big Roscoe and some of the men from church are barbecuing some ribs and chicken and a slab of beef. Robert Lee and Roscoe are lining the garden out."

"But he did not meet the plane. I waited on him Saturday morning and he never showed. When did he get here? "

"Friday night late. I was fixing to go to bed and the kids were in bed and a Highway Patrolman brought him right here to my doorstep. I got to call the Governor on Monday and tell him about that nice man. And write a letter to the Governor, too. Doing that for us in the middle of that storm."

"So he didn't wait on me. He came ahead by himself. On his own now. Out of prison. Likes to make his own mind up and do things on his own schedule."

"Roscoe has not given him any time off since he got her. I let Roscoe stay home from church this morning. Something I will not do again. But he was up with Robert Lee early. Just after the sun rose up and the Lord gave us this beautiful day, he and Robert Lee were already finishing breakfast and Roscoe was showing him all the seed packages he saved up from last year and that is what they are doing now. Lining the garden out. They been down there all morning."

I introduced myself to Ann. She had one of those beautiful, shy , and innocent smiles that only children can have. Vera and I walked out into the yard,Big Roscoe had on a pair of blue overalls and a white shirt. He was standing by two big barbecue rigs. Big silver metal drums cut in two and made into grills. Each one had a little silver smokestack on it. I could smell pork ribs cooking. There were several other men standing around the grills or sitting in lawn chairs. They all looked like they had come straight from church. Ties and white shirts with the sleeves rolled up and dark blue or black suit coats hung on the back of green lawn chairs.

One was Gorman Ballard. He was sitting in a lawn chair under a pecan tree. No bow tie today. A pair of nice khakis and an open collar blue chambray shirt. He had the same look today I had seen on my father. The look that is a combination of age and fatigue. Big Roscoe was holding court. Talking about the ribs and jiving with Gorman Ballard about his fees. Telling him the hills of Yazoo County were not a good place to find paying clients. Clients that got in trouble, yes. Clients with money, no.

Ballard grinned and told him money was not the only reason that a lawyer took a case. All the other men laughed and Big Roscoe said if he told another one that big, he would have to go back to Clarksdale to get fed and everybody laughed. I sat there for a few minutes while

Roscoe tended to the meat. Gorman was content to be Big Roscoe's straight man.

The smells were enough to make the drive down worthwhile. Pork on an open grill. Hard to beat the smell of smoking meat. He had the ribs on one grill and on the other one, a big slab of beef sat in some tin foil at the end of the grill and chicken halves were scattered across the opposite side. I could see Robert Lee and Roscoe bent over some paper they had spread on the ground. They were right outside a fenced-in garden plot a hundred yards away from where we were watching Big Roscoe turn the chickens. I walked up to see them. I introduced myself to Roscoe. He was polite but preoccupied. Robert Lee said hello and I kneeled down and looked at the paper they were looking at.

It was a large piece of white paper. A rough sketch of the garden plot had been drawn on it with a black magic marker. The rows of the garden were numbered on the paper and Roscoe was telling Robert Lee what he wanted planted on each row. I saw two rows for speckled butter beans. Two rows for corn. Only one row for green beans. One row for squash. Two rows for tomatoes. Rows for watermelons, purple hull peas, Crowder peas, eggplant, and cantaloupe were all noted on the sketch.

Robert Lee said he would go into town and get the seeds tomorrow and disk the ground up in the afternoon and set the rows later on in the week. Roscoe told him which hardware store had the best seeds. Roscoe said he was going to ask his mother if he could stay home from kindergarten until the garden was planted. Robert Lee smiled at me and told Roscoe that was something he was not getting into. Robert Lee said he was going to hold off a week or so before he set the tomato plants out.

I listened to them talk about the garden for a few minutes and went back to the house. I wanted to stay and eat a couple of ribs but I knew Janis was fixing lasagna and had picked out a good bottle of wine and I did not want to get home without an appetite. I sat with the men and soon the women came out of the house carrying pots and pans of food. The young girls helped set the food out on the tables and we all lined up for food. Big Roscoe made Gorman be last in the line and put me at the head since I found Robert Lee.

Vera sent Ann down to the garden to get Robert Lee and Roscoe. When they came up, one of the men said a short prayer that included thanks for having Robert Lee in the community and hoping he would join the church soon. I looked at Robert Lee. He was staring at the ground. I figured it would take some work to get him to go to church on a regular basis. Not that he would be against religion, but because he was just getting used to freedom and would not take to being preached at. When the prayer was over, Vera told me to go ahead and start the line. There were two kinds of potato salad, sliced tomatoes, pole beans, barbecue beans, cole slaw, candied sweet potatoes, mashed potatoes, and some kind of carrot and cucumber salad. And the sliced beef, pork ribs, and chicken halves. The beef had been cooked with a rub and had no sauce with it. The pork ribs were wet with a thick brown sweet sauce. The chicken was cooked with a rub, also, but there was a lighter, redder sauce on the side for it. After I had filled my plate, there were still sourdough rolls, pecan and chocolate meringue pie and a banana pudding.

I tried to hold back, but the food was too good to resist. The adults all ate under the pecan and oak trees and enjoyed the food and the sunshine streaming through the trees. Big Roscoe came over and asked for some of my cards and handed me an aluminum pan with ribs, beef, and chicken to carry back to Memphis. I gave him the cards and he thanked me for finding Robert Lee. He asked me how I did it and I told him it was mainly because I had some people help me and because of luck.

When I got ready to go, I had to make two trips to bring all the food I had been given back to the car. Vera followed me down to the car and hugged me again and went back to her friends and family under the restful trees. Gorman Ballard came to the car after Vera left and told me to expect a lot more business to come my way from his office in the future. He said he had a sexual harassment case he needed help on. His client was a young girl who had worked for a paving contractor out of Greenwood. He was suing the contractor for making advances on the girl and he thought things were going to get nasty and he needed some legwork done. She had been fired when she refused to go along with the after-hours sex. Because she never went back to work. That was the official reason. Witnesses to be found and statements to be taken. He said he would come up next week and bring a copy of his file and give me an advance and a contract to work from. I told him to bring his client with him so I could get some background from her as to what had happened.

I asked him if he ever went crappie fishing and he smiled and said , "Only when I am invited." I told him my father and some friends of his had a cabin at Tunica Cutoff and I thought we might be going there for a few days when my father got some time off.

I drove on back to Memphis in the late afternoon sun. When I got home, I saw my father's truck parked in front of the office. Sharon and Janet were on the balcony drinking wine. When I got upstairs my father was on the couch facing the television. He had nodded off to sleep. I put all of the food in the refrigerator and we let my father sleep until the sun had set over the River. While I had been gone, the fields across the River in Arkansas had been disked and plowed and the new rows were black and empty. The River was brown and swollen.

We sat and drank wine for a few minutes and went inside and I helped Janet get the food set out on the table. She was wearing blue jean shorts and a white blouse with blue and red piping on the bodice. When we had everything ready, Sharon went over and shook my father's shoulders. He woke up and she knelt by him and talked to him in a soft and soothing voice I had not heard before. He got up and grinned and went into the bathroom. When he came out, he said he was sorry to be such poor company, but he was having trouble recovering from the long nights.

For some reason, my appetite had returned and the spinach salad and lasagna and the wine all made me relax. Janet talked to my dad a lot and Sharon told me she was proud of me for finding Robert Lee. She asked if I had gotten any help from the San Diego Police and I laughed and said yes and told her about Elena Garcia. Janet asked me just what kind of help I got from her and my dad and Sharon laughed.

Before he left, I asked my father about going crappie fishing and he asked me when I could go and I told him I would go anytime he could get off. We settled on leaving for the Cutoff on Tuesday after work and fishing Wednesday, Thursday, and Friday of next week. He said he should get back before dark in case he was called out Friday night. Sharon said she was coming too, but she would help cook and catch up on her reading. I asked Janet and she laughed and said she would come down after work each night and drive back the next day after breakfast.

I planned on calling Gorman Ballard tomorrow and inviting him. The three of us fishing and good food and wine at night sounded good to me. And my father doing something he likes to do. The night passed too fast and when Sharon and my father left, Janet and I sat on the balcony and watched the stars and the river and the lights on the barges and talked until after midnight. When we finally went to sleep, she was lying close to me with her head next to my chest and her right arm over my chest. The last things I remembered before I finally slept were the peaceful sounds of her breathing and the sweet, apple smell of her hair.

CHAPTER FIFTEEN
TUNICA CUTOFF AND BEYOND
Ethan Cheatham.

I told Tommy Briggs and Bill Nolan about my trip to Yazoo County on Monday. We were in the office kitchen before court. They were drinking coffee and eating donuts Irene had brought in. I had fixed Janet and me omelets after my run that morning. The sky had been clear of clouds and a soft breeze from the southwest kept the humidity down. A couple of clients were in the lobby waiting for Bill or Tommy.

As an afterthought, I mentioned that I had a new case. Thanks to Gorman Ballard. I said he would probably bring me the file when we met at Tunica Cutoff on Tuesday night. Bill looked at Tommy Lee and then asked if they were invited. I said, "of course", and they went into their offices and brought their calendars back into the kitchen. Both said they could swing it. I knew Tommy Lee would bring a lot of bourbon. The good stuff, too. And a lot of food. That meant we now had five for poker.

I called my dad after Tommy Lee and Bill had left and told him they were coming. He was in good spirits. Four homicides had occurred after four p.m. on Friday and before roll call this morning and they had suspects in custody on all four and expected to charge everyone by the end of the day. He said he saw me running back from the Auction Street Bridge this morning when he was on the way to the office. He had cooked breakfast for Sharon this morning. Egg white omelet with mushrooms, onions, and enchilada sauce on the side. Plus raisin toast and coffee.

He told me to tell Tommy Lee and Bill they were welcome as long as they brought porterhouse steaks and high grade Bourbon. I spent the rest of the morning filling out my expense sheets, copying receipts, and preparing a written report on my efforts to find Robert Lee Whitfield for Gorman Ballard. It felt good to have money in the bank. A nice cushion. I still had Gorman Ballard's firm credit card in my billfold. I had forgotten to give it back to him and he had not asked for it. When I had everything ready to send to Gorman, it was past noon. I faxed a copy to him and mailed the originals down to him. I kept copies for myself, of course.

The plan for Tuesday was for all of us to meet at the Blue and White Restaurant in Tunica around six p.m., eat supper, and then go to the cabin. When I got to the Blue and White, my father and Gorman Ballard were sitting at a large table drinking coffee and talking to Carol. Whenever my father came down to Tallahatchie County and picked me up and carried me back to his place for the weekend when I was a kid, we always stopped at the Blue and White and ate. And most of the times we stopped, Carol was there waiting on tables. Her black frosted hair was always piled high on her head. An assortment of curls, some real and some not, always topped off the extravaganza.

She was over sixty now, but she still had a great smile. She was not pretty. Not now or back when I first started coming in, but she was appealing and attractive to men. She had not lost her figure. Pretty, long legs and a slender waist and big brown eyes. She was always smiling and it was obvious she had a decades long crush on my father. When I came over to the booth, she hugged him , and said, "Hi, handsome." He blushed like he always did.

Gorman asked her if she was talking to him and she said, "Even without that bow-tie and suit on, you ain't even close to cute and you are way away from handsome." She told me I did not need a menu. She knew what I wanted. My dad ordered the catfish plate with a side of turnip greens. She told me that was what I was getting, also. It just happened to be what I got almost every time I came there. Even when I was a boy.

Gorman had his glasses on and was looking at the menu. He looked lost. Carol took his menu away and said, "Relax, lawyer, I will take care of you."

When she was gone, Gorman said, "Ethan, I will bring our client up next week on Tuesday afternoon. Along with her mother. This case is not going to be as much fun as the last one. Sordid is the word to describe it. No way to dress it up. Most of the witnesses live in a ten-mile square area around Greenwood and most of them work for Ed Welker. The paving contractor. He came down here from Indiana in the fifties when he was a little kid and now he is a big dog around Greenwood. Employs a lot of people on his road crew. Not very well liked, though. Just a rich man. Someone you have to put up with. That's all. I took some notes but you won't be able to read them. What happened is that Ed groped her at the end of one of those rainy and windy March days. No one around who saw it. She left his office crying. Two women in the outer offices saw that. It happened in his office and we think the two women will come through. Then she went to the Wal-Mart there in Greenwood." He stopped talking and held his coffee cup up as Carol walked by. She gave him a look that would have slowed down a rampaging Brahma bull.

"Her mother works in the meat department and she came in crying and she and her mother went outside and she told her mother what happened. She never went back to work and her mother called me a few days later and asked me what I could do. The mother is Sue Graves. Our client is Anita. Barely nineteen. Got two years at Holmes Junior College and came back here to help her mother make ends meet. Wants to save up some money and get a degree from Delta State. You know any Graves over in Tallahatchie County when you was growing up?"

"No. Don't recall any."

"Far as I know, the only kin folks they got are over in Arkansas somewhere. Dewey. He was Anita's dad. He got killed a few years ago, hauling pulpwood. Stopped on the side of the road and was making sure his load was tight and a fellow who had just left a happy hour at a bar in Batesville did not see him and hit him. Knocked him in a ditch and killed him. The truck was off the road and it was just past sundown but there was still some light. Sue came over to the office and retained me and I got them money enough to last a while. They bought a better house and Sue says she has left a lot of the money up in the Casinos in Tunica. At least they kept enough to buy a good house. Anyway, you can start next week. Sue is fine. In church all the time. Quit her gambling. Got her feet on the ground, now. She will bore you to death now with all of that Born Again stuff. But she is a loyal client and I like her. Obsessing on being a part of the Born Again crowd is better than gambling your life away. I guess. Anita is shy. Nice looking kid. Pretty face and a nice slender figure. Says she is nineteen. She could pass for fifteen. You look at her and you get mad thinking of someone bothering her."

Gorman changed the subject to fishing. My dad had been quiet while Gorman talked about the case, but he opened up just a bit when Gorman mentioned fishing.

"You fished the Cutoff much?"

" No." Shortest sentence I had ever heard from Gorman. He wanted to listen to my dad.

"Go back to the start. The Big River had a horseshoe in it back in 1942. We had just got started in the last Big War. Two wars at once and we set out whole hog to win them both. Germany and Japan already was going full throttle with their war machines. So that horseshoe in the River was holding shipping back. The Corps of Engineers went in and blew the narrow neck of the bend in the Mississippi up and straightened the channel out. Left what we lay fishermen call Tunica Cutoff. Now the Corps of Engineers calls it Tunica Lake on the maps but no fisherman worth his name calls it that. It is about six miles from where we sit."

Bill Nolan and Tommy Lee Briggs walked in and Dad smiled and watched as they came over to the table. When Carol came over, she hugged Tommy Lee and pushed Bill Nolan down in a chair and told him he was using too much of that Brylcreem. I did not know they even made it anymore. She told them she knew what they needed and left. Soon, she was back with iced tea.

Gorman said, "You interrupted the Captain. Hard enough to get him talking. Now I got to try to get him restarted."

Dad was grinning. His eyes were not as puffy as they had been Sunday night. "Well, anyway, after they dynamited the narrow neck of the bend and created the new channel, when the River was high or at flood stage, it would restock the Cutoff with water and fish that comes in the intake chute at the lower end of the lake. So the lake is almost always got enough water in it. Last year. That was 2011 for you lawyers benefit. Last year there was a flood. Water backed into the lake from the River and caused a lot of damage to houses and trailers built on the low ground."

The food came. Everybody got the same except Gorman. He got hamburger steak with grilled onions, mashed potatoes with thick brown gravy and Crowder peas. We all got catfish filets, cole slaw, onion slices, tomato slices, hush puppies, and a separate plate of french fries.

"There is enough grease and cholesterol here to do me in, Miss Carol." Gorman said.

"Yea, and you been thinking about how good it was going to be ever since you got up this morning. Folks don't even dare to put a hamburger steak on the menu anymore. This isn't a patty or a hockey puck. This is the way it is supposed to be done. And another thing. Don't be asking for ketchup. It is already on the table. Right along with the steak sauce. Now leave me be for a while. I will bring the pie when I get to it. That goes for all of you."

Gorman said, "Now that all that is settled, go ahead on and tell us about the Cutoff, Captain. Please."

"Well, in the spring, some of the snow melt from up North comes down the river and some of that gets into the Cutoff and the Crappie start to bite in late January through April. They may be a little slow right now. But the bream may start up. We could catch crappie. Use minnows and we can try some yellow jigs. The jigs work good around the cypress trees. Yellow has worked for me more than any other color. We will stop at Charley's Bait Shop. I called him this morning. He is going to have minnows for us. We get fresh minnows every day from him. Now, we get some red worms too. Throw a pole out with a small cork and fish the worms around eight to ten feet. The bream are still a little passive. Not warm enough for them yet. As for bass, I say use some spinners. Not hot enough for top water action now."

"How deep you want us to go for the crappie?" Tommy Lee Briggs asked.

"I would start around eight feet, go to twelve as the day warms up. Start the jigs a little deeper. Keep working them on up to the top. A nice bass could follow it up and hit it right close to the surface."

And that is the way it went for the rest of the meal. Bill, Tommy Lee, and Gorman. All lawyers. Not pretentious. Just wanting to catch some fish. Dad willing to talk about fishing. Never once saying how many he had caught or how big the fish were he caught. He didn't have to tell me, I had been with him fishing here and at Sardis, Moon Lake, Grenada Lake, and countless farm ponds in Mississippi and Tennessee ever since I can remember. We almost always caught fish, but when we didn't, it did not seem to bother my father.

He always knew a place to stop for dinner and breakfast. He was happy not being in a squad car or the morgue or at a crime scene. We were eating quietly when Gorman said, "You were telling us about the flood last year and people losing their houses, what about your cabin?"

"Well, it is not mine. They got shares in it." He pointed his fork at Tommy Lee and Bill. And there are two friends of mine. One in the Police Department, one runs a body shop down off Third Street in Memphis. The five of us. We bought it a few years ago from a Memphis bond salesman. Went belly up in the eighties. One of those crashes. Ethan was just born. It is built up high and still the water come in a little. But there was no carpet to fool with. Just that Mexican tile all on the floor. Still we had to restain some of the boards and a couple of doors warped and had to be replaced and we lost three boats and motors. But we were lucky. Come fall, we just about had the lake to ourselves. The few times I could get away, I caught fish. "

"Where is the smoking section in the restaurant. I bought some great cigars, fellas. How about it, Carol?" Bill asked.

"Smoking section is out the door, go six miles west, and have at it, big boy." Carol said.

In a few minutes, she brought the pie. Three slices of coconut meringue and two slices of chocolate meringue. The meringue was four inches tall, at least, at the highest point on each slice.

"Oh, and don't bother asking me if I would like to come down to your cabin a little while later tonight. The answer is no. Has always been no. And will never be anything but no."

"Miss Carol. I just wonder how many times you been asked that question over the years." My dad asked.

"An awful lot and you know what? It has not slowed down that much and me with a grandson almost twenty-five years old. They keep asking. My grandson is coming home from Afwhateverstan. That shithole. Pardon me for saying that. But I can not think of another word for it. I am just glad he is making it home. That boy is something. He is a Marine. Says he might as well stay in and make a career of it, but they have told him he can redeploy. I think that means go somewhere else and be a Marine where they is no shooting. At least for now. Is that right, Mr. Delta Lawyer? You with steak sauce on that nice blue dress shirt. What you gonna look like when you get some whiskey in you?"

"That sounds right to me, Miss Carol." Bill said.

She started clearing the table. A short Hispanic woman came out of the kitchen and helped her bus the table. When the table was clear, she handed the check to Gorman and said, "Don't short me on my tip, lawyer, because I said that bad word. Not my usual way. To be negative. But I understand less and less of the world around me as I get older. And my own people. Americans I mean. Maybe it is a natural thing that happens as you get older. I just do not know. Oh, and Mr. Gorman Ballard, if you need some fish to carry back to Clarksdale to tell people you caught some, just call me and I will get some out of the cooler for you. "

And with that she left. Sharon and Janet had not shown up yet and no one was surprised. They were shopping for groceries in Memphis. We went on ahead and set up camp. There were three bedrooms on one side of the large cabin. Dad and I both took a bedroom and Tommy Lee had to take the last bedroom because the sound of his snoring was like a sawmill. Dad and I unchained three boats and took a five horse Evinrude and a trolling motor out of his truck and were fitting them on the boat when Sharon and Janis drove up. After we took groceries up, Dad and I came back down and got poles and rods from his truck and laid them in the bottom of the boat. Dad took a cooler up stairs. We had stopped by Charlie's Bait Shop and had everything ready to go.

We played poker until after midnight. All seven of us. Dealer's choice. Fifty-cent limit. Three raise limit. We drank Blanton Bourbon and Russel's Reserve and my dad was relaxed and had a good time. We cashed in the chips and settled up and when we were in the bedroom, I looked at my watch. It was almost one o'clock. I slept through the night and my father knocked on the door right before five.

When I dressed and went out into the kitchen, Bill and Gorman were sitting on the edge of their bunks rubbing their eyes. There were eight bunks against the far wall of the cabin. An upper and lower bunk. And four rows. It was still dark when we finished breakfast. Sharon and Tommy Lee and my Dad cooked. Janis slept. We ate fried eggs and bacon and country ham and hot biscuits with blackberry jam and hot coffee and iced tea.

Dad and I fished together in one boat and Gorman and Bill Nolan fished in another boat and Tommy Lee fished alone. Dad never talks a lot during normal times, but he hardly ever says a word when he is fishing. He points some. And gestures some. He sat at the back of the boat and took a small paddle and sculled us in to the places he wanted to fish. When it got to be light, we were trying to find the crappie with jigs. We let our poles sit for a while and stayed with the yellow jigs and spinning rods. A cooler lay in the bottom of the boat a few feet from Dad.

He moved the boat quietly through the cypress trees. By noon we had caught a dozen or so slab crappie. The smaller ones had been thrown back into the lake. I had caught two nice bass with the jigs. Each one weighed a little over two pounds. Neither would go over three. Dad said to keep them. Around noon, he handed me a salami and onion sandwich and a peanut butter and grape jelly sandwich. We fished and ate in silence. Our company was the sun and the cypress trees and a clear blue sky and a few fast, low flying clouds. In the afternoon, the crappie slowed down and we fished the poles with worms and caught a few small bream that we tossed back and a few big bull bream with red and blue and gold bellies that we tossed in the cooler.

Around four I gave up on the bream and crappie and started fishing a green tailed spinner in about twelve feet of water. I caught some more bass but they were in the pound to pound and a half range and I threw them back. Dad caught a nice bass. Almost four pounds.

He gave Dad almost an hour of hard fighting. When he got him up to the boat, I netted him and took the lure out of his mouth and held him up.

He was still fighting me. His tail was flopping and I was having trouble holding him. I looked and Dad and he made a tossing motion with his left hand and I slipped the fish back into the water. He stayed by the side of the boat for a minute and then darted down into the dark lake water.

"Nice fish. Fought hard for his size." I said.

"He did. Some eight-year-old girl might catch him later on. Hope so, anyway." Dad said.

We headed back into camp a few minutes later. After we cleaned the boat out, we turned it over and sat and cleaned our catch. We threw the guts and heads of our fish into the water at the head of our little pier and watched them sink into the water. We washed our hands off and carried our fish and cooler up stairs. Sharon and Janet were listening to music, drinking Dogpoint Sauvignon Blanc, and cooking. I could smell spaghetti sauce. Sharon was adding onions to a skillet of browning ground pork, venison, and beef. Janet was chopping a green bell pepper. There were several cloves of garlic close by. When dad walked up to the stove, Sharon told him to get a beer out of the refrigerator and stay away from the stove.

I went to the refrigerator and got us two Sam Adams Boston Lagers. We sat at the table and ate some cheese and crackers and waited for the others to come in. Soon Sharon and Janet dumped all of the meat and onions and bell pepper and garlic into the simmering sauce. When everyone was back from the lake, Tommy Lee went into the refrigerator and came out with a pan of porterhouse steaks he had left marinating while we were fishing. He asked my Dad to cook them and asked that Bill and Gorman take showers and stay away from the grill on the deck.

The spaghetti sauce was for tomorrow night. We were told not to take the lid off the pot and sample it. Janet took some of the filets and rolled them in a cornmeal batter and she and Sharon fried them while the steaks were cooking. There were lemon slices, hush puppies, tomato slices, and cole slaw and hand cut french fries right off the stove. We all ate too much but when we thought we were through, Sharon pulled out a banana pudding her mother had made for us, Again, a lot of meringue on top and layers and layers of vanilla wafers and bananas.

While we were eating, everyone except Dad talked about the fish he had caught. Tommy Lee had caught a slab crappie he swore weighed four pounds. I figured it would be lucky to go two and a half. Fish just look bigger when you bring them out of the water than they really are. Dad listened and laughed and never mentioned the nice bass he had caught and thrown back in.

In the interest of decorum, Janet was wearing a bra. And her blouse was buttoned to the top.

Something she always did around my Dad and Sharon. Something she never did when she was at home with me. She was wearing a nice sedate blue blouse and khaki slacks. No shoes. The table was full of food and it was almost ten when we cleared everything away. Steak and fried fish. Hard to beat.

In a few months, the fresh vegetables would start coming in. I hoped we could come back in early June. The crappie would be slow but the bream would bed up in the shallows and the bass would be hitting topwater lures. Fish early, rest in the middle of the day, and then get back on the lake and fish hard until nighttime. There was not as much drinking as last night. I had opened some 2007 Ramey Cabernet. We had went through two bottles at dinner and no one seemed interesting in drinking much after the two bottles of wine, the steak and fried fish were gone.

I followed my dad out on the deck. He and Gorman Ballard were looking out over the lake. The wind had picked up and the sky was dark. No stars and no moon tonight. Some clouds were moving past us from the west. Low and dark. The temperature was dropping fast.

"Might be a storm coming through. These clouds are moving fast and low and the wind is bringing us something. You can bet on that." Gorman said.

"Probably a lot of rain later in the night and into the morning. The water will be choppy and murky. Fishing will be spotty." Dad said as he walked back into the cabin.

We started the poker game back up and Tommy Lee brought a bottle of Russell's Reserve to the table with some glasses. I sipped some as we played cards. Everyone was tired and we quit before midnight. I went back on the deck and sat and watched the weather move in on us. The rain came hard around one in the morning and my dad and Gorman and Tommy Lee and I moved inside. Dad said he was going to light a fire. He figured it was cold enough. He cracked the door leading to the deck and we sat by the fire and finished the bourbon.

Tommy Lee and Gorman told stories for a while and then we just sat there and watched the fire in the fireplace and listened to the hard rain pound the tin roof of the cabin. The wind was rattling the windows some but the fire and the bourbon kept me warm. When I went to bed, Janet woke up for a minute and pulled me close to her and went back to sleep. I was tired but I lay on my back and thought about the fishing. From when we first got in the boat and slid silently into the early morning darkness all the way through the day. I tried to remember each fish I caught and each thing my father and I said to each other.

I fell asleep listening to Janet breathe softly through her nose. I woke up when it was light. The rain had let up a little but it was still pounding the roof. No use going out in that. I slept for a while and then got up and shaved and went into the big open kitchen and den area. Dad was tossing some fresh logs on the fire. It was just a small fire. But it was still comforting. After breakfast, we watched The Weather Channel and found out it was going to rain off and on all day today all over the Delta. From up in Memphis down past Greenville.

When everyone was up, we ate a slow breakfast. My dad drank coffee and talked to Sharon and me about a trip he wanted to take. Out west to the Grand Canyon and Yosemite and Yellowstone. I told him about San Diego and he smiled and said he wanted to see the great National Parks in September after Labor Day when the kids were back in school and before the first snows in Yellowstone. Sharon told me she had already made the hotel and plane reservations. They were going to be gone for three weeks. Some flying and a lot of driving.

A few minutes after one, it was still raining. Steady but not as hard as before. Dad told us all, "It is slacking up. I think I will try it."

I followed him out to the boats. We turned ours over and got things ready to go. Sharon told us to come in if there was any lightning. We left the dock and Tommy Lee was standing at the end casting out into the lake. He had a baseball cap pulled down low. He had a cane pole rigged for crappie. His line was thrown out near a cypress log that had fell many years ago. He was casting a little silver spinner and smoking one of Bill's cigars.

We fished for a few hours and caught nothing. Then Dad tossed me a top water lure that looked a lot like a minnow but had a yellow feather at the back of the lure. We started catching bass near the shore and near the cypress trees. Most were in the two-pound range. Fun but not worth keeping. At last light, I caught a good bass right up against a dock we passed on our way back. He went deep after he was hooked. Probably looking for something to snag my line on. I brought him back up to the surface and he jumped once, then wallowed a little right at the surface and tried to run again but I brought him on in.

Dad netted him and held him up. "Nice fish. Probably go five pounds. Bigger than my fish yesterday."

I motioned for dad to throw him back. He took the fish and

lowered him into the water and let him get his bearings back and when he thought he was strong enough, Dad let him swim away. We started back and another storm moved in fast. Lots of water and some lightning over in the west. It got dark before we got back, but we had a good flashlight and we could see our cabin lights in the distance.

When we pulled up to the dock, Janet and Sharon were waiting for us on the dock under an umbrella in the rain. They helped us with our tackle and cooler. We put the boat up and emptied the cooler and went upstairs. I had decanted two bottles of Il Poggione Brunello from the 2004 vintage right before we had left this afternoon to go fishing. We ate spaghetti and drank wine. Tommy Lee had caught some crappie on minnows. Bill and Gorman had stayed in the cabin. Gorman with a book. Bill with a bottle. It was hard for me to stay up long. I was tired and after we had cleaned the kitchen up, I went on to bed.

We left out early Friday morning to fish. Sharon and Janet went back to Memphis. Dad and I caught some nice crappie but we could not get a rise out of the bass. We headed on in to camp around noon. After we packed up, Dad and I drove on into Tunica and stopped and ate. Carol was there and she called my dad handsome again. I ate turnip greens and fried chicken. My dad stayed with the catfish but left the french fries alone.

We were eating pie again when my dad said, "This new career. Private detective work. It suits you. It lets you work on your own. Take your own cases. Turn the ones down you do not want and not have to put up with the regimentation and bureaucracy."

I said, "Yes. That is right. Gorman is giving me cases. Janet gives me some. And Bill and Tommy Lee give me plenty. A few trickle in from other lawyers in town. And I am saving money. Not many expenses. No rent. No utilities. Just car insurance and health insurance through the firm and a few piddling expenses. I am putting money away."

"Sharon said Janet was crying some when it was lightening yesterday evening and we were out on the lake. I like her. But that is strictly your business. Strictly yours."

We didn't talk much more after that. I picked up the check and left Carol a ten-dollar tip and drove on back home to Memphis.

Anita Graves and her mother, Sue ,came to the office the next week. Anita was nervous and shy. I walked her through what had happened. Ed Welker had called her into his office and got up out of his chair and walked behind her and put his hands on her waist and moved them up to her breasts before she got over the initial shock of him touching her. She ran out of his office and was crying as she left the office. She ran to her car, drove to Walmart and found her mother in the back of the meat market weighing and packaging pork sausage.

Her mother said she looked up from the sausage and saw her daughter crying and went outside with her and tried to calm her down. I got the names of people at Welker's office that had seen Anita run out and also the names of people who had seen her at Walmart crying in the back of the meat market.

Within a week I had everything wrapped up. Pictures of both locations and statements from the witnesses were not that hard to get. Gorman had called it right down the line. Sordid. No one wanted to talk and when they did, I got the idea they were telling me a fraction of what they knew. Gorman was happy and I moved on to other cases. He told me to keep his firm's credit card handy since he would be needing me a lot. Anita called me one day in late June. She had moved to Denver and had a job as a waitress at a busy Italian restaurant. She gave me her address and phone number and I faxed all of this to Gorman.

Dad and I went fishing again the first week in June. Got down to the cabin on Monday afternoon and stayed until Thursday night. Just me and him. Sharon and Janet came down at night and left in the early morning. Most of the time right after day light. We fished early, came back and either watched baseball or read and then fished in the late afternoon until we could not see. The mosquitoes were out and we seldom went out on the deck. We caught a lot of fish. Big bull bream and some nice bass. We kept the biggest bream but threw the bass back. We ate at the Blue and White again when we left Thursday night.

The summer was nice. Slow and easy most of the time. I had plenty to do. I turned down some business. Marital surveillance. Spying on husband or wife. Trying to catch one cheating on the other. Something about that made my skin crawl. The cases I kept were fairly interesting and I was happy. Waiting for the fall and another chance to go fishing with my dad after he got back from his trip out west.

One hot Thursday night in July, I took Janet out to the El Porton on Highland. We sat in a back booth and drank margaritas and ate chicken enchiladas. I told her I loved her and wanted to always be with her but I was not ready for children and a house in suburbia yet. It took a lot for me to say all of that to her. She smiled at me and told me everything was going to work out and for me to relax. I told her I had been a coward for not telling her before. I just could not make the jump to being a husband right now.

I told her I loved to have her over at my place but I felt uncomfortable at her big house on Mud Island. And I liked the nights I had alone. Just as long as there were not too many. The occasional night alone, she said. We laughed and drank a pitcher of margaritas. I called a cab and it was all either one of could do to stay awake on the ride home.

So we are happy. Janet and me. And I am happy. Sometimes I think of Robert Lee and Vera and Roscoe and Ann. Gorman says all he has heard from Yazoo County in the last few months has been from Big Roscoe. He is buying another store at a crossroad near Benton. Not a juke joint but a country store. Hardware and groceries and gas and oil and tires.

I have gotten my drinking under control. Janet helps me. I told her I was afraid I was on the verge of having a problem. So now we do not drink as much wine as we used to and we share a single margarita when we go to El Porton.

Gorman Ballard called me right at the end of August. Anita Graves' sexual harassment suit never got filed in court. Ed Welker got into some more trouble. He was caught by the husband of one of his secretaries in a motel out by the Interstate in Hernando. Ed and the wife in the middle of some serious sexual activity. After that the case settled on the high side. Anita called last week and said she was coming back to Greenwood. She loves Denver but the cost of living is so high she will never make enough money to buy a house. She wants to move back with her mother and go to school down in Cleveland, Mississippi at Delta State University. The plan is to get an accounting degree.

September will be here soon. Football and falling leaves. Another year of rebuilding and disappointment down at Oxford. The Tuesday after Labor Day, my dad and Sharon will fly to Denver, rent a car, go to the Tetons and Jackson Hole, then on to Yellowstone, and after a long haul to Yosemite, they will swing back to Denver after stopping at the Grand Canyon, Monument Valley and Telluride.

So, life moves on. Ed Welker is in danger of losing his marriage and his business. Janet and I are determined to make things work. Tommy Lee frets about Bill Nolan drinking so much. Bill Nolan sadly watches his lonely life drift by. He is a functional alcoholic with no motivation to change., He and I don't go out much together anymore. I stay around my apartment and watch that old River go by at night. The fields across the River are full of white cotton bolls. The sky is usually clear at night and Janet and I always try to be on the balcony with a glass of wine in hand at sunset.

Gorman Ballard lives in his office with a lifetime of memories and some quality scotch. The River is down but shows signs of rising. Robert Lee Whitfield, murderer and ex-convict, is now a father and grandfather. He is teaching Roscoe Chaney to appreciate and respect the land he lives on and to celebrate the land and its potential.

While Dad and Sharon are gone, I am going to take a Sunday in September and go back to the Chaney farm in Yazoo County. I want to hear about the garden. I want to see if Roscoe has grown any over the summer. I want to eat some more of Big Roscoe's barbecue. I want to watch the women in their church dresses and big hats bring pots and pans and platters of food to the table under the pecan and oak trees. The food will all smell good and seduce you away from any thoughts of a diet. Ann and her friends will be laughing and playing on the porch. And I want to see if Vera still smiles a lot like she did that April day when I drove down and ate barbecue at Elton Chaney's home place under a soft, spring sky in the quiet rolling hills of Yazoo County, Mississippi.,

CHAPTER SIXTEEN
MENDING THE BROKEN CIRCLE
ROBERT LEE WHITFIELD

End of Summer, 2012, Yazoo County, Mississippi. I been thinking on things. Now that the boy and his sister are in school, it is quiet around here a lot. They leave shortly after six in the morning and don't get back until after three. Riding a big yellow bus. Roscoe is out of kindergarten and is in the first grade. Ann, she is in the third. Vera is talking about having them tested at the end of the school year and if they test out like she thinks they will, she will put them in school in some advanced schools in Jackson.

Roscoe still feeds the chickens before he leaves. I asked him if he wanted me to feed them on school days and he ducked his head and said no. Ann said he liked to go out and yell at the old rooster first thing in the morning.

A lot of times, I hear his mother going in his room in the night and telling him, "Roscoe, first light will be here before you know it. So go on and get in bed and shut your eyes and go to sleep." He never answers, just gets out of his little rocking chair by the window and crawls into bed. Times have been up and down with Roscoe. Most of the time, he is full of energy and wanting to help me. But there are days, he is somewhere off in his mind and I just can't find him. He will be right there besides me. Fishing down at the pond. Changing the oil in the tractor. Going into town for feed. And it will take him a while to answer anyone and when he does, his heart is not in it. I do not know what to do. All I know is to be here and try to do right. He never sees me drinking and I do not take the Lord's name in vain around him. I do not go to the church with them on Sunday. I stay here by myself and enjoy the quiet and try to think about the week that has passed and the week that is ahead of me.

But Roscoe is going to be fine. He will make it. He just needs to put some time between him and his father's death. He is starting to fill out some and grow taller, too. Not a lot, but some. He is proud of that. The deal is this. I can take seeing people cut in a fight or shot. But to see that boy unhappy and troubled gets me in a place I never knew I had in me. He wants me to go and get his Daddy's cutting horse from Big Roscoe as soon as we buy some cattle. He wants to learn all he can about cattle and he has told his mother he would like one of those big hats to wear when he gets his horse.

We made the garden. That is what my Uncle Leon and the old-folks back home in Hardaman County used to say. Make a crop. Make a garden. We made the garden, alright. Disked the ground the week after I got here and plowed it and harrowed it until we had worked manure into the soil. We being me and Roscoe. Me on the tractor and Roscoe watching with his hands on his hips or with one hand shading his eyes from the sun.

When we had the rows all lined out, Roscoe and I went to the Twiner Feed Store in Yazoo City. They knew Roscoe. He had been in there all his life with his dad ,according to Levi. Levi is the Twiner I met. A little white guy with gold in his teeth and just a little gray in his black hair who wore blue coveralls like my Uncle Leon did years ago. Levi was my age and he listened to Roscoe and got him the seeds he needed and some Beef Steak Tomato plants and told Roscoe to plant the corn and tomatoes right by each other. He did not know why, but his mother and father had told him to do that and it had always worked for him.

When we had everything, seeds and tomato plants, a sack of oats, and some cracked corn for the chickens, all stacked up on the old wooden counter, Levi asked Roscoe, "You know what you forgot? Your daddy told you right here in this store last spring. Now think, son. What did you forget?"

Roscoe turned and went outside where the bedding plants were and came back with a tray of marigold plants. He put them on the counter and went back and got another big tray and brought it back. Nice short plants with yellow flowers on them. Then he went back and got two more big trays with orange flowers on them. Marigolds. I remembered Nora Deen Barksdale telling me when I was a kid to always plant marigolds everywhere. They kept the bugs out of your flowers and garden.

When we had everything loaded up, I took Roscoe down to a café Vera had told me about. It was near where the bridge goes over the Yazoo River and the Delta part of Yazoo County starts. The rich part. The Yazoo River winds all the way to the Mississippi and is about the muddiest excuse for a river I have ever saw. We sat on stools and ate hamburgers and fries and drank iced tea and watched our fat waitress swat flies. Roscoe looked all around at the folks drinking beer and shooting pool in the back of the café. The hamburgers were big. Roscoe had to use two hands to hold his. He could barely see over the counter.

When we had everything planted in the garden, I started to working on the fields and the flower gardens around the house. I planted a good bit of corn since I had heard Vera say she was wanting to buy some cattle later in the year. When I had the corn in the ground, I started to planting flowers in the beds around the house.

Roscoe was always there with me. After school, he would come running up the road to the house. Ann would walk behind him. He would change clothes and come and find me. This was when I first got there and he was in kindergarten. When school was out, he and Ann were always around or, at least, somewheres close.

During the late spring and early summer, I would take both of them down to the pond and we would fish. Lots of times, it would be me and Roscoe fishing and Ann playing on her phone or reading a book. Sometimes she fished, but she gradually lost interest and just stayed around the house. Roscoe loved the pond and fishing. When he wasn't fishing, he was throwing dirt clods in the water and running around getting into some kind of devilment. But the boy minded me. I would tell him something and he would mind what I said. His dad and mom had already taught him how to act.

Most times when we fished, he would stand a ways from me and ask me questions about the crops and fishing. When the plants in the garden started to get some growth on them, I showed him how to thin some of the plants out. I showed him how to chop weeds out of the garden and take care of the bedding plants and the roses.

Later in the summer, when everything was up and growing, he and I would go out every evening and gather beans , eggplant, corn, squash, cantaloupe, peas, or tomatoes. Whatever needed to be gathered up and carried to the back porch and laid out for Vera to go through and cull when she got home from work. We ate a lot of the vegetables and gave away a bunch.

One Saturday in the middle of July, Roscoe and I loaded the back of the truck up with all the vegetables, and watermelons, and cantaloupes we could. We went up on Highway 49 on the way to Jackson and when we were almost in Jackson, we set up a stand where a new subdivision had been built. We sold a lot of watermelons, tomatoes, squash, Crowder peas, and cantaloupes. Plus we had some green apples off our tree. We sold most all of them. They were apples I never learned the name of. I always have called them green apples. They start out green and when they are ready to eat, they are green. Levi Twiner calls them Granny Smith apples. Ann went with us and handled the money and made change while Roscoe and I sacked the fruit and vegetables up and weighed them.,

I let Ann and Roscoe half the money up. It was after dark when we got home and Vera was sitting in the den with her feet propped up on the coffee table. She was asleep and it was not nine o'clock. I fixed some supper up and we got her up and Roscoe and Ann talked about the money they had made and Vera looked at me and grinned and I felt happier than I guess I have ever been before in my whole life.

Now, the garden is playing out. The melons and cantaloupe and corn have stopped growing and the tomatoes are just about played out. The old mule died a few weeks ago. I do not know what happened. One day, he just did not come up to the barn to be fed in the evening so I figured there was something wrong. Roscoe had just started in school and he tried to stay home and help me look for the mule , but Vera shook her head and said no. The way she said it, the boy knew not to ask again. After I had them on the bus to school the next morning, I got on the tractor and drove around looking for the mule. He always stayed between the pond and the barn. A lot of times he was in a little stand of woods about a half-mile from the barn. Down near the pond.

But that is not where I found him. I found him dead on the old path he had beaten into the ground from the pond. The path led from the pond to the stand of woods and then on to the barn. It was just a small path, but it was worn down considerable since he had been walking it for all these many years.

He was lying on the path, about two hundred yards up the hill from the pond. When I saw him, I stopped and got off the tractor and looked at him. All around. There was nothing you could see wrong except his old gray tongue was sticking out and ants was in his eyes and crawling over his stomach. Way I figured it, he just died. His old heart quit on him in the Mississippi August heat. I put a chain on his back two legs and drug him off to the woods where he stayed. I went back to the barn and put the backhoe on the tractor and went back and dug a hole and drug him off in it and then covered it up. Buried him right beside a clump of trees he liked to stand in during the heat of the day.

When Roscoe and Ann got off the bus that day, it had started to rain and there was some thunder and lightning way off in the west and low, black clouds were blowing past us. Before we went in the house, I told Roscoe and Ann about the mule being dead. Roscoe ran on up to the house and went in his room. Later he came out and went up to the barn and fed the old brindle cow. I stayed in the tool shed and waited for him to come back. I figured it would be best just to let him be for a while. Ann was down at the shed with me. Something she rarely did. She was sitting on a bench doing her math homework.

When Roscoe came in the shed, he puttered around a while and then came over to where I was tightening the fan belt on the little green lawn tractor. He said, "What happened to the mule, Robert Lee? He never bothered anybody. Why did he have to die? Did he suffer any? That was my daddy's mule. He told me the day he left for Iraq to be sure and take care of the mule and the brindle cow. Daddy said he learned to ride on that mule when he was a boy. Now the mule is dead. Nobody ever gave the mule a name. Not even Daddy. He was just the mule."

I sent Roscoe after a crescent wrench I did not really need. I needed a minute to think of something to say. He came back and handed me the wrench. I was on my knees, bent over the motor of the little tractor, so I straightened up some and told Roscoe, "Son, sometimes people, animals, and even machinery will just give out. The mule was walking back from the pond like he always did and he just fell and died. His heart give out. That happens to people and animals. It had nothing to do with how you fed and watered him. It was just his time to go. There was no sign of him trying to get up or anything to show a struggle. The mule just lay down or fell down, one or the other. If we had been right there with him and called the vet, it would not have mattered. He was probably dead by the time he hit the ground. Or shortly afterwards. He did not suffer. He just died."

That was a lot for me to say at one time. And afterwards, I felt like

I had not said the right thing. Roscoe looked at me for a while and said nothing. He turned around and went on back to the house. That night we were all eating a quiet dinner. Some good sliced tomatoes and pole beans with bacon cooked in with them, and some chicken Vera and Ann cooked with onions and tomato. Vera and I talked a little but not much. Ann was always quiet and that night Roscoe would not talk. I cut open a cold watermelon and put some slices on plates for everyone. Roscoe ate about half of his. He usually ate his and what was left of his sister and his mother's slices.

When the plates were cleared, Roscoe sat back down at the table and asked his mother, "You a doctor, Momma, can you get me a book about the heart? With pictures. And a book with pictures showing a mule and his heart. I want to see why a heart gives out. I don't understand it. That is what Robert Lee says happened to my daddy's mule. If the words are too big, Ann will help me read it. She likes to show off what she knows. And Momma, Robert Lee says a bird has a heart and it beats a lot faster than ours. Show me why that is."

I got up and went in the den. I was tired and the Cardinals were playing and the game was just getting started. I turned on the television and Rafael Furcal was standing on second base taking a pad off his forearm and knocking the dust off his pants. He had a look on his face. Real intense. I liked to see that on a ball player. I knew Furcal from when I was in Parchman and would listen to the Braves games on the radio station out of Jackson, Mississippi. No Cardinal station came in very clear down in Parchman. I settled in and watched the game. I was tired. I had been working all day. The rain had slacked off and it made a slow steady sound on the tin roof that always relaxed me.

When the game was in the fifth inning, I went back in the kitchen and opened a bottle of Sam Adams Boston Lager and poured it into a beer glass. Vera, Ann, and Roscoe were sitting around the kitchen table. Ann was reading from a large book that Vera had brought out of the study. It was one she had studied when she was in medical school.

Some of the words was too big for Ann and Vera helped her with them. The book was black and Vera said it was an anatomy book from her Medical School days. Roscoe had his head down over the book and Vera and Ann were laughing at him because his face was close to the picture of the heart on the left side of the book. He was using his fingers to help him find parts of the heart. Then they all started laughing and I stood there in the kitchen and watched them.

Why I remember this so well is because it was the first time I had heard Roscoe laugh since I got there. I went on back in the den and watched the game and finished my beer. When I went to bed, Roscoe was asking Vera why she did not have any anatomy books on mules and horses. Books like that soon made their way into the house either by way of Federal Express from the State College over in Starkville or being dropped off at the house by the county agent or the vet we used, Dr. Alice Summers. Dr. Summers is a white lady that works on small and large animals. She is in her forties and drives a new black Ford 150. She has long blonde hair she wears in a ponytail and a voice with some gravel in it. A smoker's drawl. She came by the house one day and the way she looked at me made me think of Marci back in San Diego. But all that would have to wait till I thought it was time. Least that was what I told myself that day.

She brought a big poster of a horse with all the organs showing in different colors. Roscoe put it up in his room. She and I took Roscoe down to the barn and I went and hunted the brindle cow up and got her up to the barn. Roscoe and Dr. Alice were sitting on a hay bale looking at pictures in another anatomy book. This one had a picture of a cow in it showing where all the parts and organs were.

Dr. Summers asked me to hold the brindle cow still. I put a little halter on her and she stood still for me except for her tail. She was switching at flies with her tail. Dr. Summers and Roscoe stayed on the hay bale and looked at the book and the brindle cow for over an hour. Dr. Summers walked around the cow and Roscoe followed her. She showed him where the organs were and what they did to keep the animal alive. She told him what she was looking for when she got a call to see a sick animal. Any signs of swelling on the legs or gut of the cow. Any cuts or scrapes that might need doctoring. Then she looked in her eyes and told Roscoe the brindle cow still had good eyesight but sometimes a cow could go blind and you had to watch for it.

After she left, Roscoe spent the rest of the day inside reading the books. Or looking at the pictures. Vera would read to him when she got home. The days were long and a lot of the time I was in the cornfields or cutting and baling hay. We got three hay cuttings this year. Most of the country had drought. Bad drought that scared me when I heard or read about it. It's getting to where I do not want to know what is going on in the world anymore. Just take care of my little piece of it as best I can.

Speaking of Marci, one-day back in July, Vera came home from work one day and brought two packages home she said were delivered to her office from San Diego, California. They were sent to Vera's office, but they were addressed to me. One package had my Panama hat in it. When I opened the package, Roscoe grabbed my hat and tried it on. It fell down past his ears and Ann and Vera laughed. He gave it to me and I put it on and said I would wear it sometimes when we went into Yazoo City or Jackson.

The other package contained the rest of my clothes. The ones I had left in San Diego when I came to Yazoo County. There was a framed color photo in between some of the clothes. It was a picture of Marci and Mr. Minh standing in front of the White Lotus. Marci had on a pair of cutoffs and a white top. Mr. Minh had his khaki shirt and pants on. Marci was laughing and Mr. Minh looked like he was facing a firing squad. I put the photo in my room on the top of the chest of drawers in the corner. There was no note or letter from Marci. I guess it was goodbye. I could not see me going back out there and leaving my blood kin here when they wanted me here.

A week or so after the mule died, I was stacking hay on a trailer I had borrowed from Big Roscoe. Big Roscoe brought the trailer over and stayed to help. We were down to the last few bales in the field. We were almost ready to go in for the day when Alice drove up in the field and came over and said hello. I think she was a little embarrassed Big Roscoe was there. He got in my truck and drove off to the barn with the trailer and hay. The trailer was stacked up high enough and we needed a break anyway. We talked a while there in the field in the afternoon summer heat. She wanted to know about Roscoe. Whether he was still reading the books and looking at the pictures. She lit up a cigarette and looked off at the freshly mown field. I told her Roscoe always asked questions. Questions about the animals, the plants, the machinery, and the land. When she was close to me I could smell her perfume. It smelled a lot like vanilla. With some apples thrown in.

She gave me one of her cards and wrote a number on the back and told me to call her if I ever needed some company. I put the card in my billfold and she took me on to the barn and drove away.

Big Roscoe never said a word about her. He just asked me if I was a tired old man and if I was, his going rate for unloading and stacking hay was seventy-five dollars an hour. We unloaded and stacked the hay. All the time he was going on about his rate of pay. What he was worth. I knew he was just passing time because he was always there for Vera and the kids when they needed him, When we were through, we went up to the shop and drank a Sam Adams each out of cold bottles and waited on the kids to come home from school.

A few days later I called Alice and we decided to go to a Memphis Braves game in Jackson. I wore some nice khakis and a green and blue Island shirt and my Panama hat. She picked me up and Roscoe wanted to go, but Vera told him he could go another time and he didn't seem to mind. The Braves were playing the Blue Wahoos from Pensacola. We sat down on the third base line in some good seats she had bought online. We ate peanuts and drank a draft beer. I do not even remember who won the game. It was fun. Sitting with her, talking about the game and watching all those young men trying to make a good play and move on up to the big time.

Alice had been a Braves fan most of her life. She had grown up down near Collins, just south of Jackson. Dale Murphy had been her favorite player until Chipper Jones came along. Her folks had owned a dairy and she had went on to Auburn and gotten her Vet degree. I told her about Parchman and she said she already knew. I asked her how she knew and she said everybody knew. There were no secrets in Yazoo County. Vera had not told her. But somebody at her church told her. She knew I had been there but she did not know what for. I told her and she told me there were some things about her she would tell me after the game.

When we came back from Jackson, she pulled off in a yard of some folks that had gone to Florida for the week. She told me she had experimented with some things in college. Things like drugs and other women. She said she was a bisexual person but that she had no ties at the present. It was hard to see anyone now because most of the men were married and she had not met any women that interested her. She asked me if I had any remorse for killing Billy Ray Starnes and I said no.

There was silence in the truck for a few minutes after I said that and then she told me she liked the way I acted around Roscoe and we did not talk about Billy Ray Starnes anymore. I told her about the letter Ethan Cheatham delivered to me in San Diego from Vera and how I was going to see it through with this boy and his sister and my daughter. After a while, we started kissing some and then we got just a little more serious and I liked the way she felt. It was hard to get things right in the cab of the pickup but we found a way and when we were through, she pulled a joint out of her purse and we shared it listening to the crickets and watching the clouds in the sky.

We get out some. Usually once a week, at least. We took both of the kids to a baseball game and Roscoe has already planned it out for me to carry him to the high school football games this fall. Got them all marked out on the calendar in the kitchen. Just a few days ago, Vera came home from work one day and she and Roscoe and Ann went out to her car and brought in some boxes and I asked to help and Ann told me to watch a baseball game for a while. After supper, Ann and Vera took the boxes in my room and shut the door. Roscoe watched the game with me some but he kept going back into my room.

I was asleep on the couch when they woke me up and asked me to come into my room. When I went in the room, I saw a computer monitor and a keyboard and mouse on my desk. Ann and Roscoe stayed up for a while and showed me how to turn it on and off. They showed me how to get online and get the farm prices and the news and ESPN and the Jackson Clarion Ledger and the New York Times and CNN. When I get confused, Ann comes in and helps me. I use it some everyday. To keep up with the news and the ball scores, mainly. It is nice and I know when the bad weather comes after Christmas and before planting, I will spend some time learning more about it. Best thing about it is the fact that Ann and me talk more now. She is reserved. Not really shy. You ask her something and she will talk a lot. But she is not like Roscoe. She is like Vera.

Roscoe is like his daddy. Vera and I sat up one night and shelled peas after the kids were asleep and that is what she told me. She sees Elton in him every day. The way he is always asking some kind of mischievous question to throw her or Ann off balance. How he is interested in the crops and the land and the welfare of the animals. How he likes to get outside no matter what the weather is. All like Elton.

So now I have a nice life. Alice Summers and I are getting along fine. She accepts the fact I need to be in this house for as long as these kids are growing up. We go to her house and grill steaks outside in the shady back yard a lot. We drink just a little wine she buys up in

Jackson and sometimes we smoke a joint. Sometimes I stay the night but when I do, I get up and leave early and get back to the house before Roscoe gets up.

Alice has some nice quarter horses she rides when she can. One is a big sorrel with a high hip and a tea cup nose and a white blaze on his face. She seems content to see me once or twice a week at night. She drops by sometimes during the day when she can. If it is raining, she usually shows up and we sit in the shop and talk. She wants me to get a cell phone. I do not know about that.

I think about what Vera said about the broken circle that was her family when Elton died. Now, it is still damaged and weakened. No way I can be a father to those kids. What I can be is steady. And quiet. Somebody they can trust. Somebody they will never see drunk. Somebody that can help them understand the little world here on the farm that we live in.

Ann called me Grandpa the other day. She said it just slipped out and I told her that if that is what she wants to call me, it was fine. Now she calls me both. Robert Lee and Grandpa. Whichever strikes her fancy. I taught her how to take care of the roses this summer. We had nice ones and they are still blooming. She likes to go out in the yard and cut the stems and bring the roses in and arrange them and put them in nice vases. I told her next year she can be in charge of the roses because I had taught her everything I knew and I was tired a lot of nights when I came home out of the fields. She went online and researched roses and now she wants to plant some new plants in the fall.

Vera and I called Johnny Hixon last week and he came down to see us Sunday. He said he could get us some Black Angus for a fair price. Johnny and I walked all over the place and I showed him the fields and the fences and the pond and he said Vera's place could hold a lot more than two hundred head of cattle. You can lose a lot of money on cattle, so we are going to start with fifty and a nice seed bull.

Johnny walks slowly now. He has put on some weight and I know he misses his little brother. There is a lot of sadness in his eyes and his shoulders are starting to get stooped and rounded. He is stiff in his knees and does not look comfortable when he has to walk very far. He has so much land now, I think he spends most of his time riding in his pickup truck to and from his farms.

He was glad to see me and he asked me to come up to Hardaman later on after the cattle are bought and delivered. Soon we will have fifty heifers and a bull in the pasture. We have plenty of feed to keep them through the winter. There will be calves to care for in the spring. Another set of adventures for Roscoe. A new set of questions for me and Vera and Alice to answer. Soon, I will have to get the corn out of the field,and put it in the cribs in the barn. Big Roscoe will help me.

Way I got it figured, I got about nine more good years with this boy. Then he will get to be fifteen and start driving and seeing girls and being a teenager and he will have less and less time for me. I will show him how to take care of a car. Then, I will have the land and the crops and the animals and Vera to give me comfort. I figure Alice to be done with me in a few years or less. That's fine with me. A few months or years with a good woman is better than a lifetime with one that you can't ever make happy. A woman can haul off and leave you. But she can't take the good memories away from you. And now that is plenty for me.

Ann will be different. I think I can depend on her to always be near and to be considerate and not to forget me. That boy, you just never know. Like Vera says, when the hormones kick in, all bets are off. But I think he is like Elton in that he may stray but he will come back to this place. The land and the trees and plants and the animals are such a big part of him, I think he will farm this land. He likes to see things grow and when he gets big enough to have a horse and learn to take care of cattle, I think he may stray but he will come back and stay. Like Elton, he is getting to be a part of the land around him. More, every day.

All I know to do is to do my best with these kids. Do my best and hope it is enough. Keep the circle mended and strong. Like Vera says.

CHAPTER SEVENTEEN
ROUNDING A BEND
VERA CHANEY
AUGUST 31, 2012

Yazoo County, Mississippi. When Ethan Cheatham left the farm that day way back in April, I was optimistic about my children and my life. I have never worried about Ann, but Roscoe was another matter. He was difficult to reach. In fact, impossible for much of the time since Elton died. But when my father came home, it all changed. He had someone to follow around the farm and ask questions and do things with. Someone to heighten his curiosity about life and someone to have faith in.

After everyone had left that afternoon in April, I was sitting out in the yard and enjoying the late afternoon sun. I was tired. Emotions had washed over me like waves in the ocean ever since my father showed up on that rainy Friday night. I was sitting there under a big oak tree when Roscoe came running around the corner.

He said, "Robert Lee says the ground is dry enough to start the garden tomorrow. He is going to disk it in the morning and then go to Mr. Twiner's store and buy the seeds and the tomato plants. Let me stay out of school this week, Momma. I can make it up. We need to get the garden planted this week."

I told him no. He had to go to school. Even if it was kindergarten. He opened his mouth to argue but he saw the look on my face and dropped his head and went up on the porch and played with his sister and two of her friends that were staying over with her. Robert Lee was up in the shop. I walked up there and watched him work on the tractor for a while. He had it running and he had a long wrench in one hand and an oily rag in the other.

I sat down on a bench and asked him if it would take him a whole week to get the garden in. I told him there was no hurry at all. He said it would probably take most of the week for him to answer all of Roscoe's questions. He laughed and said he would have all the seed and tomato plants in the ground by Friday at the latest. He was settling in easily around the place. He told me he wished he had known Elton.

He said he liked him and had never even met him. What he liked was the way he kept his fences up and his pastures and the pond being all clean and neat with no trash in it or on the banks or the dock. He said the shop had every tool you could ever need and they were all in drawers and bins or hung on the walls in a neat and orderly way. He said the best thing was how the children acted. Respectful. He liked that. I asked him if I should let Roscoe stay out of school and help him with the garden and he asked me what would Roscoe's teacher have to say about that.

I had one of my two cell phones with me. I was not on call from the hospital this weekend so I only had my personal phone with me. I had Lettie Butler's number in my phone. She taught Roscoe and about twenty others in kindergarten during the day and ate the wrong things and drank gin at night. She was large. Even for today's society. She was in her late forties and lived with one of her sister's on a little farm over near Benton. I was treating her for high blood pressure, high cholesterol, and back and knee pains. But she was a good teacher. A nice soft voice and a patient demeanor. She laughed a lot. Except when I told her she should diet and lose at least a hundred pounds.

She answered on the second ring. She told me she hoped I was not coming by her house because she was sitting out on the back porch eating fudge she had made for one of her grand daughters' birthday. Just sampling it, she said. I told her about Roscoe and she said he was so far ahead of the rest of the class, he did not really need to come back at all this year. She said he was reading books she brought him from the third grade room. She said to let him stay home and help his grandfather plant the garden. She said the rows were already set in hers and she was trying to get time to get some seeds so she and her sister could plant it next week in the afternoons after school.

She told me when Roscoe came back to school, she would have a hard time keeping him quiet. He would be wanting to tell everybody how he had planted his own garden. We laughed and she said , "That boy is a pleasure, Dr. Chaney, a pleasure."

I told Robert Lee what she had said and he laughed and said they would have a good time and that Roscoe was good company and he could use the help. I went on back to the house. Roscoe was still on the porch. Sitting on one of the white rocking chairs. I can remember when he had to climb into the chair or get someone to help him up into the seat. I pulled up a chair and sat beside him. He had his head down and was not saying anything. Tough to be five years old and have to ask people so many questions and have to ask permission to do things you have your heart set on doing.,

"Roscoe, I called your teacher, and we talked about you. What we decided to do is to let you stay home and help Robert Lee put the garden in next week. Now what I want that to mean is you help Robert Lee. He knows how to do it. Don't be telling him how to do everything. Listen and learn. And Ms. Butler said when you come back to school, you would be doing a lot of talking about the garden. I want you to tone it down. After she said so many nice things about you, I do not want my son going back and being a burden to her by distracting the other children. Now will you promise me to do what I have asked of you?"

His head was up now. And he was nodding his head. "Yes ma'am. Yes ma'am," he said. We sat there for a few minutes and I asked him questions about school. There were some doves flying low over the house. They were probably going to roost in the trees in a small clump of woods near the pond. The same clump of woods that Elton's mule favored so much.

Right after I showed Roscoe the doves flying past the house, he jumped up and left. He told me Robert Lee might need some help with the tractor. He was running by the time he turned the corner of the house.

There was one other thing that happened that day that I have thought about a lot. Ethan Cheatham came up on my porch and he had a sad look on him like he was going to a funeral. And then when I told him Robert Lee was here with Roscoe, he smiled at me and I had this feeling. A feeling a woman has when she has needs and there is no one to look after her needs. Private needs. And I was ashamed later when I thought about it. But he looked handsome with his long black hair and tall, trim body, and pretty eyes. The feelings just came to me.

It was the first time I had had that sort of feeling, however fleeting, towards a man after Elton left for Iraq. The first time. And the last time. I know I can not act on those types of feelings now or, maybe, never. These children will be raised in a stable and dignified way. I can do that for them and for Elton and myself. Elton said the deed on this farm was all in error. The deed said he owned the land. Elton said no man ever owns a piece of land. Elton said this farm owns us. I never pretended to know what he was talking about but after this summer I know exactly what he meant.

This farm does own me and my family. Robert Lee and Roscoe and Ann. Maybe not Ann until this summer. She spent more time out of her room. Down at the pond fishing. Out in the yard with Robert Lee helping with the petunias and the roses and the zinnias and marigolds. All the flowers. And the gardenia bush. She went online and ordered a book about gardenias and now she wants to order some more rose and gardenia bushes for next year. She showed me this afternoon late where she wants everything to go. She told me she would not need the boys, that is what she and I call Robert Lee and Roscoe , to help her once they had dug the holes for her to plant the bushes.

And me, sure I am drawn in to the land, also. All the memories of Elton. From our improbable meeting when he called me a nurse and acted like he was not going to help me get my car out of the ditch through all the good times and up to now. Every time I hear or see Roscoe, it brings back memories of Elton Chaney. When Roscoe grows up, he will be here on this land raising crops and cattle and fishing down on the pond. He is mischievous just like Elton was when we were courting.

You do things in life. Things you look back on years later and marvel at how and why you did them. But when I married Elton, I knew what I was doing. I was getting back to the land and simpler times and simpler people. Elton did not care that much about schooling. But he read all the time. About how to farm and take care of the soil. Why you rotated crops and let land lie fallow. What watermelons grew best in Mississippi. What type of soil we have on our place. What cattle could hold their weight or put on weight during the hard, humid Mississippi summers. What crops to stay away from. All these things that go into farming the land and living on it. That was his life. And he would have never left it. Never.

I do not live in a vacuum or an idyllic environment. I am a single practitioner. I would like to bring someone in to help me. Try doing that in a poor Mississippi county. New doctors usually have a lot of debt and you can not blame them for wanting to live in an exciting city and make lots of money. I have employee problems. Absenteeism, challenges filling positions with qualified people, and establishing an attractive benefit program for them. And malpractice insurance. And finding time to keep up with the latest changes in medicine. Keeping my equipment up to date with the industry standards. The same problems doctors all over the world have.

But when I go home at night or in the late afternoon, I eat food I have helped grow. I can sit on my porch and listen to a bob white call. I can see a doe and a fawn slip across the side pasture. I can listen to my children laugh. I can smell the gardenias and the honeysuckle. When it is lonely at night, I can take small comfort from the call of a distant whippoorwill.

Soon, I will have some cattle. Heifers and yearlings. And a bull and then, some calves in the Spring. And horses. For Roscoe and Ann and I may get one for myself. Be nice to ride over the place with Robert Lee or the children and check on things. The blackberries and plums are gone. But they will be back in the late spring and I will make cobblers and jam and Ann will help me., Soon it will be fall. I can sit by the fire at night and watch my children grow up.

The way I see it, I am here for life, also. I am happy. Now that Robert Lee is here, there is more noise, more activity around the house. He is quiet but Ann and Roscoe have opened up to him. Now Ann is helping him learn some about computers. She goes into his room most every night while he is out in the den watching a ball game or playing monopoly with Roscoe. She checks his computer to be sure it is working right and then goes, several times a week, into the den and tells him about a new website she has found for him.

When Roscoe and Ann found out we were going to buy some cattle, they both asked for horses to help with the cattle, of course. We were at the supper table eating chicken enchiladas I made from scratch when they brought the horses up. Robert Lee said Dr. Alice Summers had some nice horses and she would help us find horses if we needed them. Ann looked at me, rolled her eyes, and smiled. So there is another door that will open for the kids and tie them closer to the land. Robert Lee told me later, we would need at least one horse to help with the cattle and it would not hurt for Roscoe and Ann to have horses. There was plenty of room to grow enough food to keep them in good shape without stressing the land.

Robert Lee and I talk most nights after the children go to bed. One night a week or so ago, he opened up to me. He told me Dr. Alice knew about him being in Parchman before he told her. He said that disturbed him because he knew one day Roscoe would come up the road from school with his head down and tell him the other kids in school are saying that his grandfather had to go to Parchman for killing a man.

I told Robert Lee we would tell the kids the truth if it ever came up. Ann will work it out in her brain. She is that kind. I will never underestimate her cognitive powers. As for Roscoe, he will be more emotional. But Robert Lee and I will lay it out to him as best we can. I still do not know how I can explain it to Roscoe and neither does Robert Lee. I know we can not sugar coat it or rationalize it. It happened and it was wrong. When I told Robert Lee that, he said he knew that and that is why he did not fight going to Parchman. He just did not want to die in some old wooden chair with electric current going through his body.

One of the Ten Commandments was broken. And by my father. But I know that is part of the punishment my father will have to suffer. Having to look Roscoe and Ann in the eye and admit this to them. How he and Roscoe deal with it remains to be seen. I can only wait and be strong when the time comes. I will talk to my preacher about it in the next few weeks and I can call the psychiatrist in New Orleans one day next week. Try to develop a plan. It is a problem to deal with down the road. Like Elton would say, we will round that bend when we come to it. But I think I should start getting prepared now. It could be next week or five years from now. But the day is coming. I know it.

Robert Lee never gets upset or mad. Just goes on. Like Gorman Ballard said about him many years ago. Robert Lee keeps his own counsel. Does everything internal. Maybe that is a secret of life. Just going on. Elton, like I said, was not a man of schooling. But he was smart. One day he told me we were fixing to round a bend. I asked him what that meant and he said sometimes in life you were going down a straight path and then you rounded a bend and everything was different in your life. This was right before Ann was born and I thought I would never quit being pregnant.

He was right. I had Ann right on schedule and things changed. Some of what he meant was that when you get through a problem time, sometimes you get carried into a new and exciting time of your life. I think that is what he was trying to tell me. That is the way I feel tonight. I have rounded a bend. My father is here to help me. My daughter is going to plant gardenias and roses next spring and probably take care of them for as long as she lives here.

We are going to buy some cattle later this year once the corn is all in the barn and Johnny Hixon finds us some nice Angus to raise. And then, slowly and cautiously, I will look into buying some horses.

Yes, I feel we have rounded a bend in our life this summer. Robert Lee coming to help me was the catalyst. We are all four enriched because of all that has happened during the late spring and summer. I can not tell what the future will bring, but I feel strong ,clear headed, loved, and secure in my little part of the world tonight and I am not sure you can ask for more.

ABOUT THE AUTHOR

Jerry Harris was adopted as an infant and grew up on a farm in Yazoo County, Mississippi. He rode horses, fished, hunted, and after moving to the Mississippi Delta developed an intense interest in Hemingway, Faulkner, Eudora Welty, and John Dos Passos. After high school, he attended Millsaps College and received a degree in English. Eudora Welty was the Writer in Residence at Millsaps and Jerry took Creative Writing classes from her his last two years at Millsaps. While at Millsaps, Jerry achieved recognition from the Southern Literary Festival for his short stories.

After Millsaps came law school at Ole Miss. After graduating from Law School, Jerry relocated to Memphis, Tennessee in 1969. He became a trial attorney with the Shelby County District Attorney's Office in Memphis in 1974. His specialty was Homicide cases. He was head of the Major Violators Unit, Chief Homicide Prosecutor and Legal Advisor to the Homicide Squad of the Memphis Police Department. As advisor to the Homicide Squad for 30 years, Jerry worked with detectives and other policemen on an almost daily basis. Many of Jerry's trials were broadcast on Court TV.

After retirement in 2004, Jerry and his wife, Audrey decided to move to Tucson in 2007. Audrey is an ophthalmologist who still does surgery and maintains her medical career for three days a week. Jerry has two grown children. Paige, his oldest daughter, lives in Sharpsburg, Georgia and teaches school and is a riding instructor and horse trainer. She uses many lessons Jerry taught her when she showed horses in her youth that Jerry trained for her. His youngest daughter, Alexis is a Phi Beta Kappa Scholar, who graduated from Rhodes College in Memphis and is completing her PHD at Penn State.

Made in the USA
San Bernardino, CA
21 June 2016